THE MAN WHO ESCAPED THIS STORY AND OTHER STORIES

BY CODY GOODFELLOW

ISBN: 978-88-31959-15-5

INDEPENDENT
LEGIONS

SUMMARY

Cody Goodfellow

The Man Who Escaped This Story
& Other Stories

INTRODUCTION

This is my fifth collection of short stories, so it seems as good a place as any to ask myself, *What the hell am I doing with my life? Why am I doing this to people?*

The life of a horror writer, seen from a distance, is not so unlike that of any other torturer, though instead of testing chemicals on lab animals or skinning neighborhood cats, we visit unspeakable imaginary punishments on equally imaginary people. And like most torturers, we tell ourselves we're doing the necessary for a better world—to extract the truth, punish the guilty and discover the unknown. Better left unsaid is the guilty thrill it gives us to depict these unsavory scenes, to hand down these vicious judgments, while congratulating ourselves that we've spilled no real blood. But is it any less cruel than the real kind, and are we not just adding to the world's suffering?

I once got the chance to interview John Balance, vocalist for Coil, an uncompromising and decidedly sinister experimental music act. I started by congratulating him on having produced such effectively evil music, but he groaned as if I'd missed the whole point. "Actually," he sighed, "that was never our intent at all. We were just trying to sing about the things that we love."

This was a truth so fundamental that it never occurred to me before, and one that many people misunderstand about horror. We all fear the same things you do, but when we write about our fears, they seem as dreary and miserable as anyone else's. Mere terror, the prospect or certainty of harm, death or insanity, is too easy and ugly, and yields boring, ugly stories. It's when we write from a place of fascination with the indifference of the universe, the arbitrary ferocity of nature, the savagery and saintliness of humankind, that we come closer to achieving something meaningful and rewarding, that justifies the vicarious suffering we've inflicted.

Because that's the paradox that keeps us telling these stories, and hopefully keeps you reading them.

This is ostensibly an unthemed collection, though it's impossible not to see connecting threads and motifs that suggest a deeper commonality than the hand that perpetrated them. Many of them were written when I lived in southern California and worked on the periphery of the entertainment industry, so the peculiar evils of fame and fortune are a staple ingredient; but taking a piss on the venality and greed of Hollywood is as easy and unsatisfying as railing at anything else humans do. For better or worse, Hollywood is the focal point of the world's unfulfilled desires, betraying its overwhelming hunger for escape, for transcendence and for human sacrifices to lay on the altar of our dreams, and it was for these reasons that I wrote so many, and because the pressures of fame and failure to find it warp people into unique creatures not found elsewhere in creation.

Perhaps, in spite of myself, this *is* a themed collection. The title story, saved for last, only brings into sharper relief a thesis present in all the stories herein, meditating on the need to believe our tribulations and occasional revelations must be in the service of some higher purpose, whether it's for the diversion of wanton gods, or just each other, as we burn, break and rust.

This is not idle, morbid introspection, but a serious question. When I wrote most of these, I was ridiculously well-off, married with a beautiful family in a handsome suburb, with a promising acting career; but when I looked at my work, I felt like I was drowning cats or burning anthills, creating flawed characters and submitting them to my own flawed judgment, and punishing them with extreme overkill to quell a deeper unrest. Did my readers come to me for exactly this kind of *grand guignol* kangaroo court, seeking bloody expiation to satisfy their own unaddressed anxieties? Was I giving anyone anything they really needed?

More than seeing faults in my work and the genre, I began to question the whole process, the entire medium. I ended up blowing up my old life, leaving wife and family and career and relocating to the other end of the country, where I found myself no more at ease, even if I was no longer forced to play a role ill-suited to my essential nature. Feeling at times like a character in a horror story myself, I lost or threw away more than I ever thought I'd have, but as I struggled to find real love and self-awareness, I started to see what I'd always been trying to do in a more revealing light.

If all we're doing with horror fiction is creating little arenas where we can rewrite the rules to send our enemies to a private hell, we should stop. Get a real job and a new hobby, like taxidermy or butterfly collecting. But if we're trying to understand each other, to ferret out the inner resolve and rationale of people who live and think and believe differently, to learn from those who seem to thrive in a world that leaves us helpless, or to interrogate those who seem to be the authors of our suffering, to seek love and fascination in a world woefully short on both, then we are, perhaps, doing something worthy of any audience we might win.

Naturally, I hope these stories of bad things happening to worse people will give you thrills and chills, but if they are worth reading and remembering, if they were worth writing, I hope they will give you some sense of empathy for the condemned—some understanding of how people who feel trapped or driven by circumstance are too often the authors of their own undoing, or how even the most venal villains are the heroes of their own stories—and (perhaps it's not too much to hope for) help you figure out how to be the hero of yours ... and maybe even how to escape it.

Cody Goodfellow

PURITY BALL

9:45 PM

Heat seems to radiate up from the ground, hours after sundown. Santa Ana winds like ionized dragon's breath roll over the canyons, cul-de-sacs and paved oases of suburbia.

Icy blue light from the deep end of the Schweinfurter's swimming pool paints the patio furniture and bowers of tastefully manicured tropical landscaping in mottled submarine patterns, animating the stolid rubber faces of the horned devils in tuxedos, lurking in the shadows.

The blinds are drawn and the curtains closed on all windows and the sliding glass door of the two-story ranch house. Lit only by the epileptic stutter of a TV playing music videos, the downstairs rooms seem alive and animated, but only one upstairs window is lit.

Crouching like a beast unused to walking on its hind legs, a fanged apparition skulks out of the bushes to prowl along the windows, peeking through gaps in the blinds. The flickering light reflects off glassy eyes set deep within the gnarled visage, the twisted, goatish horns sprouting from a sloping, shaggy brow.

Two more devils creep out into the liquid half-light, ignoring their leader's furious gestures. When the trio crowds against the sliding glass door, the leader impatiently tugs it open and they storm inside.

In front of the wall-mounted flat screen in the family room, blankets, pink sleeping bags and bowls half-filled with popcorn and Chex Mix. An open laptop on the couch shows the Skype logo when a devil nudges it.

A fourth devil, with a monumental potbelly, staggers down the stairs and rips his face off. "They're gone," he gasps. "Fuckin' Bonnie's passed out in her waterbed."

"Who?"

"Schweinfurter ... the mom, dumbshit. Nicole ... she's not here ... None of 'em are ..."

"Damn those girls," the leader says, ripping off his mask and crumpling it in a fist.

Still poking at the laptop, the second devil says, "What're we going to do, Ron?

"We're going to do what we vowed to do," the leader says. "We're going to find them and remind them of *their* vow."

"I can't ... I just can't believe they'd do something like this. If they're so determined to damn themselves ... To throw away everything—"

"It doesn't matter what they want. This isn't about them. This is about the promise *we* made to them. And to God."

9:57 PM

Ron Kolb ramrods his Suburban through the dithering, half-drunk Friday night traffic. Keith Slauson rides shotgun, and Bo Rieber sits in back, losing an argument with his daughter's voicemail. The girls all left their phones at the Schweinfurter house, anyway, so they couldn't be tracked.

"We should call the pastor," Keith says.

"You call the pastor every time you need to do your duty as a man? No wonder you still change oil for a fucking living." Kolb bites his lip. "I'm sorry, that was out of line."

"Forget it." The whine in Slauson's voice makes Kolb want to break his jaw. *Way out of line*, he reminds himself. *Be a man. Remember your promise.*

"Fucking whore," Rieber growls, "just like her mother."

Kolb turns up the gospel station. Running in his head, everything he knows about Hope—every place he dropped her off, all the kids she tried to sneak out or "study" with, all her friends outside of church, everything she ever talked about doing after school, that they made her skip. Maybe if Enid was smart enough to home-school the kids, shit like this wouldn't happen.

"It doesn't sting that they did it, you know?" Slauson turns down the radio. "It's that they teamed up to pull this shit, right before the night."

"You think they knew?" Rieber asks.

"Women always know when a change is coming. Down in their parts." Slauson takes something out of his pocket and gnaws on it. Peppered jerky.

Kolb gets a whiff of it and looks sideways at him just before pulling onto the highway. "You make that yourself?"

Slauson says, "Watch the fucking road."

Kolb prays for strength to be delivered from the sin that rides them all, the sin of gluttony.

10:54 PM

Cruising the neighborhood, scanning for house parties, the mall parking lots, when Tammy Slauson calls from a payphone. She's sobbing, big, whooping hiccups as she cries for Daddy to come pick her up out front of the high school. Keith makes reassuring noises into the phone, telling his baby girl to sit tight, they'll be there in a minute, Daddy'll fix everything. Then he snaps the phone in half and throws it out the window.

Tammy comes running across the empty parking lot of Santana High in the fluffy pink bathrobe she packed for the slumber party, but she's naked underneath. Rieber and Slauson switch seats and he bundles his daughter into the back.

Kolb's eyes water and his nose begins to run from the stink on her. All of them react to it, Slauson worst of all, his shame and his lust making him secrete his own ugly musk.

They were just going to swim together and maybe kiss a little, but Bobby Chesebro, her boyfriend for going on three months, he went crazy on her, and he changed—

"You did wrong, putting yourself in that situation," Keith says, but it's the Pastor's words coming out of his mouth. He grabs her hand and crushes it in his. "Where's the ring, girl? Where's your silver promise ring?"

"I'm so sorry, Daddy, I didn't want to … Those other girls made it sound like we *had* to …" Kolb watches the road. Tammy draws in a breath and whimpers, "Daddy, you're hurting me."

"You made a vow, girl." Keith clears his throat and starts again, deeper, slower, "And I made a vow to you. You promised to keep yourself pure …"

"But I did, Daddy. I got away from him …"

Keith wants to go find the Chesebro boy. He's Flatland El Cajon trash, not even a member of their church. Bo Rieber's pretty sure the boy's Daddy is in jail for hitting his wife. Kolb says no, they've got to find the other girls before midnight.

Slauson suggests this dead-end road up in the hills where they used to go parking themselves, when they were younger.

"Fuckin' houses up there for almost eleven years, dipshit," Rieber says. "*She* knows where they went. Where'd those girls get off to, Tammy?" Smiling humorlessly, showing all his teeth.

"Don't even fucking look at her," Slauson says. Leaning over the seat to snarl in Bo's face. The stripes of scar tissue shine like silver all over his scalp, through his thinning ash-blonde hair. "Keep your filthy fucking paws off her, or so help me …"

"Sure," Rieber says, "now the horse is out the barn …"

"Mind your fuckin' mouth," Slauson growls.

"Ronny, you wanna turn off the child-lock thing so I can roll down my damn window?" Rieber asks. "My eyes're watering back here, from all the—"

"Shut up." Kolb's phone vibrates, showing the location of the multiplex movie theater where Hope just used her debit card. Trying not to let his thoughts go red, he hits the freeway and cuts off four lanes of traffic.

The whore, the slut, the bitch … He'd be no less furious if it was a son he was out chasing, but trouble doesn't stick to boys. When she had taken this vow, the week after her first period, it wasn't his idea. It was *hers*. Said she was scared of the boys at school. He really believed her. To find out, on a night that was supposed to be so special, that it was all lies, and she was just like the rest …

He catches himself in the mirror and wonders if he shouldn't change clothes before he picks up his daughter. It'd be a perfect cap on a perfect evening to lose the deposit on the rental tux.

11:03 PM

The manager at the box office wants Kolb to buy a ticket to go get his daughter out of the theater. He wants to explain to him that he's not here to see a movie, but to remove his daughter from a dangerous situation she's put herself into, and that he'd rather not involve the police. He wants to rip the manager's doughy face off his skull and eat it.

All at once, the manager seems to read his fate in Ron's eyes, and lets him go in. "But I'm coming back there in five minutes," he shouts, "so don't get comfortable!"

Ron blows by the snack bar, momentarily distracted by the carousel of cylindrical meats, shiny with the same petroleum-based grease that oozes out of the popcorn tubs. It almost makes him vomit, makes him angry like a broken promise.

He finds her in the third theater. A pimply post-teen usher follows him with a flashlight, halfheartedly warning him to keep his voice down. He strides down the center aisle of some foreign romance thing with subtitles, the kind of arty bullshit Hope watches with her mother when he goes hunting.

Almost before he bellows her name, he recognizes her profile, the particular swoop of her neck as she pops from her seat and goes for the fire exit. Another figure, shorter with boyish, spiky hair, runs after her, but Ron gets to the door first, knocking the interloper down as he grabs his daughter by the hood of her sweatshirt and drags her down the sticky exit corridor, hammers the outer door open and drives her ahead of him into the alley behind the mall.

"Daddy, I didn't—"

"Shut up. The car is around the corner. March."

Her hands sweep around her like birds, trying to lift her up and fly her away. "Daddy, I didn't do anything. I just went to a movie with—"

"There's a dress in the car. You're to put it on when we get where we're going ..."

The exit door flies open behind him and he turns around, fists out but only half-closed. Another girl stumbles into the alley, holding her arm across a rather voluptuous bosom. Short hair with too many colors, and her eyes ringed with mascara. Holly Schweinfurter. "Mr. Kolb, I'm sorry … You look really nice." She giggles nervously.

Ron counts to ten. "Hope has to go to a very special event to celebrate a milestone in her life. It's a father-daughter thing, for daughters with fathers."

"Daddy …" Hope starts. Ron slaps her to silence with a glance.

"Mr. Kolb, we didn't do anything wrong …"

"Holly, go home and wake up your drunken whore mother and tell her she's got 'til tomorrow night to get the fuck out of town." In Ron's hand, his car keys jut out through his clenched fingers, just like claws. Holly goes to grab his arm and he shakes her off, jabbing at her eyes with the keys.

Ron comes out of the alley and gets to the Suburban just as Hope starts to climb in next to Tammy Slauson. Ron orders Rieber out and into the back. "Hope's riding up front."

She scoffs, "Like we're going to *talk*, or something?"

Slauson doesn't want Rieber in the back with his daughter. He has Tammy climb over the backseat into the cargo space, where Hope and her brother used to ride for hours together when they went on road trips. When everything worked …

"Where's Nicole gone, girl?" Bo Rieber's face is a fist squeezing out sweat.

"I don't know. They wanted to go meet their boyfriends, so me and Holly went to the movies …"

"You bitches planned all this," Slauson says. "Sitting around watching trash TV and listening to trash, you must've schemed for hours on how to turn *yourselves* into trash."

Jerking the Suburban across the highway, Ron whips around to skewer Keith with one clawed fist. "Way out of line, Keith. *My* daughter wasn't running half-naked in the street."

Bo chuckled nastily. "You know what they say about that Schweinfurter girl …"

Ron says, "Why don't we go find *your* girl, now, Bo?"

"Getting' packed in here," Rieber says. "Whyn't you drop me off …"

"We'll go together." Ron bites his lip.

Slauson digs in. "Who's she been running with lately, Bo? That flatland boy who got kicked off the JV team for his temper, or that kid with the hotrod GTO everybody's always bitching about … I can't even keep track …"

Silent, Ron Kolb stares at Hope while he accelerates, cutting off a river of honking, swerving smaller cars. Stares and accelerates until she whispers, "I know where she went."

11:28 PM

The church has a deal with a local RV dealer to put most of their overstock in the outer edge of the church's parking lot, facing the highway. It makes the lot look fuller and gives the sense of the church community as being laid-back, affluent, always on vacation. The building belonged to a Korean evangelical group that relocated after a financial scandal. Looking more like a futuristic prison from thirty years ago than a church, it still serves their convocation of just under a hundred quite well. More than half of them are the old group that followed the pastor down from Alaska. Some were old enough to remember before even then, before they had names.

And all of them were gathered tonight in the great hall for the Renewal Purity Ball gala. Twelve girls were going to take the vow for the first time. Their small group is growing, a sure sign that God smiles on their way of life. Their girls were to be initiated into womanhood, presented by their fathers to be declared eligible for marriage. But everyone has gone home.

The night was supposed to be a celebration of their successfully defended innocence, and Kolb still hopes to salvage something. His daughter will still go stand before the Lord, their God and declare her chastity, her abstention from the fatal sin of gluttony. And then she will go into womanhood.

But first—

They cruise the rows of RV's twice before Slauson spots the yellow glow shining out the dome skylight on an Asgardian fifth-wheel. Slauson jumps out, Rieber right behind him.

"What're they doing, Daddy?"

Kolb turns to Hope and wonders how much Enid told their daughter about the birds and the bees; about what they really are, and why God tests them like He does. Unlike a lot of fathers, he never filled her head with crazy stories to scare her into behaving. He hadn't even had the heart to tell her the truth. He only vowed to protect her innocence, to defend her honor, until she was chosen by a suitable husband. "You know you're not like other girls at school."

Her eyes go wide, the gleam off them reminding him of when all he had to do to make her smile was pick her up and tickle her. When she was a toy. "Well," she starts, stammers, "about me and Ho—"

"Wait," Kolb slides out of the driver's seat and lopes over to the door of the fifth-wheel.

Bo is peering into the frosted louver windows. "That's them, goddamit, I know it's them …"

Slauson tries, not very hard, to push him back. "Bo, you know you can't … you had yourself that operation …"

"Fuck you," Rieber elbows Slauson aside and pounds the door. "Nicole Charity Rieber, get your busted ass out here before I take it in my head to …"

The door flies apart and what comes through it hurls Bo Rieber into the fiberglass wall of a Crazy Horse Extended Camper-Lodge. He sits down hard with a chestful of broken ribs, sliding sideways as he digs a Glock out of his fleece-lined jacket. "Tried to tell you, girl … tried to save you …"

Before him, between him and his friends, still dripping and trembling from its first transformation, a low-slung torso surging with muscle, flexing talons longer than a man's fingers, hisses through fangs like box-cutter razors and bows its head in shame, just as Nicole Rieber's boyfriend comes charging out on all fours.

Bo shoots him four times in the head. One red-rimmed eye explodes and the other twitches and goes dull, but the ferocious mainspring of its rippling, powerful body drives it into the pillow of Rieber's gut and rips great steaming garlands of bowel out of him, flinging it aside as if digging a winter burrow, gulping wads of flesh down in a reflexive frenzy. It subsides and dies only when distracted from its feast by the bristling howl of its mate as she rakes his flanks, still dripping the shreds of her human skin.

Ron Kolb's daughter's hand clenches his biceps, digging in with her nails. "What are they, Daddy?"

He wants to, but he can't tell her about how it was when they lived in sin, losing themselves to hunger and fury every winter, staggering out into the reborn world every springtime, naked and red, to start over, every year. About being ruled by the animal urges, about the toil and torment of even setting out on the path to control. About how

God's message saved them all, brought them together out of the darkness and into the light. About how they left behind the long winters and lawless wasteland and found a place where they could be safe and secret in plain sight, where they could love each other and raise a family without ever giving in to the fatal, unforgivable sin of acknowledging their true nature.

Gulo gulo, they're called, slandered even by science. *Gluttonous glutton.*

Slauson puts a cheap nickel—plated revolver to Nicole Rieber's head and goes to blow her brains out. She's curled up in a ball, whining, shaking, licking away the last shreds of her humanity. Someone should tell her how the first time is the worst; how she might change back if she kills and eats a man, might turn back in a few days, might never turn back at all.

But maybe she already knows. Her claws rip up Keith Slauson's leg, boning it like a poached fish. The gun goes off everywhere but in Nicole's face. Her jaws clamp on his forearm. Slauson roars and his teeth sprout like icicles. He bites into her thickly muscled neck, ripping out tufts of wet pelt, but even as his skin splits and his humanity burns up in a fire of fur, he bleeds out and dies in her teeth.

"You see," Ron says, flipping on the hi-beams to pin the monstrous wolverine feasting on her own father's entrails, "why we take this Vow so seriously? I told you to save yourself. This is what you're saving yourself from."

"I'm still pure, Daddy,"

His nostrils flare, stealing her breath. "I know, honey."

Slauson's daughter, way in the back, starts blubbering again.

Ron pokes at his phone a moment. BREAKING NEWS: SHOCKING ANIMAL ATTACK ON HIGH SCHOOL CAMPUS—ONE DEAD, ONE MISSING.

Tammy Slauson smashes through the rear windshield and comes charging at her best friend, her shrinking skin tearing to let her red womanhood out.

He throws the truck into gear and drives around to the back of the church.

11:57 PM

The pastor is waiting for them. *Thank you, Lord …*

"What were they, Daddy? What happened to my friends?"

He wants to tell her about what God put into them, that must never come out; about how the pastor offered them a way to live and thrive and control what they were; about the doctor who performed the operation on some who couldn't control themselves; about the "vasectomy" he had to undergo, or else Enid would've thrown him out and the church would've hunted him down, because he couldn't stop going down to the border to hunt on all fours; about how much easier life became with his musk glands and testes gone, about the peace of having no choice but to be good.

But he just gets out and comes around and opens the door for her to get out and follow him. As they go down an empty hall lit by red lamps, he feels his blood thrum and sing, the heat freezing, the cold cremating, racing through him without finding that door to everything that made life what it was supposed to be. If Hope wanted to live long enough to bear children, then after she had borne a family, she would need the operation too, or she'd have to go north and forget her name.

He wanted to tell her all this as he danced with her one last time and now it's too late, but he has to believe she'll figure it out. When he takes her hand and removes the silver promise ring, she says nothing, only bows her head, though he can smell the oily fury from her ripening scent glands.

He holds out his fists and tells her to pick one. She knows how this game has always been rigged, and this time is no different. A prize in each hand, so she can't lose. Identical white gold wedding bands. When she touches the left hand with her nose, the pastor draws back a curtain.

She's a smart girl—no, she's a woman, now. She's already going down on all fours and arching her bristling back as the pastor throws wide the door of her husband's cage.

LIFE COACH

This is what happens when you lose control. The moment you start to live for someone else, you become a human-shaped hole in the world. The moment you stop making things happen and become the victim of things happening, you stop being the star of the movie of your life and you become a statistic. Or worse: a story.

You're walking your dog when a tiny Smart car pulls up and this distinguished older Yuppie couple asks you for directions. "We're soooo lost," the man says.

They've come to the right place. "You certainly are. Ditch this ridiculous car. You look like time travelers from a sad, shitty future. Get your dead parents' Cadillac out of the garage. Stop dressing young. Your desperation is like a hate crime. Stop recycling. If you act like the world will go on after you're gone, then you don't deserve to live in it now. Spend your retirement money getting some cosmetic work done, so you can stand to fuck each other. Here, take this card and tell the doctor I sent you. Not just you, ma'am … *you*. A beard is not a chin implant, sir. Now, get out of my fucking neighborhood."

It is one of the greater paradoxes of your life, that your flaming hatred of humanity has made you one of the more sought-after life coaches in LA. And here you are out on the street, giving it away for free.

Because of the dog.

Hatred is healthy; hate gets things done, but fear is not. Doubt is not. And living alone, you sometimes feel both.

When your last boyfriend moved out, all your best frenemies told you to get a dog. You've recommended it to many of your clients who want intimacy and unconditional love from something that won't talk back. You resolved to knock down your need for security and companionship in one play, and so picked out Clovis.

The rescue pit bull-dachshund-ridgeback mix struck you as intimidating and charming at the same time. His powerful torso ripples with layers of prison-grade muscle, but his stubby legs make him look more whimsical than menacing. And the ghetto shock appeal of a brutalist mutt among the purebred puppy farm lapdogs your neighborhood favors salved both your conscience and need to inspire fear. Don't let a man define you. Get a monster.

The combination of lethal strength and small-dog syndrome makes Clovis a bad fit for even the rowdiest dog parks. Clovis attacks anything that tries to sniff his ass and has to be dragged away, straining on his four-point harness and spraying froth through his muzzle.

Training made him easier to handle, but one can never let their guard down. Every morning, you run him for an hour on the winding canyon streets around your stilt-legged mid-century split-level off Mulholland. You get up before sunrise to have the streets to yourself with no distractions.

You like this neighborhood because the steep hills and busy lives of the inhabitants mean they mostly mind their own business. Anyone on the street in daylight hours is a gardener, a nanny or a pro athlete burning calories in the off-season.

But doggy dawn patrol has introduced you to more of the neighborhood than you can stomach. Every psychotic overachiever in the area keeps a neurotic, lonely bottom rattling around the house. Usually, these jet trash losers are your staple diet, but Clovis makes it hard to fraternize.

How to greet a pedestrian in Los Angeles without looking like a hillbilly: Don't Overdo It. Merely observe that it is indeed, "Morning," with no pushy wish for a good one, or even a rhetorical *howyadoing*? Angelenos hate over-sharing and obligation, and wishing someone else a good day might somehow cost you one. Also acceptable is a cool nod and chagrinned tightening of the mouth when caught staring.

You detour into the street, but they seldom take the hint. They have no control over their dogs, and they blame you for controlling yours. If they say *Good morning* and you just roll your eyes and offer a friendly warning to keep away, or remind them to pick up their dogs' filth up off the sidewalk, you get a half-baked rant cribbed from the weak second act of their doomed screenplay. Even in the best neighborhoods, talking to anyone on the street is like waking up a sleepwalker.

This is why you quit real estate. After so many years, you stop listening to what the buyer wants, and learn to mold them into the ideal mark for the property you need to sell. Subtly reshape their goals and expectations until they'll buy anything you offer. But once the deal is closed, you have to start all over with a new rube. After seven years of it, you realized you could ditch the houses and just work on the people.

This morning, you're out before six with your whole obedience kit: a six-foot length of iron rebar; a tennis ball can filled with nickels; a rape whistle and an air horn for emergencies, and four recycled plastic shopping bags for his leavings. Some trainers recommend treats to reinforce good behavior, but you never got anywhere by doling out bribes. In your skintight black Lycra running suit, with your theme music cranked up on your iPod, you look and feel like a weapon, more deadly than your dog.

It should be soothing, but even when you're alone on the street, the familiarity of it breeds worse than contempt. Every time you pass the Plantation-style McMansion with a huge, faded, guano-streaked American flag flapping under a huge birdfeeder, where they park four black Escalades on the driveway blocking the sidewalk, you have to fight the urge to leave a nasty anonymous note on their lawn jockey. You've never actually seen these people, but you dream of feeding them to a wood chipper. If trifles like this can get you so worked up, then what's the use of any of it?

As soon as you see him coming up the sidewalk, you know he'll be trouble. Doughy and prematurely bald, swaddled in baggy, holey sweats that say UCLA DRINKING TEAM, and those asinine road-running shoes with separate toe-compartments, that look like space chimp feet.

Your finely honed people-reading senses go to work: Bass player with a washed-up late 90's alt-rock band, coasting on radio residuals and sporadic scoring work for porn. Divorced, childless man-child, out delivering pee-grams with his only friend.

His dog is a young Aussie, flailing like a hyperactive kindergartener in his urge to rend, chew and piss on all creation. Your eyes nearly pop out of your head when you notice the dog is frolicking off-leash.

You clang your staff on the sidewalk to bring Clovis to heel and claim the right-of-way, but the idiot diverts into the street to pass, his dog bouncing along like something out of a Tex Avery cartoon. A parked BMW with a canvas tarp over it separates the dogs, but the Aussie stands up on its hind legs and paws at the air, then drops into a crouch with his tail stump wagging in a frisky puppy challenge. Clovis instantly forgets all his training and lurches off the curb snarling, intent on an entirely different kind of play.

Most people get the message right away, but this fool just stops in the street and says, "Hi, buddy! You wanna play, don't you?"

Clovis rears up on his hind legs, dangling by his leash like a botched lynching. You barely hold him back, slamming the rod into the concrete beside his ear as you politely ask, "Get your dog under control, would you?"

The asshole laughs at you! "My dog is under control, lady. He just wants to play ..."

"I have the right of way," you say, but the niceties of dog walking etiquette as laid out by Cesar Millan are lost on this retard. "So back the fuck up."

"You shouldn't talk to people like dogs, and you shouldn't treat your dog like a machine. Have a nice day, anyway." Loping off, he claps his hands and his dog dances around him on its hind legs, nipping at his sweatpants and tugging them down just enough that one flabby, pimpled asscheek winks at you before he disappears around the corner.

Right or wrong, the loser of any argument is the one who broods on it after the last word. When you tell your clients that, they nod as if you were a Brahmin from Shangri-La. But you hyperventilate and fume about the encounter all the way home, where you find a kilo of still-steaming dogshit on the neatly trimmed Bermuda grass parking strip in front of your house. Clovis goes berserk trying to eat it. It takes the can, the rod and the air horn to drive him back into the house.

You try all your vaunted refocusing techniques to put it behind you, but it gnaws at you all through your sessions with clients. Mrs. Mossadegh is agoraphobic and needs kid gloves, but you lash out at her and send the widow into a panic attack. Scratch yoga, insert alcohol.

You have much bigger issues on your radar: shooting another infomercial next week, and a pitch for a regular segment on a nationally syndicated afternoon talk show. But you feel violated, as if you've been assaulted in the street. How dare he raise his voice and flaunt his apathy, like *you're* the defective one? Where did this slacker shithead get the balls to talk to you like that? And his dog, his harmless happy beastie buddy, where her own dog was not a friend or even a reliable tool. And he knows where you live …

Option 1: Bag the shit, then return it to him via his mailbox. But you have no idea where he lives. You could follow him home and …

Option 2: Wait until he believes you've forgotten him, and then … Escalate.

Your heart races as you get up before five and slip into a vintage Danskin metallic green leotard, black Adidas track pants and new Saucony running shoes. You collect your platinum-blonde shoulder-length razor-cut into a brutal bun that takes seven years off your face, and put on a trucker hat that says SHOW ME YOUR TITS, all the while mentally rehearsing a menu of withering, snarky attacks for next time.

Clovis feeds off your tension, jumping on you and gouging divots out of the Mothersbaugh designer wallpaper in the entry hall. As soon as the door opens, he jerks you out onto the porch and down the stairs. He knows exactly what's bothering you, and he has the scent.

You jog down Stonebridge, Clovis humping along like a quadruple-amputee bodybuilder on a 'roid rage vendetta. You only want to spot your enemy and track him back to his lair. Merely knowing where he lives will give you parity, and the peace of mind to decide how this will proceed.

Clovis drags you from flowerbed to rock garden, whining and snapping. The puppy must've pissed everywhere, claimed the whole neighborhood. Clovis leads you up a blind cul-de-sac, then seems to lose the scent. You look over the daunting array of postmodern palaces crowding the edge of a bluff overlooking the San Fernando Valley, and your heart sinks. Your own house is prime real estate, but still a two-bedroom box on stilts facing the wrong way, like a clueless chaperone. If he lives in one of these, then he can buy and sell you. Unless he's just sponging off an old bandmate, running the Kato Kaelin act, walking the dogs and cleaning the pool.

That has to be it. Nobody rich enough to afford an eight-bedroom with a panoramic view wanders around baked with his dog at this hour.

Then you come around the corner, and he ambushes you.

He's just across the street, bouncing a tennis ball to tease his stupid Aussie puppy, who springs and bounces around like he should be wearing a cape.

"Good morning, mean lady!" he calls out. He's wearing the same clothes as yesterday.

You're not ready for this. All your lovingly prepared cutdowns evaporate. Head down, you give Clovis a taste of the rod. It strikes sparks off the pavement and rings like a tuning fork, making your hand go numb. The numbness seems to vibrate all throughout your toned, taut body.

"Is this far enough away, your majesty?" He capers around on the opposite sidewalk as you haul a suddenly frozen Clovis onto the shaggy lawn of a misbegotten Cape Cod ranch house that's been up for sale for over a year, and probably will be forever, with Coldwell Bankers rep Megan Wynner showing it. You back up under an unruly magnolia tree with blossoms like overripe cabbages. Their perfume smells like gasoline.

The idiot tosses his tennis ball down the street. The Aussie bounds after it in a flurry of matted flukes and floppy, adorable ears. Clovis growls real low, like a semi approaching a steep hill. You feel your phone vibrating in your breast pocket. You don't keep your phone there, don't have a breast pocket.

"You're breaking the law," you tell him.

"Make a citizen's arrest," he says, stroking the puppy and trying to wrench the tennis ball out of his mouth.

Fuck him, he's not worth it. Keep walking. There are ten phones vibrating under your skin. "If you want to play games with me, little boy, you better be ready to learn how grown-ups play."

"You know, maybe if you played with your dog instead of trying to play games with people, maybe you wouldn't both be so miserable …" He throws the tennis ball down the tree-shadowed street. His dumb dog goes galloping after it.

Clovis bolts. Your earbuds pop out. The leash burns your hand and whips free, as Clovis launches off the curb.

"Clovis, no!" you scream, or you remember saying it, anyway.

The Aussie pauses to clock Clovis and turns to meet him for a jolly frolic. Clovis leaps and catches the Aussie by the throat and tosses his head to snap the puppy's neck and lay bare a baffling lacework of muscles, tendons and arteries. Before you can drop the rod and get out the nickel can, before the hyperventilating dumbass can call his dog's name, it's dead meat flying in Clovis's teeth.

You would be first to admit that you're in the wrong, but in the moment, all you can feel is the grim satisfaction of the vindicated. Right or wrong, that takedown was *awesome*. If you'd seen it on YouTube, you'd have to have a heart of stone not to stand up and cheer.

We're even, you think. *Suck on that.* If it stopped here, it would be perfect.

Clovis pauses to lift a leg over his fresh kill, then turns and pounds after its owner. The retard gets maybe ten long strides up the driveway of the empty house when Clovis bowls him over, throwing his undulating torso into the wild flurry of legs and battening down on an ankle. The dog-owner pitches face-first into the shit-strewn lawn and crawls through dandelions and sun-bleached junk mail towards— what? His Achilles tendon is gone, so he isn't getting up. With Clovis on his back, he's going nowhere.

You run at your dog, shouting and waving your arms, but you stop just short of grabbing his collar. He could kill this man, but if you interfere, he might just seriously harm *you*. And then your bond will be broken. He'll have to be put to sleep.

You should do something, but your panic-stricken mind can only replay the scripts you trot out for your helpless clients. What would the celebrated life coach tell a sucker to do, in such a situation?

"Please stop! Get him off!" He screams for help, or tries to, but he can only hack and wheeze in his assassin's face. He bats at Clovis with a moldy phonebook, trying valiantly to shove it into the snapping jaws. Clovis already tore off one ear and made meatloaf of his right hand, but the coughing seems to drive him to new heights of ferocity, and he goes for the source. Fixing his massive jaws over the man's face, he battens down like a nutcracker, jerking it from side to side, looking for that telltale snap—

You yank on his choke-chain, but he won't let go. When you finally pull him off, Clovis takes half the man's face with him.

You almost blow the airhorn in his ears, but then drop it when you notice the quiet. You look around.

Thank god for Sunday morning.

The street is empty. The house next door is under construction, and the crew won't be showing up until tomorrow. The sun has just begun to climb above the grey soup of smog that obscures the valley.

Fat newspapers lay on driveways and dewy lawns. Hungover and medicated and dead to the world, the neighborhood has not heard or seen anything.

For a moment there, you felt a sickening hole in the pit of your gut, a sucking undertow that threatened to drag you into under when you needed to be at your best. But it was not shame or guilt. It was good old-fashioned fear at the loss of control, at the quicksand of consequences opening up underfoot. Every aspect of your life could change for the worse forever and ever, just because your dog had an accident.

Clovis sits at attention, oblivious to the weeping, faceless horror crawling in the weeds with a Thai bistro menu stuck to his three-fingered right hand.

"Okay," you keep saying, like the robotic voice in a car with the door standing open. You are the person anyone in such a situation would look up to. You thrive on crises. Like working out a cramp, you pace and say, "Okay," until the sinkhole in your gut goes away. You suddenly feel quite giddy, as if you just snorted pure MDMA. This situation is still yours to fix or fuck up.

Your house is two blocks away. Your chances of running home and returning with the Cayenne before someone else finds the mess are negligible. Also, he isn't dead.

He should really get to a hospital. Right now, he's grievously fucked, but will probably live. If he dies, that's the end. If he survives as a mangled sideshow freak, he'll be around your neck for the rest of your life. It'll be like divorcing a stranger. But you can't bring yourself to do it, not right here. The silence is a bubble that could burst at any moment.

And then, like you always do, you simply snap out of your funk and just start fixing it. Running up the driveway, you use the iron rod to snap the realtor's box off the doorknob and get the key. There's a Bel Air Patrol sign out front like on every house on this street, but it's weathered and cracked, and the alarm is shut off.

You kick and cuss Clovis into the guest bathroom and shut the door, then race outside to pick up the Aussie.

A huge splash of blood decorates its passage, in the shape of a big bird with wings outstretched. You almost throw up when its floppy forty-pound bulk sags like hot trash in your arms, its bowels relaxing and squirting a runny racing stripe down your leg. You run into the empty house and down the hall to the garage, drop the corpse on the concrete floor and run back outside.

The dog-owner still hasn't caught his breath. Blood and a loose flap of face completely obscure his eyes, which he tries to comb out of the way with his right hand. "Help me," he moans. His voice is reedy, breathless even for a smoker. His skin is cold and clammy. Going into shock.

You say, "I'm going to help you. Just calm down and try to get up. Let me help you inside. I can stop the bleeding, that's what's important."

"Call 911 … call …"

You get a hand into his pocket just ahead of him and take his cell phone. "I'll take care of you."

If you lived here, you'd be home now. Furnished with Italian modernist dreck from the showrooms going out of business down on Ventura, and deep pile cream shag carpet alternated with blonde hardwood floors. Empty rooms look small and yet daunting to buyers. Bad taste hides bad space. It's easier to picture living in a house if it seems like someone else is already there, and doing it wrong.

Every room has its own air freshener. The living room smells like evergreen, the kitchen like fresh cookies, the dining room like pumpkin pie.

Goddamit, he's bleeding everywhere. His flopping arms make a red snow angel on the entry hall floor. You detour into the garage and lay him on a moving blanket against the washer-dryer combo. With his shoelaces, you make tourniquets for his hand and ankle. His face drizzles blood everywhere, but it's all capillary blood—no arterial splashing, at least. He's not liable to die, but he isn't certain to stay put, either.

This could continue to spiral out of control, or you could end it right now.

Ask yourself, as you do when divining the good or evil of anything, what purpose would an action serve, and whether it could succeed. This makes it so much easier to live in a cruel and crappy world and not constantly flagellate yourself about injustices from child abuse to genital mutilation in Africa and Adam Sandler movies. Would it work? Would it get you what you want?

The backyard looks out on a steep, brush-choked canyon. Coyotes would find him and his stupid dog before anyone else, and nobody would suspect—

Jesus, it's easy to think like a villain. Is this who you've always been? Are you a bad person? No, you're a problem solver. Weak people let circumstances run them over. Problem solvers rise above, and get shit done.

Clovis whines and paws the bathroom door.

Bad person or no, you didn't ask for any of this. You could let it ruin the rest of her life, and take comfort in having done the "right thing." Or you could take the obvious solution. It's so simple, you would be betraying your deepest principles, if you didn't act on it.

Why the hell don't you just do it?

You go out the side yard and sprint home. You get a deluxe first aid kit left over from Sasha the suicidal performance artist, a smorgasbord of painkillers and anxiety medications collected from sundry other exes, and the maid's cleaning supplies from the entry hall closet.

All the way back, you tell yourself you're just going to stabilize him and try to get him to see sense about the attack, before you call the police. As long as no humans have died, there'll be no lasting fallout. You might even come out of it a hero.

He's halfway to the front door when you come back in. You go to the bathroom door and open it. Clovis comes out growling and makes a beeline for his new favorite chew toy. Wait until the idiot can smell his own flesh on Clovis's breath before stomping on the leash and stopping the dog close enough to lick his nose.

"I'll take care of you," you say again, and press a clean gym sock soaked in ether over his face. He slumps into your arms and you drag him back into the garage.

It takes an hour to stitch his hand. The severed Achilles tendon is above your pay grade—you learned how to stop bleeding and close holes from Sasha's many artistic misadventures, but you're no surgeon.

The face is a challenge you actually enjoy, like arts and crafts from summer camp. Despite your best efforts, the semicircular flap of exquisitely articulated muscle from the hairline to the bridge of the nose now looks like a slab of chuck steak cross-stitched to his head. Slather the results with Polysporin, garnish with hot pink self-adhesive bandages, and serve.

He sincerely seems to appreciate it, once he wakes up. "I'm really sorry about what I said earlier," he says, as near as you can tell. You fed him some painkillers during and after the operation, so he sounds pretty dopey. "It was very insensitive of me. Thank you for saving my life."

You blush. "I'm sorry, too … that you got hurt … but you know, you were asking for trouble."

He smiles, which would look kind of cute, if the upper left quadrant of his face wasn't swelling and turning blue. "What're you trying to do, here?"

"Why can't you admit that you were at fault?"

"Wha …?" Now he laughs, which isn't nearly as cute. "Your dog … he …"

"He's not a bad dog."

"I'm sure … under the right, um …"

"He never attacks unless he's provoked."

He smiles again, looking stupid, but now you start to think he's playing possum. "Maybe you're right. It's just one of those things. Shit happens, right? Let the lawyers sort it out. But you have to call 911."

You make a big production of thinking about it before answering, "No."

"What d'you mean, *No*?"

"We'll settle this here. Now. Between us. No lawyers."

"Lady, I'm bleeding to death—"

"No, you're not. I fixed it."

"Nonetheless …" He sniffs, wrinkles his nose. "Are you baking cookies?"

"Let's talk about *you*, okay? Your dog shit in front of my house."

"What's that got to do with anything?"

"And your dog was off-leash, and you had no way to control him, and you were playing a provocative game in an inappropriate place."

"So, I was asking for it, is that what … I got what I deserved, is that what you want to hear? I'm sorry I made your dog attack me?"

"Don't twist my words. You made my dog angry …"

"You're not angry because of your dog," he gasped. "Your dog is angry because of *you*." He looks fit to bust into a rant, but then he notices something behind you. His face cracks open, tears squirting out of his stitches. "Oh my God, Cutter …"

"What kind of name is that?"

He looks at you like you killed his dog. "Toecutter from *Mad Max*," he whispers. He looks hard at you, trying to stick something in your mind. "My name is Tom."

Great, it has a name. "I'll take care of it."

This is the nadir of your relationship. You've lost his trust. But if this were a romantic comedy, you'd be just one montage and a grand gesture away from happily ever after.

Clovis attacks when you kneel to pick up Cutter. Tearing into the limp carcass like a bag of kibble, he harries you all the way down the hall to the kitchen. He clamps down on one flopping foreleg and yanks with all his weight. You shout, "Heel, Clovis! Off! Go to your spot!" Clovis has never shown much interest in puppy games before, but he's a fiend for tug of war. The limb twists and pops out of its socket. Fur and flesh split open and lukewarm blood sluices down your leg to pool in your new running shoes.

"God damn it, *heel*" You kick Clovis and catch him in the groin. He yips and spins around snarling and for one frozen moment, you're sure he's going to turn on you.

You've never hit him before. The regimen of training and discipline ran you both ragged, but you never lost your temper. This sudden change in your relationship strikes you both mute. You back away with the corpse, reaching behind you for the sliding glass door. Clovis lumbers off to sit and pout by the front door.

You lurch across the patio, around the drained swimming pool to the edge of the yard. Beyond the low fence, a steep slope, shaggy with coastal scrub and exotic invasive weeds, plummets about two hundred feet to a dry arroyo that feeds into a storm drain. A palatial walled estate sprawls across the top of the next ridge, but there's no other visible sign of civilization. The San Fernando Valley below is completely obscured by a colorless pall of smog.

Drop the dog and it tumbles down the slope, almost instantly swallowed up by the brush. You're not a big fan of poetry, but a line from a Browning poem leaps to mind as you wash the blood off your hands with the garden hose. *And yet, God has not said a word!*

You probably can't just throw *him* away now, though. Coyotes don't give their kills stitches. The neighbors are digging a new pool. You wonder how hard it can be, to drive a Ditch Witch.

Filled with renewed resolve, you go back into the house when Clovis lets loose a torrent of barking.

The dog-owner is crawling down the hall again. Clovis snaps and growls, but not at him.

The front door opens.

A TV weatherman walks in holding a Starbucks travel mug and a big pink box of doughnuts. He looks at you like an unexpected Category 4 tropical storm that he failed to predict.

"Am I early for the open house?" you ask. "I was walking by and the door was wide open, and I wanted to come right in and make an offer …"

You maneuver yourself to block Clovis and draw his eyes away from the shambling monster in the corridor to the garage.

He smiles and nods, trying to believe you. This house has been a bomb on the market since before the recession. "That's excellent! My wife is the agent, I just schlep the doughnuts …" He drops the box on the dining room table and goes for his phone.

"You don't have to bother her …"

"Oh, it's no trouble, she's right outside, putting up signs …" He hits a speed dial button and puts the phone to his ear. "So, are you from this area, or …" His face drains of blood, leaving only the pale orange of his bronzing agent.

"Help … me …" Tom moans.

"What the hell is that?" The weatherman notices that he's standing in a puddle of tacky blood.

Clovis tenses, you feel him trembling against your leg. You *feel* his low growl, like the foundation of the house splitting in half.

You cower and scream, "Don't hurt me!"

Clovis leaps. The weatherman's travel mug bounces off his head. His muzzle clamps down on the weatherman's crotch, driving him to the floor.

You look around and find nothing useful. Your rod is in the garage. You run into the kitchen and grab every knife out of the block in a big fistful.

The weatherman is much tougher than the dog owner, and must've done a special report about surviving wild animal attacks before. He rolls on his belly and curls in a ball, covering the back of his neck. Clovis circles in a frenzy, biting and clawing and scoring superficial flesh wounds, but nothing the government would call torture.

This has gone far enough.

You jab his hands with the knives. They're cheap Chinese crap, but the sudden pricking makes his hands fly away from his neck. Before he can flip over, you plunge all five knives into the junction of skull and spinal column.

He goes rigid, humping the deep pile shag with pitiful, diminishing spasms, then sputtering, winding down, choking on his own blood. It takes a while for his eyes to glaze over. He must have so many questions ...

You sit on his back for another minute, willing yourself not to throw up, you've already got enough of a mess to clean up. If she ever hopes to clear this abortion, Megan is going to have to recarpet ...

Clovis nuzzles your hand. You absently pet him, moaning, "What am I gonna do with you," and then notice he's got a phone in his mouth, and it's ringing.

You pick it up. It's dripping slobber. "Hi, Megan Wynner? It's me, Rowena Merkel, from Encino Re/Maxx?"

Megan is, to put it plainly, a dipshit. Changed her last name from Weiner because, she said, she was afraid of offending Persian clients. "Oops, sorry, I was trying to reach my husband ..."

"And you've reached his phone, hon." You push the fruity Avon Lady pep into your voice. "I'm here with a really sweet couple who wanted to sneak in and see the house early today, and you caught us."

"Oh, well that's great!" Megan chirps. "I thought you were out of the game. Are they, you know ... serious?"

"Very, but they're really concerned about security, and I'm afraid Dan—"

"Doug ...?"

"Doug, thank you, was showing us the panic room, and he locked himself in."

"Omigod. Really?" She giggles. "He's *such* an idiot ..."

"They all are, hon. Is the alarm shut off?"

"Yes, it's not connected, but the lock ... I have the key and the combo ..." You hear the slam of the big loading door on Megan's SUV and her chunky wedge heels clomping up the driveway. "Damn coyotes got somebody's cat or something on the front lawn. I hope that didn't put them off—"

"Oh, they're fucking morons, I can assure you. He's some kind of TV personality, so be sure to kiss his ass a lot about it."

"What a coincidence! Wait, he's not at Channel 11, is he? Doug hates those guys. You know they stole his idea for the toy drive …"

She comes into the dining room and sees Clovis, his deep brown coat spiky and stained with fresh blood. She bends down and coos to him and blows him kisses. "Who's a good boy?"

You don't even have to tell Clovis what to do.

"So … do you remember ever not being a sociopath?"

Out in the living room now, why try to hide? Call any crew of Salvadoran refugees and pay them cash up front to clean this room, no questions asked, and without a moment's hesitation, they would deport themselves.

"I'm not a psycho," you mutter. You've been talking to him for a while now, and he's been so nice, and then he springs this on you … "The dog got out of control."

"But you don't seem to feel bad about what happened."

"Sure I do! You think I wouldn't rather be doing something else, right now? This is a workday for me. I want my fucking life back, too."

"Why deny it? You're just going to kill me and burn the house down or something, anyway. Make it look like me and Doug were using this place as a love nest. And Megan found out, and went all Benihana on everybody."

"That's good," you say. "I should be taking notes," but nobody laughs.

"What's your life like?"

"What? Mine?" That catches you off-guard, but in a nice way. "Oh, I don't know. It's good. Really good. I … work with people to maximize their potential, and sometimes I'm on TV …"

He smiles, waving a bandaged flipper to encourage you. "What do you tell them?"

"Oh you know, all kinds of shit … don't give up your dreams for someone else, don't be a victim … but I give it to them straight, and I tell them what I see. I don't sugar-coat it."

"So you see yourself as a …" He winces. "You got any more of those Percocets?" You give him a couple pills and a bottled water. "Thanks … You teach neurotic people how to be more psychotic, to get what they want."

"If you have to *label* everything, then maybe …"

"Sure, but what happened today should be a warning sign, right?"

"A lot of people pay therapists a hundred bucks an hour because they can't face up to the fact that they feel exactly the way I do."

He nods and smiles at some joke he refuses to share. "What would you tell me to do, in my situation?"

"Excuse me?"

He digs in his waistband and pulls out a wallet, fumbles out a wad of twenties. "Go on, I'm soliciting your life coaching skills. What should I do?"

"Put your money away." You scoot closer to him on the couch. His face is already starting to smell, and it's only been, what, four hours? "I would tell you to look at that dog, over there."

You point at Clovis, lolling on the love seat across the conversation pit from you. Something about her perfume or the overblown hairdo on Megan drove him wild, and he made a pig of himself.

"What would he do, if it were his life on the line? He would die fighting, but he wouldn't pick a fight he couldn't win."

You put a hand on his chest, gently pinning him while running the other hand up his leg. His glazed eyes bounce off yours. "When animals know they're doomed, they slink off into a cave or go under a porch and die. We have to make the world do it for us, when it's too late to dig out of the mess we've made of a life. Have the good sense to let go."

"I'm in no shape to fight you," he says.

"You never were," you say, "but that doesn't mean ..."

Your hand finds a phone in his pocket. Doug's phone. You dropped it somewhere when Megan tried to jump through the living room picture window into the front yard with her guts trailing around her ankles.

"You maggot, you called the cops?"

"God no," he chuckles. "Rich people never call the cops."

You take the phone away. The last call was to Bel Air Patrol, just over the hill in Beverly Hills. You hit redial and just start talking while you strangle him.

"Yes, my husband just called, and I don't know what he tried to tell you ... Yes, Tom *is* married. We're very private people, we don't feel the need to tell everybody everything ... Yes, maybe you *should* update his profile. Anyway, there's no need for ... Yes, he's quite high on prescription medications from an injury ... a dog bite."

He's squirming, flailing at your face with his uninjured hand. You punch him in the throat and crush his windpipe.

Relax. Take a deep breath.

"I understand there's a false call fee … We'd be *happy* to charge it to our account. And also, there've been a lot of break-ins to our neighborhood lately, so perhaps you could have a car parked on our block for a couple hours in the afternoon? It'd mean the world to us, as most of the burglaries have happened during the day, so … Fine, go ahead and add it to our account. You work on commission, right? Does that make you happy? Very good then, have a wonderful day, bye."

You've gone and done it, now. You got the last word in, so why do you still feel so empty? Now, he can't eat his words. But kicking his stupid blue face in still sounds a lot more relaxing than yoga.

Okay, enough. You've navigated this situation like a pro. Time to reclaim the day. You had things you were going to do, so do them. If nothing else, a solid trail of business calls will establish an alibi. Nobody in the midst of a killing spree pauses to work phones.

You call your agent. She's busy, but you call and call until she picks up. "Have you heard anything about the Doctor show?"

"No, but it's Sunday and the Daytime Emmys were last week, honey. Nobody's talking to—"

"I want the producer's number."

"Don't push too hard. They don't like hungry women. It scares them, and you always—"

"Give me the number, or you're fired."

She gives you the number. You go into the bathroom to look in the mirror and give yourself a pep talk. "You are a star. This is destiny. Nothing else matters, but what you make of this moment."

Take out your phone and make the call.

You smell gasoline.

A flutter in your chest, like a phone sewn under your breastbone, but this time there *is* a phone, albeit in your hip pocket. You take the dog-owner's phone out and look at it next to yours.

You answer his phone and say hello to yourself.

The doorbell rings. You go to the window and peer through the blinds at a nice Pakistani couple on the porch. The husband looks like a chemical engineer, the wife maybe a lawyer. Behind them, a discreet distance down the driveway, a couple with two-point-three kids fresh from church loiter around their SUV, eating Cold Stone ice cream and waiting their turn. On the lawn, and on every lamppost on the block, are signs in Megan's cack-handed Sharpie penmanship: OPEN HOUSE TODAY!

God damn it, after all your hard work, one little accident and you're back in real estate.

The doorbell rings like every church in Christendom heralding the Second Coming. Clovis jumps and barks at the front door, and then he looks right at you like he's not a dog at all, before he bolts out the garage side door.

You're really losing it, because it occurs to you that maybe there is no Clovis, maybe there never was, and all of this was just you, all along. It's almost a relief to find you're not going crazy, when you hear the barking and screams outside.

You go back into the living room and look around. You blow out the pilot light on the water heater and the stove fixtures.

Suddenly, it's out of your hands. You might as well lay down and have a nap. Lay your head on Tom's chest, and your ear crushes a soft pack of cigarettes, and this is what happens, you think, when you lose control. You may as well start smoking again, just to have some control over how fast you blow it all.

It's been years, and you've built a cult, if not a religion, out of your own legendary self-control.

Fuck it, you think. *Maybe just one …*

You light a smoke and take a drag and remember why you quit. This is not who you are. You're not someone else's sordid water-cooler story. You can never go home, but you won't let the bastards drag you down.

You drop it on the floor and go out the back, around the pool and over the fence, sliding, tumbling through grasping thorny brush snagging your leotard and ripping off your hat.

You come to rest in a dry creek bed surrounded by coyotes. They scatter when the explosions and fire split the sky, but they circle you, yipping and howling when the sirens come.

This is how you get control back. You don't need a dog to define you. To get back on top, you only have to take out the leader.

This part will be easy.

CAVITY CREEPS

Storage space #369 was four feet deep and eight feet wide, with a narrow, two-by-four appendix of useless "bonus space" they couldn't subdivide into another unit. It was just enough room to fit a modest human life and the body that had lived it. Filled to a height of eight feet with all of his records, books, sheet music and old instruments, there was just enough bonus space for Oscar Gurewich to sit in his favorite chair and listen to his phonograph.

This is your home, now. Don't cry, for God's sake. At least you have one … and all your precious, heavy possessions.

He was taking an awful chance. The old hi-fi was plugged into an extension cord that ran out under his rolldown door and along the corridor to the service closet, which he'd propped open with a strip of duct tape. But he had paid for this space with money he'd earned. He didn't accept charity, but he'd be damned if he'd suffer in silence. And yet so long as no one tripped over his cable, he was outwardly as silent as the dead. He almost felt as if he was stealing something.

Oscar detested the headphones, but he couldn't risk being discovered. He had never knowingly broken a law or even a rule, and he really had no other choice, nowhere else to go. The world had taken everything from him, and if he sold his things, who would want them? He would still be penniless, homeless and too old to start over, and without his music and memories, he would be less than an animal.

To dwell upon his circumstances, to honestly examine his fortunes and scheme upon any reversal, was pointless self-flagellation. The balm of Brahms' 4th Symphony soothed his nerves like no empty words ever could. In its elegiac opening tones, he found serenity, the sense that it was all part of some greater plan, but the flow soon turned stormy and defiant, making his heart race and his jaw clench.

He was on an unhealthy romantic jag tonight, having worn a hole in the Moldau and his whole Mahler catalog. Berlioz, Grieg, Saint-Saens and Tchaikovsky lay out of their yellowed onionskin sleeves, the brittle, heavy disks more like pressed anthracite than flimsy postwar vinyl. His dithering fingers fumbled the Moonlight Sonata out of the milk crate at his knee, but replaced it. He was not strong enough, tonight.

When had the world lost its taste for such beauty? One could plot the "progress" in all human endeavors over the last century against the decline of music, from insipid jazz standards to the fecal sturm and drang of modern pop music, and observe an unmistakable correlation … but which was the symptom, and which the cause?

Perhaps, he reflected morosely, the end had begun with the recording of music itself. When playing music ceased to be a magical skill to conjure fleeting melodies out of tyrannical silence, and instead became a lot of common noise that came out of a can, it lost its enchantment, its potent ability to speak to the soul … or perhaps men had sold or lost their souls first …

When Brahms himself submitted to record one of his Hungarian dances for Thomas Edison in 1889, perhaps he had seen the terrible changes the new invention would wreak. Almost buried beneath surface noise like a swarm of vicious rats, the master's muted piano work had the resigned air of a formal surrender.

As the 4th tossed and turned like a dreamer lost in troubled sleep, he laid down the photo album he'd been leafing through and patted himself down for a tissue. The desiccated clippings swelled with the droplets of his tears. Discolored memories of his years with the San Diego Symphony and as a DJ at a flurry of short-lived classical FM stations, and his last vacation in Vienna, with Elaine. They didn't come to life with the infusion of fluid. They only got wet.

Suddenly, he jerked upright and snatched the headphones off his head. Though his hearing was not what it once was and the music was turned very loud, he'd heard something intrude on his reverie, a rough pounding that spoiled the perfect counterpoint of the music. The sound didn't repeat itself, but he felt somehow guilty for retiring into the embrace of his headphones.

He knew he was not alone in trying to live in the storage spaces. He'd seen others who hopped the fence just before the office locked up, who snuck into their spaces and bolted themselves in with cut padlocks, and some vulgar idiots who left soda cups and beer bottles refilled with urine in the outside lot. Such shameful circumstances did not make men eager to bond, but in the still of the night, you could hear men weeping, raging or ranting into imaginary telephones. The steel ducts that connected the four hundred spaces with the indifferent air conditioner distilled the chorus of raw emotions into a bland, murky tone poem of despair; Ligeti's *Lux Aeterna* for condemned choir. A monotonous clicking of some loose vent or faulty thermostat regulator often sounded for hours on end when the heaters blew their rank breath of combusted dust throughout the storage complex, providing a sort of robotic rhythm section. Sometimes, he thought he heard babies crying. It was enough to drive a man to opera.

Oscar was grateful, then, for the headphones. When he looked around at the stacks of heavy, antiquated LP's in their crumbling folios alongside Elaine's corny old rhumba records and Les Baxter and Dave Brubeck 45's and the battered instrument cases, he felt like much more than a broken music teacher. He felt as he supposed those young people in their Brobdingnagian monster trucks and paramilitary SUV's must feel, breezing along in implacable bubbles of creature comfort and blathering into cell phones with one half-lidded, heavily medicated eye on the ebb and flow of likewise disengaged traffic. More and more of them were marked with a bumper sticker from a local megachurch on the tinted rear window. *NOTW*, they defiantly proclaimed, with the T as a cross that looked more like a sword: *Not of This World*. Back when someone had explained it to him, it'd seemed like the infantile height of modern stupidity, but now he wholeheartedly empathized. However high or low, hard or soft, the things of this world were an unbearable burden, and the longing to be free of them was not such a bad thing to feel.

He still had his possessions, his passions and his illusions. He had an air mattress, a gallon of fresh water to drink and clean himself, and a serviceable chamber pot. Eat your heart out, Sardanopolus. You *can* take it with you.

This was only temporary, to be sure. He still taught private lessons at Benoit Music on Ventura, though they paid barely enough to cover the storage space. He could try out again for the Los Angeles Symphony. Maybe this time, they'd deign to let him be an usher.

It had nearly killed him, lugging all this old junk into this tiny box of sheet metal, cinderblock and naked concrete, when the bank threw him out of the house on Vesper Street that he'd bought with Elaine, eighteen years ago. He'd had to make his final trip with a stolen shopping cart, because they'd repossessed the camper.

When he walked from the storage space on Sepulveda to the library on Moorpark in the morning, he passed it sitting in the repo yard, the green GMC with the Roll-Along shell they'd bought when she was laid off from teaching middle school. That was what she'd wanted, to be footloose and fancy-free for the rest of their days, but her heart wasn't up to it, and took her away before they could hit the road. Soon, the camper would be auctioned off, and someday, all of this crap would fall to some scavenger who would no doubt groan at the dismal prospect of selling it on eBay. More and more spaces were turned out, of late, once the renter couldn't be found. It was a wonder they hadn't found more dead renters packed away with the junk they couldn't pawn or part with, the best parts of them divided up long ago between the banks and the rats.

Enough. He didn't come here to wallow in self-pity. When he closed his eyes, he could almost dissolve into the music, and rise above it all in a way that made him think death wouldn't be so bad, if it was like this. If Elaine was there, and music.

The last bombastic stabs of the 4th subsided into the fireside crackle of needle on looping groove. Saint-Saens next. *Carnival of the Animals* was a juvenile parade of frivolity, but it was one of her favorites.

He dropped the record when he heard the sound again, damn it. Fists rapping on sheet metal.

His heart turned a backflip in his chest. He'd been found out. Too late to make any difference, he switched off his battery-powered camp lantern and tamped out the ember in his meerschaum pipe. What the hell was he thinking, smoking in here? Maybe if he just played dead, they'd move on. He was hardly worth the trouble, and they had to know he had nowhere else to go.

A warbling tremolo of wordless fear came through the wall, and someone banged again with their open hand. The sound wasn't coming from outside his door, but from the wall at his back.

Someone in the next space.

He'd resided in the storage space for almost two weeks now, and he'd never seen his next-door neighbor, nor had any reason to suspect he had one. Tugging the headphones off, Oscar struggled to sound courteous. "Yes …? What can I do for you?"

"Help me, please, can you help me?" Through the wall, he couldn't tell the man's age or background. The voice sounded bleary from sleep or drink or both, but there was a sour chord of hysteria in his tone that shivered the corrugated tin between them. "My light's gone out, it's dark and they're—I think they're ... *eating* me ..."

Oh dear, this didn't sound promising. Maybe the poor fellow was having night terrors, or had committed the mortal sin of the modern age, and gone off his meds. But no man is an island, Oscar reminded himself, not even at the Stor-Ur-Self Hotel.

Scooting his chair away from the wall, he knocked over a stack of records in the dark. They cracked under his stocking feet. He cursed under his breath, an old habit from the days of Elaine's swear jar. He switched on the camp lamp and winced to survey the damage. The Mahler was a loss, and Saint-Saens would have a whole new time signature. Still, he tried to be civil. "Are you in distress? I don't have a phone—"

"I need light! My batteries are dead, or—gone, I don't know, but they, they come when it's dark. I blocked my vent ... you know about that, right? But I can hear them, I think they're already in here with me, please ..."

Was he talking about rats? Oscar had never seen one on the premises, though there were poison bait stations everywhere. "I don't have any extra batteries, and just the one lamp ... why don't you open your door?"

The lights in the hall were on motion triggers, and would switch on in fifty-foot stretches of the cavernous arterial corridor outside. A security guard was on duty in the front office and occasionally watched the video monitors, but he was studying for the LAPD exam—probably not for the first time—when he was awake at all. Surely a harsh blast of fluorescent light would wake him out of his nightmare, and Oscar Gurewich could mind his own business again.

The man on the other side snapped, "What the fuck do you think I am, new? I can't do that, I tried, but it's locked! Creeps locked me in! Fucking *creeps* ..."

Well, that tore it. Oscar turned away from the wall, gingerly replaced his chair and picked up his headphones. Big, clunky old full enclosure Technics studio cans, he wouldn't have heard artillery or a Roman orgy in the next space, during *Marche Slave* or Holst's *The*

Planets. He wondered how long his neighbor had been making a drunken spectacle of himself. For surely, that was all it was …

What would Elaine tell him, right now? He didn't need to ask his memory to replay her catalog of lectures. He didn't owe this stranger anything, but he owed it to himself not to have to look at a coward in the mirror every morning.

He grabbed the nylon rope leash and tugged his door open. It rolled jerkily up into its housing, but refused to budge beyond waist-height. Oscar ducked and stepped into the hall. The fluorescent lights flickered and came on, so cold he expected to see his breath, so bright that his shadow between his feet was a bottomless hole in the floor.

He looked up and down the corridor, but of course there was nothing moving, nothing alive. His extension cord snaked past five doors to vanish into the service closet. As bright as they were, the lights cast discrete cones of sterile illumination on the floor. The dark crowded greedily around it, ate it up.

Oscar hesitated before he knocked on the door of #368. He could be dangerous, he could be sleepwalking or on drugs …

Just you go and do nothing, then, and see what that gets you …

Thanks, Elaine. He knelt before the door, and bent over the lock. The light was funny, his deep black shadow made the familiar door look like the dark side of the moon. He instantly regretted touching it. The lock was covered in some kind of septic, blackish gunk like what grows inside a garbage disposal in a widower's house. He clamped his lips tight to keep from vomiting, but he took hold of the lock and tugged.

It was one of the cheap padlocks everybody bought from the front office, but it wasn't cut with bolt cutters, like the ones everybody rigged over their unlatched doors. It fooled no one, Oscar was sure, but it let the management deny that they were a cut-rate flophouse. If the night watch wasn't practicing his sleeper hold on a CPR dummy in the office, Oscar might just get caught, before things got out of hand.

Maybe it was security playing a game with them, or one of their faceless neighbors, because someone sure as Chopin put the filthy padlock on 368 to seal him in.

Creeps, the man had said, with a particular whine of primal terror. *Fucking creeps …*

He looked over his shoulder. Nothing moved. No one lay poised to pounce on him. Then he heard a sound that made him jump back and clutch his chest. That clicking he heard from the ductwork, that faint but persistent sound he'd written off as a failing component in the climate control system ... he heard it now, but it was not a faint, faded sound. It came from just the other side of the door, which shook, just a little, as he backed up against the opposite wall. It sounded like scissors opening and snapping shut.

"It's okay, I'm sorry, I'm okay ... just go away, okay?" The man who'd begged him for light now sounded like he was counting backwards on the operating table. "Just ... go ..."

Nothing he could say could answer that, but nothing, now, could make him obey. Briskly, Oscar jogged down the hall to the closet. As the lights passed by overhead, his shadow grew long and stretched out behind him, then shrank until it puddled at his feet to seep out ahead of him again, as if it took three days to reach the closet and throw open the door.

Dark inside, but he found the switch. He'd got the supply room key from the daytime office manager and had it copied, then propped it open with duct tape. But Oscar was no bumbling Watergate burglar. He taped up the strikeplate so no one who didn't pull on the door would know it wasn't locked.

Shelves stocked with Waxie floor cleanser, Goo Gone, and industrial strength graffiti remover, next to a pile of mops, push brooms, and a bucket on wheels. He almost despaired of finding them before his eyes picked the bulky yellow rubber grips out of the mess. The ungainly weight of the bolt-cutters almost tugged him off his feet. He slipped sideways in his sweaty Argyle socks, but checked himself against the doorframe with one shoulder as he charged out into the hall.

Almost immediately, he sensed something behind him. The dim orange glow of his camp lamp was like the ember of a dying campfire in a coalmine. He kept running and all he could hear was his own labored breathing, like shovels full of wet sand hitting a brick wall. He ran harder, lurching and listing with the bolt cutters in the crook of his left arm. He risked a fleeting glance over his shoulder and saw a flash of black and yellow teeth at his back just before all the lights went out.

Still running, he whipped around and for a moment, the sixty-one year old music teacher galloped backwards like a first-string NFL receiver wielding Excalibur, lashing blindly out at the gurgling darkness.

Once he swung them, the bulky steel shears took over his momentum. It was like swinging two sledgehammers one-handed. The carbon-steel teeth caught something that checked their wild trajectory and made the blackness shriek like dry ice on metal.

Oscar stumbled. The runaway bolt-cutters smashed into a rolldown door like a battering ram on a drawbridge. Shock ripped up Oscar's hand as if the bolt-cutters had clipped a third rail.

Loud.

Oscar's left ear shrieked like a cheap alarm clock. The echoes rolled away down the infinite corridor and came back mushy and mingled with shreds of the blood-curdling falsetto scream he'd let out.

And then, just as it occurred to him that he was still running backwards, he tripped on something stretched across the hallway. His feet flipped out from under him and he flew ass-first into the dark. His arms flapped up to shield his head just as the floor cracked his tailbone and compacted his lungs into the back of his throat.

Rolling into a broken ball like a drowned spider in a bathtub, he could not defend himself, let alone speculate upon what had attacked him. A burning breath like a draught of liquid nitrogen made him cough and retch on the concrete.

Someone in a nearby space shouted at him to shut the fuck up, they had to work in the morning. He gasped an apology before he remembered his own troubles.

Something had attacked him in the dark, and he'd quite palpably hit it. His mind told him it was a dog, emphatically pushed pictures of big black Rottweilers snarling and baring yellow teeth, and it would be easy to accept them. It was no less terrifying, but it added up. The storage place had bought some guard dogs, or strays had wandered in, or—

No. What he saw, however briefly, overwhelmed any reflexive rational explanation. It wasn't a dog, or a man, or anything like anything he'd ever seen, before. It was something *Not of This World*, as the born-again Yuppies said.

And it was still somewhere, very close by.

Nothing was broken, thank God for small favors, but he wouldn't be sitting in chairs for a week. He rolled onto his knees and dragged himself upright, clutching the wall and wheezing. By the murky lamplight, he saw that he'd tripped over his own extension cord, and the bolt cutters lay splayed open on the floor about eight feet away.

You old fool, he scolded himself, you've got yourself all wound up over nothing …

Something darker than darkness lay or squatted at the very edge of the lamp's feeble corona. The light glinted off something. An eye … No, it had no eyes. Only teeth.

His knees shook. He was too terrified even to run, but when he finally took a step, it was towards the thing, and another, slowly, testing the phantasm for a sign of life. At last, he bent, head swimming, to grab the bolt-cutters. The prone figure hissed at him and backed into the curtain of opaque shadow. Coward, he thought, but he crept backwards with the bolt-cutters brandished like a cross against vampires.

He went to his own storage space and picked up the lamp. The feeble yellow light hurt his eyes. How long had he been in the dark?

It was harder to pry himself out of his own space again. His hand caught the leash and started to pull the door down. A man was in the next space, and he needed help. They were discarded and damned, but they were yet human beings, and to ignore another would only prove that he was not fit to save, himself.

Outside his space, the corridor felt hotter. He went to #368 and held the lamp up to the soiled padlock, then set it on the floor to apply the bolt cutters. The serrated teeth nipped through the cheap aluminum lock like it was made of cheese.

Something banged into the door, just opposite his face. Oscar fumbled the bolt cutters, then held them up like a club as he squatted to grab the handle, then threw the door up as hard as he could.

It jerked to a stop at chest-height and wouldn't budge further. Oscar took a step back. A nauseous stench rolled over him, like mildew and carrion and raw sewage poured into a space heater.

The dingy sheet-metal walls were plastered with clipped photos and maps from *National Geographic*, along with the pages of a Gaugin coffee table book. Everywhere, the sunny, honey-colored windows into another world gazed down in blind dismay upon this one.

His neighbor lay on a Coleman air mattress with his head at Oscar's feet. In a red T-shirt and red pajamas, he looked like someone sleeping in their own home, and for a moment, his beleaguered, lost stare was enough to make Oscar back away and apologize as he reached to shut the door.

But then, no matter how much he wanted not to, he still saw the things that crouched over the art lover, and brazenly continued with the business of eating him.

They were two or three feet tall, but hunchbacked and bent on all fours. Their skin a glossy, bubbling black like roofing tar; lean, crooked limbs dragging bloated bellies and propping up wobbly, ponderous heads, which were nothing but bulging jaws and jagged teeth.

He could see no eyes, ears or nostrils. Huge incisors and tusklike canines as thick as Oscar's thumbs were jammed in like a drawerful of steak knives, and as they busily gnawed and nipped chunks off the man, they made that insidious clicking sound he'd heard night after night. The sound of them gnawing, eating their way through this building, and through its nameless, faceless tenants.

"Go away," the man moaned. "It's fine … doesn't hurt …"

Two of them dismantled his legs, while two more gnawed on the exposed bones of his arms and gobbled the loose, weathered skin of his neck.

Long, grooved black tongues licked out to lap up the sluggish blood flow, and somehow, Oscar's reeling mind supposed, they must be drugging him. Their saliva was some kind of anesthetic, for how else could he still be alive and trying with a skeletal vestige of a hand to wave Oscar away?

Repulsion drove a hot steel rod up his spine, turning fear to fury, as he forced himself to accept them, to acknowledge that they were real. They were unacceptable, but they were most definitely of this world. They were the very essence of the goddamned place.

A fifth creep squeezed out from behind a tumble of art books and gurgled at him, extending its quivering tongue like an invitation.

Maybe it didn't hurt. Maybe after everything else he'd been through, maybe being eaten, becoming nothing, would feel *good*.

I doubt it, thought Oscar Gurewich. He swung the bolt-cutters in a reckless downward smash that crushed the head of the advancing creep into its sunken shoulders. The others gasped and clicked and leapt over the prostrate feast with bloody, fat-marbled flesh in their teeth.

Oscar turned and banged his head on the roll-down door, raced blindly back to his space through a flurry of stars. Stumbling over his turntable and falling into the opposite wall, he rebounded and reached for the door leash. They came surging in before he could close it, and set to work on his legs.

He kicked out at an impossible jolt of agony, throwing a squealing creep into the rotator for Elaine's old Leslie organ with a thick strap of Oscar's outer thigh in its mouth. He dangled on the edge of shock, but the pain was like a knot that simply untied itself. A cold, tingling euphoria suffused his trembling flesh with the promise of escape. It wasn't so bad, after all, to be eaten.

The others climbed him, and he sagged almost willingly under their rubbery weight. He felt claws at his neck and fetid breath stirring his thin, silver hair, and teeth shredding his clothing, yet he couldn't move a muscle.

It figured that something like this would be the end. The world had been taking bites of him for so long, stealing his wife and his livelihood and his home. At every turn, he had clung all the tighter to his things, to the false cocoon he'd secreted around his raw, unfinished form.

Elaine had loved him so much, it killed her. He knew that, always had, but never admitted it. His clinging to his records, his books and his junk had smothered her spirit, and when he could not tear himself away, she had sickened and died before he even realized he was losing her. He hated himself for the relief he'd felt, when he realized he wouldn't have to abandon all that stuff, to live in the camper.

He barely felt the teeth clamping down on the crown of his skull, skating across bone as they peeled off his scalp. But he felt his heart breaking, and his tears came flowing down so thickly he couldn't see where he was swinging the bolt-cutters. In his head, he heard only the invincible rhythm of Verdi's Anvil Chorus.

The fanged cutting head demolished an orange crate filled with Wagner and Handel and sent a creep spinning. The creep on his back shredded the sleeve of his cardigan sweater and tried to chew off his arm, but he flung it headfirst into the cinderblock wall and chased it with the cutters, smashing its crooked spine out between its chattering teeth before it hit the floor.

Spinning on his heel, greased by blood streaming down his leg, Oscar chopped down a stack of Elaine's old novelty records. Yma Sumac, Martin Denny and Spike Jones took wing like clay pigeons. The bolt-cutters spun out of his grip and caromed off the wall. There were still more of them than he could count, and more dropping out of the open duct overhead. Out of every crack and cavity in the sad tomb of his life, they slithered and skulked, snapping their cleaver-teeth and crowding him into the narrow, coffin-shaped bonus space.

His life was forfeit long before they showed up, but Oscar Gurewich was nobody's food. He looked around at all his things, all the music that had both set him free and buried him, all the heavy, dusty things he had mistaken for the stuff of life itself. All the terribly flammable shit …

In his pocket, he thumbed the lid off his monogrammed silver Zippo lighter. A silly affectation he'd found in his stocking one Xmas, though Elaine loathed the smell of his pipe and cigars. He struck the flint and tossed it into a crate of sheet music.

The antique yellow paper ignited like potassium powder. The creeps cowered, hissing, as he flung flaming paper into every corner of the storage space. He kicked a creep away from his wounded leg, then heaved a tower of ancient Mozart limited pressings on top of the snarling abomination.

The fire took root among the crates and oiled cases and bloomed in earnest. Creeps melted like wax and burst in the flames, or scrambled back up into the duct with their asses ablaze. Alarms rang in the corridor and sprinklers spurted unevenly outside his space. The vents sucked smoke and fluttering embers into the central duct.

Oscar looked around him. He didn't feel like he was burning, but he smelled bacon underneath the reek of broiled sewage. The thought of trying to save any of it made him laugh until he coughed. He didn't belong to any of this stuff. He could remember and play any of it that really mattered. But he turned and reached into the mounds of flame, digging by memory until he found the familiar grip of an old instrument case. His clarinet, the one he'd played in the symphony when he met Elaine.

He snapped up the case and patted out plumes of smoke on his sweater. Backing away from the furnace roar of his life burning up, he noticed that he'd grabbed the wrong goddamned instrument. The grubby, rubber-banded grip was attached to the case for a beat up old tenor saxophone that Elaine had bought for him at a yard sale, back when they courted. A loud, vulgar horn that Mozart might've loved, but which had always seemed to Oscar to be the flatulent, razzing death-knell of the classical era. Well, to hell with it. He had to play something.

He picked up the bolt-cutters and shambled down the corridor past bleary-eyed refugees in thermal long johns, down the stairs and out past the front office, oblivious to the security guard who tried to stop him, but then screamed, "Jesus, you've been scalped!" and puked on the sidewalk.

Sirens wailed and blared as fire engines and police converged on the storage complex. They'd be busy for a while, maybe all night, if they found the nest of creeps.

Feeling neither the cold nor the pain of his many wounds, Oscar Gurewich tossed an imaginary dollar into an imaginary swear jar, and walked down Sepulveda to get his fucking camper back.

HOWL OF THE SHEEP

She couldn't wait to change. Hours before moonrise, she stripped and took to the streets.

Looking for a fight.

On her own, but she wasn't alone. High school kids prowled and pissed in the alleys in Berserker war paint, pounding beers and painkillers to numb the coming change, or just pounding each other and anyone passing by in full-throated anticipation of it.

Vanessa itched with burning sweat that burned like her pelt coming out early, but she made herself walk down the street towards the park. Running would only attract them, and whatever they did to her before she changed would be permanent.

She was stupid to be out alone, but the impending change had been working her mind for days, and she couldn't wait at home any longer. The raging intensity of new sensations, the slippery, sickening nature of linear thought, made it impossible to control herself, but at least it focused her previously scattered impulses. She no longer knew what she was, but she knew what she wanted ...

This was the last full moon of the summer, and Vanessa meant to make the most of it. The rest of the girls on her football team would want to go play grab-ass games like hunting rabbits in the canyons or scrapping with stuck-up cheerleader bitches, but next week, they would start at Schwarzenegger High and try out for the JV Berserkers squad. Everyone knew that high school was different. The sports were co-ed. They would be fresh meat.

Her friend Hannah's brother Heath made first-string varsity his sophomore year. Varsity played Full Moon Ball. He got his foreleg ripped off in the first game against Valhalla and it grew back stunted, and all his dreams of playing pro ball were dashed.

High school was serious. To survive and thrive as Berserkers, they would have to come in with blood on their paws.

To that end, Vanessa had simmered upon a course of action, but her febrile teenage mind could not cut through the bullshit and make itself clear. Now that she knew what they had to do, she only hoped she could find her friends and transmit the urgency and excellence of her plan, before it was too late for words.

She was in the office—for fighting, again—when Richard Pilcher's mom came in to see the principal, only that afternoon. They closed the door, but Vanessa scooted her chair up close and pressed her ear to the claw-scarred Formica. Mrs. Pilcher started sobbing, until the principal growled at her to harden the fuck up.

He apologized, reminding her it was that time of the month, then explained, "Your son's condition is not all that rare, Mrs. Pilcher, but it's pretty unusual for someone with his condition to survive this long––"

"His father was an alpha pack leader—"

"And what does *he* have to say about his son's retrograde development?"

More sobbing. "I don't know … I was r-r-r—*casually impregnated* … in the *daytime*." Wow. Ms. Pilcher almost used that dirty, illegal whine-word, *rape*. She should have been proud. Less than half of adult Americans could change at will, and maybe one in ten could do it in sunlight.

"That's just too bad, Ms. Pilcher, but facts are facts. Richard shows no ability, or willingness, to change. His grades may be top-notch, but he flunked the physical aptitude tests. He flatlined on the instinct tests. And he's a fucking *vegetarian*, to boot. He's not one of us. And if I send him on to high school as he is, I'll be ringing the dinner bell …"

The secretary shooed Vanessa away from the door, but she had already heard enough to set her head spinning.

Richard "Rabbit" Pilcher was the smartest kid in school, but he was a freak. Long before the first twinges of puberty sharpened their senses, everybody knew there was something wrong with the scrawny, nearsighted kid whose torrential dandruff fluttered after him like skywriting.

Vanessa was briefly his friend in kindergarten, and had to pound him almost daily until fourth grade before anybody forgot about it.

The abuse only got worse after the other kids got their first changes in middle school, so he kept to himself. He spent all his free time reading the few unburned books in the library and twanging away on a queer little mandolin thing, when he wasn't running from a beating.

She saw Richard on her way home. He sat high up on the jungle gym in the playground, half-heartedly ducking clods of mud and rocks some kids from Norris Elementary threw at him as he read another of his infuriating books. No pictures, just words like dead bugs in a row that came alive in your brain when you looked at them. Ugh.

Perched up there with his head down, too scared to run away from a pack of hairless cubs, Pilcher didn't look so smart.

"Whatcha reading, Rabbit?" Vanessa shouted.

Without looking down, Pilcher waved and held up *The Foxfire Book*. Cool enough title, but the cover was a plain brown snore: *Hog dressing, log cabin building, mountain crafts*, zzzzz.

"Looks like a pretty shitty book," she sagely observed.

"No, actually, it's quite—Oh, I get it." He sat resigned as Vanessa threw the punchline. He brushed the curds of month-old wolf shit off the book, then wiped his glasses on his scarf. The scars on his neck and hands were flushed and angry as Richard Pilcher himself never was. Bite marks and claw-stripes from all the kids who tried to make him one of them.

The Norris kids howled and high-fived. Vanessa asked, "You got any special plans for tonight, Rabbit?"

Shaking as if it was winter, Pilcher said, "I was thinking I might try to get out and do a little hunting ..."

That cracked Vanessa up, but later it made her mad, because she couldn't think of a smart retort. But as the sun went down and the electrified darkness of the Bright Night began to fall over the howling town, she knew what she had to do.

But first, she had homework.

U.S. History was Vanessa's favorite subject, after PE. Her textbook was thinner than most coloring books.

History made simple: Once, the world was complicated by the weak and the weird, and overwhelmed, it ground on towards its own destruction, until one full moon twenty-five years ago, when the revolution came.

They called it a plague, but it would be the cure for all that ailed America. Nobody left alive was positive what caused it, but the shady data from that first fateful full-moon election night pointed to red meat, domestic beer and cable news as contributing factors. The brave patriots who first rose up on all fours and tore out the throats of the weaklings in their midst were proud core consumers of all three, and little else. The armed forces were routed from within, but resurrected with new purity after savaging the feeble civilian hands that had starved and misused them for centuries.

When America emerged from its first cycle of the Werewolf "Plague," thirty-seven percent of the population had fled to Canada or been eaten, but the remaining whatever percent restored a new order and integrated a golden age of freedom in the true spirit of the Founding Fathers. And not those fruits in the powdered wigs, either, but the *real* founding fathers, who first swore the sacred blood oath of the pack in the forest primeval.

Still quarantined and shunned by the rest of the world, America had returned to its purest core values—and one or two nights a month, it lived them.

Vanessa recklessly blasted through the word searches in her homework and copied her Bible verses, then scarfed down the steak tartar Mom left for her, and stripped down to her shorts.

Mom and Dad were off to the Santee Drive-In again, and hadn't invited her along. The stress of raising a girl in a world of wolves had left them tearing each other's ears off, and ever since she could fend for herself, they went out wilding on mule deer at the Barona reservation or rutting with strange mates at the drive-in at least twice a season.

When the sirens began to bay all over town, most of the howls that answered it were from thickened, bestial throats. Vanessa was already in the park, sniffing trees for the spoor of her friends, when the fat, mustard bulk of the harvest moon first peered down on them over the shoulder of Cowles Mountain.

She dropped to all fours and buried her face in the parched brown grass. Wrenching agony wrung the last gasps of humanity out of her mind, flooded it with pain so pure it obliterated any trace of self. Vanessa ripped the grass and dug into the dirt with her knurled, shrinking hands, and rolled on her warped spine to kick all four twisting, trembling limbs at the sky.

In Health class, they told you how to handle the changes and showed a stupid video, *What's Happening to Me? (2nd Ed.)*. It was a painful but natural part of growing up, just like whelping pups or honor killings. They talked about their estrus cycles and their wet red dreams and practiced their breathing, but nothing could have prepared her for this. And each time, as her human body grew up, it hurt worse. As if she wasn't changing into a wolf, but giving birth to it.

When it was over, she could barely remember her name, or who she was. The sudden unfolding rush of the world, the scintillant brightness of the moonlit night, the blazing mosaic of heat and the sweet scents of predator and prey made her forget the pain, pushed her ever farther from the pimply, nervous, two-legged thing she'd been before.

She bounded around the park, chasing other young wolves and marking everything in sight, when she finally scented her teammates. They came bounding up in a bunch, panting and yipping as if from a raid on the boy's locker room.

She hunched down on her forelegs and snarled, daring them to run after her, but their anxiety pricked her nerve. They were spoiling for a hunt, and rats and raccoons were for kids.

Damn. What had she been thinking? What was it that seemed so important just a while ago?

The black-faced wolf who always ran at her wing, her best friend … Hannah, right … reminded her. In her mouth, dangling from slavering jaws, she carried a dead rabbit.

In PE, they teach you everything you need to know: the breathing exercises to ride out the initial trauma of becoming a wolf; the mnemonic tricks to hold onto some crust of one's human self; the do's and don'ts of prey selection and courtship. The thing they didn't actually teach you, was how to actually *kill* something.

It should come naturally, and in a natural world, no doubt it would. If you were the lone predator and lord of all you surveyed et cetera, you'd run across all kinds of small game in the scrub canyons around town. But there were a million or so werewolves in San Diego County, and they had exercised their 34th Amendment rights to the hilt until nothing but rodents ran wild in the hills. The only game bigger than a rat that Vanessa had ever run down was the hobbled baby deer at her coming-out party, last year.

But she hungered to be something more than another bitch at the back of the pack, or a gray, skeevy mutt alone with a litter like … like Richard Pilcher's mother.

Rabbit.

Her mind was a scarlet fever swamp, but while she chased her tail through it, her divine animal body raced ahead of her mates over fences and down the game trails of extinct coyotes to the bluffs of lower San Carlos. The trails stank of sugary lupine piss, but they didn't see another wolf. It felt heavenly to dig her claws into soft sand instead of clicking on pad-punishing concrete.

Most of the tract homes out here had burned down or been abandoned as their owners either got eaten or moved to better digs. A few houses were occupied and had electric fences and huge halogen lights on motion detectors. Dog breeders and other malcontents lived on the bluffs, but they were out wilding with the rest, tonight. If there was anyone still on two legs by the light of the full moon, they had to be more mole than human, by now.

The Pilcher household didn't leave a light on, but Vanessa knew he'd be home. Ms. Pilcher was a fundamentalist, and did her wilding at the First Lunar Revival Temple in Allied Gardens. They rolled in thorns and broken glass to keep themselves from enjoying the glories of becoming a beast.

Stupid. So stupid …

She'd heard all the tall tales about what it was like to eat human flesh. The laws were foggy about charging people for crimes committed in animal form, and no humans had been seen on full moon nights in San Diego since Vanessa was a cub.

They said that if you ate human flesh, you might never change back. She knew they said that just to scare you, but she wished it were true. If she could, Vanessa would never change back.

The bloodthirsty whirligig in Vanessa's streamlined skull skidded to a stop at the chorus of howls from before and behind her. The trail petered out on a cactus-studded ridge overlooking a ghost town of empty cul-de-sacs and naked foundations. Nothing stirred or shed heat anywhere in the terraced gulch below, but she could smell the goatish spoor of their prey in tantalizing traces of his sweat, piss and even blood in the sand, where he'd run home like a hunted thing from school every day. They all could smell it, and in their quickened state, it drove them crazy.

It was a wonder every wolf in the zip code hadn't scented Richard Pilcher and circled his door; but werewolves were like any other animal. Once they started chasing the nearest vermin or licking their own balls, they forgot whatever cares troubled their two-legged selves. Vanessa was simply gifted, or perhaps not so lucky. She barked and bit her mates to silence and led them down through the brush and burned-out cars choking the ravine, down onto the cracked blacktop game trail of Golfcrest Avenue.

Slinking from pothole to pile-up like quicksilver shadows, they fanned out and surrounded the crappy stucco two-story tract home on the corner. She didn't know why anyone would stay out in the middle of nowhere, in such a shithole. Unless they had something to hide …

Hannah bolted for the front picture window, but Vanessa bit her ear hard enough to draw blood. They circled each other for a tense moment before Vanessa stared her down and reasserted herself as the alpha.

Behind the curtains blocking all the upstairs windows, she saw the glow of candles. Downstairs was dark, and probably booby-trapped. He'd be up there reading, thinking himself safe.

Vanessa padded cautiously into the yard, hugging the rusty chain-link fence and sniffing for traps. Strange urine trails clouded her palate. Not wolves, and not human, either. An ugly smell, it chafed her nose and bristled her hackles, but she wouldn't let the doubt turn into the crippling animal fear that would turn her away. She skulked past the garbage cans and the locked-down garage to the backyard.

A drained swimming pool had been filled with soil and turned into a nice little vegetable garden. Bear traps lay all around it, and the perimeter fence was electrified. Crispy bird carcasses lay everywhere to bear witness to the effectiveness of the voltage. The ground-floor windows were boarded up, and the back door had a ten-key box on it. A big dead oak tree stood close to the house, and a thick jute rope dangled from its highest branches. It stank of how he got in and out of the house.

Digging her claws into the iron-hard bark got her nowhere, but when she backed up and charged it, she was able to get halfway up the trunk before a wire noose dropped over her slim snout. She snapped at it, but it drew snug around her throat, then fed her enough electricity to power a rollercoaster.

Vanessa yelped and went ragdoll. She fell from the tree, but missed the ground. Swinging by the wire noose like a fish, Vanessa danced to the yipping panic of her pack.

Vanessa bit the wire. Fresh jolts shot through her teeth and turned her whiskers to ash, but she fell to the ground and sounded the alarm.

So much for hide and seek.

Vanessa shook herself and crept up close to the back door. A flapping pet entrance in the bottom panel let something small and sleek dart out into the yard, hissed and sprang over the fence before she could catch it.

Vanessa stuck her head through the pet door, bracing for a shotgun blast to the face, but she saw only a jungle of uninhabited clutter. Squeezing painfully through the low, narrow hole in the door, Vanessa stalked the Pilcher house.

Her snout wrinkled in repulsion at the ammoniac reek that saturated every fiber of the carpet, every stick of furniture, the overstuffed bookshelves. She only recognized the stench from the scratch & sniff cards in Health class. Cats. Incredible. They were supposedly wiped out before she was born.

These people were *freaks*.

She heard her mates outside, baying and scratching all around the property. Her simmering fear went away at the sound. She was not alone. The pack would back her play. Almost immediately, a chorus of yipping and the clang of steel jaws snapping on clumsy paws and snouts sent her cringing into a corner.

She pissed on the crumbling plaster until the smell made her feel in command of at least of tiny piece of the world. Before something else could catch her, she darted up the hall, and climbed the stairs.

Weird. His weak, deviant smell was alpha, here. It was a cloying, musky goat-smell, devoid of even the faintest trace of tangy predator edge that every boy in school exuded even at the bottom of his cycle. She quivered with rage, but it only masked something deeper, that even her worldly-wise animal self could not explain.

She knew he was anything but helpless here, that his retiring, sheepish public clothing had been only bait, but she didn't care. She knew what she had to do next. She was ready to kill.

He stepped into the hall and jumped back as if electrified. Dressed all in black with a white plastic sheep mask on, his legs tangled up and spun him around like a top. What a spaz.

She unleashed a proper roar that pinned him to the spot, then pounced. Her jaws wide to seize his neck, she hung above him in the air for an instant.

Her snarling snout smashed into glass and crashed through a mirror, instead of hot, soft flesh.

He stood in the open doorway to her right and watched her fall through the angled mirror and the hole in the floor and into a darkness even her wide, dark-adapted eyes could not penetrate.

She landed hard on cold concrete. Her left foreleg folded under her funny and snapped cleanly through her auburn-black fur. Shrieking and licking the sweet marrow, Vanessa could try to climb the walls or she could heal, but not both at once.

Growling and gagging on tears as the bone set itself, she turned and looked up at the hole in the ceiling just in time to see Richard peek down at her and drop something on her head.

A net snarled her flailing limbs and bit into her furry hide with teeth that stung her to paralysis. The barbed hooks woven into the net were pure silver.

Suddenly, the room was filled with light. Headlights painted the walls of the garage. The door opened with a grating skirmish of bent metal, and an army of remote control trucks squealed out of the garage and down the driveway.

Vanessa barked to summon her mates, but those who weren't caught in traps were too bewitched by the lights and wailing sirens of the speeding RC cars to heed her call.

They raced barking into the street after the cars. Hannah shagged one before it jumped the curb. It exploded in her mouth and blew her snout off. She quivered and rolled up whining, but the others were too far-gone to notice her. They raced out of sight to end in muffled bangs and whimpers in the dark.

Richard came down the hall and entered the garage. He wasn't wearing a sheep mask, anymore. He had a long, tapered snout, big, batlike ears and twinkling, opalescent yellow eyes. She recognized it from magazine pictures and museum dioramas. It was the face of a coyote.

And it wasn't a mask.

"I hoped you'd come," he said. Kneeling beside her, he took out a huge, serrated combat knife.

She growled warningly, but the sound came out like a purr. Her foreleg was shaky, but the bone felt strong under her. Any movement caused the silver hooks to dig deeper into her pelt.

Set deep under a sloping brow covered in fine copper-blonde fur, his yellow eyes twinkled at her. She ached to have his heart in her mouth, but that head-spinning something else swelled up inside her, almost smothering her pain, and transmuting her hate into something else.

"Lie still, Vanessa. Yes, I know it's you." Laying the flat of the shark-toothed blade against the downy fur of her throat, he skinned back his jowls from his needle-teeth as he let her think he was about to kill her. "I could always kind of tell," he said, "when you were picking on me with the others, that you were different from the rest. You knew I was different, too."

Petrified, she trembled under his gentle, tawny hand. He slid the razor-thin knife up the net, slitting it like pantyhose to set her free. Delicately as a mother, he pulled the hooks from her hide and scratched behind her ears, making them throb and ooze arousal scent. The goatish stink of him no longer made her hackles rise; now, it had taken on a whole new meaning.

He worked her nerves like the strings of his instrument, settling the tension and stealing away her pain, so that she felt only the queasy wash of strange sensations pouring out of her loins. She burned for words, but her wolf tongue betrayed her, straying out from her jaws to lap at his paw.

"I'm not like the rest of you," he said, "But I'm not weaker. I'm a child of Coyote, the Trickster God, who was the lord of this land. We control how often we change," he added, pinching her with the opposable thumb on his paw, "and how far. I've been hiding among you to find someone who was special, to run with me and hunt wolves as wolves hunted men, forever and ever. Does that sound crazy?"

His gently relentless paws stroked the sweaty softness of her belly. She lifted her throat to him and turned to present her inflamed hindquarters. Whimpering as he mounted her, she felt no defeat in surrender.

He was her first, and nothing about it felt like the Health videos said it would. His thing was all wrong, and far larger than a canine's ought to be, and it didn't shoot out of a sheath or lock inside her, like she expected. But neither was it the kind of gross doggy-style mounting that she'd always dreaded. He drove her mad with his dexterous forepaws as he thrust with a maddening delicacy into her trembling hindquarters.

At long last, Richard uttered a tortured howl and spent so deep inside her she felt his seed racing through her heart. She howled deliriously, whined with a joy too powerful for human words. She had come here to kill this strange boy who haunted her dreams, and discovered so much more. He was not weaker, but just different, and so much smarter, than the rest. Instinct had drawn her to him, and now she had found a mate like no other, her destiny could only be something awesome.

Still stroking her, he smiled wide, his pink tongue lolling out like a broken party favor. His grin got even wider, and he reached up to pull his ears back until his grin split his face apart. Ripping off the furry mask and peeling away the gooey gum that held it in place, Richard Pilcher spat out his coyote dentures and grinned at her with his blunt, crooked rabbit teeth.

His muscle-melting massage turned into a bee sting between her shoulder blades, and frigid fog poured into her bloodstream.

She tried to get up, but couldn't even make a sound. Skinning off the furry paw-gloves, Richard turned to face the shadowy figures watching from the corner of the garage. "So, how was that?"

They had no scent at all. They wore black dappled fatigues that rendered them completely invisible to her until they moved. They shed no heat, and their faces, behind big goofy black sheep masks, might have been figments of her drugged, despairing mind. Apparently, they'd watched—and *ewww*, videotaped—the whole thing.

"Points for originality and daring," one of them said, "but hardly a challenge. These suburban bitches are dumb enough to fall for anything."

"She's as smart as they come, out here," Richard answered, and Vanessa felt sickened at a tremor of love for him, even now. "I can't stay here, after this."

"Fine then, kid," said the other black sheep. "But wrap it up. We've got to be out of town before the moon goes down."

Richard turned back and sat beside her. "I'm sorry about all of this, Vanessa. I wish I could take you with me. But you're just not all that special. But mostly, I'm sorry this isn't going to hurt."

Out came the knife, slicing into the tender flesh under her ears and plowing a red furrow down her shaggy flanks to her tail, as neatly as any diagram in the Foxfire Book.

But Richard was wrong. It hurt like hell.

His sheepish smile was wet, warm and wicked, and it might be another trick, but she could see the wolf inside him. He might be immune, or he might just have it so locked down, that it never came out to play. But it raced behind his eyes, just the same. He only looked like a sheep on the outside.

"Ask yourself," he said in a jocular tone, his knife chattering off the shivering bones of her ribs, "why you have to be dumb, to be strong."

The day after every full moon was a National Day of Rest. Only the 7-11, the churches, the butcher shops and the emergency rooms were open in town. Most folks slept in until noon, when the NFL preseason games from the night before replayed. The Chargers looked to have a decent offensive package for once, but the Raiders sacked the quarterback in his own end zone, cracked his ribs and ate his heart for a safety. He was expected to miss the rest of the season.

Vanessa woke up in her bed, and stayed there.

The next day, she tried to weasel out of school, but Mom made her go. She wore a hooded sweatshirt to cover her bald head and the scabby, itchy pink mess of her half-healed back.

Hannah's parents let her stay home. Lucky bitch got her face blown off, but at least she didn't know what really happened in Richard's house.

Everyone was talking about Richard, but there was no announcement in homeroom. His desk sat empty. Someone with a radio said the Sheriff was investigating and would make an announcement, but it was pretty obvious what was coming. The bloody rags in the house matched Richard Pilcher's scent. His murderers were not identified, but from the lingering stares she got as she slinked down the hall, Vanessa thought she had somehow got the credit. Richard's devious black sheep friends must've turned on him.

Unless it was another trick, she thought uneasily, and he was still out there. She should tell someone what he really was, and about the danger he posed, and warn the world that he wasn't alone.

She could do this and still take credit for killing him, maybe. She was still chewing this over when the intercom razzed Health class and ordered her to the nurse's office.

That was a new one. Fights and trouble, she knew, but the nurse's office? She wasn't sick, and the nurse wasn't allowed to give out anything stronger than aspirin, anyway.

Two Sheriff's deputies and a bunch of angry, red-eyed parents huddled in the back of the room. She really didn't believe any of it could be about her, until she saw her father sulking among them.

So they were spotted at Pilcher's house. So what? Full moon nights were like Carnival in Rio. Crimes of passion didn't count for shit. They would probably just hit her for a stool sample, and when none of Richard's teeth or toenails came out in the wash, she could come clean. Anyway, she'd be entering Berserker country as a celebrity.

The Sheriff came over with the nurse and requested some privacy. They took her behind a screen and he ordered her to strip. Vanessa howled, "Daddy!" but he didn't intercede. "Just do what they say, honey."

She stripped and the nurse slipped on rubber gloves and gave her a pelvic exam. The pervy Sheriff stood close enough to spit his tobacco juice into her, squinting at her junk like it was modern art until her last atom of dignity floated away on the wind.

"Looks like a natural girl to me," the Sheriff finally said. *Gee, thanks, Sheriff. So glad it's finally official.* "Now missy, I suppose you better tell us what you remember about last full moon night."

Vanessa snarled, "Fuck you sideways." The nurse backhanded her off the gurney, then yanked her up by the hood.

When they saw her freshly scalped head, the Sheriff said, "Ah shit. Now it adds up." He ordered Vanessa to get cleaned up and go back to class. The nurse slapped the Red Man out of his jowl. He reluctantly took off his hat and apologized, then explained.

Hannah, Bristol and Britney each came back to their respective homes yesterday morning torn up and tired and pleading total amnesia on the entire night. But after they all ended up at the hospital, they grudgingly gave her up. Any loyalty was out the window, anyway, after what she allegedly did to them.

They all told the same story. Vanessa—or someone who looked and smelled just like Vanessa—had come and sprung them out of traps or saved them from bleeding out from their toy car injuries ... and then scalped them.

The whole pack blamed her.

She'd have to change schools. Her clique was ruined. "It was him!" she screamed. "Rabbit! I mean, Richard Pilcher!"

"That's impossible, miss," the Sheriff said. "He was attacked in his bed, and his remains dragged out into the canyons. By the volume of blood at the scene, we're pretty sure he was in no shape—"

"It's a trick! He's still out there! And there's more of them ..." She got up off the gurney and came at the Sheriff with her cracked nails out. Dad and the nurse grabbed her and held her back. "He's smarter than you and he doesn't need to change, but he's out there, and he's not alone, and he's going to come back ..."

The Sheriff asked the nurse to give Vanessa something strong to help her relax, and then left the school with his hat on backwards. Dad slipped out in the commotion without saying goodbye.

The nurse gave her a pill and stroked Vanessa's flayed back with chubby, rough palms covered in tufts of wiry black hair.

"You'll be back to normal in no time, sweetie," she said. Her nostrils flared and took in Vanessa's scent. Her orange eyes bugged with alarm, but then she smiled, as she realized the strange blood she smelled on Vanessa was not on her claws, but in her belly. "On second thought, I suppose congratulations are in order ..."

BLIND ITEM

If you know me at all, you know I'll publish anything. Doesn't matter if it ruins lives, or if no one believes it, or even if it's true. But I won't put my name to this.

If you don't know me, so much the better. I take pictures of celebrities, but not at phony functions where they stand around like action figures against that endless corporate logo wallpaper. I'm more of a big game hunter. I stalk the wily beasts in their native habitat. Nobody can read and none of the stars can talk, and every publicist uses the same robotic verbiage to honk out their empty spin, so my pictures *are* the story. When I drop shots of an A-list sitcom daddy with a reputation as a lady-killer gobbling WeHo hot dogs instead of tacos, my editors know they won't have to lawyer up, because I've got somebody's scalp in my claws. Sometimes, the star's management buys the shots and buries them. I've burned more celebutards than tanning beds. It's the only thing about this job that still gets me excited, I freely admit. It reminds me why I used to love them.

I used to see those searchlights sweeping the night sky like God and his angels were expected any minute, somewhere across town. Maybe it was just a movie premiere or a used car sale, but I ate up the hype like secret vitamins. I vowed to do anything to get inside that light and see what all the fuss was about.

I'm not just a pest with a camera. I trained and worked for years as a fashion photographer. Nobody in this town knows more about how to make them look good. Nobody tries harder to keep them relevant, but they spit on us.

I eat their hate like Wheaties. I did not get into this business to get laid or be anyone's friend. And I sure as hell don't want to be famous, any more than the guy who shot that running, burning Cambodian girl would've wanted to share a napalm shower.

We get the celebrities we deserve, and somehow, no matter how flashy the package, no matter how loud the crowd cheers, we know we're getting ripped off. Marilyn Monroe isn't as hot as most second-string underwear models, but that thing she became for 1/100 of a second at a time made her a goddess. Doesn't matter if she's dead; what you see in her eyes is still out there, looking for you.

They don't make them like they used to. Stars, I mean. Dead-eyed decoys is what they give us. Bait in a badly camouflaged trap.

But I digress. This is not a memoir. I'm only the camera, but I burned the original disks and I'll take the prints to my grave, so I have to tell it.

This is about her …

(I won't use her name. Don't need the headache, and don't need to, because you *know* her. Or you think you do. It's a lie that the name is the same as the thing. Call her name, and they know you want her, but something very different from the fantasy will come to collect. Names claim nothing in a place where everybody drops Ecstasy and renames themselves every time they sober up. There is no name, no word, for what she really is now, anyway.)

A perennial star of tube and screen a few years ago, but now the queen of tabloid smears, superior court dockets and basic cable reruns. Whether she's getting caught shoplifting on Rodeo Drive or puking in the River Phoenix memorial gutter out front of the Viper Room, she's still America's crab-infested sweetheart. For a culture conditioned to both crave and despise fame, she's a career-long car crash, and nobody looks away, nobody learns a thing. Tabloid snaps of her three-way coke orgy at the Satori rehab chalet in Sedona opened bigger than her highest-grossing feature. The bitch ran over my foot and broke my toe in her Maserati at Coachella last year, but I didn't press charges, because her dumb, drunken antics bought me a BMW.

She came out of the Marmont an hour before last call Friday night, and alone. A sure sign of impending drama. She was still supposed to be in rehab. Her erstwhile girlfriend was spinning at Cannes, and she'd been implicated with a married X-Games athlete two weeks before. She'd dyed her hair red again. I'd hated her as a blonde. I remember I felt like singing.

The usual goon squad followed her to the curb, snapping taunt-pics and shaking her down with ugly, blunt questions. You never know when you'll hit a nerve and get the target to go Full Metal Britney on your ass. But she just weathered the lightning flashes and hit her cigarette like sucking venom out of a snakebite, her glassy rape-gaze orbiting the moon. The valet brought her silver Italian snob-coffin and she peeled out east on Sunset to turn up Laurel Canyon.

I followed her into the hills. She didn't see me, but she drove like she did. She scorched the wafer-thin racing tires on the hairpin curves and blitzed every stop sign to the top of the hill, leaving a mile-long burnt-rubber autograph. I followed her through the last stop sign before Mulholland, and the dark of One AM turned into a red and blue high noon.

Down in the flats and in the Valley, it's a lawless, nonstop demolition derby, but go up into the hills in a cheap piece of shit car or a Mazda pickup full of lawnmowers, and you'll find the cops thicker than tumbleweeds. A cloud of fear-piss hangs around every half-hidden stop sign.

My BMW should've earned me a pass. But the cops all know her, and if I was following, they knew me, too.

The cop—young, chiseled Latino sportscaster type—rapped on my roof with his baton, then on the glass to show me he'd chipped my paint.

Spared me the speech, wrote me up for Failure to Stop, Reckless Driving, and searched my car. Unscrewed the telephoto lens of my Nikon and dropped it in the gutter. *Blar-har-har, no coke in here …*

Finally, when our little make-out session was over, he advised me to go home and stop stalking respected citizens, smashed out one of my taillights, and wished me a magical evening.

I didn't ask why they didn't pull her over. That would've nailed her down for me to shoot, and any way they handled it would reflect badly on LAPD's sterling rep. The class chasm is so deep and so wide, you can't hide it, so why try? But the groundlings in the cheap seats want to see up the skirts of the immortals, and all the other side really has to sell is carefully orchestrated peeks behind the curtain wall. It's why I pull down 200k per annum and spend so much on lenses the size of elephant trunks.

I sat parked on Mulholland for a while, letting the dregs of adrenaline cook off before I did something dumb. I should go back down the way I came and take the 101 home to Studio City, but the smashed taillight might get me pulled over by Highway Patrol. The only smart play was to take the narrowest, darkest side street into the Valley. I decided to risk slinking down Mulholland to the 405, instead.

Ogle the palaces, chateaus and fuck-fortresses of the gods, and try to remember why I once wanted to be like them.

The view was for shit, the sparkle of the Valley lights drowning in smog and brushfire smoke, a nebula of attention-starved nobodies twinkling like they were further away than the stars.

It's still beautiful. It can still knock you sideways and make you fall in love with it all over again. Just to set you up for the next time it fucks you …

Mulholland wriggled and noodled to its terminus at Skirball and the 405, but all the onramps were blocked off and a Caltrans crew was tearing up the Sepulveda bridge. I stayed on Mulholland and crossed the gridlocked river of diamonds and rubies. Getting worked over by fascist cocksuckers always brings out the aesthete in me.

West of Sepulveda Pass, the hills get even wilder, and the McMansions retreat behind shaggy landscaping and rusty wrought-iron gates. The high tide of TV's golden age crested here and rolled back to leave a lot of aging freaks in their crumbling stucco villas, popping pills and watching their cracked swimming pools turn into primeval swamps. Past a couple megachurches and a fire station, the scrub brush and coyotes take over. I could've turned down Calneva into the Valley, but I didn't want to go home. Something didn't want me to. It wanted me to witness what I saw when I came around the turn overlooking the vacant lot behind Bel Air Presbyterian.

Pepper trees and scrub pines crowded the edge of the lot, but they didn't quite hide the squad car parked under them with its lights off.

I looked away and hit the gas and then the brake. If it was the same cop, I was already boned. But then I saw I'd struck lucky. He already had someone pulled over. In the split second before I passed it, I almost gave myself whiplash.

Her silver Maserati.

There's no place to park out there, so I just pulled onto the shoulder around the next bend. Traffic? There was none. I got my starlight lens and my stealth Nikon. It's covered in matte-black grip tape, and it can render a clear image in pitch blackness that makes the Pam & Tommy sex tape look like the Paris Hilton sex tape.

The sandy shoulder rose up into a ridge that overlooked the dirt lot, but there was no cover. Odd thickets of exotic wild grasses rose almost shoulder-high on the other side. Scottish heather, Russian thistle, pampas and bamboo linked arms and tried to tear my clothes off like adoring fans with thorns for fingers. My leather jacket fared okay; my jeans and running shoes, not so much. I made enough goddamned noise the cop should've spotted me, but when I finally got within fifty yards of the parked cars, I saw he had his hands full.

And she had her mouth full.

She gets arrested a couple times a year, but the cops pull her over a couple times a month. If there're no paparazzi around, they let her off with a warning. She's beat every rehab program in the country, and her stupid soap opera saga clogs up the courts and the jails like a kilo bindle of coke passing through a smuggler's gut.

Every peeper on my beat knew the cops had to get some kind of payback for letting her slide, and now I had it.

The setup was so perfect, I would be looking for Satan's lawyer with a contract to sign, if I were a religious man. But I told myself it was just the dumb luck of the doggedly obsessive, and started shooting.

The cop could've been the same asshole who shook me down, in the ghostly greenish murk of my light-gathering lens. He leaned against her door with one hand clamped on the back of her head. Deep auburn hair veiled her face, but there was no mistaking that profile.

Saying something nasty to her in a throaty growl, he thrust into her until she choked on him. Her hand came up, but circled his thigh, clinging to his utility belt, pulling him deeper.

I switched the camera to video and tried to creep up close enough to capture some audio. I got something better. For just a second, her eyes lock on the lens and she slow-burn bats her lashes, as if to say, *you're next, little boy …*

God, what a whore. It must've chafed her, to turn down that Vivid contract last year. She loved it like only a tranny who's fooled a dumb sailor can love it.

The cop had to work pretty hard, to remind her she wasn't supposed to.

"Watch the fucking teeth!" he shouted and tried to pull out, but she wouldn't let go. "Your mouth feels like a frozen turkey's asshole, what's the matter with you?"

I had edged up until I was twenty feet away, propped in the fork of the pepper tree like a nearsighted sniper. I was watching the action, not my footing. A fallen branch or some shit crunched underfoot. I dropped to my knees and dove into the brush, but he saw me.

"Freeze, fuckhead!"

I started to run, what was he going to do, shoot me with his dick hanging out?

"*Stop, or I'll fucking shoot you!*" I turned to advise him of my rights, but he didn't come running. Not right away.

She wouldn't let him go. Her tiny fingers hooked in the leather loops of his belt. He slapped her so hard her head rebounded off the steering wheel, but he was the one screaming like a car alarm. He backed up tucking his junk in with one hand and trying to draw his gun with the other, and tripped on his own feet.

I started to come back down the slope into the trees again, shooting video of the cop trying to get up. His legs were like noodles, but superior training won out, and he managed to draw his gun and point it at me, then her.

"Out of the fucking car!" He turned back to tell me to get on the ground, but by then, I was halfway to the next zip code.

Deciding not to shoot me in the back, the cop finally came loping after me. He let out this low moan when he ran, with one hand holding his crotch and the gun swinging like a winged thing on a tangled string.

He popped off two shots, wild and into the air. I juked left towards the road and a huge stand of prickly pear cacti, then turned right and tumbled down a loose gravel slope.

Camera in the air, I skidded down the rock-studded cheese-grater on my right side. Thunder crashed and a blinding flash took my eyesight. It was all so fucking ridiculous ... *she* bit him, and he was shooting at *me?*

I rolled rolled rolled, and he came tumbling after me. I hit my head, my shoulder, my ass, but I kept the camera safe. I'm a fucking professional.

I crashed into a sagging chain-link fence embedded in high weeds, grateful but pinned down for the cop.

He crashed into me and tried to grab me with his sticky black hands. His gun was gone, lost somewhere on the slope. He was like a last-call drunk, ridiculously strong but totally uncoordinated, trying to wrestle me to the ground and get an arm around my throat. All his authority, all the wonderful toys on his Batman belt forgotten, he was just a big man who wanted me dead.

I've got into shoving matches with bodyguards and publicists and Event Staff more times than I can remember, but I've never had to fight for my life. The cop had me pinned against the fence and put every ounce of his huge, donut-batter ass behind strangling me.

I hit him with the only thing I had. My camera is a digital, but the casing is carbon steel and graphite. You can bust a padlock with it, and still shoot a decent fashion spread.

The first hit split his eyebrow. His head whipped back, his fist spasmed and tried to tear out my trachea. I hit him again, again, I don't know how many times. When I finally stopped, my camera was slick with blood and bone chips. The cop wheezed into my face like the last squeeze of syrup from Aunt Jemima's head. I pushed him off me and then fell on top of him. He didn't get fresh with me again, but his corpse twitched under me like a Magic Fingers bed for a while. His little partner still stuck out the flap of his fly, gushing blood like a garden hose. It wasn't just scraped; at least half of the head was missing.

"You fucked up everything," she said, right behind me. I jumped back and brandished my camera. I almost threw it at her, but she had the cop's gun. It took both her little hands to hold it up, but they didn't tremble. It might've been resting on a surveyor's tripod.

"I didn't do shit," I shot back. "This is *your* mess, this is, this is ..."

I was knee-deep in a dead cop. His blood was all over my camera. His blood, hair and brains were under my fingernails.

She cocked the gun. Wiping white powder from under her nose and blood off her chin, she looked nothing like the doe-eyed lost little girl fame had thrown under so many buses. This was the Teflon-coated nymphet with a safety razor under her tongue, the brazen bitch-goddess she fleetingly channeled for a fistful of fashion spreads and a couple movies, before it burned her out.

"It's *our* mess, now," she said. "You've got to help me ..."

"You're out of your fucking mind! This is a *cop*! You couldn't pay me to—"

Barefoot, she leapt down the slope to give me a quick lesson in swallowing unwelcome cylindrical objects. The hot barrel raised blisters on my lips. "You're gonna help me make this right, and you'll get what you want ..."

"I can go home?"

She looked up at the stars, then smiled at me ... not the dazed smirk she mustered for red carpet petting sessions, but a real smile. It looked like something stolen. "You don't want to go home."

We took a while dragging the cop up the slope, because *we* didn't do it. I pulled him up by his ankles. She supervised.

I followed her Maserati in the squad car. The dashboard camera was, obviously, disabled, and the radio was pinging with calls for the car I was sitting in. I didn't pick it up. I just drove the car, and she drove me.

We went west on Mulholland for another mile, where the only signs of humanity are the realtors' signs offering imaginary lots on the wild hillsides. We turned up an unmarked private road and passed through an open gate that swung shut like a varmint trap when we passed through it. The Maserati bounced and fishtailed up the narrow, rutted dirt track, and I stayed close.

She said she knew what to do, and where to go. She had a plan. How stupid was I to buy into that? I'd made a fortune off her harebrained coke-whore clown show. She had a plan, and I had 2nd degree murder all over me.

The road squeezed through a narrow, wiggly canyon for a quarter mile, then emerged into a bowl-shaped valley filled with gray water, enclosed in high steep sandstone cliffs crowned with windowless castles. It hugged the shore of the reservoir until the far side, where it curved up to terminate before an old Spanish bungalow that looked like the last of the red-hot lovers' silent-era love nest. Even under the too-bright starlight, it had that weird, amputated glamour of a scene from old movies. I knew I'd seen it a hundred times. But no one came out here, and even the blind houses on the peaks looked away.

She got out of her car and stepped into her punish-me pumps, lit a cigarette as she hobbled down the cobblestone driveway to wave me out of the cop car. "Get him in there ... Leave the keys in it ..." She sounded spacey again, lost little girl coked out of her mind and playing director. "*They* got me into this mess, they can fucking well get me out ..."

"Where the hell are we? Who's going to fix this? You can't even get into Disneyland anymore, I don't think they're gonna help you cover up a murder—"

Her eyes went glassy and her bottom lip trembled, just like a baby's. Screaming, "WHY ARE YOU ATTACKING ME? WHO'S SIDE ARE

YOU ON?" she bashed me in the ear with the cop's gun. I got out of the car, enough of her shit, gun or no gun, she was going down.

She backed away, that weird, cold calm back in control. "You're just like the rest of them, then. Fine, no skin, you'll get what you want. You'll get what everybody wants. Pop the trunk."

I did like she told me. Dragged the body out of the trunk. I didn't remind her cop cars had GPS and LoJack and shit, and I didn't remind her that we were both looking at capital murder. I just nodded in time with her wound-up whining about how nobody understood how hard it was to be "on" all the time, nobody cared what it did to you, they just howled for more and then laughed at you when you crashed to earth. But she knew what to do, she had a plan. They finally let her in on the secret, and if I hadn't fucked it up for her, she would already be golden.

Wonderful. Cult bullshit, the only thing in Hollywood more boring than drugs.

The doors and windows were boarded up, but the storm cellar doors stood wide open, and a buttery yellow light spilled out from somewhere deep inside, like someone had set it up for us. I looked around one more time for hidden camera crews and found none, but now the place we were about to enter looked like the one-room schoolhouse from *Little House On The Prairie*.

The stairs were too steep, and I dropped the body when I saw the man waiting at the bottom.

The cop somersaulted down the stairs, leaving splashes of blood on each tread, and did a hilarious face-plant on the checkerboard tile floor of the cellar.

Old and familiar, like that one old guy in all those old movies, and dressed in a vintage black wool suit and jodhpurs. He stepped back to keep his patent leather shoes, like little shiny hooves, out of the mess, but otherwise, he seemed cool with the dead cop. Looking right through me, he nodded at her as she prodded me down the stairs. "We're expected," she said, in that flat, tone-deaf tone she used whenever she read her lines from off-camera cue cards. "I come here of my own free will, but I will leave when glory is finished with me."

"As you will, madame," the butler replied in a dusty Prussian purr and clicked his heels, then backed into an alcove. He didn't help.

Did I say it was a cellar? It was fucking Carlsbad Caverns. Crimson flocked wallpaper and gilded mildew and legions of faded, stained headshots covered the walls. All the great ones from the last eighty years. Uprooted fixtures and piles of crushed velvet furniture under yellow sheets made a mountain range against the far wall, but the main attraction was long gone.

A huge sunken circular dent marked where something impossibly heavy once sat in the center of the room. Only a rusted drainpipe, about eighteen inches wide, stuck knee-high out of the floor.

"All the great ones came here," she whispered. "They had parties here, can you imagine? Only the greatest stars, and they came down here and they climbed into a huge marble bath together. Fuck, what must that have been like?"

"Silent movie orgies, great. Buster Keaton and Fatty Arbuckle pouring the pork to Clara Bow and Lillian Gish. So what?"

"They weren't just orgies, shut the fuck up … they were offering themselves up to something greater than their own greatness, okay? My agent told me it was the reason the movies came here in, like, 1910 … they woke it up and it made them bring it, like, offerings? Some were sucked dry and eaten up, but the others—the *crème de la crème*–they were remade, right? Into *stars* …"

Scanning the Dorian Grey headshots grinning through mold and cracked glass, I saw nothing but Hollywood royalty. *The great old ones …*

She knelt before the drainpipe, then spread her slender legs and wrapped them around it suggestively. I hated myself for wanting her.

Her eyes went crossed for a moment, method acting bullshit, summoning the Muse. Finally, she stuck her fingers down her throat.

Bulimia? Really? And me without my camera. She flipped me the bird and retched up a lawyer's paycheck's worth of booze and sushi. Something bigger choked her for a second, clung to her teeth when it came out. I guess we all know what it was.

For a long time, she just sat there wrapped around that pipe like a crackhead, making some noise down below her diaphragm over and over, like it had to be some kind of name. Occasionally, she gagged and spat down the pipe, looking for the butler, but nothing happened for long enough that she began to think this was some kind of horrible mistake. Whatever magic might've granted wishes and made superstars there once, you only had to look at TMZ or the *Enquirer* to know it was long since out of business.

"What was supposed to happen, honey?" I asked, real soft, in my warmest, fuzziest personal assistant voice.

She pointed the gun at me like she'd never seen me before, and how did I get in her bedroom? Then, finally finding her method, she split wide open. "I DON'T KNOW! I did everything right, but the stupid cop wouldn't come up here with me, and *then* you showed up ..."

"If you don't want people like me to follow you, you could always go get a real job ..."

"You think this is funny? I'm just a big joke to everybody ... I suppose I deserve this, though fucked if I could tell you why ..." She dropped the gun and crawled across the floor like a broken-backed cat. "I just wanted to *be* something, just to feel for real what all those assholes thought they saw in me ... Everything I did was just to keep up with it, to capture it and become it ... I just wanted to be loved ... by something larger than myself ..."

By now, she was at my feet on hands and knees, and she started climbing. I don't need to tell you, this is the moment most paparazzi fantasize about. These out-of-control beauties are all flaming bags of damage, and the worse they get, the harder they look around for someone to save them, and anyone they've seen more than once starts to look like an anchor.

All I ever wanted was to capture that momentary flicker of beauty and make it immortal. If she only would have let me in before, I could have saved her career with a photo shoot ... or at least saved for history a snapshot of perfect beauty on the edge of the ledge.

Broken, weeping, she was crawling to me, her hands searching up my thigh and seeking my belt.

The perfect shot I'd thrown away my life for, and I had no camera. I tried to kneel and pick her up. We should get the fuck out of here. Set the cop car on fire and run away to Mexico, and then the Maldives or somewhere else with no extradition treaty ...

I thought that. Believed it. I saw it in her eyes when she looked up at me, saw the glossy blackness of her pupils as holes only I could fill, felt her needing me to protect her, reverence her, possess her ... forever.

I fell hard to the floor and she swooped down on me, ripped my pants down and descended on my cock like a hawk on a squirrel.

Her mouth was colder than it should be, yes, and I could feel her teeth, but that cop was clearly some kind of blowjob snob. With her breath, she transmuted it to a bar of gold, and with the merest stroke of her tongue, she quickened it into a solar flare of pure plasma energy.

I enjoy a good blowjob as much as the next guy, but this was something else. This was the fulfillment of the promise those lips had made to every man in the free world, and delivered only to a lucky few whenever she blew an audition or her meds ran out. And it *was*, it really was, too good to be true …

I'm not ashamed to say I didn't last as long as it took you to read this sentence. But she didn't let go, and I didn't go soft, and it only got better.

Someone was watching us. I know that feeling. I *cause* that fucking feeling. I looked around just like the cop did in the moment before he saw me.

Something had answered her call. Maybe not what she was expecting, but I don't think she cared.

They came out of the drain. First this oily, eerie rainbow light, and then …

They looked like the fat, corrugated hoses on honey wagons, the trucks that drain port-a-shitters. But they also looked like the soft, stinging things on a sea anemone. I could see through them, see the light they were pumping out, and the stuff they were taking in.

One of them coiled around the cop like an anaconda, and went down his throat. Something came pumping out of it at high volume, bloating the body until his chiseled face bulged and his badge and buttons popped and skipped across the checkerboard floor. I watched it and did nothing because … you have gotten a blowjob before, yes? You're familiar with the transaction, at least? Okay, then.

Abruptly, it stopped filling him up and suddenly reversed the flow, sucking out the fluid and everything else, the liquefied insides, until only a knurled rag of jerked skin and soft, floppy bones in the blue-black uniform was left.

Another colorless, see-through cable snaked across the room to disappear behind her. Still shaky from *grand mal* orgasm #4, I got up on one elbow to see where it went.

For a silly second, it looked like she'd grown a tail. It glowed like radioactive maple syrup was coming out of it, pure rainbow starshine, and it was literally shining it up her ass. But whatever it was doing to her, it wasn't trying to digest her.

I pulled myself back, but stopped when I felt her nibbling teeth get serious, her tongue making me forget we were ever two separate animals. I stopped fighting, but I started wondering what was really blowing me.

I looked around for something to persuade her to let me go, when another cable reared up before me like a cobra. Its mouth looked like a lamprey without the charm. Hooks bristled as it turned itself inside out and lunged for my throat.

I caught it in my hand, but it was slick with slime and sludge from the dissolved cop. Pouting, collagen-pumped lips blew me a sulfuric kiss, wafted stench like the ocean floor and the grease trap of a deep fryer up my nose. Even so, I almost let it do what it wanted.

It slithered through my grip, but I grappled and twisted it around until, writhing and puckering like a sphincter with teeth, it latched onto her throat.

Her adorable teeth gouged me but let me go as she gagged on the acidic torrent pumping into her neck. Rolling away from me and trying to tear the lamprey off even as the fragile contours of her face swelled to the shape of a baked potato.

At the other end of her, the changes were just as drastic. Flabby jailbait legs ripened with well-marbled muscle and strained out, growing longer and stronger out of a perfectly toned, heart-shaped ass. Her rack had always been pedoliciously underdeveloped, which deficit of maturity she'd corrected with woefully unsubtle D-cup bolt-ons. Now, her renascent cleavage ejected the saline and silicone like lanced boils, then regrouped and blossomed into bouncing, perfect, natural breasts. Her ribcage unhinged like a snake's jaw to make room for new vertebrae to support the udder perfection up front, and the two extra ribs she'd need to do that impossible thing Marvel superheroines and Varga pinup girls do with their hips.

From the neck down, my trashy nymphet had been remade into Raquel Welch. Upstairs, though, the skin split like a rotten rubber mask and red-gray bile soup jetted out to scald her shaking, maddeningly expressive hands.

And here, I'd always thought she couldn't act.

I crawled backwards across the checkered floor, watching it try to eat and anoint her at the same time.

The whole cellar shook in the grip of at least a 5.0 tremor. Headshots fell and shattered and mirrored glass rained down from the ceiling.

I thought about getting the gun for all of two stupid seconds. I wasn't going to shoot anyone, but anything between me and the door was going to get fucked up. The butler stepped out of his alcove with his hands out like he was catching a little kid.

My windmilling fists crowned his head and chest and sickeningly soft belly. He didn't just drop, he imploded. His head deflated and shrank into his shirt and his hands retracted up his sleeves. The motheaten old suit slouched to the floor, hiding whatever had filled it until it slithered down the Romanesque rathole in the back of the alcove.

I ran up the stairs on all fours, into the dishwater predawn light. Down the road past the Maserati and the squad car. Not stopping to look behind me at the chateau/prison/schoolhouse/Gothic manor that collapsed into itself with a sigh like an Oscar envelope filled with anthrax tearing open, or the reservoir slopping over its banks like a tub full of fat asses. Down the dirt road and over the gate. Down Mulholland past the white-haired lady jogger, the retarded cyclist and the blind dogwalker, each of whom stopped to take my picture. Hiding my face, I ran past them all, to where my car still sat parked on the shoulder.

Home.

No cops were waiting. No detectives came to my door. I didn't go outside. I thought I could outrun it, but the *E! Breaking News* came on while I packed my suitcase. In three minutes, I decided I was not going anywhere.

She was out of rehab early, and looking better than ever. TMZ's sheetsniffers pimped rumors she spent the time in a spa and under a surgeon's knife, but by God, she got it right, this time.

"She's back, rested and ready for a second chance," the closet-case anchor snorted, but it wasn't a recovery. It was a goddamned resurrection.

Rosy cheeks and clear, green-gold eyes and not a trace of the eyebags, nic-stained fingers or ghastly pallor we'd all come to know and loathe. No protoplastic lampreys wriggling under those intriguing, engaging features.

I switched to the local news and waited for the cop. A brief, heartfelt eulogy for the LAPD officer killed instantly just before 4AM, when his patrol car went off a bridge in the midst of seismic retrofitting at Skirball Drive and plunged into early pre-rush hour traffic. The bridge will be renamed the Charles "Chip" Stillwell Overpass, when it's completed in 2014. In this town, there's still more than one way to get famous.

I know I'll never leave here alive. When it gets dark, I can see the searchlights out there, searching for me. Even in broad daylight, the soft-focus rainbow glow is coming from the storm drain out front of my apartment.

I don't think it'll make any difference, but I deleted all the pictures, after making a couple prints. The compositions are nice—*Rodney King Behind the Green Door*. If anyone in this shitty city deserved to know, or if it would make any difference, I'd send them to somebody, but maybe that's what it wants. This thing is old and sick, and more than half-forgotten by a new Hollywood that goes through reality stars like a bug zapper. She's revived the old school, and her rise will be christened a revival of the sirens and chanteuses of the Golden Age of the studio casting couch system. You will all fall down and worship, and it won't need to hide what it does to me when it finds me, because nobody will be watching anything but her.

NATASHA HATES A VACUUM

Natasha was pretty sure the Azerbaijani cabdriver cursed her as she got out on the corner of Coldwater and Ventura, lugged her belongings out of the Sultan Cab and counted out the fare from her beaded wallet. She was not used to taking cabs, indeed they frightened her—the ridiculous expense, the greedy meter, the cabdrivers who figured they could treat her like trash—but she didn't want to be seen walking the streets with the vacuum cleaner. Anyone who spotted the dumpy, forty-two year old Latina in her faded pink sweatsuit would know her for a housekeeper, and would conclude, quite rightly, that she was also a thief.

In all her years as a cleaner, Natasha had never stolen anything from an employer. *What happened today was just an accident*, she kept telling herself. *I thought I was doing good.* Maybe she still was, and maybe she had lost her mind, and her job in the bargain.

Limping north on Coldwater, she risked calling Tia Blanca again on her prepaid phone from the cleaning service. It had been chirping and vibrating like an angry baby bird in her purse, but she couldn't answer it. If she could only catch Tia Blanca and take the vacuum to her, then she could face the consequences. Perhaps, they would even be grateful.

No, not the people on the hill. They appreciated only her labor and her silence. For them, even a few insincere words of gratitude cost far more than money.

Jesus, please make her pick up, Natasha prayed, but when her prayers were answered, she almost hung up. A frenzy of diabolical accordions icepicked her ear, and she thought it must be the vacuum playing tricks on her again, but then a wheezy old woman's voice cut through, commanding the infernal din to cease. "Bueno, I have been expecting your call …"

"Really? Then who is this?" Even in her dire predicament, Natasha still got irked at Tia Blanca's theatrics.

Tia Blanca consulted the spirits in her Caller ID and turned up her hearing aid, while Natasha yipped with terror when the vacuum cleaner was snatched from her grasp. She spun on her threadbare sneakers, planted her weight on the ball of her left foot and nearly fainted from the pain. Her huge purse filled with cleaning supplies slammed into her hip and knocked her on her bottom.

The infernal machine lay supine on the otherwise deserted sidewalk. The wheels had stuck in a crack in the pavement.

Just an accident.

"Natasha, are you still there?"

Picking herself up, she felt tempted to just run away, leaving it on the street. It was no more her responsibility than anyone else. "Tia Blanca, I need your help ..." It almost came out right there on the phone, but she choked it back, along with tears. When it came time to put it into words, she could not accept that even Tia Blanca Villalobos, the crazy old *bruja*, would believe her.

"Is it very serious?" The old crone's voice went girlish.

"I have run afoul of a very bad spirit," she said, as plainly as if admitting to the flu. "It has killed two people that I know of, but everyone will think I did it ... I need to ..."

"Don't come up here," Tia Blanca said. "My grandson's band is rehearsing for a wedding up here. Meet me at the taqueria on the corner. I'll bring you something to ward off the spirit, if it should come upon you again."

"That's not going to be enough," Natasha said bleakly, but she finally picked up the vacuum cleaner and hop-jogged to the next corner, and the *Gallo Negro #3* taqueria, already in sight. "I have it here with me."

By the time Tia Blanca came in the door, Natasha had gone through three orders of menudo. The three loud white kids at the corner table took no notice of her, but the boy at the counter and the pregnant girl in the next booth sneered at her empty plates as if she were a pig. But she hadn't eaten any of it.

"I thought you were above superstitious nonsense, Natasha Altamorena." Tia Blanca slid into the booth across from her and popped her arthritic knuckles. If she enjoyed anything more than the diversion of someone else's problems, it was seeing a skeptic eat crow. She looked long and wide and hard at Natasha to read her aura. Her eyes opened so wide, Natasha could almost see her inner light reflected in the old woman's huge bifocals. At last, she said, "This won't be easy or cheap. But I can do it for you."

From her straw purse, Tia Blanca took out a bunch of *botanica* candles and lit them, each off its own kitchen match. Over the painted faces of the Orishas, Tia Blanca had glued images of their earthly incarnations, which she'd clipped out of *People*. As she arranged her portable shrine and stocked it with candy and cigarettes, she chattered of the upheaval in the spirit world—Chango had deserted his faithful but clingy wife Oba to cavort and breed with his kindred spirit Oya, the slut. In her bitter jealousy, Oba had forsaken her duties as the guardian of marriage and made a string of scandalously bad romantic comedies. But the signs and portents in the tabloids hinted that Chango was again texting his former wife and might be considering a reunion.

"It's not like that," Natasha said, waving at the shrine. "The stars on the hill can't help me."

Clicking her tongue, Tia Blanca lectured, "Why else would they raise up such beautiful, empty vessels and shower them with glory, if not to invite the spirits to come into them and sample earthly delights?" She took out a knotted handkerchief and gingerly unwrapped it to present Natasha with an egg. "You need not believe, you have only to ask, and they will answer."

"But it's the stars on the hill, that cursed me. It's—"

"Bring me more meat, whore," said the vacuum cleaner, "or I'll make you sorry."

She was already as sorry as she could be, but she put her plate on the floor beneath her table. "You're a thing," she said. "You can't eat." Though she knew this wasn't true. It had to be putting it somewhere, and its canister should be filled many times over. Why was she having a conversation with this thing? After what it did …?

Tia Blanca looked at the possessed appliance as she would an unruly toddler or a flatulent dog. "You're something special, eh?"

"I am a fire too hot to be contained by any mere mortal vessel of shit. I will burn a hole in this world and suck all of your miserable kind down into the abyss—"

"Enough." Kicking her plate away from it, she planted her right foot on the vacuum to keep it from rolling away.

"This is the work of a very powerful devil," Tia Blanca hissed. A cigar appeared in her tiny, shaking hand. She lit it and blew smoke over the vacuum cleaner when the counter boy was refilling the *horchata* machine, then stubbed it out in Natasha's iced tea. "Tell me what happened. Don't leave out any names."

Sadly, there were no juicy celebrity names to drop. Natasha had worked for In the Pink Cleaning Service for three years, and cleaning houses in the Hollywood hills for nearly half her life. She didn't hire out independently because her English wasn't good enough and she didn't have a car. She'd had a car, but her son Hector wrecked it. In The Pink picked her up every morning at 5:30 in a minivan packed with other sleepy women in pink sweats and delivered them to different palatial estates and cliff-hugging glass castles in Bel Air, Sherman Oaks and the canyon enclaves of the Hollywood Hills. Unlike most services, they didn't leave their maids to hike down into Van Nuys or West Hollywood to catch a bus, but they had to be taking in four times what they paid them.

The money wasn't much better in the hills than anywhere else, but in these times, regular working people only hired maids to serve drinks at their holiday parties, or to clear out dead relatives' houses. Natasha had learned to work around them and their hare-brained instructions, and never gave them a real reason to complain. She never looked at the gossip magazines or watched much TV, so she never got starstruck. But maybe it did give her a little tickle of superiority, to scrub the toilets of the immortals.

Today's house was like all the others, inside——huge and empty and sterile, like a museum or a church of the self, with vast, hideous paintings everywhere and great vacant plains of green Carrara marble downstairs, and a loft with two master bedrooms carpeted in white angel hair. (Nothing odd? Nothing personal? Only boxes of rubber surgical gloves in every room.) Floor-to-ceiling glass walls overlooked some private, pastoral Los Angeles, where mule deer and coyotes and even a mountain lion frolicked in an oak grove, and a musclebound naked man with hair like Samson stood in a hot tub, shooting a bow and arrow at a target.

Though she had worked for her only today, the young blonde woman was far from Natasha's favorite client. She drifted around the house in a medicated haze, exhausted from changing dresses every hour, and left half-empty teacups everywhere. Coffee was bad enough, but with tea, every cup left a little bloated corpse, and if one wasn't diligent in tracking them down, they quickly became putrid cups of mold. She constantly asked Natasha if she "wouldn't mind" doing a task, a confusing trick of English idiom that Natasha never answered correctly the first two times, no matter how she replied.

Though she wouldn't recognize them, she doubted either of them was famous, let alone the breadwinner. Actors were always moving in or out of their dream houses. Everything in this house was precisely and obsessively arranged, and had been for long enough that the sun had burned silhouettes of the furniture on the interior walls. Only producers, lawyers and pharmacists had that kind of security.

After sanitizing the kitchen and bathrooms, dusting, and washing the windows and laundry, it was nearly two and the lady of the house was nowhere to be found.

("Did they have a bidet?" Tia Blanca asked. In every bathroom, she was told. How many? Six!)

Natasha didn't dare look at the backyard again, so she noisily hunted upstairs until she found the vacuum cleaner. This was the most discreet way to avoid an ugly scene, as everyone would know where she was.

It was a very strange machine, and right away, Natasha didn't trust it. It was one of those bagless European things that looked like a weapon stolen from the future. It sang like a castrato choir and collected the tufts of dog hair into a special reservoir, where it was woven into a dense mesh basket suitable for displaying dried flowers.

She made short work of the hallway and the bedrooms without seeing anyone else naked, but when she came to the end of the hall, she found a door standing open that she hadn't noticed on her first pass. It had no knob or latch, and was set into the wall like a secret entrance. The thick white eggshell paint had a single pinhole at eye-level for a tall man in it. She remembered no special instructions about avoiding any rooms. If she skipped it, she could get into terrible trouble, and it wouldn't be the first time she saw something she shouldn't.

If her curiosity had been pricked by the odd door, a quick sweep of the room failed to titillate. A single black leather egg chair sat in one corner, overlooking creation from a godlike aerie. The walls were lined with framed primitive carvings of men and women with animal heads doing nasty things. Ashtrays on every table and shelf overflowed gilded butts on the carpet. And in the center of the room, spreading almost from one wall to the other, an old, lumpy rug of rudely combed wool, stained a deep maroon that was darker than black. Its fringe of long white tassels lay as straight as courtroom evidence, as if someone had to comb them before they could enter or leave.

Nothing else. It seemed perfectly reasonable that she was supposed to dust and vacuum the room. Why else would the door have been left open?

The fancy light-scattering museum glass over the carvings was practically bearded with dust. Clouds of it floated in the air, making her cough and entertain unworthy fears. Dust was mostly hair and skin. She would never know these people's names, but she would carry them home in her lungs.

She emptied and polished all the ashtrays—eleven of them. Emptied the wastebasket into a burn bag. Squeegeed the windows. It should've taken only a few minutes to vacuum the rug. If she hadn't stepped on something sharp that went through the sole of her sneaker and into the ball of her foot the moment she turned the vacuum on, she would be home right now.

It felt like a tiger's claw in her flesh, its thickness and sharpness an intruder against which rubber, flesh and bone were as butter and lard.

She screamed and sat down hard. The vacuum snapped upright, still running on Shag setting on the odd, nubbly old Berber rug. Its regular sinusoidal threnody abruptly turned to a braying, howling honk that meant it had sucked the area rug into its intake and gotten blocked. If she didn't get up and shut it off, the motor could burn out, but her impaled foot demanded equal time.

There was indeed a hole in the sole of her shoe from which a few straggling droplets of blood flowed, but it had felt like something much, much worse.

Flipping the corner of the rug over, she instantly found the culprit. A plastic placard lay face down under the rug with a long, thick tack through it. On the front, it said, STAY OUT—DO NOT ENTER in eight languages.

Her bloody footprint on the rug was a big, glistening splat of bright crimson, but far from ruining the rug, it seemed to seep into the thirsty threads and spread out, rejuvenating the crusty maroon expanse to give it the appearance of a rippling pool of fresh blood.

The vacuum howled on, so Natasha didn't hear the lady of the house screaming at her from the doorway. She wore a lavender silk kimono and she was hysterical, and probably not for Natasha's welfare.

The blonde *gringa* slapped and pulled at her to get her out of the room like it was on fire, cursing her all the while, though Natasha couldn't understand a word of it. Steeling herself against the pain that still made her want to throw up, she tried to get up and turn the vacuum off.

The blonde was way ahead of her. She tried to shut it off, but couldn't find the button. Her hysteria redoubled, she whirled around in circles twice, then went for the cord, where it was plugged into the wall opposite the door.

What happened next was just an accident. It could happen to anyone with so little self-control. The blonde leapt over Natasha and went for the cord, but somehow managed to trip on it, wrap it around her ankle and in a howling panic, stumbled into and through the glass wall, and out of sight.

The cord whipped halfway out of the socket, but the vacuum roared even louder. It started to roll backwards towards the broken window, but then stopped with a weird jerk. The frayed gray rubber cord stretched taut over the window's jagged mouth.

Before Natasha had begun to even answer the question of where she had gone, the big naked man entered the room, dripping wet and demanding answers. Natasha had to cling to the wall to bring herself halfway upright, only to be thrown back on her behind by the angry, naked man.

Punching at air, he ran over to the window and let out a horribly high, desolate wail. Then he started jumping in place, but his feet wouldn't leave the puddle of water he stood in. The frayed cord jumped and twanged between his feet for a long, sickly stretch. His anguished cries became an endless, ululating shriek that finally drowned out the vacuum.

The big naked man dropped to the floor, still twitching. His thick, veiny neck, stretched over the teeth of shattered glass, began to leak. The vacuum's unbearable racket fell off to a faint rattle of ruined gears that sounded too much like a nasty laugh.

Natasha got up and said twenty rosaries, then twenty more on her long, slow trek around the room. Her ears still screamed with a dull blue tone of brutalized eardrums. Her foot burned like she'd stepped on a scorpion. She clung to the wall for support, but she was mortally afraid of touching the rug, which had changed again, and not, she thought, for the better.

It looked like it had when she'd come in: an ugly old rug from somewhere she'd never heard of. She couldn't even find the spot where she'd bled on it. Nor could she see any trace of the deep maroon color. It looked drained, consumed, the color of cigarette ash.

There are things you don't want to see, but must witness, for they are God's inscrutable work. (Like when she had to identify Jorge's body after he fell off a ladder and electrocuted himself installing a huge nativity scene in Beverly Hills.) There are other times you must avert your eyes and stop up your ears, lest the Devil, by temptation or despair, gain a foothold in your heart. (Like when her dead husband's answering machine was overloaded with passionately grief-stricken calls from three strange women.) And then there were times like this, when the question must be answered: How bad can it possibly be?

It was worse than bad. No monstrous fate concocted by the perverted man-children who wrote slasher movies could have been more wantonly cruel, so calculated to show what a bubble, a joke, was the human body.

The enormous house stood up out of a plunging hillside, surrounded by cacti that someone must have picked out to ward off burglars and paparazzi. Huge gray-green starbursts of iron-hard sawtooth blades, like spiny tank traps. The lady of the house had plunged head-first into the central spine of a massive blue agave cactus. It went up her throat and emerged south of her navel, while four more speared her neck and chest to peel her like a banana. They held her in place even after the cord retracted and snaked back into its housing in the canister of the vacuum cleaner. It stood right behind Natasha, mechanically slurping the cooling blood off the floor.

"We should leave," it said.

"And you just took it away with you?" Tia Blanca said. Her eyes darted from the vacuum cleaner to Natasha as she crossed herself.

Natasha didn't want to, but the vacuum cleaner was persuasive. It made it impossible for her to see any other outcome but her arrest for a double homicide. It offered her things, made promises, if only she would carry it away. So she called the cab and came down here.

"What did you think *I* could do?"

"Drive it out, send it back to Hell, how should I know?"

"And leave you the only suspect in the murders?"

"I never harmed anyone! I didn't touch them. The police are like magicians, now. They will see the truth."

"They won't look, when they can blame a Mexican." Tia Blanca rummaged in her purse for a while, but clearly, she was just keeping her hands busy while she searched the deeper, darker corners of her memory. "I can't cast out a spirit, unless I know its name."

Natasha shook her head.

"But it promised you a reward—"

"Yes, anything I wished for."

"You didn't make a wish, did you?"

"No, no."

"Devils only grant wishes when they are trapped, or when summoned by one who knows their true name. It costs them a little of the black fire they stole from Creation to grant a wish, and it takes something from the one who makes the wish, too. When they've given themselves away until there's nothing but a mouth and a bad attitude, they can still grant little wishes, but they're only tricks and lies. Did you bring me here to help you negotiate a deal with this devil?"

"No, Tia Blanca," she said too fast.

"Wonderful. Throw it in Tujunga Wash, if there's water in it. Better still, the ocean."

"But … it's not mine. And it's a really nice vacuum. If someone finds it, it swore it would make me suffer."

The vacuum belched, filling the taco shop with the stench of melted plastic and scorched blood. "Bring me over to that pretty, gravid slut, there. I would have milk from her te—"

"Quiet! You unclean spirit, by all the saints and incarnated orishas, I command you to speak truthfully and clearly—"

"In truth, I will have milk or blood from one or both of you, this day."

"What manner of thing are you? I command you to answer."

"I have been called rakshasa and djinn, dybbuk and devil. I was among the first-born and favorite of the Creator, later betrayed and forgotten by Him. If you know my name, then I am your humble servant, but if you know it not—"

"You are powerless, little devil. Tell us your name."

"I tire of this game, bitch."

"See? Just like I told you. Trapped for so long, he used up all his real powers, long ago. He doesn't even remember his true name. He probably doesn't even have a body, anymore. Just a nasty ghost of something that was never really alive."

The devil refused to rise to the bait. "Natasha, your flesh is overripe but not yet rotten, it is a tragedy to waste it. The loneliness in your blood is strong enough to get drunk upon. I could bring back your Jorge … he writhes on a flaming dungheap, but you can rescue him—"

Furiously scribbling upon a Post-It note pad, Tia Blanca hissed, "Don't listen!"

"Or I could make you so beautiful you could have any man … so irresistible they would kill or die to lay in your shadow …"

The reticulated hose popped off its rack and fell onto the table like a dwarf elephant's trunk, edging closer to her hand … "You don't have to say it aloud … only whisper it to me, and it is done—"

"Do something!" Natasha whimpered, shoving the hose off the table.

Tia Blanca slapped a sticky note on the vacuum canister and said something in Latin. The note had a spiky six-pointed star with lots of tiny dots and symbols around and inside it. Steam like boiled sewage escaped from every orifice of the vacuum, but it fell silent.

"Seal of Solomon," Tia Blanca said.

"I knew you'd know what to do!"

"No, dear one. We're fucked. If we can't get rid of it now, sooner or later, it will get what it wants."

"And what does it want?"

"To get out, to be free to do evil. Who knows how long it was trapped in that rug? We must think—"

"There's no time."

Tia Blanca tapped her nails on the table. "Maybe we should discuss my fee now."

Natasha pointed out the window and slid over in the seat. She grabbed the neck of the vacuum cleaner and yelped, jerking back with a stifled scream. Blisters rose and burst on her palm. A shiny swath of her smoking flesh was stuck to the vacuum's handle.

Tia Blanca reached for her friend, but then she looked outside and almost started to bolt out of the taqueria, herself.

A black limousine stopped out front and a thick black man in a suit got out and walked into the taco shop. He went to the kids and whispered something to them. They were gone before he approached the pregnant girl, who beat a retreat behind the counter with her boyfriend.

Another man got out of the limousine and came into the shop. A white man.

"Oh my God, I recognize him!" Tia Blanca said. She flushed and smiled in spite of everything. "Why didn't you say you worked for—"

"Don't say my fucking name," the white man said, in perfect, patrician Spanish, down to the Madrid lisp. Impeccably dressed and groomed, he looked like something that had escaped a terminal cancer ward. Bilious yellow skin glared through wisps of tinsel-silver hair. He coughed continuously as he crossed the taco shop to stand beside their booth.

With a gravity that commanded awed silence, he snugged his tiny hands into a pair of surgical gloves, took out a packet of Wet Naps and thoroughly wiped down the seat beside Tia Blanca. Then he took out another Wet Nap and wiped it down again. And a third. Then he did the same with the table.

Then he sat down and changed into a fresh pair of gloves. His hands splayed out on the table and shook. His fingers were yellow and shaky like he was holding dice. Scowling at them, he slipped on a pair of heavy leather gloves before he deigned to look at either of them.

"I watch your show every day," gushed Tia Blanca. "You must wear a lot of makeup—"

"Shut up, cunt."

Even Natasha recognized him, though she couldn't recall his name. He had hosted that same game show since she was a little girl, and he never seemed to age. For the last six years, they shot a Spanish version with real Latino contestants, and he hosted that one, too. He looked a lot taller on TV. His manners were better on TV, though.

He also looked twenty years older than on TV. And right now, he looked about a cup of coffee away from a fatal heart attack.

"Sir, I beg your pardon. "This … evil thing killed your wife and … her friend. I was afraid, but I thought—"

"No, don't apologize," Tia Blanca interrupted. "She did nothing to your family. Your wife wouldn't have mourned *you* for very long, by the sound of it."

He tried to take a deep breath to shout, but his lungs weren't up to it. "You have fucked up the balance of my life beyond all recognition." His anger was squeezing him, so he had to let it go. "My relationship with Corinne was complicated. But don't think I didn't know what was going on in my own home."

"He's barren," Tia Blanca said, pointing at his light. "You poor, damned man! You wanted a child so badly ..." She covered her mouth, deliciously scandalized.

The white man could care less. "You triggered a silent alarm in my office at the studio the moment you entered my study. I have a video record of you leaving the crime scene, but I won't give it to the police. I will pay the very expensive private service I used to track you down to exterminate your whole fucking bloodline, then to go down to Mexico and make a picket fence out of cousins you never knew you had, if you don't give it back."

"You just want it back? I don't understand. It killed your—"

"You fucking idiot, look at me! This isn't *me*, this isn't what I'm supposed to look like ..."

"It was always strange," Natasha said. "Your show's been on for—"

"Thirty-two seasons. Six Daytime Emmys, and thirteen fucking *TV Guide* Quality Awards. That was my first wish. See, you have to be careful what you wish for. They're crafty motherfuckers. This one said it was trapped in the rug by King Solomon himself. I bought him at a bazaar in Katmandu ... I think ..." Looking lost, the white man bit a leather-sheathed finger. Two of his teeth were missing. His gums were grayer than his hair.

"I wished for fame and fortune and security and the good will of millions. And I knew show business, so I made sure it was for a long, stable career with guaranteed ratings. And it made me a goddamned *game show host*.

I made a deal with a devil to spend half my life giving out shitty prizes to drooling morons who couldn't complete the crossword on a Happy Meal box. My show plays in thousands of nursing homes, you know. They say it's the last spot of excitement in a lot of people's lives. Waves of invalids check out when we go into reruns, every year. No shit."

He coughed, long and hard, wiped his mouth with a raw silk handkerchief. What he saw in it alarmed him. "Did you know you had to trade something? I didn't. It told me to hold something dear to me in my heart when I made that first wish. Nothing much, just a memory, a little thing that I loved less than having a perfect life. You just think of it once, and then your wish comes true, and it's gone."

"That's very terrible, sir," Tia Blanca said, almost sincerely. "What did you give up?"

"How the fuck should I know? *I gave it up*! Something I remembered, something I used to be able to do. Maybe it was my capacity to love. My first wife left in the middle of Spring sweeps, and all I cared about was that the ratings went up seventeen percent. Corinne was my fourth.

"I've given up so many other little things since then, it hardly matters, but the wishes have been all smoke and mirrors, ever since that first one. Illusions go a long way in this town, but look at me. I'm not supposed to look like this!"

He looked around the empty taco shop. The black man stood outside the door, a walking CLOSED sign.

"You might think it's the key to getting a better life, but believe me … you don't want to step into the ring with it. It's insane. Doesn't even remember its own name. You can't hope to control it, you can only try to aim it at somebody else, when it's hungry."

"So, you just want to take the vacuum cleaner and …?"

He reached into his breast pocket and took out a wallet. "I'll pay you a bonus to say my wife sent you home early, and you saw nothing. Better yet, get the fuck out of this country, and don't ever come back." He held out a tightly folded roll of the cleanest, newest money Natasha had ever seen. "Just take it and go home, Natasha."

She started to reach for the money, but Tia Blanca grabbed her hand. Hers was hot and sweaty. "Don't take it. He'll frame you for the murders. Or just wish for both of us to get hit by a car or shot by the cops for killing his trophy *puta*. For knowing …"

The white man shook his white head. "I don't want anyone else hurt. I just want this whole sordid catastrophe to disappear. That's what you people do best, right? Make a big mess, then disappear."

Natasha bit her tongue, but the blood rushed and roared in her ears, and she came as close as she ever had, to talking back to an employer.

"Don't take his money, Natasha."

The game show host slapped their hands apart. "Stay out of this, witch! If your chicken-killing peasant voodoo works, why're you all still scrubbing toilets?" He sighed and put the money back in his pocket, then peeled off the Seal of Solomon Post-It note and flicked it at them. "Good night, ladies. Forgive me if I don't kiss either of you."

Tia Blanca looked like she was coming down with a fever. She'd been right about sending the sick man away, but it wasn't like the old *bruja* to turn away money.

He slid out of the booth and grabbed the vacuum by its handle, tugged it like it weighed a ton. The black man held the door for him, but he only got halfway across the taco shop before he noticed the cord wasn't coiled neatly around its flanges on the back of the canister. It trailed back across the grubby orange tiled floor to disappear under the ladies' table. He gave the cord a weak tug, but it wouldn't come out of whatever it was plugged into.

Like a rabid dog, Tia Blanca came out of the booth and across the floor to tackle the game show host with the cord still dangling out from under her skirt, screaming, *"None of you shit-worms knows my name!"*

The bodyguard came through the door with an automatic drawn and leveled at Tia Blanca. "Get down sir," he grunted, and shot Tia Blanca four times.

With spit?

The short, stout old woman never broke stride until she hit the sick man in the gut. He folded over her like an empty suit, going down in a tangle with the now inert and probably broken vacuum cleaner.

Tia Blanca ignored the bodyguard. Steam came out of the holes in her torso, as if from a ruptured radiator. Her eyes boiled out of her head and black flames licked the holes, but she ignored this, too. She clung to the game show host and pressed her face to his until the flames burned his eyes out, too. He screamed and kicked, powerless to resist her. The bodyguard shot her four more times, but two of the bullets went through her and into his boss.

"Fuck this job," he said, and went outside to call somebody.

By the time the game show host stopped moving, Tia Blanca had been all but consumed by the black flames. No mortal vessel could contain it, the devil had said. *I will burn a hole in this world—*

With the black blazing head of a tiger, Tia Blanca stood upright on matchstick legs and staggered towards the counter. Natasha curled up in her seat, too afraid to pray. The game show host hadn't wanted children, but then it occurred to her that maybe the devil could enter an unborn child and be born again into a new body. Perhaps it could even grant real wishes again, throw around the kind of power that Solomon, with all his captive demons, once wielded. And with a new name, it would be totally under the control of its new "father."

This did not all occur to her in a flash of purely intuitive understanding. It leapt to her as Tia Blanca threw herself at the counter, where the pregnant girl stood, frozen in an ecstasy of breathless terror.

Without thinking any more, Natasha scooted out of the booth and moved to intercept the devil. Tia Blanca's charcoal skull showed through the black flames, which had begun to gutter for want of fuel. The tiger roared, "Out of my way, hag! It is not God's will that I fade—"

Taking her life in her hands, Natasha reined in her tone and found her quiet, humble maid's mask to hide behind. "You'll burn up the baby, sir. It already has a name. But if you go inside my womb ... into one of my eggs ... you could start all over ..."

Tia Blanca crawled closer. The flames eating her were colder than dry ice. "You're ugly, old and fat. Out of my way ..."

Holding her burned hand to her belly, Natasha promised, "You can name yourself. I won't double-cross you ..."

Tia Blanca reached out to embrace her in sable flames. Natasha withstood it, felt the awful attention of the devil roving over and in and out of her until it found a healthy egg bigger than all the others, and gushed out of Tia Blanca's spent form to possess it. Smitten with its own cleverness, it began to gloat at its power over her, when it suddenly realized it had been tricked, perhaps even worse than when King Solomon trapped it in an area rug.

Tia Blanca's egg trembled in her wounded palm as its contents spun round and round, searching for a crack, a seam, a corner, but finding only itself.

"What is this thrice-damned prison? Treacherous cow, I'll rip you open—"

Carefully, Natasha took the quivering egg out of her pocket with a handful of napkins. Smeared with blood and skin from her burned hand, it must have looked like a part of her to the stupid, desperate devil.

"They're coming for you, Natasha," said the egg. "Wish yourself to safety. I can make it all go away for you … then we can start fixing your life. Think of all the things you'll wish for."

Even now, Natasha was tempted. She could have everything she never dared to want, and she had to many painful memories, so many wasted years, to trade, that giving them up would almost be a bonus wish.

She almost wished for a Sharpie pen, but she found one on the counter before the words left her lips. She quickly scrawled a hasty Seal of Solomon on the egg.

"I don't wish for things, devil," Natasha said. "I work for them." Passing around the counter, she slipped out the back door of *Gallo Negro #3* like a shadow, just seconds ahead of the cops. She stopped only to offer a prayer to the Orishas on the hill, and to drop the egg into a big pot of boiling water.

THE TELL TALE PARTY

An hour before sunset on New Year's Eve. The dead paraded past the window, milling on the corner of Hollywood and Western outside the Cabeza De Vaca Steakhouse in the lobby of the Hotel Conquistador, waiting for the light to change.

"Sorry, but there's just no fucking way I'm hiding out tonight …"

Clink of a dessert fork on empty glass brought the waiter and maître d' running with refills. Mineral water and Orange Fanta. "No, hiding is when people are *looking* for you, and you want to be found. Nobody's looking for you. You're dead."

The dead outside were celebrities, apparently disinterred from Hollywood Forever Cemetery, down on Santa Monica. A charred Bogart and a syphilis-raddled Chaplin smeared chocolate syrup and clown white on the glass. Alfred Hitchcock slavered over Nick's mutilated steak, then waddled off after Tippi Hedren, who did the Watusi in the bike lane while festooned with stuffed ravens. "Hey, she's not even dead yet … Is she?"

Trudy snapped her fingers in his face. "No. But you are. You've finally dropped off everybody's radar. Not even Fallon's still cracking on you. Now, it's safe to start to rebuild."

"That's why I need to get out …" Lost little girl eyes gray as soft-boiled eggs, Marilyn briefly mistook Nick Stratton for the President. Her voluptuous lips left a scarlet smear on the glass, but then the light changed and they all lurched off the curb into traffic. "There's no such thing as bad publicity. Fuck, I probably make more money off people who hate me."

It was a pretty huge zombie walk; they'd been slouching past the window since right before Trudy cancelled his first drink order.

She fork-tortured her blackened ono in macadamia nut glaze, looked accusingly at his barely dented thirty-dollar cheeseburger. "I put aside all my other clients' needs for the last three months to get the iceberg out of the ocean liner and set it back on course. They love a spectacular fuckup, but you have to beg for redemption and you have to show them it's possible for a spoiled piece of shit to make good. You blow off sobriety again and publicly show up in all your old haunts … after what you did …" She didn't finish.

"What I did … was make a boring awards show entertaining. I said I was sorry …" A white-faced phantom in a black sheik costume pranced up and vomited giallo-bright blood on the window next to theirs. The manager ran out to chase him off. "What the fuck was that?"

"Rudolf Valentino," she said.

He let the tension dissipate a bit, put on the deeply contrite expression his acting coach called the *O* Face (for "Oprah," not "orgasm") "Look, I know I don't deserve your support. It was never the drugs or the booze, it was the fame. It's—"

"The worst drug of all, I know. The ones who don't self-destruct like you did, they all had to come to the realization that they deserve the love and success that they've earned."

"I earned it. I deserve to win. My therapist never stops telling me so. It's not about that …"

"You're not going to find self-respect at a party, Nicky."

"Trudy … Like … I was a motherfucking *Mouseketeer.* I was in a fucking boy band that made Milli Vanilli look like Van Halen. If I haven't slashed my wrists by now … *Oh … my … God …"*

Trudy turned around to look at what Nick was staring at. She tried to cover his eyes. "Oh shit, don't look. What an asshole. Don't give him the time of day, honey. I'll call hotel security …"

Nick slid out of the booth and ran out of the gloomy steakhouse and the seedy lobby with Trudy's supersonic shrieks barraging him. He hit the totally anachronistic revolving door just as the zombie in the tablecloth-toga lurched into the crosswalk. Wearing his trademark bright red Ray Bans and carrying the severed arm of a pretty girl still clutching a Golden Globe Award, he turned to marvel at Nick coming at him at a full run. YOLO written across his chest in lipstick by some anonymous wag at the after-party, after someone discreetly knocked him out.

Throwing his arms around the zombie's waist, Nick hoisted him into the air and danced around. "Oh my God, Nicky, I'm your biggest fan!"

The zombie walk's photographers swooped in and snapped a brace of pictures before Nick dropped his zombie doppelganger on the hood of a Star Safari bus, high-fived him and ran back inside the hotel.

Trudy was out in the lobby with her phone glued on, probably with the cops.

"I think I'm my own best publicist, anyway," he said. "You're fired."

She followed him to the men's restroom door. "If you fire me again, I'll quit."

"*C'est la vie …*"

"And then I'll *talk*."

Nick looked around, then came rushing over. "You fucking work for me …"

"I am *invested* in you. I won't let you tear that down. You will stay in the hotel. You'll post a short Twitter and maybe an Instagram clip humbly declaring your New Year's resolution to clean up your act, and you'll toast the new year with sparkling apple cider."

"Here?"

"Here. It's a lovely old-school Hollywood place …"

Look around: at the new silver and burgundy paint sprayed over grimy gilded Spanish colonial vomit. Recent investment had gentrified the hotel halfway out of the gutter, but sad-sack monthly residents still lingered in the lobby like ghosts of celebrity abortions. "It's a shithole."

"See that man over there?" She pointed at a crudely carved cigar store Indian in a cheap sharkskin suit, holding up the water cooler beside the front desk. "That's the hotel detective. Isn't that a scream? I told you, this place is old-school. It's his job to keep you from leaving or receiving visitors. We're going to ease you into the mea culpa talk show circuit and wash you squeaky clean, and then *maybe* we'll get you stunt-cast in a cheesy Netflix-original show, but if you fuck it up …" She didn't finish.

"Maybe I can get the house dick to score me an eighth of gorilla glue …"

"Go upstairs. Rest. If you want to get high, I've heard some really great things about autoerotic asphyxiation."

⁓

"Dude, you gotta hook me up."

Nick on the phone in the restroom, the signs of a bygone era. Ashtrays and a swing-out shelf for personal effects in the toilet stalls, and swear to God, the handicapped stall at the end had a bidet.

"I'm climbing the fucking walls, bro. Why can't you?"

"*I just can't … bro, like … I'm going out of town …*"

The restroom was movie-palace lavish, eerily clean and stocked with paper towels and a miniature drugstore. The tiled walls were encrusted with autographed headshots of an endless procession of cap-toothed, blow-dried, grinning, vamping, desperate dudes with phony names like Shadoe Stevens and Cork Proctor.

But unlike almost every other public restroom in Hollywood, this one still had an attendant hovering around the sinks. Only the oldest, dustiest places—the Palace, the Mayan, Musso & Frank's—still had them, and they seemed like a relic left to police the place, rather than a service. Half the time, Nick couldn't go at all for knowing a grim old black guy who'd held down the stool since the Kennedy era was lurking right behind you, waiting to slip you a hand towel for a fat tip, maybe sell you a splash of Vitalis, an individual cigarette or a stick of gum for a buck.

Not that it mattered today. The attendant was blessedly absent when Nick came in.

"Just say it …"

"*Please, dude … just … let it go.*"

"Is it the cops? LAPD don't give a fuck. Not about white kids on white powders, dude. Come on … I'm fresh out of the joint … I'm not asking you to front, I'm not asking for weight …"

"*I'm sorry, man, I just … It's like … it's a bad time. Sketchy in the extreme.*"

"Who is it? Just tell me."

"*Everybody. When you get down to the people who matter, this isn't a big town at all, you know? People know people, and they … you know, when somebody crosses the line, it's not like there's a trial on TV or anything, you know … You just know you're out.*"

"So, after all I fucking did for you … How many good customers did I hook you up with, Bryce?"

"*Fuck, I'm sorry, man, just … don't call back, okay?*"

Artie Shaw's rendition of "Song of India" leaked from a coffee-can speaker in the ceiling. Outside, the restroom door opened with a gulp of refrigerated air rushing out. Jesus, it was sweltering out in the restaurant, why was it so cold in the fucking shitter?

"Hey, #3," said a low, smoky voice, "nice kicks you got in there." A wooden stool creaked amiably as someone took up the perch between him and the door.

What the fuck? Nick lifted his feet off the black and white checkerboard tiles. He was still wearing the cheap, shitty Vans slip-ons Trudy bought him after some assholes in rehab stole his good lama-leather moccasins. Shit was worse than county, yo.

Whatever, just:

–Finish up with Trudy.

–Blow this shithole.

–Keep working the grapevine until something pops up. A score, a party, a screwed-up middle-aged cougar with a medicine chest full of magic … New Year's was Christmas for freaks. Unimaginable kicks abounded, somewhere out there. He was suffering from a terminal case of FOMOphobia, the endemic disease of the entertaining class: Fear of Missing Out. He couldn't help cramming everything he ever wanted into some mythical party that wouldn't let him in. Visualizing the shit out of this motherfucker. Where the fuck was it?

Business at an end, he fumbled with the stainless steel cowling over the toilet paper roll before realizing it was empty.

Son of a … He was just clearing his throat when a massive hand in a spotless white Bugs Bunny glove popped up from under the barrier, holding up something just inches from his nose.

"Compliments of the house," said the man on the other side of the door.

Nick took the roll. "Thanks …?"

"Powerful sorry, boss, but I had to go back to the supply closet for more paper. Third time today …! If I didn't know better, I'd think some folks was stocking up for some *mischief*, later."

"Uh, yeah, sure. You saved my ass there. Heh …" Wiped and kicked the lever to flush. Shuffled his feet, eyes on the latch holding the door shut. What was he afraid of? He had a ton of black friends.

Fuck it. He opened the door and ambled out, eyes fixed on his reflection in the huge mirror above the sinks. The attendant sat in his niche beside the last sink and the lobby door. He was an animated shadow in the mottled light from the mock torches set into the walls.

Studiously ignoring the presence beside him, Nick checked himself in the mirror. He'd put on some weight in rehab, but the bags under his eyes, the hollows of his once-dreamy cheekbones, made him look more like the ghost of himself than the zombie jackoff he'd accosted outside.

His eyes were glassy, red, but not "brightly empty as the headlights of a hellbound minivan," as some queer at *Rolling Stone* had put it.

Tired, haggard, hopeless. Sober. Forgetting all else, he stared into his own eyes and made his most sincere face and mouthed his only line. *I just want to go back to work—*

"Looking sharp, young blood," said the attendant. His voice, like velvet tearing, came from a crack in the wall. "Not going to get into the high-tone places with those sneakers, though."

No choice but to look at the guy, now. Nick let his eyes rove over the racks of breath mints, vanishing creams, pomades, single-serve mouthwash, antiperspirant and cologne, shoe polish, gum, toothpicks, cigarettes and sheepskin prophylactics. He didn't recognize a single fucking brand. He dropped a dollar in the tip jar. "Yeah, I'm staying in, tonight. Doctor's orders."

"I hear you, brother," the attendant winked. "Why go out when the baddest party in town's just upstairs?"

Nick looked at him then. He sat well back in the alcove and he wore black slacks and a deep red jacket, so all you could see was the reflection off his wraparound shades, and the glint of the gold crutch on his front tooth when he grinned at Nick.

"Sure," Nick said, brain scrambling. "This place is a morgue. Who's throwing a party here?"

"Big tipper like you, I know I seen you at the movies before. Thought you got you an invitation already, boss."

Toss another buck—no, a five—into the tip cup. "My e-mail got hacked, bro, so like, I never got mine. But like, where, uh …"

The attendant leaned forward on his stool, but the shadows still hid his face. His gloved hands twisted the lid off and onto a can of Shinola shoe polish. "Oh, everybody who's anybody knows about Mr. Belasco's New Year Parties, boss. The old Conq ain't on nobody's star tours, but if they knew even the tamest shit the guests got away with back in the day, it'd make this place infamous. Oh, the things they do up there'd pop your cock like a thermometer in hot lava."

Chuckling, he added, "But you can't go round asking the help, you understand. We sworn … to … *secrecy.*" He retreated back into the niche as he said this last with such exaggerated Screamin' Jay Hawkins theatrics that Nick stopped pushing.

"How much are the smokes?"

"Ten cents apiece," he said. "Sorry, I know it's a bite, but I can't charge per flush …"

Nick had plenty of black friends—three on his last album, two in his last movie—but he never felt right laughing at their jokes, when half the time he felt they were laughing at *him*. Anyway, ten cents … Everybody else wanted a buck, at least. He dropped a dime in the cup and took an unfiltered Camel.

"Thank you, boss. Wish I could tell you more, but I ain't seen none of the brothers serving the party, 'cos they come in through a service entrance up the rear to the El Cortez Room, up top." He put his hand over his mouth. "Shit, I said too much already. Boss, you too smooth. I bet you talk your way in just fine."

Smiling, Nick put out his hand, drunkenly grateful. "What's your name, bro? You're pretty cool." He figured he'd wash his hand again in his room.

The attendant dropped the shoe polish tin on the counter. "Name's James, but most folks just call me Shine." Took Nick's soft, clammy hand in his mahogany paw. Calluses sanded his fingerprints off. Wouldn't give it back. "Used to shine shoes in the lobby back in the day, when folks wore proper leather kicks."

"You been around this place a while, old man?"

"Since I was little. Sure, ain't much now, but back in the day, all kind of famous folks came here to let their hair down. Ol' Declan Cummings, you 'member him? King of the Vitagraph Living Bible Series … Got a powerful taste for the snow … Cut up two sporting girls and jumped off the roof when the men with the butterfly nets came to take him away."

Shine held out his hand in a way that compelled Nick to follow suit. "My good friends know I can get *anything* they need," he said. Something Shine slipped into his hand soaked up all the sweat from Nick's palm. "You tipped me too big, young blood. Here go your change …"

"Right on," Nick pulled his hand back, bounced off the counter slipping free. There was a folded-up dollar bill in his hand. "You're a good friend, Shine."

"Compliments of the house, boss," Shine said as he left.

Some yoga dick in rehab once tried to tell Nick you didn't need drugs to get high. You could just mentally recall the state of intoxication and bring it back like a memory, without poisoning yourself. That was the worst part. Sometimes when he did something right, or when nobody took a picture of him fucking up for once, he felt a little goose of good vibes and soon as it started to slip away, he needed a bump of molly to keep it going, and then all he could fucking think about was scoring …

Trudy didn't even want him smoking cigarettes, because they just set up the cycle. Whatever, the smoke would kill the ants crawling all over his brain. He asked the desk clerk where he could go to smoke. The fat slob looked back at him like he'd asked to be taken to the hotel's leader. So much for old-school …

Nick called his bluff and lit up, jauntily strolled to the elevator. The nicotine was nothing like the brain-tuning miracle he needed, though it took the dismal sheen of grinding anxiety off everything for a while; but that wasn't why he felt so good as he punched the button for his floor. There was an odd chrome-plated stool set into the wall of the car beside the brass panel of buttons, but thankfully no monkey-suited asshole with his hand out.

No, he felt good because he had a party to go to.

A bellhop got on with him at Three. Short old guy, sweaty, his lower teeth chiseling skin off his harelip.

In his pocket, Nick started to unfold the dollar bill in his pocket. That old bastard in the restroom was a trip, alright. *Anything*, he said, for his *good* friends. Place like this must be mobbed up, must be maybe why they kept fuckers in the toilets. Suddenly, it made perfect sense. In his pocket, something spilled out of the folded dollar. Shit! It felt like sand, like talcum powder, like—

He took his hand out of his pocket. The bellhop ate his lip. There was something gritty and white on his thumb and forefinger. Turning away, he rubbed it on his gums.

He nearly beat the elevator to his floor by ten seconds. Praise Jesus! Little Nicky can walk again!

When the elevator opened, he limped out pumping his fist in the air and nursing the pocket with the holy of holies in it.

The doors still had keys—old metal fucking keys, he almost had to call Harelip back to help him open it. Inside, he rushed into the bathroom and took out the folded bill. It was a tiny origami pitcher with a pinch of glittery white stuff in the folds. Setting it down with a jeweler's precision, he turned his pocket inside out and fingered about half a gram of something special onto the chipped green tiles. After tweezing the lint and hair out of it, he took a moment to reflect.

At every turn in his life, he had gotten everything he had (and lost) because he took every door that closed in his face, every dick who told him he had no talent, every good friend's hot mom who brushed him off, as a challenge to be overcome. If he truly regretted anything he had *not* done, he certainly couldn't remember it.

Rehab told him that was self-destructive thinking, punishing himself because he felt, deep down inside, that he was a fraud. The other doctors had told him his brain was broken, wrote him a prescription for a strange new antidepressant every week, and got his autograph for their "niece." His problem wasn't drugs, they told him, but an archaic reliance on wildcat pharmacology.

Using an old Blockbuster Video card (for its rigid, sharp-edged lamination and resistance to dust and scratches, second only to a real safety razor; accept no substitutes!), he flayed every flake off the dollar, scraped Washington's wig off and reamed the seams of his pocket while he watched E! and then local news. His cavorting in the zombie walk had failed to go viral. Fuck everybody.

Flipping around on the castrated hotel basic cable loop, he settled on Mexican MTV, then turned on his iPod, plugged it into the cheap bedside alarm clock.

Almost a hundred days since his last taste.

He was buzzing so hard on anticipation, he snorted two fat lines of it before it hit him: *This isn't coke.* Not molly. Not crank … H?

He didn't care.

He put his head down on the counter, running in place through a long commercial break. His brain raced in circles like stunt motorcycles in a flaming cage. He did another bump of it and then said, fuck it, and finished it off, but all the way through those last fat lines, he was thinking, MORE.

He flung himself back on the bed, thunder in his chest and ball lightning in his brain. Painted gingerbread men slam-danced on TV. He couldn't hear the music over the pounding of his own heart. It jitterbugged against his sternum like a Skrillex drop. He rested his hand on it, his other hand flopping against the wall to stop the bed spinning.

The beat he felt was coming through the wall. He couldn't hear it, but he could feel it permeate him so thoroughly that it drowned out his own racing heartbeat.

He muted the TV, the iPod under his pillow, his phone, the AC. He still couldn't hear it, but he could feel it in the bones of the hotel, like a freight train was racing in the basement ... or like someone was tuning up a motherfucker of a sound system.

The rush topped off on a cloud so high above sobriety he could drop a penny on it and burn a hole in it, but leveling off felt like losing. In rehab, they kept hammering at you that drugs were a crutch. Maybe for some people, but if you were doing it right, drugs were stilts. Motherfucking rocket boots.

He had to find out where this Belasco dick was throwing his Halloween party. He needed a costume. And he had to get some more of that shit.

Now.

He had a hundred in cash, but Trudy took his bank cards and all but one puny credit card with like a fifty dollar daily. A kid's credit card. How did they expect him to become an adult, if they treated him like a kid?

Washed the chalky, alkaloid stuff down with a glass of tap water that gagged him.

He got in the elevator with a hot Catwoman and a hotter Lily Munster. Fire licked up his spine. Catherine wheels spun in his balls. He simmered inside; bubbles percolated up through his molten insides, tickling the inside of his skin like the opening stages of a GHB binge, but his mind raced with laser-guided precision to the exact strategy to get these hot ladies back to his room.

"Hey, is the party 60's TV themed this year?" Knees knocking. "I'm going as Zorro and my date got held up at a photo shoot ..."

Lily and Catwoman laced hands and giggled deeply into each other's eyes until they hit the lobby.

Damn, maybe he should go to the party dressed as a chick.

The desk clerk said there was a Halloween Superstore of the kind that popped up in the husks of recently deceased bookstores all over town every year. Fuckers spent nearly as much on costumes and candy and decorations and partying as they did on Christmas. Plots for horror movies he could write and star in and rhymes for a Halloween-themed rap disk jumbled through his forelobe between him and the door so he almost danced with the hotel detective.

"Really 'pologize, Mr. uhhhh … But uh … y'see …"

"I can't leave?" Out on the sidewalk, he saw a couple of his old friends, the paparazzi, leaning against parking meters with their cameras trained on the door. He recognized Mansour, the terrorist who egged him into the homophobic tantrum that cost him the lead on a Disney Channel series.

"Your people thought it would be prudent for you to take it easy tonight …"

The exchange didn't have to go much further. Nick read it in the house dick's piggy eyes. *Start shit, kid, please. I'll pants you for the photogs out there, call my pig friends and we'll clobber your ass and 5150 you in County overnight before your "people" find you, and you'll beg them to take you to jail after a night in the observation ward …*

And he'd nod because he'd walked that particular plank before. "I just need to make a personal fucking phone call and find a costume at the fucking store around the corner, dude. You can walk me over there. We'll hold hands."

The hotel dick had Shar Pei eyes and razor-stubble on his forehead. Nick could hear it growing. He pointed at the front desk, where a clerk obligingly held up an archaic landline. "Dial Nine to get out," he said.

"Eat me," Nick said under his breath behind his hand, and went to the restroom. His buzz all but trashed. The door was propped open by a big placard on an unwieldy wrought-iron stand that said, in elaborate Gothic script that the toilets were both CLOSED and CERRADO.

The dick conferred with the desk clerk, who made a retarded, mocking face and pointed at his nose. They laughed. Nick ducked into the restroom.

The lights were off. "Shine?" he whispered. "Hey, bro …" *Shit shit shit …*

He slipped sideways on a floor slick as mineral oil. He kicked a galvanized tin mop bucket, recoiled from the bright clatter of it rebounding off the wall. His hip hit the counter hard enough to bend him over and bang his head on the mirror.

The fuck?

By the feeble stream of light from the half-open door, he saw a faceless white shape lurching towards him from Shine's alcove. He threw a punch and dented the chrome hand towel dispenser. He bit back a scream, clamped his jarred fist under his other arm.

"You look like a fella," Shine said, "loses a lot of fights with the mirror."

Nick spun around and reached out towards the sound. His hand found gritty wet strands of matted hair, like septic dreadlocks. A mop.

He must be tripping. Nobody else was here. He couldn't figure out where the light switch was, so he took out a lighter. By its fitful, buttery yellow glow, the black tiles gleamed, and his reflection gaped at him, giggling. Maybe Shine left his goods when he went out on break.

He had to come back, it wasn't even dark yet. They'd keep the fucking restrooms open on New Year's Eve, right? He looked over the counter, but all of Shine's sundries were in a big wooden box with a padlock on it.

He had to come back. He had to …

Then he saw the little, flat Shinola tin tucked between the shoeshine box and the tiled wall, just under the dented hand towel dispenser. The same one he'd twisted in his hands as they talked, then put it down and palmed off that bindle to him.

The lighter had grown hot in his hand, and started to throw out little blobs of melted plastic. He pocketed the tin and held up the lighter to illuminate his way across the treacherous wet floor.

He looked down and saw the checkerboard pattern was gone. He was standing up to the tops of the soles of his sneakers in tacky, black-red blood.

Screaming for Jesus, Nick barged through the door and kicked over the CERRADO sign. He ran across the lobby to the desk. The clerk looked at him distastefully, holding a placating hand up to forestall the old lady he'd been helping.

"In the bathroom, man, you gotta come, there's—"

"There's what, sir?"

Nick looked around. Everyone was staring. They could see everything he'd ever fucked up.

He looked down at the floor, at his shoes. They were wet, covered in suds and they smelled like industrial cleanser. "I'm … I … I'm so sorry …" but he was laughing too hard to finish.

"Do you require assistance to your room, sir?" So they knew. Of course they did, they knew they were dealing with the only guy on drugs in the greater Los Angeles area.

"No, that's cool." Tossing a five on the desk, he said, "Just point me in the direction of the El Cortez Room."

The clerk stared at the sweaty bill like it was a tampon. "Pardon me?"

He made a face at the old woman until she stopped staring. "The fucking ballroom, man." Winking, he pushed at the five like maybe he just hadn't noticed it.

"I'm really sorry," the clerk said with tired relish, "but I don't know what you're talking about."

"When does Shine come back on duty?"

"Who?"

"Shine, man ... the, you know ..."

A big black bellhop passed close behind him, bumping him against the counter. "I don't care how famous you are, punk. Watch your fucking mouth, 'fore somebody knocks it off your face."

"Mellow out, dude," he said. Fuck it. Now people were staring and taking pictures. Even the mummies in the seats, the lifers, were staring. One old black guy with a scabrous beard like a silver skin disease shook his cane at him.

The devil came strolling in, turning Nick's head. These fuckers knew where it was at. The guy was maybe fifty, Nick didn't recognize him but felt instantly like he should, he had that kind of face and affable gravity about him. In a white tux with understated horns artfully affixed to his forehead, and he went for a double-dip on the tanning bed to get the color right. The witches on his arms were thousand dollar-a-night escorts; Nick thought one of them was a Ukrainian cunt named Martina.

Nick flicked the five at the desk clerk and glided off in their wake. Wracking his brain for the guy's name, he hung back until they detoured past the steakhouse to the elevators. He swooped in just as they got into the car. The devil rolled his eyes as he asked them what floor.

"The top floor, of course," said the devil. He fingered something in his vest pocket he'd probably hoped to snort before Nick barged in.

"You guys going to the party too?"

"We're going to all the parties," Martina said, grinding against her sugar daddy. Did she really not recognize him? She was a coldhearted pro, alright.

"Why go anywhere else when the real party is right here, right?"

"Do I know you?" the devil asked.

Bite back the first ten, no twenty, responses that leap to mind. This asshole could be somebody. "No sir, but I'll bet your nieces know my work." He winked at Martina, who turned and said something without any vowels in it to her coven-mate.

"Do I need to know him?" the devil asked his witches, and they laughed even louder.

The door opened and the devil got out with his entourage. Nick followed them down the hall, ears pricked for music, laughter, bouncers, flashbulbs. The floor was silent as a miser's wake. Looking suspiciously over his shoulder, the devil strutted down the hall to a suite and glared until his witches found the key and opened the door.

"Don't go downtown on Martina, man," Nick said. "New Year's comes but once a year, but herpes is forever!"

"Go fuck yourself, loser," said the devil, slamming the door to his suite.

Fuck them. Fuck them all. He didn't need them, or anyone else. Nobody helped him get rich and famous who wasn't trying to use him. He got everything he had, everything he'd lost, by his own wits.

Close your eyes.

Open your ears.

Breathe deep.

He couldn't hear it, smell it or see any sign of life in the empty corridor, but he could feel it in his feet, that ponderous, stampeding beat. It pulsed up through the floor's dingy rose-gold carpet. It thudded and throbbed through the pipes in the walls like water, like electricity, like gas ...

They couldn't keep him out. It was way too late for that. He needed a costume.

On the wall facing the elevators, a conquistador's helmet and breastplate were mounted on a big redwood plaque on the wall with two crossed sabers. Giggling at his dastardly genius, he ripped the plaque down and ran for the roof exit. Slapping his forehead, he thought, *It must be up here*. It's the only place that makes sense ...

The door was locked, a big sign declaring NO ROOF ACCESS, but it gave way easily when he threw his shoulder into it. He smashed the plaque on the stair railing, splintered the wood and pried the helmet loose. It was cheap tin, but still heavy. The breastplate he buckled on over his Ed Hardy sweatshirt. The swords he swung and clashed against each other, cackling like Errol Flynn as Captain Blood.

The music soared and practically knocked him back down the stairs. Squealing, squawking brass seemed to both cheer and mock his appearance. He threw out his arms and then crossed the swords in a dramatic gesture he hoped the paparazzi were catching, he stumbled up the stairs, threw the rooftop door open and leapt into the fray.

The wind whipped at him. The silence was devastating. But for the moaning of air conditioners and the blaring of a car alarm somewhere fourteen stories below, the rooftop was utterly silent, totally abandoned. He wandered across the roof to the ledge and looked down on Hollywood Boulevard.

Klieg lights swept the sky in front of the Mann Chinese, the Egyptian, the Bowl and the Palladium. A rooftop party on the W was shooting lasers into the sky and a helicopter circled Vine as they tried to get some wasted guy off the top of the spire atop the Capitol Tower. Limousines, Lyfts and cabs packed the streets like lard in an artery, triggering mini-strokes as pedestrians in club wear or funky costumes spilled out into traffic, throwing candy into open windows and spraying each other with champagne and squirt guns.

Everyone in the world was doing something without him. Maybe Shine was just fucking with him with all that crap about secret parties. This place wasn't a hangout for anyone who mattered since long before Nick was born. He needed to get the fuck out of here, find some friends who still remembered him, and get into a real party. He had to get back into circulation again, if he was going to get back on top. The ache of it came cracking up out of him, that ache of being unimportant, of being unobserved and invisible, of being nothing.

He wasn't nothing. He had all he needed, whether or not he had anyone to share it. His hand clasped the tin in his pocket. He'd get a couple bumps of this shit in him and get his ass back out on the block, house dick or no house dick …

"Whatever the problem is," a girl said, behind him, "don't, like, jump, like, *right here* …"

He jumped, nearly backing over the ledge. Catwoman and Lily Munster were huddled in the lee of a rooftop water tower, trying to smoke a joint in the hot autumn wind.

The party comes to you, Nick thought. "Hey!"

"Fancy meeting you here," Catwoman said.

"It's fancy meeting me anywhere," he said, clanging his sword off his breastplate. Lily Munster looked annoyed, but Catwoman giggled. "You girls break any resolutions yet?"

"All tricks and no treats," Catwoman said, coughing up hairballs of smoke. "Don't mind my friend. You can jump if you really want to."

"Thanks," he said, "but I'm on my way to a big private party. Where you girls headed?"

Lily looked daggers at him, but Catwoman said, "We were on the list for Viper Room, but it's overbooked and those Kardashian assholes are there, and there was supposed to be this big thing up in the hills, but *somebody's* afraid to go, so we're just bumming around the boulevard ..."

"Well, I've got an invite to a party right here in the hotel, but I'm having a bit of trouble finding it. My friends are putting it on, but they're not answering. If you girls were up for checking it out, I could totally get you both ... in ... and maybe if you wanted to help me out with some party favors. I mean, I could do it all myself, but my heart would probably explode. But if that's what you girls want ..."

"Do you have a room?"

"Follow me."

They did.

⁂

The TV was still on, iPod still blasting. Nick went straight to the bathroom, telling the girls to help themselves to the minibar.

"There's no alcohol in here," Catwoman whined. Lily Munster took the remote and started channel-surfing. Nick unscrewed the lid off the Shinola tin, holding his breath. It'd be a hell of a nasty trick if it turned out to be full of shoe polish. But something inside rattled dryly inside, his hands shaking so bad the fistful of bindles flew out of the tin and went into the toilet bowl.

Biting back a high screech, he scooped them out of the toilet and dropped them on the counter, blotted them with toilet paper. They were folded up in bills, so the flax had repelled the worst of the water. Six little bindles, folded tight as origami birds. He pried one open, trapping his hand against the counter so it wouldn't shake too badly. The silvery white grit spilled out onto the counter with a tiny, musical tinkle. It wasn't crystal meth, he figured that much. Had almost a psychedelic quality like molly, but the paranoid megalomania that blossomed in its afterglow was deeper, darker …

He chuckled nastily. If it worked half as well on these bitches as it had on him, he'd be lucky if they even made it out of the room, tonight. Cursing himself for a fool, he wondered if Trudy wouldn't take pity on him and have an assistant send him a video camera.

Fiending out, chopping the lines until they were fluffy white clouds, he called out, "All aboard!"

Lily Munster—Nick had pointedly forgotten her real name—came in first, wordlessly took the rolled-up twenty out of his hand. "Help yourself, babe," he said, slipping out of the bathroom around the outthrust curve of her hip.

Catwoman—Roxane, he reminded himself—had peeled her black rubber bodysuit partway down and was sprinkling talc into the crevasse of her—wonder of wonders, seemingly natural—cleavage. "Getting sweaty in here," she said, with that insecure giggle that quickly got on his nerves. One thing he couldn't stand, it was people who had to sneak in a fake laugh at their own jokes. But you couldn't hate the tell itself, because without it, how would you know who would cave in and put out?

"It's not gonna get cooler," he said. "You're welcome to take a shower … Are you a guest at the hotel?"

"Heh … no. We're just cruising, looking for a good time." Raising her voice, Roxane shouted, "Hey, what's taking such a long time in there? If you're on the phone with that bitch …"

"No need to shout," he said, pressing a bindle into her hand. "There's plenty for everyone."

"Oh, you're so thoughtful." Kissing him on the cheek, she unfolded the bindle and dug the nail of her index finger into its pocket. "So, wanna hear something funny?"

"Always." He chucked the heavy helmet onto the desk, taking out the phone.

"Donna thought you were someone *famous*." Finger to her nose, Roxane sniffed a pile of the stuff off her long black lacquered nail. "You aren't though, are you?"

"Well," he said, venting steam out his ears, how dare this bitch do his drugs and shitcan him in the same breath … "I'm famous in some circles, infamous in others …"

"What *is* this shit?" she asked, her voice taking on a weird nasal tone like her septum just disintegrated. He reached out to take the bindle but she coquettishly pulled away, leaving him huffing the talc wafting up from her sweaty bosom. Her sweat smelled like pickles, for some fucking reason, he wondered if there were drugs enough to make that sexy, to make him not notice. "You kinda look kind of like that one guy, you know … that kid on that show …"

She stuck her nose into the bindle and snuffled greedily. "God, I don't know what's in this shit, but … *God damn* …" She got up on the bed and gyrated to the beats drooling out of the iPod. The reflected light dancing across her skinny ass and the stark convexity of her bush made his mind race, made him almost forget the drug, the other one in the bathroom.

She asked him what it was like, being famous, so he told her.

It was like a particularly devious level of Dante's Inferno, the whole game was. Like, you were on fire all the time, but react to it, bat at the flames and people say you're going crazy. Devils followed you everywhere, dogging you by making a living of stealing your likeness. Psychos thought they knew you, thought you owed them everything. But complain about it and the little people tore you apart, because they thought you were in Heaven, and better show the proper gratitude.

No, being stalked by tabloids was not like being sexually assaulted. No, dealing with Twitter haters was not like going to war. They don't pay to see you act, hear you sing. They pay to fantasize about being you. They're paying for your life, so you need to keep it like an open house or a hotel room. Anyone can come in and imagine they're you. Keep telling yourself you don't feel the concentrated envy burning you up like that Fukushima place. Try to live one day with professional strangers sniffing your shit and psychos who think they know you, and assholes everywhere underfoot trying to rip you off, and see how long you can keep your mouth frozen in that Xmas Morning smile.

She twisted and fucked the air, peeling the black rubber down to reveal a pair of pillowy, pale breasts outraged with cat-scratch ligature marks, her jutting nipples impaled with steel barbells. Sniffing and licking the flattened bindle, she forced a hand down the front of the suit, moaning.

Something she said he was trying to remember, something about a party in the hills they ought to be going to, but *fuck that shit …*

He lay back on the bed so her long, shiny legs straddled his face. He took out his own bindle, grinning at her and beckoning for her to sit down.

Then he heard the crash. Glass shattered, sang and shattered again. "Fuck, hold on," he growled.

This other one had better not queer the deal; if she wasn't going to join in, the least she could do was lay low and stay out of the way.

He came around the doorframe to find Lily Munster slam dancing with his bathroom. She'd already taken out the big mirror over the sink and just as he skidded into the room on his stocking feet, she rebounded off the counter and went backwards through the pebbled sliding glass doors of the shower stall. Her arms spun like propeller blades, flinging glass shards and the crumpled towel rack hardware at the ceiling.

Nick dropped and wrapped an arm over his face. Glass cut his cheek. He cowered for a few moments, throat swollen shut. When she didn't move, he got up and took a cautious step towards her.

Lily Munster lay on her back in the shower. A big bloody starburst split her forehead. A shard of mirrored glass jammed into her left eye filled her gaze with his lipless grimacing reflection. Everywhere the white Goth makeup had wiped off, her skin was cyanotic goosebumps. The gritty powder mingled with copious rivulets of blood from her broken nose, making a pink froth around her crimson, waxy lips that made her look rabid.

He flattened against the wall, crushing his heart in his hands, thinking, *Don't die … not here …*

Nothing he could do was going to fix this. He backed out of the room and closed the door. Just before he returned to break the bad news to Roxane, he heard the rhythmic thudding of her head slamming into the ceiling.

She was still jumping on the bed, but now her movements were like a piston or a battering ram, the crown of her head leaving little spiky coronas of blood on the textured stucco every time she bounced.

"Jesus, Roxane, cut it out!" He dove for her legs, but she launched herself off the bed headfirst into the flat screen TV.

Maybe she thought she was jumping through a window. Maybe she wasn't even thinking that far ahead. She head-butted the pane of glass and rebounded back onto the bed, deflated across the trampled comforter, twitching like something smashed on a windshield.

Oh God, they were both ... they both ... in *his* room. With his shit. They did his shit, and they both just dropped dead. *Fuck you, Rob Lowe, you thought you had problems?*

He splashed tap water in his face. It was even skunkier than in the bathroom, with a gamey quality underneath that oily aftertaste that he almost recognized. It must come from that big tower up on the roof. One more reason this place should be knocked down.

He had to get the fuck out of here. He patted himself down for his wallet and phone, planted his key in Roxane's chunky DG-knockoff bag and went for the door with his phone to his ear, calling room service.

When he opened the door, he noticed something on the floor at his feet, just as the desk clerk said, "Conquistador," in his ear.

"Yes, um," he said, stooping, falling really, onto the orange envelope where someone had slid it in under the door. It might have been there when they came in, he was hardly looking for something like it.

"Yes?"

You Are Cordially Invited ...

"Uh ... I lost my room key?"

"Are you asking me, sir, or telling me?"

To A Very Private Costume Party

"Telling you, bro. Maybe on the elevator, there were these skeevy chicks. Anyway, I'm going to be out and about, but I'll come by to pick up a spare ... later ..."

He hung up, looking at the invitation, listening to the music he could hear now, quite distinctly, coming down the hall.

10 PM until dawn in the El Cortez Ballroom.

He roamed the halls with one hand on the wall. He worked systematically from the fourteenth floor down. Pausing to cup his ear at every door, to touch every exposed pipe and load-bearing column, sword ready and trembling to run somebody through.

He tried calling every number he could remember. He badmouthed Bryce's answering service until it cut him off. He tried reaching Trudy until the phone died and he tossed it out an open window onto Hollywood Boulevard.

Whenever he was alone in a hall, he fidgeted in his pocket and lost a fight with himself and sniffed more of the stuff from a bindle. It didn't matter. It couldn't kill him. He wasn't made like them. Only one thing could kill him and that was being nothing. Forgotten. Nobody. Like you.

It was hiding from him. Moving around. Taunting him. He'd hear it downstairs, hear thumping bass and the collective roar of an ecstatically wasted crowd. Someone was vamping atop a stack of bass amps, maybe stripping or getting sucked off by an eager groupie in full view of the crowd. That's how he would play it …

Almost whimpering with joy, he'd run for the stairs and totter down them, nearly falling in his eagerness, and he'd bust through the fire door to find another empty hallway with maybe a room service cart parked by a door with a ruined dinner for two on it, maybe an escort sneaking out of a darkened room, counting cash or appraising a stolen wristwatch. Silence of drunken snores and air conditioning, of fluid and breath seeping through bodies and building, of a night surrendered. Was it midnight yet? He was almost afraid to look. And then, between one breath and the next, he'd hear it or feel it, coming from just above his head, or up through his feet …

Towards the bottom, it got harder and harder not to pound on the doors and shout, "Happy New Year, bitches!" and offer them some of his killer candy.

When he finally reached the lobby, the desk clerk was fast asleep and someone had drawn a mustache on his face. It was long after midnight. He went for the exit but boomeranged when he saw the house dick outside, smoking a cigar.

He went to the elevator and pushed the button, but the doors wouldn't close. He took out a bindle and did a quick one-and-one—

"Whatcha got there?" He turned around and around, but he was cornered in the dead elevator. The detective crowded him into a corner and took the bindle out of his hand, tasted the powder and started laughing. "You know this stuff'll give you cancer, right?"

"Huh?" Nick's heart hammered his sternum. "Please don't call the cops—"

He held up the bindle, only now it was a little pink paper Sweet & Low packet. "Saccharine causes cancer in laboratory rats. It was in all the papers." The house dick balled up the bindle in one meaty fist and pocketed it. "I'll show you to your room. Get some sleep—"

Before he realized he was even doing it, Nick had driven the conquistador's sword into the detective's belly, run him through to the hilt and left him sputtering on the floor of the elevator.

The restrooms were open. He went into the men's room, manifestly eager, with no plan. Maybe it would be good to offer to pay for the shit, but not before getting to the bottom of the whole bitches-dropping-dead side effect.

Ducking low as he passed the stalls, looking for feet, he approached the sinks, intent on the hunched black figure on the stool in the niche. "Having a nice New Year's, motherfucker?"

The attendant leaned forward like a turtle coming out of its shell. Nick bit his tongue. It was the old black man from the lobby, the one who shook his cane at him when he asked about—

"I know who you lookin' for," said the old black man, under his breath like he hoped no one would hear, and touched the side of his nose.

"Where is he?"

"Oh, it bein' a holiday, I imagine Hardy's tryin' to get wherever the action is, just like you."

"There's no action in this place, old man. Where's the dude who was working in here before?"

"Regular fella went missing yesterday. I volunteered to hold it down like I used to, back in the day."

Something at the back of Nick's throat twitched, seeking escape. Nick shook his head. "I don't care about ancient history. Where's the El Cortez Room?"

Half a cackle, half a cough. "Oh, ain't that some history, though! Ain't been no ballroom since '66, not after what happened. Yessir, they promise to keep your secrets here, but everything comes out, sooner or later. This place got a powerful hunger for fame its ownself, and it never wants for folks who think they ain't gonna get burned."

Nick twisted round at a glimpse of something in the mirror coming up behind him. He took the invitation out of his pocket and jabbed it at the old man. "I got this."

"Oh son, put that away and go home." Taking the invitation out of his hand, the old man opened it. The paper was faded and warped with water stains. The date of the party was barely legible, but it said more there than it had when he first looked at it. The date was December 31 ... 1965.

Taking the invitation back, he stared fixedly at his name on the envelope. "I've got nowhere else to go. I can't even go back to my room ..."

"Go somewhere, son ... Go *anywhere*, and pray they forget your name."

He was a breath away from begging. "Shine, he said—"

"Shine was my uncle," he said. "Got me this job, but it was never big enough for him. Sold hop and grass and coke out this restroom with the hotel's blessing. Keep the party rolling, right here in this room, 'til a vice dick who didn't get his cut once took it out on James ... threw lye in his face and took him to jail.

"Did a stretch for holding, but they couldn't nail him for dealing, it would've hurt the house. He put up such a stink, they hired him back when he got out. Wasn't a week before New Year's ..."

"You're making shit up, old man. Where's the fucking party?"

Behind the old man, in the darkness of the niche, a crack of red-orange light appeared, haloing his nappy silver hair. "Oh Lord, no," he said, "please, Shine ..."

The crack of light widened, became a doorway. Music spilled thought it, laughter and smoke. Nick took hold of the old man's shirt and yanked him off the stool. His arms came up like bundles of breadsticks, his weight so much less than he expected that Nick effortlessly flung him across the restroom. He slammed into a stall door and fell backwards, bent horribly over a hulking porcelain altar.

Nick looked at his hands, sick with panic, but the light fell full upon him and the music drowned out the sound of his racing heart. Donning his conquistador's helmet, Nick pushed the invitation into the bouncer's apelike paw and entered the party.

It made no sense, at first. He passed through the doorway into another restroom. Lit by red shaded lamps, it was packed almost two-deep with cowboys, pirates, sheiks, Draculas, centurions and astronauts who snorted and sniffed and slurped drinks from the sink, waiting in snarled, incestuous lines for the stalls. He shoved into the crowd, cutting towards the wall and looking for the door.

The floor was ankle-deep in piss and shit, paper cups and condoms and syringes. The other men happily babbled and cackled in each other's faces, while a few of them mechanically groped and kissed, chewing cigarettes and cigars, rubbing their raw, inflamed noses and twitching at every grotesque sound from the stalls, but it was obvious no one was ever going to get inside one.

Dodging the embers of lit cigars, he realized he recognized them all from the headshots in the restroom. Desperate impressionists, nameless ventriloquists, dipsomaniacal magicians, creepy comedians and everywhere, angry, chattering, strung-out alcoholic actors. Talking about upcoming gigs on Merv Griffin and how everybody who did the USO tours in Nam came back with crabs and if they were a new species, they should name it after Bob Hope.

Nick fumbled along the wall until he reached a corner and an arched doorway. He gratefully squeezed past some sleazy shithead babbling about how they should go out to this old movie cowboy ranch in the Valley where these hippie chicks stoned on acid would do *anything*—

Nick tugged the door open, shoving bodies out of the way, and squeezed into the passage.

It wasn't even a proper room, really. It was a broom closet. Shelves stacked with institutional-grade toilet paper, hand towels, Bon Ami and lye soap, floor cluttered with buckets and mops and push-brooms and a big, scuffed wooden crate with a black rubber footrest on the top.

Nick started to turn around, but a huge white spider of a hand collared his neck and slammed his head into the shelf, ringing the helmet like a bell.

"Happy New Year, youngblood. Welcome to the party."

The helmet slid down over his face. He couldn't stand up. Shine bent him over the mop bucket and tore off his jeans.

"Back off, motherfucker," he shouted, but it came out a pathetic, crippled whine.

"Shut up, bitch," Shine said, "you all mine now." Something cold and rigid slid up the crack of his ass, making him jump and try to climb the shelves, but his legs went to water under him. His stomach cramped up so bad, he could feel every bite of the thirty-two dollar cheeseburger returning to haunt him.

"Think you big shit, think folks oughta worship you. Maybe every cow that go up the ramp to the killing floor think he gone get crowned king of the cows, too. You in my VIP now, player."

Eight hundred pounds of weight crushed him down. The gloved hand on his neck bent him in half, until he could almost kiss his knees. Shine barely breathed hard, but Nick heard a fizzing, popping sound and smelled an awful chemical stench coming from the attendant's face. "Shine, man … James …? Please …?"

Nick stopped struggling. His head was ringing, he was dead, this was hell, but it all went away when Shine finally penetrated him. The intrusion was a spear of chill outrage where he could afford to feel it least.

"You ain't shit, boy. *I* should be famous. New Year's Eve fifty years ago, I killed sixteen famous white folks, and nobody ever saw my black ass again. I'm the original magical motherfuckin' Negro."

Helpless, incoherent, Nick was most horrified at the hot wash of ecstasy that bloomed out of his prostate, at his own cock growing shamefully erect; but otherwise, he was spinning on the cold, merciless skewer that plunged in and out of him until his bowels reversed course like the Nile in an eclipse, the chyme in his intestine and the half-solid fecal pellets of yesterday's lunch evacuated out his mouth and nose, into the bucket.

Nick couldn't stop convulsing, even when the straight razor hove into view, cutting his dismal world in half. "Nine motherfuckers came in here and stayed forever. Six more had that same hot shot you lifted and dosed them fine jailbait girls with. Methedrine and rat bait, boy. See, the hotel fixed it so them dead rats went over a cliff up in the hills in a big party bus. Couple B-list punks and some agents and managers and white trash who would've given the Conquistador a bad name."

I'm dead, Nick thought, and I'm in Hell. The brutal rod kept sawing at his spasming colon. He tried to remember how to pray, but he'd never had to do it on camera.

"Yeah, you getting it. You all mine, now, like all my bitches."

At last, when Nick was sure he could feel the cold invader jabbing the bottom of his arrhythmic heart, it slid out and out and out of his twitching, torn rectum, leaving him to shudder and shamefully ejaculate into the mop bucket.

Nick tripped on his pants and fell sprawling in sewage. "Fuck you, you dead black motherfucker …" Throwing out a grasping hand, he only succeeded in smearing his shit on his rapist's neatly pleated trousers.

Shine laughed and brandished a push-broom, shoving the shit-caked handle into Nick's face and painting a sloppy chocolate mustache under his nose. "Liked that, did you? I wouldn't fuck you with a white man's dick." Sliding his white-gloved hand distastefully down the shaft of the broom, he collected a handful of shit and smeared it on Nick's cheeks and forehead, into his eyes and ears. "Now you look like the help." Smoke from his sizzling face obscured his features, but not his malicious grin.

Nick could barely stand, even with the restroom attendant's help. He fell to his knees under the weight of the wooden box Shine dropped in his arms. The septic stew from the overflowing toilets sloshed around his ankles. A tiny balloon of poison floated by. Nick picked it up and hid it in his mouth for later.

"Now get out there and shine some shoes."

"You can't make me …" Nick moaned.

"*Already* made you, youngblood. Already broke you." Planting his huge, shit-caked wingtip in Nick's lacerated ass, he propelled him back out into the red restroom.

They roared. Kicked him until he curled into a ball in the sewage. Put cigars out on his scalp. Put their shoes in his mouth for him to lick.

Forever and ever and ever …

Until dawn.

⁎

From burnhollywoodburn.com
JAN. 5, 2015 @7AM/PDT

All you poser celebrity washouts, take note: **THIS**. **THIS**, you LaBoeufs, you Spearses, Sheens and Kardashians, is how you do a full-on celebrity meltdown.

Take it away, **LA Times:**

The bizarre manhunt for missing actor/singer/tabloid fodder Nick Stratton, 23, ended as strangely and abruptly as it began this morning, when Hollywood Sheriff Dept. tactical team located Stratton trapped in a crawlspace between the walls of the lobby and the adjacent parking garage that was once the legendary El Cortez ballroom, where he has apparently been hiding since he was last seen the night of Dec. 31, shortly before midnight.

LAPD and Hollywood Sheriffs responded to the hotel's calls early on January 1, after hotel security supervisor Charlie Hovis, 53 was found dead of an apparent stabbing in an elevator car; Grover Washburn, 72, apparently beaten to death in the lobby restroom; and two unidentified juvenile girls in Stratton's hotel room, both dead from alleged drug overdose pending a toxicology screening, although investigators located no drugs or paraphernalia on the scene.

Stratton was also sought in questioning pertaining to the disappearance of Hardag Kafsanjian, 47, the restroom attendant assigned to the restroom, and whose drowned body was discovered yesterday in the hotel's rooftop water-tower.

Stratton's management (who declined to be interviewed for this article) cooperated in the search for the troubled celebrity, but he appeared to have vanished without a trace until hotel cleaning staff reported hearing what sounded like rats in the walls.

HSD spokespeople could not explain how Stratton got into the crawlspace, and the wall had to be dismantled to extract him. Stratton was transferred to LA county jail's medical observation ward, where he is described as alternately unresponsive and hysterical.

Workmen also came across the remains of another unidentified man who had become trapped and died in the same crawlspace several decades before.

Though the hotel was closed to guests for the day, the Conquistador will reopen tomorrow. The hotel management declined to address the tragedy, but inside sources say they're thrilled the scandal has put the once-notorious Hollywood hangout back on the map, and plans may even be in the offing to bring back the old El Cortez ballroom, with its unspeakable Halloween parties.

So that's the official story, but of course there's more … Anonymous Eye #357 was working in the Conq when Stratton was taken out of the wall.

He was wearing **blackface [see attached image]**.

No shit.

Maybe trying to hide from the cops over the two teenagers he poisoned and the rent-a-cop he stabbed in a desperate attempt to position himself for a *Pirates* franchise reboot, ol' Mr. "Never Givin' up On U, Boo" crawled into a crack and covered himself with his own poo. The mugshot pics are ugly, but our sources say Stratton was hunky-dory until he tripped and walked into every doorknob between the restroom and the Sheriff's van that took him to county. And he wouldn't stop trying to clean the Sheriff's boots with his tongue. Perhaps the most incredible detail is the preliminary tox screen, which showed nothing stronger than soda pop in his system. Shine on, you crazy fucking diamond!

And to top it all off, cops say Nick showed clear signs of "rectal foreign object penetration." But like everything else about Nick Stratton's career, it appears to have been self-inflicted.

Some say Nick Stratton was ripe for a comeback. I say this was his destiny. He set himself on fire for us, losers. What have you done for him, lately?

The Conq is doing well … The Nick Stratton Murder Tour is already blowing up, and any rumors to the effect that this website has any financial stake in the sale of Conquistador Corpse Water is totally unfounded bullshit.

[CONQUISTADORCORPSEWATERAD.017.JPG]

AND THE ANGEL SING

Tuesday
April 3, 1945

The prayer before supper that night, their third in the rafts, started out the same as it had before. Colonel Rowse led them in grace.

"Heavenly Father, we thank you for this bounty, and we pray for deliverance from this slough of despond. We surrender our pride and we throw ourselves on your infinite mercy. We do not deign to know your plan for us, O Lord, but we beseech you humbly for water, just enough to keep ourselves alive, if that is your design."

The seven men bowed their heads over steepled hands, watching their dinner gasp out its last in their laps. They'd caught a dozen of the ugly little fish out of the school of hundreds that skimmed under their raft, using nets made out of cargo webbing. Mostly eyeballs and spiny fins, yet something about their struggles made it vital to eat them alive. But they waited, and gave thanks.

Crushed into three rubber life rafts bound together by rope, they rode the rolling swells of the Pacific somewhere between Hawaii and the Marshall Islands, but in their hearts, the colonel reminded them, they sat in God's lap.

In the lead raft, Captain Ogilvy, Sergeant Wilcox and Corporal Hooper lay with their legs in a pile and their arms draped over the pontoons of the raft, which boasted of a seven-man capacity, but must've been war surplus from Munchkinland.

In the middle raft, Colonel Rowse, Lieutenant Mundt and Private Gordesky were no less crowded, what with Gordesky's crudely splinted broken leg and the empty food hamper and the Colonel's personal effects. Corporal Trouba brought up the rear in a rubber dinghy little bigger than a bedpan. Trouba's ribs and both arms were pulverized. He moaned and sobbed and argued with the sky, but the rest of the crew of the C-47 Skytrain they called Calamity Jane would have traded places, just for the solo berth.

"And Lord, we know that not all of us here have let you into their hearts, and we beg most of all, for you to shine your light on them brightest of all, and break the chains of their sinful pride. If this is a trial set before them, and we your agents in driving the lesson of your love home, then we accept that task, O Lord, if it will hasten our rescue … in Jesus's name, we pray …"

Captain Ogilvy bit back a retort, but Hooper tugged his widow's peak and said, "Amen, sir, except for that last part."

"Beg pardon, son?"

"Well, you've been leading us in prayer three times a day, and speaking up for us to God, and calling our rations holy communion … Why can't I just have the cracker and the wine?"

"Don't," Ogilvy warned. Hooper was studying to become a lawyer when he got drafted.

"I'm of the Jewish persuasion, sir. We don't have a messiah. Not yet, anyway …"

Col. Rowse closed his eyes for a moment. His heavy, measured breath whistled in and out of his flared nostrils like a pressure cooker venting steam. "I'm well aware of your people's refusal of the savior, Corporal. But that doesn't make it so." Nodding, he went on, "In Jesus's name …"

The crew repeated his blessing. "Sir, I must protest. The First Amendment prohibits a religious test …"

He went on, but it was wasted on the Colonel, who ordered Ogilvy to shut him up.

Ogilvy muzzled him with his hand and got bit. Hooper foamed at the mouth. "You're not even a chaplain!" Hooper stood up in the precarious raft. "We may be lost on the ocean and hopeless of earthly rescue, but for your information, Jesus said that we should pray in secret, in private. Matthew, 6:6."

The raft tipped back. Wilcox grabbed Hooper and pulled him back down. Hooper stumbled and fell straddling the starboard pontoon.

"So you know your Bible, at least," Rowse gloated.

Hooper squeezed tears out of his eyes. He was about to say something, maybe apologize, but then he looked down into the water.

The blue waves went white and parted like lace. A massive tiger shark leapt out of the water and bit into his leg, just below the knee.

Hooper howled. He grabbed Wilcox's arm. Dagger teeth gnashed and ground until they met in the marrow of his thigh. Dragged by sinew and shattered bones, he slipped out of the raft.

Ogilvy and Wilcox locked arms with him until the raft almost flipped over. Ogilvy kicked at its blunt snout and black striped flanks. Rowse and Mundt both fired pistols into the churning red foam. Hooper's eyes rolled back in his head. His body jerked, fingers dug even tighter into their arms. They let him go. The red water closed over his head.

Nobody said anything for a long time. "Well, I'm afraid I don't know any Hebrew," Rowse finally said. A couple guys nervously laughed.

They ate in silence. The brilliant salmon sunset backlit a marvelous flying fortress of wine-dark rain clouds on the horizon.

"Praise Jesus," Gordesky shouted, "it looks like rain!"

⸙

Wednesday

Ogilvy had to remind himself with every breath, not to attack Rowse's evangelical furor. The thrice-daily prayers had become the guiding light and inspiration for his crew after the plane went down, especially Corporal Trouba, who had suffered internal injuries in the belly turret.

"We must stand together before the Almighty," Rowse liked to say, "or we will surely each die alone." He'd written these words in his inspirational memoir, *Angel on My Wing.* The crew was thrilled to bits to fly the celebrated World War I ace from one atoll bivouac to the next along with their supply drops, and all of them bought a copy.

The C-rations, Cracker Jacks, candy bars and cigarettes were long gone, but they still had a gallon of fresh water in each raft. In the hope of converting any "heathen natives" they might encounter, the Colonel had a box of Saltines and a bottle of wine blessed by a chaplain at Pearl that he gave out after prayers, "just for morale purposes." Only Hooper and Ogilvy had refused them, but now his stomach growled at him to convert.

The crew knew each other pretty well, but after they'd talked baseball, cars, movies and the likelihood of rescue to death, the rafts had turned into a confessional. Things they never told each other, things no man should share with anyone but his priest, they'd told. At first, Ogilvy had tried gently to make it stop, but they'd just as gently told him to shut up. All of them but Rowse, who just sat there listening, encouraging them to "make a clean breast of it." Rowse was the last one with cigarettes, and he'd rationed them out to reward the best confessions.

It bound them together before God and under Colonel Rowse, but separated them from their captain.

Though they'd done little more than lay in the rubber boat for four days, moving only to try to catch fish or prevent pressure sores, a bone-deep fatigue, the overripe fruit of terror and despair, blossomed and claimed them.

Wilcox had already confessed once, but he still had some lingering guilt about the redhead he bedded in Melbourne, before they shipped out. "Tits like flippers, but oh man … she was like a bucking bronco, stay on eight seconds, and you'd win a prize, beg pardon, Lord. Y'know that corny Johnny Mercer tune about the angels? That was our song, I tell you what. I got a hand up her dress right there on the dance floor. It's crazy, but last night, I thought I heard her singing to me out there, in the—"

"That's enough, Mark," Ogilvy said. He was staring into the water as if into the bottomless depths of a flawless sapphire. They floated on a mirrored desert, but underneath was a world as deep as the sky. He searched until his mind filled the azure void with sharks and Zeroes.

Rowse sat up and stretched his rangy, sun-blistered arms. "Believe I'll go for a little swim. Care to join me, Captain?"

Ogilvy shaded his eyes to scan the surrounding water for fins. "I don't know how good an idea that is, Colonel …"

"There are no sharks out there." It sounded more like a command than an observation.

Ogilvy pulled himself up, ashamed at the luxury of space Hooper had left behind. The water was cool and inviting, until he slid into it. The brine bit into his broiled skin with a million tiny teeth, but he welcomed it. It cleared his head.

Rowse belly-flopped and bobbed to the surface like a big red walrus, chopping the water with powerful, easy strokes. "You boys try not to sail off without us, now." The crew pursed their cracked lips to whistle "When the Saints Go Marching In," to help them find their way back.

Ogilvy kicked and clawed after Rowse, nursing his cramped legs. The old man was way out ahead of him. His shaggy white mane dipped in and out of sight among the jumbled surges of the tide. Ogilvy's stomach clenched, but he couldn't show fear. It would not just ruin him with his men, but somehow, it was feeding the colonel.

He'd worked out what he wanted to say, but before he could catch his breath, Rowse growled, "If you want to give the orders, you go ahead, Captain. But if you want to come between these men and their God, I'll have something to say about it."

Ogilvy fought to keep the rolling quicksand waves from tossing him into Rowse. "I just don't want to lose another man to a stupid mistake. And these men aren't dead, yet. They need more than a 24-hour prayer vigil. We must not give up hope, but we must not give up trying—"

The Colonel rolled on his back and floated effortlessly. In the water, his bulk was buoyancy. "You blame me for what happened to your man, or do you blame God? We'll be rescued or we won't. It's in God's hands."

"I beg to differ, sir. It's in *our* hands, yours and mine." Ogilvy struggled to keep his head afloat. Every kick felt like he was telegraphing *Come & Get It* to the sharks. "The important thing is to stay focused and stay alive. You're propping up the boys' spirits pretty good with prayer ... But you've got them expecting a miracle—"

"I'm fighting for their *souls*, Captain. Their bodies might survive, but I've seen what men can do in situations like these. Men without hope, yes, without fear of God, are no better than beasts." In the molten sunset glow, the thick white hair all over the man's body gleamed like a golden fleece.

"I know my men a bit better than you do, sir. And I hardly think one needs church to keep from turning to cannibalism. What's more—"

The Colonel rolled over on his back and flexed his arms, forcing air out his nostrils. He smiled indulgently, but his anger carved bestial angles in his round, jovial face. "I wouldn't expect you to understand, Captain Ogilvy. 'Decline to State.' That's as strong as the form lets you put it, but you marked it up pretty hard. You must've been raised Catholic. Were the nuns too hard on you? Did your big college education make you think you'd outgrown your faith?"

"What the hell did you read my file for?"

"I wouldn't fly with someone who doesn't trust in the Almighty, but war is war, and your record looked solid. But you were riding for a fall.

God struck you down, and these poor boys had the bad luck to be stuck with you."

"With all due respect, sir, that's hardly what happened. We were struck by lightning—"

"Ha! Well, there you go!" Rowse swam up close to Ogilvy, his powerful hands strangling the water. "You'd rather play the Devil than go creeping to the cross, eh? Suits me. This game's a lot more fun, with a Devil."

Behind the orange fire of the sun's reflection, his eyes were flat black disks, showing only hunger. When his guard was down, something prowled in the colonel's smile, that would not think twice about seizing Ogilvy and holding him under until the bubbles stopped.

"I offer them hope, when no earthly hope remains. What can you offer them, son? This is out of all our hands. It's in His."

Ogilvy backed up, but the buffeting waves held him helpless. He scanned the plunging horizon, but he couldn't see the rafts. *Pick your battles.* "Alright. But I've been watching the stars whenever the skies cleared up, and I know our position."

"We talked this to death already, Captain. You figured out where we are, without a map or a sextant?"

"I've been flying these parts long enough, sir, and the native Polynesians did it for centuries. I've been taking compass readings. We can't be more than a few hundred miles east of Christmas Ridge and the Line Islands. If we got the boys rowing at night, we could still—"

"You could fill them full of false hope and run them ragged so there wouldn't be enough left to feed a shark."

"Sir, the current is pulling us east as we speak. There's nothing east of us until the Panama Canal."

Laughing, the colonel kicked lazily back toward the rafts. "You don't know where we are, Captain. And you can't really believe we can just pick a direction and paddle for home. Not out of this. Because if you think you're the master of your destiny, then where were you on Sunday morning, when your plane fell out of a clear blue sky and dumped us in the sea?"

Nothing in the nets for dinner. They said a special prayer for Trouba, who begged for a priest, when he made sense at all.

"God has a special purpose for us all," Rowse preached. "I know in my heart what my purpose is, and it's to save men who can't or won't heed the call. Those men are sick in their own sin as a beast in its own filth, and yet they call it riches, knowledge, power."

Ogilvy said nothing, but his teeth worried away at the meat of his cheek. He had seen the beast Rowse kept at bay, today. If he threatened Rowse's faith, he would corner the beast. What then?

"Body of Christ, amen," Rowse said as he fed Trouba a soggy Saltine. The corporal had thrown up all the water they'd given him, but somehow he kept down the cracker and a mouthful of wine. A miracle …

At dusk, just after they finished singing "Nearer My God to Thee," the golden face of the waters sparkled with tiny chains of ripples. A flock of flying fish jumped into the boats. Laughing and cheering, the boys caught handfuls of them.

"God works in mysterious ways, his wonders to perform. He has decided that we should live another day. Give thanks, boys."

Bullshit, Ogilvy thought, but he mouthed the words and ate with the others.

Holy Thursday

They awakened to find themselves engulfed in mist. They wrung out half a canteen each from their sodden clothes, and ate the last of the flying fish for breakfast, after a lengthy morning prayer.

Ten minutes after they said, *Amen*, it began to rain.

"Hallelujah!" Rowse cried, and the others echoed him. Under his breath, Ogilvy said, "He probably does that when coffee comes out of a coffeepot, too."

Wilcox punched him in the throat. He didn't look at his commanding officer before or after. He didn't say anything. He just shot a quick jab and crimped his windpipe.

"If it is a miracle, what's it hurt to believe it? Just keep your goddamned doubts to yourself from here on out, I'm warning you, sir."

The rafts jerked as the nets snared something longer than the whole raft convoy. The lead raft nosed down into the rushing water and was swamped. Ogilvy flipped over the top and hit the water headfirst. Wilcox clung to the raft, praying, "Please God, please."

Ogilvy tried to dive after their first aid kit, but the flawless sapphire water turned pitch black, cold and thick as concrete. His ears popped and his lungs smoldered when he bumped into something.

The big gray body sent him spinning, skin smooth as glass. He expelled his burning breath in a scream of bubbles and chased it to the surface.

He clawed at the pontoon of the raft, but with nothing to kick against, he could only flail in the water. "They're down there! Wilcox, help me!"

Wilcox took his hand, but didn't rush to pull him into the raft. "You lost our fishing net."

Ogilvy dug his fingers into the Sergeant's arm. "Pull me in, goddamit, there's a shark down there—"

"You don't believe in him, but you'll curse him. And you lost our medicine."

"I didn't lose anything, Wilcox! Let me in the fucking boat!" He tried to throw his leg over the pontoon, but they were weak, floppy meat. His thrashing would only bring them faster. He needed to calm down.

"Help your captain, Mark," Rowse said. "Judge not, lest ye be judged."

Wilcox didn't meet Ogilvy's eyes as he dragged him into the raft.

⸺⸺

Evening prayer.

Mundt checked the food stores and found all the Saltines missing. Mundt accused Gordesky of eating them.

Gordesky was an altar boy in Yonkers. He fumed, "Why would I eat them? They were the communion wafers, Lieutenant. It'd be a mortal sin—"

"They're just crackers," Mundt barked, "unless a priest administers them, right? Not like that would stop a chow-hound like you, Gordesky."

"Well, what about you, *sir*? Me and the Colonel were sleeping all afternoon. Begging your pardon, *sir*, but you're just a Lutheran. They're just crackers to you, and you're an officer, so maybe—"

Mundt growled, "Are you accusing *me* of stealing the crackers, Private?"

Ogilvy had slept for two blessed, dreamless hours after swimming with the colonel. Sitting beside the arguing men, Rowse had his hand on the food locker, and his eyes off on the horizon, plotting his next sermon and licking salt off his lips. "I'm not angry, boys. Just disappointed ..." Salt and crumbs?

"Quiet, both of you!" Ogilvy snapped. Rubbing his eyes, he stared at the blue on blue horizon until he was sure of what he saw. "Sharks!"

The shifting plain of water tilted to become a wall of glass studded with sleek black shapes. Dozens of them.

"Come on then, you devils!" Rowse stood up in the raft and fired a shot at the armada of scythe-like fins. The rest took up oars and leaned away from the pontoons.

The white water turned to shaving cream. Trouba's tiny dinghy bobbed and danced as sharks passed under it, homing in on the rippling waves of agitation from the terrified men in the big rafts.

"It's every goddamned shark for a hundred fucking miles," Wilcox snarled, then added, "Sorry, sir. But that fucking Jew Hooper rang the dinner bell for them."

The middle raft bucked and slid sideways. Rowse almost fell out, but Gordesky caught him. A fourteen-foot hammerhead reared up from the froth and sank its teeth into the port pontoon. The heavy, oily rubber popped like a bubble and shredded in its threshing jaws. Water rushed into the raft. Mundt and Rowse both shot it in the head, but the hulking shark battered the raft like a runaway torpedo.

Gordesky smashed his oar over the monster's back. He slid across the tipping raft on his splinted leg and fell on top of the hammerhead. He threw out his hand to Mundt, who caught him and screamed for help. Rowse threw his body over the food and tried to reload his gun.

Ogilvy watched all of this out the corner of his eye, as he and Wilcox fought off waves of tiger sharks. Ten feet long, at least, their black stripes danced in the churning water. Ogilvy jabbed their snouts away from the raft, but he wondered at their markings. He must have sunstroke, to study this trivial detail of something trying to eat him. They weren't stripes at all, but bands of black diamonds in irregular, arcing bands down their perfect bodies. Sleek, like the perfect airplane, hundreds of millions of years in the making.

Ogilvy looked at the middle raft. The great hammerhead whipped and tried to disengage itself from the sinking rubber snare, but two black tiger sharks were shredding its helpless flanks.

A shark caught his oar in its teeth and yanked him halfway overboard. He jerked backwards into Wilcox, who bumped or shoved him into the water.

Ogilvy hit the water and lost the oar. He kicked and thrashed back to the surface. Bodies bumped into him. Silver, black-banded skins stroked him like cat's tongues. *God no,* he thought, *not like this—*

He inhaled a gout of seawater and sank like lead, gagging on fire. His foot touched something, and he kicked off it. His fumbling hands seized on a fin, a tail. Literally climbing out of the water on the bodies of sharks, Ogilvy vaulted back into the raft.

"Help me, Jesus, please!" Gordesky screamed and clawed at Mundt, who hung on to Rowse, who clung to his footlocker. The tiger sharks ate their way into the trapped hammerhead until they met in the middle. The hammerhead roared silently and rolled off the raft, taking Gordesky with it into the midst of a feeding frenzy.

Screaming, "They're eating me!" Gordesky dragged Mundt and Rowse towards the submerged edge of the raft. Still hacking up seawater, Ogilvy leapt onto the starboard pontoon of the middle raft and grabbed Gordesky's broken oar. Driving the jagged shaft into the hammerhead's gills, he tried to save Gordesky. The private looked right through him to reach out to Rowse.

Rowse's gun went off in Ogilvy's left ear. He jumped back, sure he'd been shot.

Gordesky jerked away as if shocked, clutching his chest and tumbling off the hammerhead. Bloody foam and teeth closed over his screaming face. His hand darted out to wave at them with no fingers on it.

"You son of a bitch!" Ogilvy wheeled on Rowse to find the gun in his face.

"Get back to your raft, Captain."

At their feet, a dozen sharks battled for scraps of Private Tommy Gordesky. The rafts shook on the heaving sea, but they were not attacked again. They drifted away from the feeding frenzy as if they were already dead, or marked by God, for someone else to eat.

Rowse reached into the water and fished out a gobbet of meat, and immediately sank his teeth into it. For all he knew, it was Gordesky, but Ogilvy was too tired to go for another swim, right now.

No more Body of Christ, but Rowse gave them all a double belt of His blood, shed for thee.

Ogilvy lay in the raft alongside Wilcox, but he did not sleep. At least, he did not feel himself sleep. He dreamed he heard beautiful voices singing hymns, way down in the sea.

Good Friday

No rain, no ships, no planes.
No fish.
Hot.

"Even you, Captain. He can spare miracles for even one who denies him." Rowse and Mundt lay straddling the starboard pontoon of the middle raft, which rode low in the water under the burden of the colonel's footlocker. "What did Private Gordesky do to deserve his fate? Only God knows—"

"You murdered him." Ogilvy's throat was parched and swollen halfway shut. He had some water left, but he had to hold it. He'd offered it to Wilcox, who had a raging hangover from the wine, but he refused. He stared into the water, mouthing the words to that corny song.

"Your lies shame the devil! I saw you fall into the sea, and the sharks spat you out! He delivered you, and yet you still deny him!"

"Mermaids," Wilcox whispered. Urine and the blood from his cracked lips was all he'd had to drink since the last communion, unless he'd been drinking seawater.

"Rowse shot Tommy in the chest, Wilcox. In cold blood. Isn't there anything in the Bible about that?"

"She's out there," Wilcox mumbled. "Don't you hear her?"

"I am an old sinner, son," Rowse crowed. "I make no bones about that. The Lord makes and spends us, as per His own higher purpose."

"I don't want to hear your purposes, Colonel, or His."

"In his fear, the boy would've taken us all down. He was a good boy, who made his peace with the Lord for his moment of weakness. But I won't hear you accuse me of murder."

Mundt stared into the water. "The Colonel saved my life. Gordesky was already dead. And he was a thief."

The sun got stuck at noon and camped there for a year. No rain, no wind, no fish.

Hotter. Sharks circled like vultures under glass.

Nobody had moved or spoken for several hours when Trouba died. He hadn't stirred since his last communion wafer, but he suddenly arched and sent tremors through the raft convoy.

For a moment, Ogilvy envied him. He'd slept through the whole damned thing.

Rowse delivered a eulogy, but turned the sermon on Ogilvy. "Your doubting will be the death of us all. God has a plan for us, even you. Especially you, I think."

His mind chased itself through hoops, drifted on seas teeming with monstrous visions—his whole fighter wing vanishing in a cyclone of steel over Manila, as if the hack cartoonist who scribbled this funny paper of a war had just erased them; Pvt. Gordesky, smiling and walking on red, shark-infested water, "just like Jesus!"

"Hey Colonel, she's here!" Wilcox hung over the side. He threw his arms around something in the water. Ogilvy reached out for him, blearily moaned, "Wilcox, don't—"

"So long, suckers!" A sleek gray shape rose up to kiss Wilcox's grinning face off. Before Ogilvy could even react, the sergeant was gone.

Rowse delivered a heartfelt eulogy. Ogilvy screamed, "Balls!" in the middle of it. Rowse ordered him into the aft boat. "If the Captain can't abide the stink of us Christians, maybe he'd prefer Corporal Trouba's berth to himself."

"You go to hell."

"Ha! There're no atheists in foxholes, Captain! Get in that raft, or I'll shoot you in the leg and let you swim back to Hawaii. You're so sure you know the way ..."

Ogilvy refused.

Mundt cursed him. "You're damned, Captain, you're drowning in fire, and dragging us down! Get out the boat!"

Ogilvy turned to appeal to Wilcox, but of course, he was gone.

Mundt jumped into his raft. Ogilvy caught the blade of the oar across his temple.

He toppled into the water. Kicking away from the raft, he looked down and saw something the size of a fighter plane pacing him.

Rowse pointed the gun at him, but was all smiles as he paddled back to the tiny dinghy at the tail of the convoy.

The raft almost spilled Trouba's corpse in the drink on top of him.

"Mind you don't lose Corporal Trouba's remains, Captain. He wanted to be buried beside his mother in Perth Amboy, and I'd like to honor his last wish."

Ogilvy clung to the side of the raft. Corporal Trouba was a short but stocky guy. He lay on his back with his hands across his chest, which jutted out at odd angles like a bag of broken furniture. "You're insane, Rowse. Why don't you just drop the mask and show us what you really are? Why can't you just kill me, too?"

Colonel Rowse laughed and laughed until the last light died and he looked like a big shaggy dog, perched on the drooping edge of his raft. "I want to hear you admit that you don't disbelieve, Captain. You just hate Him. Well, you don't have to love Him. You just have to recognize who is in charge, here."

Ogilvy heard the water come unzipped behind him. Mundt giggled, "Here come de judge!"

Ogilvy screamed, "God damn you!" and threw himself into the raft on top of Trouba's corpse.

That night, it rained.

Saturday

Ogilvy awoke to the ungentle rocking of the raft. For a second, it felt like Sunday morning at home, with the kids sneaking up on Mom and Pop, and the dog pulling the covers off the bed …

He rubbed his eyes. It was still dark, but the eastern sky had begun to fade.

A twelve-foot bull shark tugged almost playfully on Trouba's trailing right arm.

He heard someone singing hymns. It wasn't his crew. The dinghy floated alone on sloping, slanting swells like an endless field of rooftops.

Fighting nausea and panic, he rolled Trouba's corpse out of the boat. The water boiled and went red. The bull shark whipped around and leapt out of the water as something below bit off its tail.

Almost playfully, the pack of tiger sharks devoured Trouba and the crippled bull, but never touched the tiny raft. The black diamond swirls around their fins and tails were not natural markings, but stylized bite wounds, sacred scars.

Swarms of remora and smaller fish swooped in to mop up the debris, but the tiger sharks followed and circled the raft like guardian angels. The current flowed faster now, dragging him along like a crumb on a vast blue tablecloth.

They must have cut him loose in the night. He didn't remember sleeping, but he must've dropped off into a coma on top of his radioman's corpse. Amazing, what one could adapt to, and call natural …

Trouba had been laying on an oar. Also, the wrappers from two sandwiches, four empty C-rat tins, three Cracker Jacks boxes and an apple core. He doubted Trouba had enjoyed any of it.

Ogilvy felt a lot less guilty, now, about stealing the Communion Saltines. He'd only done it on a whim to cheese off Rowse, but then he'd lost them when the raft flipped.

He had failed his men. He was half-asleep at the stick when the plane went down. He had let them fall under the sway of a lunatic. He had failed to keep them alive.

The sun rose like a fever. Its first tentative rays struck his arms and chest like the lashes of a whip. He paddled with the current until his emaciated muscles twanged and tore under blistered skin. He hunched over and tried not to retch up the last fluid in his belly. He had to catch up to them, save his men from Rowse—

Fins darted around him as he rowed, doubled and trebled and turned into a *kamikaze* fighter wing, lost forever in the mirror of the sky. Sharks flew overhead, too—tiny, white ones, screeching at him to give up and die.

No, damn you, I won't. He cursed the sun in a hoarse croak.

You must be up there after all, busting a gut at our pitiful antics. This has to be for someone's entertainment. Good comedy like this can't just go to waste. Uncle, I say unto Thee, and mea maxima culpa, I admit it. I'll never love you, but I kneel, I bow, I humbly acknowledge your everlasting power. Do with me as you will …

He paddled until his arms revolted and he dropped the oar and fell into a stupor. He heard singing down in the sea, and knew they were angels.

Just let it be for something, God. Just let there be a reason …

Sometime after nightfall, he woke up to an old familiar friend, the sounds of shooting and shouting.

He opened his eyes and checked his Bulova watch. Almost midnight. The rolling, moonlit hills of quicksilver parted and sucked him into a momentary valley, and he saw them.

The rafts rode the high shoulder of the next swell. Rowse had maneuvered Mundt into the sinking middle raft, and now held him at gunpoint. He heard them shouting at each other.

"Mundt! Stand down!" Ogilvy searched for the oar, but it was gone. He paddled with his bloody, ragged hands, screaming at the top of his lungs.

They didn't see or hear him. Mundt shouted, "Colonel, I relieve you of duty!" It must've been painful for Mundt, to realize he was wrong. But not as painful as Rowse's response.

He fired a flare gun at Mundt, who caught the phosphorus round in his mouth. Jets of scarlet sparks blew out his cheeks and backlit his eyes for a horrible instant before it sprayed out his eye sockets.

"Damn you, I'm over here!" The ocean turned over under Ogilvy's raft like a restless sleeper, lofting him down a sheer slope and into the midst of the rafts.

Rowse broke open the flare gun and calmly reloaded it. In the moonlight, his teeth looked like little knives.

Mundt folded and fell into the sea. Ogilvy saw the Roman candle of his skull merrily fizzing underwater as he sank out of sight.

When Ogilvy was thirty feet away, Rowse fired. Ogilvy dove. The flare punched into the nose of the raft and melted it.

He felt the water alive with them. His muscles rebelled at the furious exertion of swimming the gap. The fear of drowning, being eaten or shot in the back held no power over him, anymore. He was driven by one thing the god of this world should have applauded: revenge.

Something surged under him and threw him into Rowse's raft. He crashed into the colonel and brought down both fists on his face. Rose dropped the flare gun and flopped back, grabbing his heart.

Ogilvy cuffed him across the face. "You were right, Colonel! God is real! You want to meet Him?"

"No, please God, I'm an old man …"

Rowse curled into a fetal ball. Ogilvy threw him over the side and lay down in the raft. He heard hymns from deep down below, felt it through the raft, and he thought he heard Col. Rowse singing along.

Easter Sunday

Ogilvy woke up to see white sharks in the sky. He rolled over and looked around. He was alone. But he was alive.

It's a miracle!

The boat rocked like a cradle on the shore of a black beach. Ogilvy looked into the shallow water for a long, heart-frozen while, then lurched over the side, but found his legs quite unable to hold him up. On elbows and knees, he wallowed out of the surf and planted kisses on the sand.

A tiny desert isle of naked lava rock with a few tortured thorn trees, a cluster of huts made of scrapped canoes and whalebones, and a low, blunt hump of a volcanic mound, with a ramshackle clapboard shack on it. A church.

Ogilvy lay back and melted into the sand. An insect alighted on his forehead and drank at the oasis of tears from his left eye. His hands couldn't get the trick of brushing it away, and that was just fine. But he was not at ease in his mind, for he felt unseen eyes peeling him like an onion.

He rolled over to find the girl right there, smiling shyly down at him. Her long black hair, almost auburn at the ends, cast a veil of blessed shade across his face.

"You came! We prayed for you, and now you've come! Now no one will doubt."

Captain Ogilvy smiled up at her. She was a beautiful young lady, somewhere between fifteen and forty, the way Polynesian women often were. Draped in a gaily colored sackcloth muumuu, her lithe curves reminded him how long it'd been since he saw or touched any woman. Never one half this beautiful. He felt drunk. "You speak pretty good English for a dream come true, ma'am. What island is this?"

"I am Kalei." She knelt over him and put her hands on his chest. They were tiny delicate things, with no fingers. "You are Christian, yes?" Her glossy black eyes searched his with earnest need.

He nodded absently, looking out at the ocean. "Born again, just yesterday. Our plane crashed, and we—"

"He sent you!" She jumped up. "We pray to you come every Easter just like Father say, but you not come! But we love you, Jesus. We never give up hope."

"I was otherwise engaged …" He fogged out her crazy chatter as he saw three boys come bounding down the beach to frolic in the surf. "Hey, what gives?"

The oldest child was maybe twelve, the youngest only six or seven, but only one of them had legs. The others hopped along on stumps and their fingerless paddle-hands.

Another miracle. He'd washed ashore on a leper colony.

They found something in the surf. Dancing and clapping their fins, they hauled it out onto the black lava shore.

It was most of Col. Rowse. It threw up an arm picked clean as a chicken wing to fend off the boys.

"Don't touch that!" Ogilvy got up. He felt faint. He had to get away from here—

"Come, we make ready!" She tugged his arm eagerly, but then hobbled up the beach to the huts. She had no legs below the knees. He noticed the patterns of scars down her thighs, around and above the shiny scars of her amputation. The scars were stained black from lava dust rubbed into the wounds. He pulled himself to his feet and walked after her.

Embarrassed and horrified, he saw the children and the girl with new eyes. They weren't lepers. They'd been eaten, a bite at a time, by sharks.

He shuddered with fear and shame. Theirs was not a sudden ordeal, but a daily struggle. The ocean was infested with sharks. There was nothing else to eat.

The children laughed as they pulled Rowse's mouth open by his straggly white beard and stuffed a sea urchin into it. He danced on the sand. The children played a game of trying to ride him in his death throes.

Rowse was a beast. God had dealt with him. He had nothing to fear from these people. They loved him. They thought he was Jesus. Who was he to tell them they were wrong?

Ogilvy asked to see the priest, the chaplain, the missionary teacher. "Or the doctor. Surely, you've got to have a doctor or a nun, if you're, uh …"

"We pray for you to come," she repeated, at the end of her pidgin English lessons. But she gamely tried to explain. She led him to an empty hut and lay him down on a mat of woven human hair and fed him cool spring water and spears of candied shark meat. Her strange accent slowly melted, and her voice became almost manly.

They were the grandchildren of Ka-moho-alii, the god-king of sharks. Driven out of their sacred caves at Molokai by jealous tribes who feared their mastery of the sea, they turned away from their true nature and swore to live and die on land, for Ka-moho-alii had forgotten his grandchildren.

"We had to leave Molokai, and the sea brought us here. We had no choice but to eat the devils of the sea, even as they ate us. We were hated and forgotten by all, when the Father came to us." With a fingerless hand, she indicated the ruined chapel on the hill, and then pointed at a framed picture on the wall of the hut.

Through corrosion and salt crystals, he saw hollow, haunted blue eyes in a wasted, ascetic face and a straggly beard. *Jesus*, he thought. It was a mirror.

"He taught us the Word of the Lord, and it was good, for Jesus would come to heal us and end our hunger. We studied and were baptized and our warriors took Holy Communion, and they were born again."

A croaking, barking riot erupted outside the hut. Kalei tried to fend them off, but they would not be denied. When they came piling into the hut to worship him, he thought he had nothing to fear.

They hopped like frogs out of a French kitchen; they humped over the black sand like caterpillars and snakes; they led blind, faceless monsters who hummed "Ave Maria" through naked, sun-bleached bone and teeth filed to needle points.

Leprosy, famine and the sharks had whittled them down to shiny gray shark-shapes that slithered and hobbled towards him and groped his salt-crusted rags, and called him Jesus.

They herded Ogilvy out into the moonlight with their mangled stumps, urging him up the path between fluted fangs of lava rock, towards the church.

Kalei walked beside him. "The Father saved those who came to him, but there was not enough of him to save us all. We prayed to God to let us return to the sea and swim with our blessed brothers in Paradise. We prayed for a real miracle. And now, he sent you!"

"No, you can't believe that!" Ogilvy shoved her aside, stumbled over maimed children and broke for the beach. He couldn't heal them, he couldn't do a miracle. This was a cruel joke, it was a nightmare he'd conjured up to punish himself for breaking down and begging God to save him. The last refuge of a scoundrel ...

His raft lay on the shore, but all around it, the shallows churned with slashing fins and mutely roaring mouths. A tiger shark twice as long as Ogilvy was tall beached itself on the shore. Another leapt out of the surf and lolled on the sand, gills flapping.

Ogilvy backed away from the lacey foam of the waves. Four, six, eight tiger sharks lay between him and the raft. Their flat black eyes goggled out the sides of their huge, torpedo-shaped heads. Their mouths gaped from ear to ear with row upon row of gnashing bayonet teeth. The islanders bowed to them and covered them with leis of obsidian and bone, reverently touching the raised black scars incised into their flanks until they turned and thrashed back into the surf.

Ogilvy shaded his eyes and stared at the crosses erected at the end of the beach. A skeleton hung from the nearest one. Rowse's corpse hung on another one, what little was left of it. The islanders kneeling before his cross were convulsing as if they'd ingested poison or drugs. They rolled on the sand, crawled into the shallows, thrashing and tearing at their arms and legs with their teeth. A naked child too young for him to say if it was boy or girl yanked a dangling loop of Rowse's intestine, causing his slack mouth to open and close, silently praying, *forever and ever, amen ...*

Legless women and children clamored around Ogilvy, lifted him off his feet and carried him to the crosses.

Too weak to run, too tired to fight, he surrendered himself unto their hands as the warriors lifted him up to be bound to the arms of the cross. Kalei climbed up on their backs to whisper in his ear, "Say the words, Jesus."

Ogilvy thought back to the last time he went to Mass, before Dad came back from the Great War and said if the bastard wanted a cheering section, He should become a football player.

The ones that devoured Rowse had all crawled into the ocean.

"Take this and eat, for it is my body," Ogilvy said, and they repeated it. Kalei kissed him.

"Body and blood of Christ," he repeated.

She kissed him and probed his mouth with her tongue.

"In Jesus's name," she said.

She bit his lower lip and peeled it off with a toss of her head, skinning him down to his chin.

He screamed, "Jesus!"

With teeth already growing longer and sharper in her mouth, she pried his jaws wide and bit his tongue. It burst in her mouth like a juicy plum and deluged her graying, scaled face with hot arterial blood.

He let them do it. He tried, with his last red breath, to bless them and admit his sin, for now he knew that God did indeed hear prayers and work miracles, but God was a shark.

WE WILL REBUILD

On the three-month anniversary of V-D Day, some residents of Ocotillo still came out to wave or put Old Glory up on their porches as Deputies Snopes and Bascomb rolled up the nameless main drag in their armored cruiser, siren blaring to lift the curfew.

"Happy Death Day, suckers," Bascomb hollered.

"Leave 'em alone," Snopes said. "Everybody loves a parade."

Bascomb made V-D Day medals out of Xmas ribbon and teeth for the occasion, but only Bascomb wore his, along with his Army Purple Heart and the special citation for the Battle of Calexico Wal-Mart, two weeks ago. A Wal-Mart greeter's nametag hung from the ribbon; HI! MY NAME IS SOLE SURVIVOR.

Verna Schepsi swept the sidewalk in front of the feed store, but it was a fool's errand. The particles of ash that still rained down out of the sulfurous yellow sunrise were like downy snowflakes, merging into gray dust devils battling in the empty street.

Chubby Beckwith lumbered out of the Circle K and waved at them when he got to the end of his chain. Chubby was a good kid, always kept a fresh pot of coffee on back when they had it, but he got grabby when they stopped to top off the cruiser once, so they had to chop off his hands. It was all legal, the papers on file with the judge.

"Wanna go out to the canal and look for deadbeats?" Bascomb was crocked early and itchy today, because his wife got into it with Taffy, their Doberman pinscher. Reluctant to put either of them down, he was damned if he wasn't going to shoot something today.

"Waste of ammo," Snopes replied. "Besides, we got to go out and change the sign."

The sign marking the Interstate 8 off-ramp used to read OCOTILLO; ELEV. 47; FT. POP. 220; GAS FOOD LODGING. As soon as the dust settled after V-D Day, they revised the list of amenities with big stenciled red NO's, and shortwave and CB frequencies to call those inside.

Snopes had the idea to borrow the scoreboard numbers from the little league field. He displayed the number of the alive with the black numbers for the home team, and the number of the dead in the red for the visitors. The score was not encouraging: 32 to 67. Gabe Gonzalez got bit by his daughter last night, and after they woke the judge up to sign the order, she was put down. Everyone pretty much knew what he was trying to do when he got bit, so no one was overly exercised about it.

Still and all, a pretty normal day …

Bascomb wanted to tack a 1 in front of the black number. "If any more gangs come looking for shit, we got to look tough."

"When the Army comes, we got to look meek, so they don't just bomb us. You heard on the radio what the Marines did to them rich dicks in Palm Springs."

Snopes went up the road with his binoculars to check the perimeter. Ocotillo straddled the I-8/S.R.46 junction, snug between the Anza-Borrego mountains, studded with fractured granite boulders, and the dusty, drained lakebed of the Imperial Valley.

Nothing alive or dead had come up the 8 or down from the hills in over a week. Gangs and deadbeat stragglers from the conflagration that destroyed El Centro and Calexico still dribbled in from the east, but deadbeats couldn't cross the canal; burnt up with hunger and half-mummified by the desert sun, most of them dissolved like soda crackers in the swift current. Everything on wheels stopped where the deputies had blown the I-8 overpass at the canal, and either turned north on the 46 or abandoned their vehicles to plead for food and shelter.

After that doctor from La Jolla, nobody had been granted asylum in Ocotillo. When they let him in with his wife and three daughters, they thought they'd turned a corner; but three days later, the shitbird gassed himself and his whole family with their propane tank. The house blew up and burned down both its neighbors.

People from the cities couldn't handle desert life, before or after Day Zero. Nothing out here had changed. There had always been laws on the books for dealing with aliens. If they were from outside the town's jurisdiction and had nothing to offer, they had to be treated accordingly.

A couple deadbeats had wandered into the minefield along the highway a while back, and parts of them still tried to crawl through the tumbleweed snarls of razor wire that flanked the interstate and encircled the town. The fields were clearly marked for living and dead alike, cardboard signs and rotting, chattering heads on pikes, but nobody took time to read, anymore.

Vultures and crows feuded over the last scraps on the skeletons of the latest live invaders—a small herd of runaway horses that had blundered into the minefield around the abandoned Pernicano ranch. The yard sale scatter of long, elegant bones and stringy flesh looked like the ruins of something built to fly. Sometime ago, he might have seen something sad or beautiful in it, but now the waste of meat just made his mouth water.

In the crisp heat haze of the quickening day, everything seemed to squirm with a tortured thirst for blood and sweat. Snopes went back to the cruiser. With sheet metal and chain-link fence for windows, it was already a sweat lodge inside. Bascomb was in the driver's seat, hooting at the radio like football was back. "Hell yeah!"

Snopes pushed him over and got in, turned back down the off-ramp. Bascomb loaded shells into the shotgun and stuffed the rest of them in his pockets. "Dead wetbacks!"

They passed Chubby again, who waved a stump at them as he chewed on the other. Mrs. Chesebro wandered her dusty yard in her housecoat, looking for her cats. Next door, Chet Bamberger strained at the end of his leash to get his months-old morning paper. He wore only a wife-beater tank top—second-skinned to him by yellow seepage, and drizzling maggots out his armpits. His muzzle was splashed with bright red blood, which, since his own was black and clotted in his feet and ass, clearly solved the mystery of the missing cats.

Bamberger was unemployed, and lost his license for a third DUI coming back from the Golden Acorn casino, so he and the deputies knew each other pretty well. He liked to tune up his wife, but she never pressed charges. He beat up Connie in Pal Joey's Bar on V-D Day, and got locked up with some deadbeat tweaker from San Diego who'd crashed a stolen car on the off-ramp. The tweaker bit Chet, who died but got up and ate two of his cellmates.

Chet was one of the first dead locals to stir, and Snopes put four bullets into his torso that night. He sorely regretted that he didn't know, back then, that you have to shoot them in the head. Order was restored, Connie took him home, and he hadn't attacked anyone since. How they stayed together under one roof with no AC was a mystery to

Snopes, but their problems were none of his business, until someone formally complained.

At the stoplight, Ocotillo tried to show that somebody really believed it would be a proper town, once. A shabby little bandstand and a pocket park once sat in the middle of the road, but now, the town square was a field of black, greasy ash. A sun-bleached and smoke-blackened banner hung over the street, reminding him to catch the Ocotillo Settlers' Days festival that should have started last weekend.

The town hall was a sturdy whitewashed brick monument to itself, with a sheriff's station, courtroom, mayor's office, basement holding cells, and a broom closet that doubled as a library and civil defense shelter.

V-D Day was mostly peaceful in Ocotillo, until the panicked mass exodus from San Diego swept through with the dead in its wake. Half the town bugged out for the hills, while the rest hunkered down in attics and cellars, or the town hall building.

Ocotillo was overrun and picked clean. Sheriff Lorber and the deputies holed up on the town hall roof when the remaining civilians fled or went down in the shelter. The dead converged on the town hall, wading into the ankle-deep gasoline pool the Sheriff had drained into the square, and gawking up at them as they tossed road flares.

When the fire died down, the wave had crested and fallen, and the remaining deadbeats were easy to put down or contain.

Judge Dooling came down from his ranch that morning, and since the Mayor was dead, he took over and restored order. Painting the town hall white again had been the first order of business.

The people in the shelter weren't so lucky. When the power failed and the water pressure dropped, rats boiled out of the toilets and bit them in the dark. All the rats had feasted on the bodies in the streets, and were rife with the bug that made them walk and eat.

Whatever still knocked around inside was too dumb to work the hatch, but the Judge ordered them to open it. Three deputies had family in the shelter, and at first, they were just happy to have them back. Espinoza ate his gun that night, after executing his dead wife and his mother. Benedetto got careless, and was bit by his son. He looked happy today, when he and his family lurched out of their trailer for morning chow, or at least, happier than when he was alive. Bascomb and his hogbitch wife fought almost every night, so for them, nothing much had changed at all.

In all, they identified seventy-nine walking dead residents, and sixty-three living. Getting the deadbeat locals to go home was easy; once chained down in their houses or at their jobs, most just did more or less what they always had, knocking around aimlessly until chow time, or until live meat got too close. Putting the muzzles on, though, was a king-hell bitch.

Deputy Mark Snopes had no family in town. He came over from the San Diego Police Department two years before, and was damned lucky to have a job. The cop mentality—us versus them, with any civilian more or less one of them—ground on his nerves. He tasered an enormous lady shoplifter when she got aggressive with him. She turned out to be five months pregnant, and miscarried.

In a burg like Ocotillo, it was the same problems, but smaller and simpler. Half the town out of its head on drink or drugs or God, and beating on the other half; shitheads and deadbeats passing through, littering and shooting up the signs; and wetbacks, creeping over the border and eating all the livestock. But it was better than the city. The desert took care of those who couldn't take care of themselves. You knew who the good people were, and the right and the wrong of a situation was always writ plain. Now, more than ever …

Snopes swung the cruiser into the town hall lot and jumped out. Bascomb called after him, "Fuck you, then, I'm driving!"

Betty Olson saw him coming, and unlocked the door, then locked and bolted it when he barged through the saloon doors that led to the courtroom. "I wouldn't" she whispered. "The generator's out, so he's in a mood."

Snopes didn't knock. The courtroom was darker than the other rooms, with no slits cut into the boards over the windows, and no lamplight. The dark was all violet fireworks until his eyes adjusted to the pinprick spider webs of daylight seeping into the courtroom.

In the stifling heat and silence, Snopes believed he could feel something scratching, like claws, on the concrete underneath his feet. Somewhere in the room, the dispatch radio crackled.

"Your Honor, even if there *was* something out there, we got bigger shit—beg pardon, sir—issues, to contend with, and I'm worried about Bascomb—"

"He's worried about you, Deputy."

"I can't see you, Your Honor."

A match flashed and kissed the mantle of a Coleman lamp on the judge's desk. "The dark makes it feel cooler." Only the gavel, drinking glass, revolver and pale, liver-spotted hands came into view. "If we had gas to spare for the generators ... but never mind. You wanted to resign, then?"

"You know I don't. I take this job seriously, and since Sheriff Lorber got bit, me and Doug are pretty much the only law left. But this patrol duty isn't going to solve anything. We're just wasting gas."

"Deputy, the migrant illegal traffic through this area is more of a scourge now than ever. You saw, yourself, what they did in Seeley and Calexico. You'd like to see them gather at the wire, I suppose, and overrun us again?"

Snopes couldn't lose his temper with the judge, but the way he tied you up with his questions made his head hurt. "I'd like to clean up the mess *inside* the wire."

"What mess is there? What haven't you been reporting to me?"

Snopes came closer to the light. The outline of Dooling's head floated in the dark above the perfect black of his robe. Hairless, blank as the moon. "Your Honor hasn't been outside in a while, so far as I know, but I have, and I file reports on everything. Five of our people got killed this month alone in, uh, domestic disputes—"

"*Nine* died this month, don't you mean, Deputy Snopes?"

"No sir, the other four were already—"

"They were citizens of this town, each and every one, never forget that. We take care of our own."

"Sir, we have a responsibility to the living to protect them from the dead ... don't we?"

Judge Dooling looked Snopes up and down, his bifocals and his dentures winking in the yellow light. "Deputy, do you know why the dead got up three months ago?"

Snopes felt as if the courtroom at his back was packed with laughing ghosts, laughing at him. "No sir, I don't."

The judge clucked his tongue, a dry baby rattler sound. "Then how can you say you know what will happen tomorrow?"

Snopes headed for the door. "I don't get it, Your Honor."

Dooling's chair creaked. "You are the arm of the law, young man, not its brain. The police have ever had the thankless duty of standing between the citizenry and their own worst impulses."

"Your Honor might take a different view of the law if he ever got off his fossilized ass and tried enforcing it." That was what Snopes wished he'd said. Instead, he said, "Yes, your Honor."

Dooling's voice got higher and louder as Snopes walked away. When Snopes stopped at the door, it went down low, but the superb acoustics of the courtroom delivered it to his ear. "This could be divine retribution, and it could be a disease, Deputy. But tomorrow, if it is a disease, there may be a cure; and if it is the judgment of God, then we will go to our greater reward with our sins against the innocent and ill weighing heaviest in our hearts."

Snopes tried hard not to shout. "Your Honor, Bascomb and I are more than ready to take care of business with a clean conscience—"

"Have him start with his wife, then, would you, Deputy? You haven't lost anyone, so you can't relate. The state can't presume to write the law, but should act to preserve order and normality, until the rest of the world does likewise."

"Right, everything's normal."

"Yes, if we say so, and we do. We have restored order, and we will rebuild our town. Now there's a mob of illegal aliens massed somewhere around the fence. See to it."

Snopes left, stopped in the library to get a tripod-mounted M-60 and two extra belts. Judge Dooling was also a retired Brigadier General in the National Guard, and had the keys to the armory in Seeley. All the heavy stuff went out to blockade the 8 to the east, to stop the deadbeat armies marching out of Mexico. Nothing came back.

Snopes got blindsided by the daylight when he went outside. He slipped on his shades. Bascomb hung out the window with his arms wide for the machinegun. "OK, you can drive."

They drove south, down the perimeter to where it swerved east to parallel the interstate. "All clear, shit!" Bascomb growled, and cracked open a blood-hot beer.

Most of the ash came from El Centro, Calexico, and Mexicali, which the Marines torched with fuel-air bombs a week after V-D Day. They boiled over like anthills doused in gas, never-ending waves of deadbeats, scorched black and ravenous. The Marines got eaten or bugged out, and that was the last they saw of any order outside their own fence.

Snopes went up the canal to where the fence picked up at the trailer park at the north end of town. He cut across the back end of Bascomb's yard on the cul-de-sac. Bascomb waved to his wife, who drooled and banged on the bars of their bedroom window.

They followed the fence along the canal and turned north, and were almost back to the main drag when Bascomb called, "Wetbacks!"

Snopes braked on the shingled dirt road beside the abandoned Milbank ranch, which stood half in and half out of the perimeter. Donnie Milbank was a small-time TV minister, and when the Rapture found him still on earth, he packed up the family in the Winnebago and hauled ass for some born-again survivalist enclave in Texas.

Where the fence circled behind Milbank's stables, he saw twenty or thirty ragged scarecrows loping across the dead brown lawn. They shambled jerkily through a gap in the razor wire, where it was trampled flat.

Snopes jerked to a stop. The nearest wetback was inside the fence, not ten feet away, flannel and denim rags caked with mud and dust and blood, claws outstretched, slack jaws snapping in dumb, bottomless hunger. Bascomb jumped out, laid the M-60 across the hood and opened up.

Bascomb hosed them down like leaves off a driveway, walking the spray of lead across their midsections to slash them in half and pile them up against the wire.

Snopes stayed behind the wheel, but opened fire with the shotgun. He saw big scoops of meat lifted out of heads and chests and knew he was connecting; at this range, how could he miss?

It was hard to hear with the atomic-typewriter clatter of the machinegun, but when Bascomb finally stopped to reload, Snopes could see how a few survivors tried to run for the open desert. He could hear how they screamed and cried and prayed.

His stomach filled with nightcrawlers and battery acid. "Stop! Bascomb, Doug, Jesus Christ, stop! *They're not dead!*" He hit the siren and jumped out, ran around the cruiser to knock Bascomb down, because his partner just laughed and kept shooting.

Snopes tore down the gun and shut off the siren. If any got away, he didn't see them moving.

Bascomb got up and dusted off, punched Snopes in the shoulder. "Fuck you thinking, fucker? You wanna die?"

"Didn't you hear that? They were fucking screaming!"

"They were screaming in *Spanish!* They're fucking wetbacks, dude, and they look pretty fucking dead now. Come on, let's clean up."

Bascomb covered while Snopes checked for survivors. There were none, and nothing got up. The bodies lay in mounds like wet laundry in the gap, which they'd made by throwing plywood from Millbank's stables over the wire. There were nineteen of them, as near as he could tell, what with their being blown open and running into each other like a casserole. He saw two women with babies in slings, and another who might've been pregnant.

"Give me a hand, asshole," Snopes said. He turned and vomited into the dust, wrapped a bandana over his face. They rolled out some tarp and got them ready for the chow wagon.

The bodies were pitifully light, skeletal, blistered skin flaking away, but they had walked out of Mexico alive. "We gotta get this shit in the chipper before lunchtime," Bascomb said. "Stiffs'll think it's Thanksgiving."

"Your wife'll be so happy," Snopes said, "she might even let you get some."

"Fuck you, Mark. Least I got something to come home to …"

They lifted one by the hands and feet, and were trying to sling it over on the tarp without spilling its innards, when Chet Bamberger came limping across the yard, with his chain and a chunk of drywall dragging behind him.

Like all Ocotillo's registered dead citizens, Chet wore a chain and a leather muzzle with a bike lock on the back, and only a tiny hole for eating. They were fed slurry and carrion from the chow wagon, but said supply had petered out as even the dead stopped coming down the road.

Chet wasn't wearing his muzzle.

"Oh fuck," Snopes cried, and let go of the corpse's feet.

Bascomb let go a hair too late, and blundered into the piles of razor wire. He shrieked, "Eeeeyagh!" and jerked up, but the curling steel teeth snagged his uniform and flabby back and dragged him into the thickest of it.

Snopes's left hand went out to pull Bascomb free, while his right tried to draw his gun. Neither effort met with much success.

Chet ignored them. He ambled over to the pile of bodies and squatted over one, lifted a neatly bisected hemisphere of a woman's skull and slurped at it like a slice of cantaloupe. Snopes had smashed in Bamberger's grill when he put on the muzzle, so the slobbering hole under his nose had no teeth in it.

Somehow, this only made him more repulsive, more threatening. His crumbling gray hide was pocked with burns and brands, and carved words. A Camel Filter butt jutted out of his left ear, and his right ear was melted off. With no TV and no Indian casinos down the road, Connie had been forced to take up a new hobby, but nobody had filed a formal complaint, so who was he to judge?

The jingling music of the approaching chow wagon echoed through the streets. "Music Box Dancer" today, thank God. Snopes didn't know why, but if he heard "Do You Know the Way to San Jose" one more time, *he* was going to eat somebody's brains.

Chet's eyes were pointed at Snopes, but they were as vital as soft-boiled eggs, and was there any remorse in them, any horror, at what he'd become? Was there any spark of anything worth saving, in the rancid mayonnaise behind those dead eyes? Had there ever been?

Snopes drew his gun and shot Chet Bamberger through the left eye, and then, because it wouldn't close, through the right.

The chow wagon pulled up in a cloud of dust. Something about the old ice cream truck always creeped Snopes out, even when it still sold ice cream. Now, with racks of chainsaws, baling hooks and flamethrowers and a wood-chipper in tow, and all the Rocket Pop and Dove Bar stickers slathered in sunbaked blood and clouds of ecstatic flies, the chow wagon only brought relief; somebody else to clean up this mess.

"Murderer! Fucking murderer!" Fists drummed on Snopes's back, ineffectual against his bulletproof vest, but knocking him off-balance when he tried to help Bascomb get free.

Connie Bamberger kicked Snopes in the crotch. He tripped and fell on the body pile. His hand snagged in a body cavity and half a baby spilled down the back of his neck.

"Murderer! Arrest him, Doug! *I want justice!*"

They grabbed him when he came into the courtroom. It was dark, but he recognized the deep-fried roadkill smell of Torres, who ran the Indian Skillet across the street, and Sturtevant's livestock stink, McBride by the whiskey on his breath. Bascomb unsnapped his holster and took his gun.

Connie Bamberger sobbed uncontrollably on the witness stand. Judge Dooling sat at the edge of the lamp glow with his hand on the revolver. "Now, Mrs. Bamberger has given her sworn testimony, and her complaint has been reviewed."

"What is this shit?" Snopes shouted. "Get off me, it was self-defense."

"Witnesses say otherwise. Mr. Bamberger was not aggressive, and the illegal aliens' refuse was going to be processed for feed, in any event. You took a citizen's life in cold blood, Deputy. You broke the law, and it is very clear."

"That's not the real goddamned law! It's not murder! Chet was already dead!" Snopes struggled in the arms of the other men, but Bascomb jabbed him in the back with his own gun. As his eyes adjusted to the light, he saw the gloomy courtroom was packed with people, half the surviving town gathered to watch.

"All of us are equal before the law, Mark. I can't sentence you to death, but you've shown that you cannot be trusted to wield force in our defense. We'll have to ask for your badge."

Someone ripped it off his uniform. "Fine, take it and fuck you all."

"Excellent. And now, Doctor, tie off his arms."

Snopes bucked backwards, throwing Sturtevant into Torres, and driving Bascomb back into the door. His gun went off into the ceiling. Snopes jumped for the door, but Bascomb was quicker, and smashed him across the back of the head. The lamplight turned into a golden lava lamp glow, and he collapsed on a plastic tarp.

Dr. McBride was a veterinarian and a drunk, but he was Ocotillo's only medical authority, so he tied Snopes off at the elbows, and pumped him with a syringe that made the trippy light into a pointillist cloudscape.

"Son, I'm sorry as hell," McBride whispered in his ear. "We all know why you did it, but there's gotta be law, and the law's gotta be blind. My son, he's dead, but he's walking, so who's to say he won't get better? If we let you go on like you done—"

Judge Dooling banged his gavel. "Don't badger the prisoner, Walter. Deputy Bascomb, proceed."

Bascomb still bled from divots the razor wire gouged out of his neck, scalp and arms, but he did not hesitate to drag his partner's right arm out across the floor and step on the wrist, heft the axe and slam it into the inside of Snopes's elbow.

From head to toe, he was bathed in lightning. Screaming blood and vomit and streaming tears, Snopes tried to fight, but he couldn't even get the breath to scream for mercy when they tugged the other one away from his chest and chopped it off, as well.

A little blood oozed out of the tourniquets, but Dr. McBride cauterized the stumps with a blowtorch and pronounced him sound.

The gavel banged again. "Court is adjourned. Deputy, leave the defendant where he is. I'd like a word. No, touch nothing …"

Snopes lay there, watching the silhouettes of the people he'd sworn to protect and serve file past the tarp. The sight of his severed arms, splayed out in front of him like spare parts from a model kit, was very unsettling; but he couldn't remember why until he reached out to touch them.

He still couldn't scream, but he found it very easy to cry.

When the courtroom was empty, Judge Dooling rose from the bench, shuffled over to Snopes, and knelt beside him.

"I know you think this is very cruel and unusual, Mark, but we all have to learn to submit to something bigger than ourselves."

Snopes' response was garbled, even to himself.

The judge sighed, touched his shoulder. "You think this is insane, but you are fortunate not to be able to understand. You probably won't remember this, but I wish you would, so you could see how wrong you were, as time goes by, about the risen population of Ocotillo.

"The dead are not wholly incapable of recovery, Mr. Snopes."

Dooling brought his face down closer to the deputy and picked up his severed left forearm. He stroked Snopes's face with his own fingers, then took a bite out of the meaty belly of the exposed muscle, just above the clean cut at the elbow.

"We *are* getting better," His Honor said around a mouthful of flesh. "Order has been restored. We will rebuild our town, and it will be better than it ever was, with equal liberty and justice for *all* its citizens."

Snopes had all but blacked out. His last clear memory was of the Judge wiping his blood-slick lips, taking the scorched stumps of his arms in his hands, and licking them with his gray, ulcerated tongue, just like a stamp.

But he heard him get up and say, "You're free to go."

BLOOM WHERE YOU'RE PLANTED

Peggy Krogh worked in a florist and spent nearly all her spare time gardening, but it was never what she would call relaxing. To cut the tender stems of flowers, or to work the coffee-black soil, was like untangling the raw and pulsing mass of her own knotted nerves in her bare hands. Each buried node of tension released a burst of latent anger, like the bubbles of a drowning man's scream. Sometimes, she would not realize how angry she was, until she'd shattered a terracotta pot or crushed the delicate stalk of a plant with her nervous, impatient hands. But she knew of no other way to exorcise the tension, and had found precious little release in her own backyard garden. Only in her father's greenhouse, had she ever known true patience. But she had not been there, since he went away. Would not be here now, if her mother had not suffered a minor but paralyzing stroke.

As a little girl, Peggy was patient and generous with all living things, but she got in trouble for breaking nearly everything she touched. Mother called her clumsy. The therapists made much of her suppressed rage, but couldn't be bothered to trace it to its source. Dad took her into the greenhouse. Forbidden territory all her life, so many fragile, precious living jewelry. Her father took her hands and held them up like blown glass treasures. "You're rough with things because you're afraid of being rough with people. Afraid of your temper. And you're angry at people because you're afraid of them. Peggy, look around you. What do you see?"

"Your plants." She was bored and hot and flushed and kind of nauseated, the way she always felt when someone tried to make her think about herself.

"You have to be careful around them, too, because they're alive. Just like people and animals. But they'll never tease you, baby girl, and they'll never ever lie."

When Dad left, he took only a couple of prize orchids and some plumeria stalks from his garden. Mom wanted to knock it down. Peggy interceded, but it was too painful to go back. There was too much of Dad left in the place, and she could not transplant a dwarf palm or mount a bromeliad without smashing something.

Two years, since she last came into this place, and even longer, she guessed, since her mother did any real work, here. The sterling roses and tulips in the front yard were her pride and joy. She only used the greenhouse to store her tools.

When they let Mom out of the hospital, they impressed on Peggy how much her mother needed her, now, and how she'd be like a different person, because of the stroke. Her body had catastrophically failed, and she was trapped in it. Until she regained some range of motion beyond the spastic control she enjoyed over her face and one hand, she might even seem to resent her daughter, but this was only a common response to such trauma. They might know a lot about medicine, but they sure didn't know fuck-all about her mother.

The greenhouse was a mess. The windows were cloudy with water deposits, and a thin scum of moss and slime mold coated the inner panes of the roof, casting a milky green pall over the failing sunlight that found its way through the gingko tree and rotting leaves. When she tugged the door out of its crooked frame, a sheet of condensation shook loose from the ceiling and splattered fat green droplets everywhere in a momentary tropical downpour.

Once, Mom and Dad had gardening in common, but she didn't pretend to like Dad's plants. The tropical species he loved were too fragile for the Bay Area, and required too much fuss. When Mom looked at the oddly angled branches with their lizard scales and lurid, waxy petals sweating nectar on knobby stalks, they seemed to remind her of something she hated.

But Dad lavished care on his babies, and passed his love on to his daughter, if not his green thumb. They used to blush at the soft, brown sound of his voice, and grew eagerly towards his touch. Peggy loved them desperately, but her love was mostly unrequited.

She was stunned to find the entombed greenhouse plants alive and unruly, if in dire need of maintenance. Only the cuttings in the one-gallon pots on the worktable had perished. Bromeliads dangling from the roof by fishing lines had bloomed into bushy spherical starbursts bigger than her head. A riotous orgy of orchids thrived on the driftwood substrates scattered everywhere, and had spread up the glass walls to catch the weak winter sun in slender green fingers. The succulents had overgrown their pots like fat men out of their trousers, bearded with dew and winking a myriad of bizarre flowers.

The awesome cluster of staghorn ferns hanging suspended from the swaybacked roofbeam would have to be cut down, soon, but the paradox of its bloated mass floating overhead, shrouded in tufts of dried elephant ears and rigid green antlers like a misfired hybrid of plant and animal kingdoms, was oddly soothing. As was the prospect of all the unfinished work, left open and begging her to pick up where Dad left off.

The small potted ferns and cycads were all rootbound, pots cracking or overflowing, and she started spooning them out of the brittle plastic pots and prepping the old potting soil. Untangling the knotted bundles of roots like a surgeon transplanting hearts on an assembly line, she had to make her big clumsy hands gentle.

Remarkably, it worked.

The fragility of her charges transmitted a temporary grace to her hands that soothed, by creeping degrees, the buried galls of unresolved anger in her ungainly body. She worked until sweat soaked through her tracksuit, turned on the lights to beat back the gathering gloom, and looked around for more work. Mom would need to eat and have a turn on the bedpan, soon, but Peggy wasn't ready to face her.

A big plumeria in a ten-gallon pot in the far corner looked ready for cutting. One of Dad's favorites, it was choking itself with abundant new branch growth, and rife with furled new flowers. When Dad tended it, the blossoms came out a pale cherry-cola sunset hue that drained away to ghostly white after he left. Six of the branches would survive transplantation.

She filled some three-gallon pots with soil and worm castings, and went to move the huge plumeria closer to the light. Kneeling before the glazed clay pot—*lift with the knees, lummox*—she put her arms around it, but it refused to budge. Rocking from side to side, the pot finally came unstuck from the brick floor, only to break apart in her arms.

God damn it! She checked herself only a split-second from hurling the clay shards off into space. She would shatter the greenhouse, or kill more plants, if she wasn't careful, if she didn't contain her anger. This was not her fault.

The soil crumbled away from the roots of the plumeria, which had thrust right through the bottom of the pot and bored into the crevices in the brick floor underneath. The potted plant had become a tree.

Peggy knew plants communicated sophisticated messages with chemical secretions. Cut flowers released a burst of vegetal pheromone—a scream, as they were beheaded. "They don't make a sound," Dad had told her, "but they surely feel pain when you hurt them. They cry out to each other. You can't hear it, but if you're very still, you can feel it."

As Peggy cut the branches and slathered their stumps with Rootone, she felt them communicating something to her, but it was not pain. This work gave her no peace at all, for the message that soaked into her from the cuttings was that her father was dead.

Mom was in the checkout line at Safeway, arguing with the cashier and the assistant manager over her double coupons, when a blood vessel burst behind her right eye, and she slumped over the disputed purchases on the check stand conveyor belt.

Mild stroke. She could move her head and face, and had limited sensation down her right side. Though she couldn't speak, she could hear and understand. Her face was wracked with palsies, but her right eye showed perfect comprehension.

When Peggy brought her dinner, she changed the channel from *Law & Order* reruns on A&E to *Law & Order: SVU* reruns on USA, and tried to watch the episode while feeding her. Mom was getting more nutrition out of her IV drip than the tepid Manhattan clam chowder, but Mom had always loved to eat, lived to eat, so Peggy fed her.

The crimson soup dribbled from her slack mouth, but her eyes were bright carpet tacks of reproach.

"Sorry, Mom, I'm not a very good nurse, am I?" Dad used to call her his nurse when she assisted him in a delicate operation, like grafting apricot branches to their plum tree. But in her own mind, she was always more like Igor, the hunchbacked assistant of Dr. Frankenstein. Late night creature features; another sacred Dad activity Mom never shared.

"The roses in the front are a total loss, I'm afraid. The sprinklers must be leaking under the beds, because the roots were all rotten.

They literally fell over when I pruned them. And the snails and slugs have the run of the tulip beds in the side yard. I know how you feel about pesticides, but I'm not too wild about crawling around picking them off by hand ..."

Mom's eyes drifted to the TV, heavy lids drooping. Peggy changed the channel to an *ER* rerun on Lifetime. Mom closed her eyes tight.

Peggy took the tray back downstairs and loaded the dishwasher, then retired to her bedroom with a new romance novel and her Sudoku puzzles. She didn't open them, though it took her several hours to fall asleep.

Peggy went to work for a few hours the next morning, so she missed the nurse's visit. But a note on the kitchen counter spelled out her new medication regimen, and a pointedly capitalized addendum— MARGIE WAS VERY CHILLED ALL NIGHT ... KEEP WINDOWS CLOSED!

A smiley face at the bottom stood in for a signature. The simple, brittle message left Peggy baffled and breathing hard, fighting tears. Who did this bitch think she was? Coming into her house and telling her how to take care of her mother. The heat was cranked up, and Peggy hadn't opened the windows. Mom got a wild hair up her ass to repaint the whole house in eggshell white last year, and half the windows were still taped shut. Here and there, the old color that Peggy picked out with Dad when she was nine, Strawberry Milkshake, peeked through where she failed to mask the doorframes and outlets.

Mom napped, snoring like a broken toy. Peggy almost slipped on the Indian rug in the living room as she raced out to the greenhouse.

Though it was cloudy and had rained just before dawn, the greenhouse was sweltering. A constant drizzle of condensation fell from the ceiling, drumming on the leaves and making the flowers nod their luxuriant heads. When she stood still, she could hear them growing.

The plumeria transplants were a miracle. The stumps on the tree had each put forth an inch of fresh green stem, terminating in the little blood-red knuckles that heralded new flowers. The cuttings themselves were shaggy with new leaves. Emerald green, richly veined like the wings of a flying reptile, but the leaves were nothing compared to the imminent blossoms.

Peggy had researched every soil additive known to horticulture, even resorted to importing volcanic ash from Hawaii, but she could never crack Dad's secret, and restore the vital tropical hues that faded when he left.

The flowers had not yet opened, but already, their fragrance seeped out and made her feel almost drunk. The furled petals had a burnt violet tinge that reminded her of sunsets, sea anemones and sunburned skin, of that trip to Hawaii. Mom was sick all week from overdoing it the first day, and Dad took Peggy snorkeling at Hanauma Bay until they both looked like boiled lobsters, until the sun went down in purple flames of exactly the color of these flowers.

Peggy did no work. She just stood at the worktable, breathing the fragrance of the flowers and reliving the memories that carried her away to the wordless knowledge of how her father died, and who killed him.

Mom was feeling feisty at dinnertime.

Peggy brought in a tray with a bowl of beef broth and some juice in a Cookie Monster sipper cup. Her breath turned to frost in the frigid air.

"Dear God, Mom, how did it get so cold in here?" She went to the windows and found them both wide open. The wisteria that climbed up the side of the house had thrown shoots over the windowsill, glossy green ringlets dripping purple pendant blossoms clung to the interior wall and wrapped tightly around the cranks that opened the windows. Their rich, fruity fragrance saturated the chill air pouring into the room. It was strong for wisteria; in fact, it didn't smell like wisteria, at all.

She pried the vines off, wincing at the paint that peeled off the wall and windowsill, and cranked the windows tightly shut. "There, all better."

Mom grimaced and made a fart sound with her mouth.

"Not nice, Mom. I'm trying really hard to take care of you, you know." She came over and sat beside Mom. The soup was too hot. Mom scalded her lip with the first spoonful, and sprayed it across the tray. Peggy had to blow on each spoonful and hold it patiently to Mom's mistrustful mouth. Every slurp might have been poison, the way she took it in, but they finished just as *Wheel of Fortune* ended and *Jeopardy* came on.

"Okay, I have a little surprise for you." Peggy took the tray out into the hall, and came back with a three-gallon pot in each arm. "I'm so sorry about your roses, Mom, but I wanted you to have some life around you, to cheer you up ... I thought they'd bring back some nice memories, and they do smell wonderful, don't they?"

She set one plumeria on the dresser beside the TV, and the other on Mom's nightstand. The furled flowers looked like tiny missiles. Their rosy hue deepened from pale orange to dusky merlot as, with an audible pop, several of them opened up all at once.

"Well, look at that! They like you."

Mom's good eye rolled up and down the nakedly phallic stalk of the plant, mouth working as if to spit at it. When she looked at Peggy again, her eye was wide with fright. Her right hand trembled on the comforter, a broken bird trying to fly from a cat.

Peggy stroked Mom's face to smooth the twitching nerves, and kissed her on her beetling brow, put the TV remote in her good hand. "You get some rest, Mom. You're the strong one. You never run away from a fight. That's what Dad always said."

She sprang her other surprise on her way out of the room. As she reached out to switch off the TV, she took the framed picture she'd found in the garage and placed it atop the TV, so it stared squarely down at Mom, obstructing the discreet crucifix and the needlepoint samplers on the wall.

It was a picture of Dad on the beach at Waikiki, clumsily framed by Peggy so Diamondhead lurked over his shoulder like a second head. Dad, grinning like a fool, teeth too white against his sunburned skin, cutting a caper in the surf.

Mom dropped the TV remote, but it hit the floor and flew apart as Peggy turned off the light and shut the door.

Peggy threw on her bathrobe and sneakers and went down to the kitchen to clean up. The box of Corry's Slug & Snail Death on the counter perplexed her. She must have brought the poison into the kitchen this afternoon, setting it down by accident next to the Nutra-Sweet when she thought she heard the doorbell. She'd dumped a bunch of the stuff in the tulip beds today, but why had she brought it inside?

A chill climbed her spine and clenched her bowels, but it wasn't fear; it was a sickly deviant of Christmas anticipation.

It was brutally cold outside, but it would be hot in the greenhouse, and she had so much work to do, before tomorrow …

She slept poorly, and woke up several times from a lucid dream, thinking she'd heard Dad's voice calling out, "Pancakes! Get 'em while they're hot!"

There was no one in the kitchen, of course, and the RN would not stop by until after lunch. She really should take a shower. She felt grit and dirt in every wrinkle of her face, and under her fingernails, but there was no time.

The door to Mom's room stuck in the frame, squealing when she forced it open. The air was hot and stifling, so rife with scent that she figured Mom must have spilled a bottle of perfume.

Peggy sat down beside her mother and tucked a napkin under her chin. "How are we feeling today, Mom?"

Mom's eyes were bloodshot marbles rimmed by yellow crust. She looked as if she hadn't slept a wink. She looked as if she'd been crying. Good.

Mom had no use for the runny poached eggs, but sipped eagerly at the orange juice. In between drinks, she seemed to be trying to make the same word over and over, but Peggy couldn't read lips, any better than minds. Peggy held the cup to her mouth until she sucked air bubbles, then took the tray away.

She dropped it on the floor at the sound of Dad's voice, right there in the room. "Tell her about the other surprise, honey."

Peggy looked at the twin plumeria plants, then she looked at the picture.

She looked at the dense clusters of flesh-hued flowers.

She looked at her father's sunburned, smiling mouth.

Stepping over the tray, Peggy left the room. She came back with a wheelchair.

"I thought it would be good for you to get out of bed and see some familiar faces. What do you say?"

Mom said nothing, but her lips skinned back from her teeth in a silent scream. She tried to make a fist and hit Peggy, but only succeeded in wrapping her arm around her daughter's neck as she scooped her up. Mom was no skinny Minnie, but Peggy had been working all night, and her tightly coiled muscles were equal to the task of heaving Mom's inert bulk into the chair with authority, if not delicacy.

Sour, sick breath whooped out of Mom's lungs in an alarming gust when Peggy dropped her. Peggy wrung her hands and turned her back to count to ten. Mom was not a thing. She was a person. Patience, not anger, was what she needed. She would do nothing to harm her mother. Like any good daughter, she only wanted to bring her parents back together.

Peggy wheeled Mom out of her bedroom and down the hall, through the living room and out the sliding glass door to the patio. Mom rocked in the wheelchair, so Peggy had to catch her shoulder and hold her in place. The rubber wheels sunk into the damp lawn, but she forced it across the backyard to the greenhouse.

"You remember how much Dad loved to work in here? It used to make you so jealous, remember? Of course you do. When he wanted to leave, you made sure he never could, because you couldn't stand the thought of him, or anyone else in your life, being happy."

⁂

She opened the door and pushed Mom inside, rocking the chair onto its back wheels to lift it over the threshold and roll it up alongside the ziggurat of bricks she'd built in the night, and the hole that she'd dug.

The earth underneath the bricks had been soft, but almost totally choked with snarls of roots. As she locked the brakes of Mom's wheelchair, she put a hand on Mom's head and wrenched it so she had to look into the hole and face squarely what lay there, exposed like a beating heart.

"He loved you for as long as he could. I don't blame him for wanting to leave you, Mom. You hated yourself for being an unloveable, bitter old bitch, but you hated me more because you made me into you, do you even know that? I almost think that's why you did it, because you were jealous of me, that Dad loved me, when he couldn't love you."

In the hole, the soil parted and something made of gnarled roots and malignant bulbs and bloated lobes of mold burst out of a rotten shroud and reached out for its mate. It did not move, so much as it *grew* out of the grave. The sickly sweet scent of it was like perfumed chloroform, its popping blossoms puckered lips and winking eyes. At the heart of it, a pulsing clot of rootbound tumors split in a grin.

Dad told her once, that every plant has at least as much of its mass beneath the ground, as above. The idea tickled her as a girl. She imagined she could see with her x-ray eyes a mirror world beneath the soil, of trees thrusting down into the earth, and secret flowers in the soil …

A keening cry came from Mom's violently shaking form. It might have been a plea, or a denial, or even a greeting to her long lost husband.

Peggy could think of nothing more to say, so she kissed her mother once on the lips, and shoved her out of the chair.

No therapy could provide this kind of closure.

Peggy drunkenly backed away from the hole as the earth tumbled and closed over them. She needed a nap, before she could put the bricks back in place.

Crossing the lawn in a daze, she dimly picked out the sound of the phone through the giddy jumble in her head.

Probably that nurse. She wondered if she would tell her just what had happened. Maybe she would, just to bring that facade of smug condescension down around her ears.

She wiped muddy sweat off her brow as she shuffled by the phone in the kitchen. Let the machine pick it up …

"Hello, you've reached Margaret Krogh," the outgoing message began, Mom pausing awkwardly to check the preprinted card that came with the machine, "but I can't come to the phone right now, so please leave your name and number, and a brief message—"

Outside, the lawn rippled like a lake in a high wind, waves of motion beneath the earth rolling out from the greenhouse.

The beep sounded, and an impatient voice swam up out of squalls of AM-radio static to stuff Peggy's heart with dry ice.

"Hello, um … I know this isn't the right way to do this, but I just got the news about Margie, and I know you must be there, Peg. I have so much to tell you, that I just ... damn these machines ... *Dos mojitos, por favor? Pura vida* ..."

The wall bulged beside the phone, cracks running up the plaster like roots burrowing through yielding earth. The cabinets burst open and disgorged glasses and plates into the sink.

A vine burst out of the wall in a shower of paint flakes and spurted a bouquet of bruise-hued flowers in her face.

"Sorry, I'm in the bar at the airport in San Jose ... in Costa Rica ... I'm flying into SFO tonight, and I hope ... I hope we can—"

Peggy picked up the phone and huddled in a ball in a corner of the kitchen. The ether-reek of the flowers lulled her into a stupor. Warm, pleasant sensations, like the reflection of happy childhood memories, spread out from her gut, poured into her with the roots embracing her from holes in the linoleum tile under her feet.

Peggy pressed the phone close to her mouth. "Daddy?"

THE FREE SCHOOL

They wanted a meeting on the Ocean Beach boardwalk in daylight, out in plain sight. It'd been so long, I was surprised they were still afraid of me. I should've known better.

I got there ten minutes early, parked on Voltaire and walked down to the beach. An hour before sunset on a perfect late summer day. A trio of twelve year-old skaters with bleached rat-tails called me an old cunt and threatened to slash my tires if I didn't buy them cigarettes. I ignored them as I walked and smoked. If I showed them my knife or my guns, I'd have to use them. When I was their age, just having an imagination was dangerous. Now, they've all got someone else's, and every sheep thinks it's a wolf.

I cruised past the lifeguard tower at the end of Newport to try to tip over any ambush. No doubt they were watching and giggling in that breathless, bored way that was the closest they could come to sounding like real children.

The flashbacks came harder than I hoped. Even with my guard up, footprints in the sand twisted into scripture. Ultraviolet sunset rippled and roared louder than the puny material ocean, the twin secret seas of Isness and Otherness lapping at the crumbling pillow fort of my private reality. Gritting my teeth on briny strychnine, I settled on a rare stretch of the seawall with no transients camped out on it, next to the snack & bait shop at the foot of the stairs to the pier, which still had a sad antique motel on it. *Sleep On The Waves*, said the sign.

I fished around in my leather coat and found my lighter and a fresh pack. I must have been getting old, because they were sitting right in front of me for a minute before I noticed them. Another five before they deigned to notice me.

Ariadne and Boy were building a sand castle. High Medieval French confection, with lacy curtain walls and flying buttresses like seagull's wings that Ariadne molded effortlessly to prop up a chapel. Boy knelt and gouged tunnels and crypts out of the foundations of the castle until it became a Swiss cheese fairy fortress, yet it refused to collapse. It took me a while to recognize the castle as the Lerner & Loewe Camelot. The game was to build up and undermine it until it fell or the tide took it. It was one of the Teachers' favorite exercises.

I knew what to expect, but it still made me a little lightheaded, seeing them playing in the sand again, their golden hair sun-kissed to sheaves of spun platinum, their cherubic features pink with mild sunburn but unblemished, unwrinkled, though they'd been out here building castles almost every day for over thirty years.

If I stared at them long enough, I thought I could look down at myself and see a girl's hands, with henna flowers and spooky Tibetan eyes drawn up and down my arms. But my hands were still nicotine-yellow, wrinkled and horny with calluses, short but sharpened nails tipped in black lacquer, the unfiltered Camel a few seconds from burning the scar tissue between my fingers.

I had finished my smoke and started a new one when Boy finally left the castle and climbed the seawall. A jogger ran by in an iPod bubble, and a young guy with too many tattoos and a big African gray parrot on his shoulder lurked like he wanted to sell me some grass. I radiated malignant vibes at him until he wandered off to hang out by the women's showers.

There's an old framed photo in the children's room at the Ocean Beach public library, of a tow-headed boy flying a kite off the edge of Sunset Cliffs. The sun makes a silhouetted cipher of his face, but the way the light haloes the boy's wind-tousled hair stamps him as God's favorite mirror. The unofficial symbol of OB so many carry in their hearts—eternal youth in an endless summer. God help them, if they ever cross paths with the real one.

When His Majesty finally deigned to address me, I got up and brushed the sand off my tingling ass. My legs felt freeze-dried. "Buy you an ice cream?"

Boy forked his fingers at me. The lifeguard tower was closed and nobody was looking. I gave him a cigarette and lit it. He sat on the seawall and sucked half of it down in one drag, watching the ocean.

The waves were sloppy and weak, but a few clueless packs of diehard surfers straddled their boards out past the breakwater, waiting for a proper swell or a townie with a brand-new board. The rip current here had a reputation for drowning outsiders.

They would never ask anyone for help. For them to reach out to me, it could only be the very worst. Boy might be revered for his wisdom, but never having gone through puberty, it took a lot for him to get over himself.

"He's hunting us ...?" He spoke with that infuriating Cali accent that makes every statement half a question.

"Call the cops."

Boy sulked, a chain-smoking Hummel figurine. "Can't, okay? It's complicated, and like ... it's *your* mess, anyway."

"Remember your lessons, Boy. We only own ourselves."

I almost mistook his fury and fear for childish pouting. It's an easy mistake to make—once. Boy flicked his cig at my eye. I barely dodged it. "Don't quote the Teachers at me, Miri. We lost so fucking much because of *you* ..."

A quick look around, and I hoisted him up by the neck of his filthy tie-dyed Moondoggy's shirt. "I owe you nothing, got that? You brats ran me out of Never-Never Land, so when *you* ask *me* to come back and save your asses, you might try to pretend you have some manners ..."

He just dangled in my grownup grip, his hooded gaze so venomous, if his eyes had met mine, I do believe one or both of us would have had a seizure.

More ashamed than frightened, I let him drop to his bare feet. The shower stalls behind him were covered in hand-drawn, Xeroxed HAVE YOU SEEN ME? flyers. Children, dogs, cats and parrots were given equal billing, but some of the parrots offered the biggest rewards.

"You never belonged with us, Miri. You always wanted to grow up and join the other side."

"Damn right I did." *And look at me now!*

"Your anger is a ball and chain," he said with a Cheshire cat grin, "that keeps you from ever reaching enlightenment—"

"My anger is still pretty useful to you. How many?"

"Lakshmi and Lennon. And no one's heard from Nova and Nimrod in almost a year."

Four missing. Jesus Christ. "Nimrod and Nova still like to get adopted for the winter? Maybe they found a good home and decided to stay. Sooner or later, even never getting old gets pretty old."

That made him smile. "They vanished, just like the others. Everybody who loved them *knows* they're gone." The pout kicked up a notch. Was it supposed to sting?

"Then why in God's eye did you wait so long?"

Looking lost, Boy just held out his fingers. I passed him another cigarette. I may have burned his fingers on purpose.

"He's only taking Free School kids?"

"We think so. We saw nothing he doesn't want us to, because he's invisible … just like us."

"So it's safe to assume he knows what you are."

"He *knows* all of us, Miranda. We've seen the bus cruising OB and Point Loma …?"

"What bus?"

"The Freedom Bus …" He hit the cigarette hard and blew a tornado in my face, but that wasn't what brought tears to my eyes. "It's a Teacher …?"

I didn't believe him, and I told him so. Because if he hated me as much as the others did and the Teacher story was true, then he'd probably tell me it was just a Class B fondler, and pray I got myself killed.

"Stick around or go back to wherever you hide, but you'll see him soon enough … right behind you." Boy looked me in the eyes and put the weight of the world's pain behind his stare. I knew the trick, but it still pushed my buttons.

"So saving you is saving myself?" I didn't need to remind him about the Teacher's *shaming of the sharers* ritual. "Our fates were detangled the day the Free School expelled me, Boy. This is *your* karma, not mine."

The last reddening rays of the sunset speared those perfect blue eyes and let me see what lived behind them. The guise of a beautiful ideal child, the kind anyone would buy an ice cream cone for, withered away. His aura was a blacklight garbage disposal. "When you murdered Sky," he said, looking full into the sunset again, "you pushed all of us off the edge, into the Isness. We never stopped falling." It was the first thing he said that didn't sound like a question.

He kicked away from the wall and strode off down the boardwalk. "Finish it!" he called over his shoulder.

⸙

The streetlights stuttered and blinked to life as I drove back up Newport to check out the old main drag, already sporting golden coronas of evening mist, but the creamy glow fell on almost nothing I

170

recognized. The Strand Theater was now a fabric store, and Char-Burger was a Jack in the Box. Moondoggy's and The Black still had a monopoly on everything a surfing hippy needs to put in his head, and nobody had put up a Winchell's or an Urban Outfitters, but something was missing. Ocean Beach had lost its soul.

The Space Man.

He was old when OB was new, with a white, flowing beard and skin like jerked shoe leather. He wore a plastic bubble helmet and a Buck Rogers bedsheet for a cape when he rode around the boardwalks, alleys and backstreets on his tricked-out Schwinn beach cruiser at all hours of day or night. Never seen off his bike unless he was surfing, the OB Space Man was much more than the local holy fool. He was an insane guardian angel, a talisman against all the big-city evils we hoped to keep at bay. He wasn't a Teacher, but we were taught to hail him as an Illuminated Master. I wondered when he went away. Did he die when the magic faded, or did he just disappear, when the town no longer wanted or deserved his protection?

OB is a backwater beach town that never quite noticed it was surrounded on three sides by a major metropolitan city. A host of subtle geographical barriers divert the tourists across the San Diego River to Mission Beach, the neighboring coastline we ceded to the invaders. Only cars with Arizona plates got broken into. The cops never even knew they weren't in control of the situation. We policed ourselves, and only let them bust the ones who didn't belong.

Look at me, saying, *we*. I hadn't lived here in thirty-five years. I didn't recognize any of the faces I saw, or half the houses. Everything I loved was long gone. The baby boomers hereabouts believe that if they just watch their bad cholesterol, keep up the yoga and try to understand their kids' music, they can stay young forever. The only truly magical thing their generation ever achieved, they have completely forgotten, even as it walks among them.

I merged onto Sunset Cliffs and turned into the lot at the edge of Robb Field, a good-sized neighborhood park and sports complex on the edge of town. The new playground was a padded puzzle of obtuse angles in the gathering gloom. Nothing risky or reckless, nothing like a mountain, nothing to fall off or fight for. But at least they took down that damned rickety slide …

It's always the ones who wring their hands demanding that someone defend, protect or educate the children, who are the most ruthless murderers of childhood.

They don't have that big rusty spiraling monster corkscrew slide anymore, with the shingles of sheet metal studded with rivets that nipped every kid who ever slid on it. Aside from the height and the danger, what we loved most about it was the tiny booth at the top, a clubhouse surmounted by an onion dome minaret with a jaunty metal flag. It looked too much like a castle not to provoke the occasional game of King of the Mountain. The Teachers discouraged competitive male power games until they felt the Flow was right, and then they trained us to *Become the World* for each other, to bully and trip each other up just as the square world always would, given half a chance.

I really didn't want to do this. I was over it, I'd put it well behind me. But with nothing else to hide behind, it was all too easy to let the flashbacks carry me far from shore, to let the tide take me back to that day.

The day I got expelled.

Sky was one of the Teachers' kids, but not even he knew which one. Golden child, born in the house of Aquarius. Next to him, Boy was a toadstool. He made fun of my name, one day. It wasn't what made me mad, but it was the reason I gave the Teachers for why I kicked him off the ladder at this very playground. He landed on his face and broke his neck. The Teachers dithered until it was too late to take him to a hospital, and he died. The next day, the Teachers went away and never came back.

While my mind floated back out of my head, my hands took up the bag from the fabric store. Without my help, they took out two long, thin wooden dowels and laid them perpendicular upon my lap, then, with a strand of rainbow yarn from the remnant bin, I bound them together and began to make a God's Eye.

The floodlights over the nearby tennis courts flipped on to radiate spokes like flaming prayer wheels, throwing the shadows of the playground equipment into harsh, spidery relief in the purple dusk. I heard a sinusoidal drone like sitars and rattlesnakes coming from somewhere in the cavernous depths of my car. I stared and stared through the unwelcome acid flashback as I wound the rainbow yarn over and under and through, meditating upon all that was here once, but now gone.

I said my mantra until I saw not only the corkscrew slide with its castle clubhouse, but also, suspended in the Technicolor western sky, the body of a perfect boy trying to fly.

It floated over the horizon like a corneal imperfection, flicking across the darkening sky when I blinked, but I was beyond guilt or dread. Once summoned, the memories came flooding back into my nerves and muscles and bones, the memory of being young.

Easy as falling off a bike.

I flicked my cigarette out the window and rolled it up. I checked the mirror before I got out, but I couldn't see over the dashboard, anymore.

I slid out of my boots, rummaged in the bag on the passenger seat and took out a pair of old Hyde leather high-top roller-skates and strapped them on. Middle-aged me is no size 0. My short, shapeless black dress draped around my ankles like a witch's smock.

I still felt old and tired and flushed with a menopausal hot flash, but I also wobbled on legs half as long as they were an hour ago, and to anyone on the street, I was a spooky little eight-year old girl skating home, sure to catch hell for missing dinner.

All the beach bums had retreated to their bungalows, watering holes and beachside campers. Raucous dancehall reggae belched out of a neighborhood pub, but I only had ears for the Lost Flock, and they did not disappoint.

As I skated down the empty, moonlit street, I noticed the parrots on the telephone lines, watching me.

Parrots can live a century in the wild, but they'll chew themselves to death in a cage in a matter of weeks, if they get bored. Local idiots buy them for a conversation piece, a piratical accessory to spice up their slacker ensembles, and they're always surprised when the miserable birds fly away.

I climbed the slope by wishboning my skates on the crooked asphalt for six grueling blocks. I passed the place on Saratoga where we used to take morning lessons in the basement. The old redwood schoolhouse was razed to the foundation and replaced with some cokehead lawyer's idea of a Mediterranean villa.

I wondered if it was haunted. What we learned down there should have left ghosts. I passed the lush wall of hibiscus hedges surrounding the gang's old clubhouse. Quiet inside, only nightlights glowing in every outlet of every room.

Ariadne and Boy got adopted in '81 by the Lloyds, a nice old hippie couple who used to do lightshows for Jefferson Airplane, and lived in their big house on the hill as their grandkids until both the Lloyds got cancer. Boy did the Kevorkian treatment on them and most of the class moved in to squat. They kept a stable of burnout adults as pets to pose as guardians, to cook and clean and handle money. Some of the Free School kids still crashed with them, but none of them could stand to be under one roof for too long, any more than they could stand to grow up.

Turning on Del Mar at the top of the hill, I stopped at the corner and looked down at the town. The fog had rolled out of the ocean and engulfed the beach in silver cotton candy. Lights and music and laughter echoed down alleys, but the town was falling asleep. Nothing out here cruising for trouble, but me.

For the first couple blocks going down Del Mar, I slalomed in tight curling loops to soak up the speed. The asphalt was a jigsaw puzzle of buckling plates, because it kept subsiding and sliding down the soft, sandy hill. My skates caught the grooves of the street and sent me scrambling, but I never fell. When the speed got too much to allow for maneuvering, I turned my toes to the ocean and just *rolled*.

I shot through an intersection in front of an old Mercedes convertible that practically stood upright on its front wheels braking as I passed, close enough to snap the hood ornament off.

My heart pounded so fast, it would have killed me, if I was still fortyish, but none of it felt real enough to hurt me. If I died, I might just wake up in my car at Robb Field, or in that shitty hotel in Warsaw, where I took Boy's terse, desperate phone call.

I jumped the curb and shot through a bank parking lot and crossed Sunset Cliffs Boulevard where the streetlights were dead. A police car was parked at the corner, lights churning to make jerkily animated purple panic out of the still night, shaking down a VW bus with surfboards on the roof.

No reason to think he would come out tonight, except for the excellent bait Boy was fishing with. Coasting down a side street lined with saloons, rundown Airbnb squats and all-night Laundromats, I passed homeless folk singers busking on every corner. I tossed change in every crappy guitar case to rack up quick karma points.

I heard a raucous squawking overhead and followed it south on Cable, then seaward on Santa Cruz, then back north up Bacon. The parrot flock numbered in the hundreds, green and gold, scarlet and turquoise wings in an angry rainbow. Nobody ever saw them after dark, and nobody knew where they roosted. If they were still out and about, then their hometown was in distress.

I turned on Niagara ahead of the flock and rolled to the end of the street and the head of the pier. Candy-colored lights flickered through drifting veils of mist. Fishermen crowded the pier's rails, tending four reels apiece and bringing in stunted sea bass marinated in Tijuana sewage. I took off my skates and knotted the laces to make them into a bolo, then hobbled down the stairs to the beach.

The sand glowed a faint silvery blue in the misty moonlight, but the darkness under the pier was like a curtain. The bonfire smoldering among the black, barnacle-crusted pylons only illuminated itself. A daisy chain of ragged sleeping bags lay around the fire. The pillars hid men who came out as soon as I got too far from the stairs to run away.

"Hey, little girl, you look lost," said a jolly, department-store Santa voice. "You wanna drink?"

"I'm looking for my Dad," I said, trying to sound helpless. "We live in, like a school bus? But it wasn't parked where it was supposed to be, and—and—please help me find him …?"

The drunk came closer, making *there-there* noises, but he looked over my shoulder at someone else. He grabbed me by the hair and raised the bottle in his hand like he would hit me with it, but I whipped my skates into a cyclone and parked them in his crotch.

He released me and dropped vomiting in the sand. His friends turned back into shadows. I jumped over him and went under the pier.

The urchins were mostly still asleep, huddled in filthy, duct-taped bundles around the dying fire. A cozy, romantic little bolthole, except for the chill draft, the stench of the rotting sea, the endless flow of predators and the splatters of parrot-shit everywhere.

I tiptoed around them until I'd scoped them all out. "Wake up! Who needs some extra cash?"

One by one, the grubby heads popped up, matted Mohawks and smeared mascara and a few haggard wino-faces, eggplant-purple with skin cancer and burst capillaries and ground-in street dirt like stains seeping out from the bone. Once, I might've found half the Free School down here, and no adults. OB was supposed to be closed to these creeps. They preyed on kids … sometimes on *our* kids. When they do, everybody's sorry.

"Winos," I pointed, then waved inland with a fistful of fives. "Go back to El Cajon." Bus fare in their grimy paws, they lurched out of their beds.

The rest of the campers were teenage runaways and slumming college kids. I turned to leave, hoping none of these clowns would force me to draw down on them, when a jaded girl with a magenta suedehead hairdo and charred bomber jacket gave me the evil eye. I let my eyes unfocus until I could see her aura like a wreath of burning black-red roses around her head, but I was seeing double. I dropped a burning two-by-four on her sleeping bag.

Yanking the smoldering bag up by its toes, I dumped the girl out, and the other one I figured had to be in there with her.

Of all the Free School, I probably hated Aurora and Electra the most. They weren't sisters when they joined, but they told everyone they were when the Teachers sent us out to beg for alms. And they came to look more alike, until they wore the same face, a plastic pixie mask, empty unless it was laughing at you.

They had flirted with puberty, but they still looked like nine-year old waif twins under all the ugly things they'd done to themselves to pass for adults. A tackle box of piercings in lips and tongue clamped their mouths shut better than I ever could, and tattoos of burning roses spilled from their necks down their arms to cover the backs of their hands, for those who couldn't see the bonfire of their aura.

Easy to forget they were bigger than me, now.

Electra pulled a knife on me, but I stepped inside it and broke her nose with the skates. The crowd made catfight noises as I dragged Aurora away from the fire by a dangly earring and shoved her into one of the slimy columns.

She tried to scratch me. "I'll cut you so bad, they'll hear you screaming in Alpine, you fucktard." She was bigger, but I wasn't woozy on painkillers.

"Leave it out, Aurora, won't you?" A closer look at her face told me too much. "Your philosophy could use a touching-up, sister. The herp isn't supposed to stick to you like that, is it?"

"I'm still innocent in here," she hissed, hand on heart, and she was right. Even all shaved and pierced and rife with parasites, she still pulled off the beautiful illusion she had something left to ruin. She wasn't a vampire—good God, who'd want to put up with all that shit? She was young forever because she made the world believe she was.

The collective unconscious is a wishing well, and while that bath of wishful thinking did nothing for the wishers, it did everything for us.

Aurora rubbed her eyes and stared at me, only just now realizing who I was. "Miranda? Is it *my* turn now?"

Finally. "I'm trying to help," I told her.

Aurora put her fingers in her ears and sang, "La-la-la, bullshit!" She seemed to grow. I closed my eyes and bit my lip to keep from getting any smaller. "He told me it was a Teacher. You think he's making it up?"

She made a flu-shot face. "The Teachers went away because of what *you* did, Miri. You're the one with blood on her hands. And now you come around posing as one of us, talking about Teachers. Is that how you got close to the others?"

I asked for an explanation. She pouted and tried not to cry and I realized she really thought *I* was the killer.

Nova and Nimrod never came back from surfing in San Felipe. They usually stole a sailboat and returned by the end of summer. Nimrod hated Boy like poison for some long-ago slight nobody else remembered. Lennon and Lakshmi disappeared last week, and Boy started in about the Freedom Bus. Nobody else saw it. "Now you show up, it all figures."

"If this is bullshit, Aurora, I'll end you myself."

She rocked back on her Doc Marten heels, almost tipping over. "That's the only trick you know," she sneered. "Nobody else wanted you to come back, Miri. He always said if he needed to, he could get you to kill again. Your buttons are so big, a blind monkey with boxing gloves could work you."

"Thank you for that lesson." Nothing I didn't already know. "You should be grateful to whoever's hunting you, Aurora. Whoever they are, they're trying to teach you something."

Then I coldcocked her with my skates. How big are my buttons?

Nobody followed me up the stairs to the street. The wind blowing in off the ocean made a balloon of my baggy dress, and my skin tried to crawl up my asshole. My teeth chattered with the cold, but mostly, it was rage. I'd never laid a hand on a kid—another kid—after Sky.

Out of the original class of twenty-three, five of us had died or disappeared over the years, all by misadventure. How many of those had been Boy's dirty work?

But if he was culling the herd and using the family scapegoat to wash his hands, calling me out here was suicide. He couldn't expect me to flail around without finding something, but maybe that's what he wanted. To be killed by a caring professional.

I sat on a bench to put my skates back on. The other benches were all vacant, except for a body buried under a mound of damp newspapers on the next one.

I would grow up, get the hell out of here and never come back. Right after I stopped at Boy's place.

Maybe Aurora wasn't just shooting off her mouth. Maybe Boy was telling the truth. And maybe this was all of them ganging up on me again, like they always used to. Maybe she knew I could never find the bus if I was looking for it … only if it was looking for me.

I had strapped on one skate and was unlacing the other when I heard a dry crackling and saw a flock of newspaper pages take wing on the evening breeze.

I turned around and saw the pusher with the gray parrot and a few lonely midnight strollers on the pier before I saw the empty bench.

I whiplashed around to look at the street. A piebald school bus, camouflaged with layers of graffiti, glided out of the fog at the head of the pier and coughed to a stop blocking the street. Down the side in twisted orange letters streaking into one another because we took off down the highway before the paint was dry: FREEEEEEEEDOM.

Before I could get up, my head was wrapped in a velvet bag, and iron arms enfolded my tiny body.

The bag reeked of skunky weed, patchouli and incense, but mostly chloroform.

I held my breath, but the arms squeezed me tighter, crushing the breath out of me, then releasing me just enough that I reflexively gasped. Saturated velvet clamped over my mouth and nose as my assailant held me close and crooned in my ear.

"Shhh, Ida, rest now. Do you want to hear a secret?"

I didn't completely black out, but I was a laundry bag in his arms as the big man carried me off the pier to the end of Niagara.

I heard the drowsy diesel engine and the squeal of the sliding door, the ratcheting rasp of the brake release, and Donovan playing on an eight-track through blown-out speakers. I was dropped on the floor on my head and we were rolling.

Who says you can never go home again?

So.

My real, given name, is Ida.

Short for Florida. Where I was born. Even a whole sheet of blue sunshine blotter acid couldn't give my parents an imagination. I hated *Ida*, but flat-out refused to answer to *Flo*, let alone to my full name.

One of the first things the Teachers made us do was choose new names. Recreating yourself made the world see you on your own terms.

Next subject.

I have, on occasion, killed people for money. I only take objectively reprehensible contracts, and I reserve the right to renege at any point. I've never had to kill bystanders or witnesses, I leave no evidence, and I never directly contact a client. The Free School taught me well. The few ripples I leave on the Web get wiped away by other caring professionals. I live out of a suitcase. I own nothing I can't replace with a phone call.

I work for fair rates on a sliding scale. The former GRU official-turned-snuff film mogul I capped in Newark last month brought in almost a hundred thousand, because of the visibility and risk. I once topped a Texas oil executive who kept and bred slaves in Africa to hunt for sport for plane fare and a sizable donation to UNICEF. I believe in nothing, but just in case, I do just enough pro bono work that my karma is fucking gold.

I might have become what I am without the Free School, but I never would have succeeded at it. Whatever they intended when they made me what I am, with my nature and the skill-set they gave me, I wasn't really cut out for much else. I take only what I need, and I try to leave the world a better place.

Our parents stumbled out of the ruins of the Age of Aquarius and they saw the establishment backlash on the horizon like a crewcut tsunami. They pegged the Cointelpro sharks circling among them, and they wanted to save us, to keep us perfect and innocent and pure forever. So they gave us to the Free School.

Others, they found on the road, and some they rescued or "liberated" from their square parents because their light was too brilliant to ignore.

I can't remember much of anything about my parents or life before the Free School. That was the *very* first thing they taught us—to forget everything before, to become holy orphans, children of the universe, swimmers in the Isness.

As vivid as my recollection of the Free School years, I hardly remember anything about the Teachers, themselves. Smiling, longhaired, featureless faces radiating blinding psychic sunlight, speaking in silent golden voices we heard in our hearts. They loved us more than life, but there was always a gentle remove, a soft psychic barrier so we wouldn't get attached. *All mortal things will fail you*, they said in our heads as we slept. I don't think anyone else remembered them, either, but nobody would admit it.

We have an elaborate system of secret dogma that only a child could understand. A junky stew of hippie folklore and quantum physics, Jung's psychology and Paracelsus's alchemy, it is complex enough to take up a whole mind, but simple enough, once mastered, to fit in a bird's brain. Some of us could whisper a Secret to a seagull and bind it to follow them around like a humble acolyte after a guru.

It was bullshit, but it worked. When Corky joined our School, she was bald, almost a naked skeleton from chemotherapy for leukemia. The Teachers had us sing for her every day. Within a year, she was healed, reborn as Lakshmi.

We were a cult, but nobody died or even got hurt until Sky. True, they pumped us full of LSD and stranger drugs every day, but they never abused us, never stole from us that innocence which they had sought to cultivate into Godhead: a portable Garden of Eden, populated by feral, immortal Eloi.

They taught us everything worth knowing in an hour a day. Mathematics, physics and biology. The great artists and composers, the great plays and philosophical writings from Epicurus to McKenna. The rest of the time, we traveled and played. And it was through play and laughter, that they taught us—no, they *made* us—magic.

Roaming the back roads of the nation in school buses and postal jeeps, they taught us to surf the collapsing wave between Isness and Otherness, and pluck what could never be out of what is like fish from a stream. They showed us how to be invisible, to steal whatever we needed and go on rides for free at amusement parks. They left us in Death Valley for a weekend, tripping so hard we couldn't tell the empty desert wasn't Disneyland. By making us live off trash from rest stops and dumpsters, they freed us from pride and gluttony. By teaching us to meditate, they made us open our third eyes and take control of our bodies—and the minds and bodies of others—and showed us how to hold time hostage with laughter. *He who laughs last, lives forever …*

The body, we learned, was not just the vehicle for the mind, but the material expression of the soul. They taught us to be what we wanted the world to see. They taught us that age, like every other aspect of the body, was a state of mind. *You're only as old as you feel …*

I cannot prove anything I've claimed. All I have is a birth certificate for a girl named Florida Warren, born November 12th, 1960, reported missing in 1969 and never found. From the day I was initiated to the day the Free School closed its doors in June, 1979, I didn't age.

We believed in the Secret Laws of the Teachers, and so long as we believed, we did not change. I was expelled, and now I take cholesterol medication and worry about lung and breast cancer. I still believe in the Secrets, but they don't believe in me, I guess. In the right time and place, I can still hear the roar of the secret seas and for a while I can still fake it, but my soul got old.

It's not that simple, of course. What the World wants is always greater complexity, greater corruption. We didn't rebuke or refuse knowledge, but to stay young forever, one must remain innocent of all the things that kill the child to create the adult. If ignorance alone was the key to immortality, America would be a nation of blind idiot gods.

What is the Last Secret Law? How is it taught, shared, taken away, and what were we supposed to do with it? We have no fucking clue. The Teachers made us miracles, but they taught us nothing, and then they went away.

I woke up to find myself tied to a rusty metal wall. My brain throbbed like a rotten tooth. Rainbow paint chips sifted in my eyes when I tried to move.

The bus had changed very little. The seats were ripped out to make a long, narrow lodge divided by motley curtains into three chambers. The stained-glass windows tinged the interior indigo and aquamarine, the walls plastered with pages of Latino bibles infected with Santeria and UFO abductee imagery. The intricate mural of the Kundalini serpent still ran from the front to the back of the ceiling, and if I peeled the pages off the walls, I could see the petrified strata of collages we made out of old news and fashion magazines—a blue, eight-armed Twiggy, J. Edgar Hoover as a crass satyr with Manson's head sprouting out of his crotch, kooky haikus we made up and scrawled everywhere on the road from Nowhere to Knowhere.

The bus was parked. Through the beaded curtains on my left, I saw the empty driver's seat. Behind the patchwork walls blocking the rear of the bus, I heard someone doing something over a hissing camp stove. I smelled hashish and formaldehyde and blood.

An old man sat across from me. He was tall, but emaciated like a galley slave. A filthy white beard, yellow with drool from toothless lips, hung down to his concave belly. He looked like a mummified yogi with his long grasshopper legs tucked under the antlers of his pelvis, and his hands folded, mantis-like, in deep meditation. His eyes were cloudy blue, sightless marbles, his toothless mouth quivering with silent laughter.

I reached out with my bare foot and kicked him. He didn't react at all, but the curtains flew apart and a crooked little man in a surgical mask and smock got in my face with an acetylene torch. "Don't you *dare* touch him! Do it again, and you'll *burn!*"

Speechless, I shrank back against the wall. The snarls of rubber surgical tubing around my wrists and waist stretched and flexed when I tried to get up, but the slipknots only squeezed tighter, until my hands went numb.

"Take off your mask, Miri. I know it's you, and I know how old you really are—"

"Why don't you take *yours* off?" I asked, but it was just something to say. I really didn't want to see.

He pulled it down under his chin and closed in until his sweat dripped in my eyes. Spontaneous reactions tell you everything.

I didn't say, "Please don't kill me," or "I'm so glad you're alive, and I'm so sorry." I just said what I said right before I broke his neck in '79. "Get off me, Sky."

"*You're not the Teacher, here!*" he screamed. "*You don't get to make the LAWS!*" He was still a little boy with long, curly golden hair, but it was falling out or curdled into grimy dreadlocks, and his features looked like a badly abused antique china doll. He wore a patch over his right eye, and a scar deep enough to hide a roll of dimes clove his forehead and cheek. "D'you ever stop to think about all the pain you caused?"

"You're making it hard to think," I said, "waving that thing in my face."

Growling and weeping in a choked falsetto, he lurched forward and singed away most of my bangs with the torch. "Oh, by all means, think on it now." He turned off the torch. His aura was an onionskin, brittle and brown.

I let out a deep, heavy breath. I could feel myself getting older and uglier. "You got any cigarettes?"

"I should hate you, Miri … for what you did to me … for destroying the School … but I forgive you, because—"

"To forgive is divine, right?" My right hand—wrinkled, nicotine-stained, cramped—tore free of the surgical tubing. Before Sky could react, I smashed the heel of my hand into the Teacher's nose. He obligingly sat still for it, then settled back against the wall. The blood that trickled from his caved-in face was barely pink.

Sky screamed and threw a scalpel at me, but it bounced off the wall behind me as I charged him. If he had resisted at all, I would've snapped his neck. But he just sat down on the floor and sobbed.

Now I was just an old woman again, standing over the little boy I broke so badly he could never grow up. "We thought you were dead. They told us so, Sky—"

"You believed what they told you. I was paralyzed from the neck down. But I got better."

"Why would they lie about that? Why would they just—"

"Please, Miri. They saw everything that happened as a shift in the cosmic balance. We were just an experiment. I was a new challenge. But I would take all their attention. So they decided to leave the Free School behind."

They took him down to South America and they experimented with focusing the global unconscious energies on healing his spine and remaking his soul. He slept for three years, and when he woke up, he could walk.

"What about …?" I pointed to his eye.

He flinched, but then forced a brittle laugh. "They said I had a spare. They learned what they wanted to learn, and moved on to the next thing. They left me in Peru. It took a couple years to escape the orphanage, and ever since, I've been tracking them."

Maybe I did a better job of hiding my tears than he did. "You should have come home. The School would've taken you back."

"I didn't want to go back to them! Didn't you ever stop to think about what we were supposed to become, what we were supposed to do in the World? The Teachers hoped we'd grow up to be the kind of leaders their revolution never had, the golden children who'd save humanity from itself. But we never grew up, and now we're barely even human. Only one of us graduated … you. I wanted to be a Teacher …" He pointed at the blind man. "That's what he was … You don't remember Bill-Eddy?"

I wracked my brain but came up empty. "In my dreams, they don't have names or faces." He nodded, smiled at this. "What happened to the rest of them?"

He scowled and stuck out his tongue in a weird spasm. "I never found the rest of them. They ditched Bill-Eddy in Costa Rica. He was blind and his mind was gone. He remembered nothing at all."

The old man called me Ida when he snatched me. Only the Teachers and our parents knew our real names, and my parents died of a heroin overdose in 1975. "So he's just a puppet? You made him kill the other kids?"

"Nobody could tell me what they did to us, Miri. Nobody could tell me how to turn it off." He drew back the curtains.

He'd turned the back of the bus into an operating theater, complete with ceiling-mounted cameras. Charts everywhere: anatomical diagrams of the brain and nervous system, Indian acupuncture charts showing the chakras and the spine as a fiery serpent. The old bookshelves were lined with file folders and medical and metaphysical and anatomical textbooks, and labeled jars with dissected brain lobes and spinal cord segments … LAKSHMI, LENNON, NOVA, NIMROD …

"None of them could show me how to free myself." He shook with fury at me, as if even this was all my fault. "How did *you* do it? How did you *forget?*"

"I never did. I accepted what I did wrong that day, and I just got over it. You could try facing up to your mistakes, Sky … Is that why you're doing this? You think you can flip some switch or eat somebody else's brain, and just turn into a man?"

I patted myself down. Aging thirty-five years in a few minutes will give anyone a nic fit. I caught a glimpse of my face in a blood-flecked mirror. I didn't look forty. I looked fifty and change.

"They believe you grew old because you killed me …" He laughed. "Or because you were cast out. Well, I *was* cast out, and I *have* killed.

And I … can't … grow … up!" Sky came back to me, holding a lethally long acupuncture needle. "I don't want to be a little boy anymore, Miri. You and I, we were supposed to do something, be something, that would have changed us both into what they were looking for. All the others failed. You walked away from that day, but I never got over it. If I can't grow up, and I can't forget … I don't want to go on—"

He ripped a book off a shelf and flipped through it, tearing pages and throwing them to the floor. "Do you know about the structural differences between normal human brains and ours? Not just the developmental ones, but the evolutionary ones? Have you ever let anyone take a good look at your brain, Miri?"

"No."

"I thought I could reverse it, and if it was just karmic, then I had that covered, too …" Like a toy winding down, he rattled around, picking up a scalpel, a bone saw, a jar with a severed child's hand floating in it. The hand was porcupined with needles, and when he carelessly set it on the shelf, it curled into a fist, poised to knock on a door. "But I learned something that made it all moot. We all have fathers. I don't mean the horny goat whose semen made half of you, but the man upstairs, even if the stairs only go up to the attic of your skull. We all have that inner father who gives out or withholds his love. They took ours away, but—"

"What do you want from me, Sky?"

He came over and knelt in front of me. A lost little boy. Who'd killed and dissected four of our classmates. "Just a kiss, Miri. That's all I wanted—"

"Don't start. I was only nine …"

"You'd been nine for ten years—"

"Don't, please." But I owed him that much. That's all he'd been trying to take from me, when I kicked him off the slide. He deserved to be punished for his crimes. I kissed him.

His lips were cold and chapped, stiff as a cigar store Indian's. I felt a surge of pity. Was I really the *only* girl he'd ever kissed?

He sat back, eyes closed, trying not to lick his lips. Handed me the needle. "Finish it."

The first faint light of sunrise was coming through the stained-glass windows, just bright enough to show me the silhouettes of children outside, faces pressed to the glass.

Sky put the needle against his forehead. "I don't want to see anymore. Close my third eye, Miri. Please …"

This wasn't an execution. It was a reward nobody could deserve.

With the heel of my hand, I drove the needle through the surprisingly thin wall of his forehead and thrust it to the hilt in his forebrain.

Sky sat back with his eyes rolled up to contemplate the trickle of blood from the needle in his head. He looked happy. He gurgled.

I found my skates and climbed off the bus. It was parked in the lot next to Dog Beach. A few campers and flophouse sedans with whole families packed into them were lined up across the lot, but nobody took notice of the gang of children swarming around the bus.

I hadn't seen so many of them in one place since the day I was exiled. They surrounded me, hands up and curled like cat's claws. Stray dogs with coldly glowing eyes lurked just behind them, expecting a meal.

I didn't dare look them in the eye. They wore matching soccer uniforms. They looked like a ten & under team waiting to take the field, except for the absence of hovering helicopter parents. I supposed I could pass for their coach, but nobody's mommy. This would be a brilliant disguise, were it not just before dawn on a rainy Monday morning.

I looked out at the ocean, where the early-bird surfers had paddled out past the rock jetty to catch the northwest swell, lounging like sea lions on their boards. I couldn't see them, but on the wind, I heard the lost parrot flock.

My schoolmates had learned nothing else in forty years, but now, they knew there was no law against spilling blood. But when I looked in their eyes, I almost started laughing. *He who laughs last—*

I could *see* them. Bent, toothless Baby Boomers in tie-dyed rags, dead-eyed and spent from living four decades in a magical lie.

Their illusions had mine beat by a mile. They'd fooled themselves all this time. *Don't stop now.*

Voice cracking between puberty and a coronary, Boy pleaded, "Please, Miranda … Just go …"

Only as old as you feel …

I could feel my hair turning white. I had paid for every stolen day. And with me around, so would they. "Summer's over, kids. School's back in session."

They complained. They thought I was taking over. They should be so lucky. I pushed them aside and tossed my skates in the trash, started hiking back to my car. Robb Field was only four blocks away. I wanted to run. I wanted to be far away before they met their new Teacher, but I turned and stopped to watch as the Spaceman of Ocean Beach emerged from the bus in his wetsuit.

His features were eaten up by an aura like a solar eclipse, and twice as hazardous to the naked eye. From a distance, he was a boy with a hole in his head surfing on the backs of kneeling geriatrics, but in his presence, all other men would feel like little children, afraid to crane their necks up to look him in the eye for fear of going blind.

He did not look back as he waded into the waves where the San Diego River flows into the Pacific Ocean at Dog Beach, with all the stray dogs paddling in his wake; not like a man swimming, but like a wrestler challenging his opponent, certain of victory.

I walked backwards along the riverbank so I could watch him. He grappled the waves until the twin secret seas cried for a rest, and the Free School children tore off their clothes and disappeared after him into the heaving gray surf.

DUST MADE OF WORDS

"Hey, kid! You like to read books?"

The boss's brother was waiting for Jim Newcomb when he brought the trash out to the dumpster behind the Aeneid Bookshop, near the bowls of kibble they put out for the feral neighborhood cats.

He was so dirty that tiny green sprigs of grass sprouted from his matted salt and pepper hair and behind his ears. The goatish angles of his sweaty, sunburned face had an absurdly regal cast to them, like his profile belonged on an ancient bronze coin, and his voice had the distracted bullroarer drone of an aphasic shaman. He clearly didn't realize he was in any way abnormal, or that he was wearing one muddy work boot and one New Balance running shoe. He wiped his hands on grimy white painter's pants and a torn sweatshirt with an old bumper sticker plastered across the chest. In English, Greek and Egyptian hieroglyphics, it said NO MORE ALEXANDRIAS!

Newcomb had expected him to ask for or offer drugs, but this sublimely obtuse question caught him off guard. "No, I'm only in it for the money ..." The awkward silence set like concrete until Newcomb added, "Sure, man, I like to read books."

"That's cool, that's cool." Nodding contentedly, the vagrant added, "But you know, you're doing it wrong."

"Oh ... really, now?"

"Yeah. How fast do you read? Because I see you reading the same book day after day, but you buy maybe five, ten books a week. You finish about one a week, right?"

This was getting kinda personal ... "Most of the time, yeah ..."

"So, if you live another fifty years, you'll maybe read another five thousand books, and you probably won't remember a tenth of a tenth of them. But what if you could absorb everything you read like it just happened to you, like a dream that jolts you awake with a stranger's name on your lips …"

"Yeah, um … That'd be … cool …?" *Check please*. The storeroom door was about a mile away.

He lived in a cargo container behind the bookshop, and he had been arrested twice since Newcomb started working there. *Domestic disturbance, public nudity, shoplifting …*

Scratching his head, he came even closer, like he wanted to whisper a secret. "Let me put it another way. Have you ever read a whole book in one day, when you had like a broken leg or a raging fever, when you're too sick to do anything else, and your head's a ship on a storm-tossed sea?"

It seemed safest to just nod.

"At that dosage, language turns psychotropic, man, like *transformative*. So like … what if you could have that total, holistic literary experience not just in one sitting, but in the space of *one breath*?"

Virgil, the store's owner, hated giving orders, but he was unequivocal about one thing when he hired Jim. *Stay away from my brother. If he asks you to do anything, the answer is no.*

"I gotta go back in, man," Jim said to the mismatched shoes. "Cal's out getting coffee. Baird's by himself."

"Fine, I understand. You're afraid. I tell you, man, I used to be like you …"

Jim used the wastebasket as a shield to push through to the door. "I don't know, man. I've never smoked crack."

The vagrant came after him so fast, he crashed into the door when Jim pulled it shut, screaming, "I don't smoke *crack*, you ignoramus. I smoke *books*!"

Jim came in just as Cowboy Cal finished reading aloud, and he and Baird sat back on their stools like poets in an opium den.

The last words of Valgovind's Boat Song soaked into the walls of the bookshop like perfume into raw silk. It was the hour after the magic hour, when the sunlight pouring in the narrow windows turned to wine and made the columns of drifting dust into billowing purple curtains, and the only customers in the store came for a nap.

"Splendid," Baird said. "Let's have another."

"I dunno, man." Cal squinted, holding the antique book up to the light. "I still think they fade a little, every time you read them." The purple words were like ancient grape juice stains. "Besides, I think it's turning one of us into a woman."

The book was one of the rarer volumes from the vault—the real one, not the flashy safe full of elaborate fakes behind the counter. Mummified in buttery, bone-yellow vellum slowly crumbling to creamy dust, paper of crushed papyrus that crackled like a dying fire. The poems were ornate, decadent exoticism, not entirely convincing 19th century fakes of Sufi love poetry, but when read aloud from the book, they had an intoxicating effect on anyone in earshot incidental to their quality.

It was far from the rarest, but one of the most interesting. Alongside the signed firsts of *Naked Lunch, A Scanner Darkly, A Farewell To Arms* and the promotional advance of Vonnegut's first novel, there were many arcane items impossible to put a price on— *The Double Shadow* signed and doodled in by Clark Ashton Smith for Robert Bloch; the Fig Leaf edition of *Oil!* with Sinclair's inky fingerprints on the cover; or the brief handwritten letter by JD Salinger. One that held a particular dread for Newcomb was an early 20th century keepsake diary in which someone had pasted over every handwritten line with a continuous Dadaist word salad snipped out of lurid old crime magazines and a German geometry textbook, forming a 200-page proof of corpses and murders, the unifying formula of the universe as an infinite crime scene. The black, buzzing madness of it was like plutonium.

The store was empty, or might as well have been. It was almost, Baird dryly observed, as if Los Angeles had finally invented some superior form of entertainment that rendered books obsolete.

The owner was camping on Easter Island for a three-day solar eclipse rave, so Jim, Baird and Cowboy Cal held down the desk. A big sign over their heads said, *Discard Your Thirst For Books, So That You Won't Die In Bitterness.* If you could name the author without recourse to Google, you'd get a discount. A bell pull rope behind the register was supposed to release the "roses of Heliogabalus" on cheaters, but the trapdoor in the ceiling was stuck.

Cowboy Cal was a stuntman in the Seventies. His specialties were fistfights, setting himself on fire and falling off buildings. He chronically got into shouting arguments with difficult customers. Jim saw him get nose-to-nose with a Randian who'd had a meltdown over the price of a signed *Fountainhead*. Cal took a deep breath and closed his eyes while the customer painted his face with flecks of spittle and tortured invective, and then he head-butted him right above the eyes, as surgically precise as the icepick jab of a lobotomy. Catching the customer as he swooned, Cal left him propped up against Communism and went to get a coffee. When he came back, he squeezed both the customer's earlobes, causing the customer to awaken with a jolt and no memory of the preceding ten minutes. "You must've fainted," Cal said. Getting up with a confused, mistrustful look, the customer wandered out of the store and never came back. Cal was, in the owner's estimation, worth ten polite clerks.

Jim studied his colleagues' means of fending off customers, but he despaired of coming up with anything half as good. He had taken to carrying empty plastic wrappers from chips and cookies in his pockets, which gave off loud crinkly noises to subtly imply that he was wearing adult diapers, and thus couldn't be trusted.

Reuben the Peeper was poring over every book in Erotica with his oversized magnifying glass. He might flinch around the section until closing, or he could remember in the next minute that his senile mother was waiting for him in his truck, and he'd scoot out like an arsonist from a fire.

Lord Fontanel had nodded off in his customary chair behind the bargain trestle tables. With an antique hearing aid the size of a Sony Betamax stuffed in each hairy ear and a white loafers-and-belt ensemble, he was the quintessential crazy old man, but he also wore a child's sparkly magenta bicycle helmet. Baird insisted it was because his fontanel never closed over.

The Aeneid was the loneliest place in LA when it was full, a mute onanists' orgy, all those wallflowers locked up in their own fantasies, so obviously alone and lost. But when it was empty, it was almost more than he could take. Like a church filled with ghosts. The air breathed itself, the yawning pause in an eternal conversation, the dust was made of words, and all of it commanded his complete attention.

The store's hundred and twenty-eight thousand titles endlessly vexed him, because he was a voracious but glacially slow reader. It took a week of feverish effort to get through even the slimmest mid-century crime novel. At the job interview, he told the owner he hoped to use the shop to research how to become a great writer. The owner said his plan was like hoping to become a great chef by studying sewage.

The phone rang. "You may answer it," Baird said, as if blessing a marriage. When the owner was out of town haunting estate sales or following a Secret Chiefs 3 tour, Baird was in charge. A gnomish, pale man stooped over a small potbelly with a patchy white beard that only accented rather than hid a grievous harelip, Baird was absolved of answering the phone for the foreseeable future after having talked a neurotic customer out of suicide when she asked him to read Kevorkian's instruction manual to her over the phone. This was an especially heroic gesture on the part of someone who hated humankind more than anyone who'd ever stood trial in the Hague for genocide, and he still couldn't forgive himself.

"Why are you conspiring to keep the books I need hidden ...?" Jim pinched his earlobe to preemptively revive himself. It was Yuri. "I have rumors heard, that Cat-Lady's library of Enochian magic is being fumigated, prior to putting up for sale. Why do you hide them?"

"We're afraid you won't keep coming back and calling every hour, maybe ...?" Yuri was the current *bete noire* of the store, or aspired to be—the celebrated Most Difficult Customer. Yuri was mostly harmless, but he was almost annoying enough to qualify.

The library in question was a set of Crowley books that some crazy old widow had sold them. They'd be worth a fortune if they didn't reek of cat urine. Currently, they were packed in a special extraction box filled with activated charcoal and cat litter.

Compared to the other four practicing (and feuding) black sorcerers who had strict appointment windows to forestall another curse-duel, Yuri was an amateur.

Newcomb put Yuri on "bad" hold. The phone system was put together by a rogue telecom engineer who wired the store in trade for a signed Syd Mead print. It had multiple hold tracks that jacked into a loop cassette deck in the back room. Track One, for the polite customers, usually played something soothing like Bach's Goldberg Variations or Ezra Pound reciting his *Cantico del Soleil* in his odd, piercing tenor. Track Two was for the ones who wanted *Turner Diaries* and bondage porn mailed to a prison, or who tried to get you to research their kid's overdue term paper over the phone. Right now, Yuri was enjoying a mix of Newcomb's drunken gay neighbors murdering "Muskrat Love" in the shower intercut with Nurse with Wound's "Spiral Insania."

Jim tried to ask Cal about Yuri's book, but he was still so high off the fake Hindu love poetry that even simple eye contact caused a Sanskrit giggling fit.

A woman in a smart silver pantsuit came in asking for books on management and tax codes. Baird told her, "No business, no computers, no law, no politics … it's the best of all possible worlds."

"So, you don't have anything useful," the woman shot back.

Baird got down off his stool, gleefully popping his knuckles. He lived for this moment. "*Useful?* Madam, we sell books of art, drama, music, history, philosophy, science, metaphysics, mythology, classic and genre literature and comic books. We sell people the tools they need to successfully pass for human beings."

Cal blew her a kiss as the woman flipped them the bird and stormed out. "And these are the twelve percent who allegedly *can* read," Baird said. "Idiots don't know Ha Jin from Ma Jian."

"Not yet, Yuri," Jim said into the phone and hung up. His attention was a dandelion seed, adrift on the lightest currents of air, floating amongst the dust that seemed to waft about him like the ghosts of Turkish houris.

A breathtaking redheaded woman came in, and he picked up a stack of reshelves to follow her until he saw her face. Her hair was so long and thick that even at this late hour, if he were to finger the braid that spilled down her back, he knew it would still be cool and wet from her morning shower. He would never talk to her, not even regular helpful clerk stuff, but he couldn't stop picturing himself washing her hair, strangling her with it and eating her fingers, which weirded him out, but also gave him a raging boner.

These are not my thoughts, he thought. He didn't know why it happened, but it usually coincided with finding a badly misshelved book in True Crime, and sure enough, he found a weathered copy of Browning's *Dramatic Lyrics* jammed in between two books on Issei Sagawa. He stuffed some earnestly loopy paperbacks into the Hollow Earth section, then recovered Sports, Martial Arts, Gambling and Oddities. The Oddities aisle collected the assorted topics the owner didn't like, but still carried so people wouldn't bug him, like childrearing and wine.

He wandered a couple more aisles and came to a massive nest of stacked books beside Astrology. Somebody had built it over hours of idle reading, then crept off without buying anything. It was always the metaphysics and astrology people, the ones in the least control of their lives, who left him the biggest messes, but it was hardly the most annoying of his duties. He had standing orders to "disorganize" Architecture every day, with vague but shrill warnings about what would happen if ever the seldom disturbed section were to successfully "re-alphabetize" itself.

Jim recovered the section and shuffled back to the counter.

Baird was reading the sports page and sipping his diet cream soda. Cowboy Cal braced him about whether or not any new customers were passed out in the reading room.

"Just …" Eyeing a customer waiting at the counter, Jim hesitated to use Lord Fontanel's proper name. Instead, he gestured to the top of his head. "You know who."

Among Cal's less pernicious obsessions was his compulsion to photograph any customer who napped in the store. He'd been doing it for as long as he worked there, entertaining the notion of a coffee-table book to be titled, The Magic Hour, but the likelihood of a class-action lawsuit kept the dream from becoming a reality, so far.

When they shared a joint after closing, the owner often expounded on the store's mystical properties, which could be communed with by napping in the store. But while outwardly peaceful, a nap in the Aeneid could change or destroy lives as wantonly as any Greek god. For every success story—like the halfway house weirdo who used to read and nap all day and apparently used chaos magic to become a top-rated local realtor—there was one like the former Broadway director who tried to learn a new language every month, and went incurably, barking mad in Cherokee.

"What about a mad scientist-type," Jim asked, "who tries to build a perfect woman out of the best parts of his victims?"

"It's been done," Baird murmured, and rattled off an Edwardian penny dreadful, two comic books, three Grand Guignol plays and six films from '38 to '97.

"So, before I can even come up with an original story, I have to read everything that's ever been written."

"No," Baird said, with that monumentally tired tone he took with only the very densest customers. "There *are* no original stories. All you have to do is make them forget all the times they've already read it. You've only got to find a way to make it *feel* new. And you can't tell anyone about it before you do it, or you'll never do it."

A young actress from the improv theater down the block bought an armload of dollar plays and celebrity biographies and a coffee table book of *matryoshka* dolls from the bargain table. Baird just nodded as she gushed over how cheap their prices were. When she'd gone out the door and picked up another armload of junk from the free boxes, Baird laughed like an owl coughing up mouse bones and said, "Poor fool has no idea what books *really* cost."

Jim thought he knew what Baird meant, so he laughed, too.

"Everybody thinks they can be a writer," Cowboy Cal said, "and all they got to do is make shit up. Everybody only has one real story to tell, if they're not stealing."

"Don't listen to him," Baird said.

"When even one of your Nobel Prize winners actually has to make up something out of whole cloth, it nearly always goes to hell. With love and luck, everybody can tell one great story, then they should quit. The truly great ones tell the same story over and over, or they're good at stealing other people's stories ... or they're secretly a cabal, like Shakespeare."

"Don't start that shit again," Baird rumbled.

"What's the deal with Virgil's brother?" Jim asked.

Cowboy Cal dropped a massive stereotaxic atlas of mouse brain wafers so it thunderclapped on the glass countertop. "No comment."

"He *was*," Baird said, dipping the *was* in arsenic, "the most sought-after bookbinder in Los Angeles." He pointed at the fakes in the display safe—the impeccable John Dee *Necronomicon*, the decoded Voynich Manuscript, the autographed first edition of *The Bible,* the *Dr. Seuss Kama Sutra.* "Studied in England, was on retainer to UCLA and the Getty. The first time he snapped, he got caught fencing Marlowe and Jonson folios from Powell Library for drug money. It was like a Jacobean revenge tragedy with crack-whores."

Jim knew the rest of it. The brother moved in out back, where he argued with his girlfriend constantly: screaming, throwing things, rough makeup sex. He often had to tell customers that a bad improv troupe was rehearsing next door.

After a suitable lull, Jim slouched out of his chair. "I'm gonna go shelve."

"Stay away from him," Baird said. "He's King Midas in reverse. Everything he touches turns to egg salad."

It was particularly hard for Newcomb to shelve fiction, because he couldn't clear a cart without finding an armload of treasure he couldn't afford and would never get around to reading. Also, far from inspiring him, every book he looked at made it harder to kid himself he would ever be a real writer, because he didn't smoke.

He couldn't, really. Allergic. He'd certainly tried hard enough. All the *real* writers and artists, the ones who suffered and burned with genius like some fabulous alien fever, smoked. In their portraits, they held up a cigarette as a totem, a candle the Devil gave them that fueled their brilliance and measured their fleeting time on Earth.

Maybe Cal was right about Shakespeare being a secret cabal of people. Jim had the temperament and the observational acuity to be a great writer, but lacked the focus and drive and stuff to write about. Maybe the other half of a brilliant writer was out there now, looking for him.

Alone, he wasn't even much of a reader. It was at such moments when he came up against his humbling limits that he most badly craved some kind of fatal consolation prize.

"Hey kid, come here," said a voice. Jim dropped his books from the top of the ladder he was standing on. They flapped and shed their jackets and crashed to the dusty hardwood floor like dead birds.

"Imagine a perfect golden tapestry … something too beautiful ever to have been touched by human hands. Fragile as a spider web, a gift from the gods, or maybe your subconscious elves spun it while you slept, and you can only glimpse it with your mind's eye through the keyhole of your conscious perception. Try to touch it, and you'll end up with a fistful of fucked-up nothing. That's what an inspiration, a truly *great* idea is.

"Now, to get it out, to express it, to make it real, you've got to take hold of a single thread and pull it through the keyhole as a string of words and weave it into a story, just so the reader can tear it apart again, pulling it into *his* brain. *That's* what a book is."

Jim tried to simulate understanding, but he was too enthralled by the thing looming behind the owner's brother to do more than nod.

The machine looked like one of the pretentious prank installations at the Museum of Jurassic Technology. A big Plexiglas dome was clamped onto the butcher-block table, with cumbersome rubber gloves protruding into it like a high school chemistry workstation. A pair of menacing old compressor pumps were bolted onto the floor, and a tangle of tubes emerged from the dome to terminate in an Army surplus gas mask.

"Y'know how a vaporizer works, right? The plant matter gets heated almost up to the point where it combusts, which releases the plant's essential oils as a vapor. Inhale, and it goes directly into the bloodstream."

He'd heard of it, alright. All the baby boomers were getting them because it was easier on their lungs. It extracted THC from a bud without scorching it, so one could conceivably resell the buds after they'd been drained. Jim had been burned more than once by pot vampires.

"Same thing, basically, except this form of vapor has to be excited by exposure to electromagnets and stuff ..."

"So you're just inhaling the vapor from a book? It's just bleached paper, ink and glue ..."

"How'd you fool my brother into hiring you? Books aren't paper, they're encoded fucking *dreams!* Reading them only lets you access them through words, but subatomic particles, man, they each contain a holographic fractal resonance of the whole. They're *ideas ...* and passion and inspiration and—Just put on the goddamn mask, man."

It smelled like green cathedral dust, with a hint of that burnt crayon smell like when he turned on the heater for the first time in winter. A fan built into the dome started to whir and the disagreeable smell seemed to open up and inside was a perfume of flowers so potent that it overran one sense and invaded the others, as music, as color as something tickling him all over ...

It was made of words in the same way that a tornado is made of air. It was like music, only more so. A sense that the words were alive, and they *loved* him.

He breathed in and became breath, atomized, and the book was inhaling *him.*

He once tried a sensory deprivation tank because some guy at school told him it was like instant Nirvana—total negation of the self, oneness with the universe—but he just worried that he was going to pee in the warm, salty bath until he fell asleep. No, he could only liken it his brief tenure at an office job, when he and a buddy inhaled the pressurized stuff in the cans that they used to blow dust and crud out of computer keyboards. The hideously unhealthy mix of nitrous oxide and chlorodifluoromethane would expand some random passing word until it became a *world,* even as your body shrank and was annihilated, and you were completely transformed or subsumed into something else, until you came to on the floor a few minutes later, acting like a caveman or a giant squid or a mad Aztec priest trying to sacrifice your cubicle-mate with a stapler.

This was more than that.

Most wondrous of all was the seamless unfolding of the book's meaning and message out of sensory impressions, how the cascade of words manifested as phantom stimuli that in turn became emotions and ideas and memories—not just the story and the language, but the ghosts of the author and their life, the grand design of the universe inscribed by a generous, fragile hand.

Pressed into the words, mixed into their ink, were the sweat, tears and bloodshed in their creation … the torment and release of dreaming, conceiving and typing it … Sparks of inspiration and doldrums of doubt, the final manic push to the end, the endless gnawing of revision …

And the writer's hand passed overhead like a storm and became the sound of the ocean and he stood on virgin earth like freshly ground coffee under a rainbow sherbet sky, and the ocean—

Lacy azure waves rolled in perfect rippling rhythm to caress the shore, like the echoes of a dance at the bottom of the sea. The foam rushed up and over him and met the rolling red waves of lava cascading down from the volcano at his back, and the ocean cracked and shot forth a wall of steam like the birth of a storm. Bright as star-stuff, a jet of raw white magma roared up out of the cataract in the earth, and raking the indigo sky, it became a swaying girl with flowing smoke for hair and a skirt made of steam, a fiery avatar of creation and destruction whose terrible, luminous beauty ever threatened to engulf the idyllic island paradise.

And as if through a trapdoor, he fell into *More*. The words unfurled into a dizzying gallery of dreams that he plummeted through like a stained-glass maze, the rhythm pulling like gravity until he found the ground again.

It was euphoric, but it wasn't long before he realized he inhabited the Hawaiian fantasy of an unforgivable hack. Exotic local caricatures showered him in an endless mugshot parade, their naïve foibles and amusing nut-brown features rendered in a patronizing singsong cadence that felt like riding a merry-go-round backwards. The scenery collapsed into a mass of fool's-gold *déjà vu* in his brain, and something else loomed up out of the wreckage.

Behind all the facades was the life of the book itself, and here, the dreamy panorama of synesthesia came back around to pummel him with counterfeit scent and stolen memory. The briny tang of the pages was not the salt of the ocean, but of tears, as he rolled in the undertow of a terrifying honeymoon, reading the silly poems for comfort as he tried to hide from the shame and guilt of the marriage bed.

His eyes were streaming when he took off the mask. The owner's brother made a derisive snort.

"What the hell was that?"

The mad bookbinder lifted the hood and held up a faded aquamarine hardcover with no dustjacket. Odd faint speckles like raindrops dappled the dull boards. Jim took the book and flipped to the title page: *The Island-Hopper*, a collection of Don Blanding's insipid poems from 1938. "They used to give them out with leis to every tourist who steamed into Hawaii."

Jim said, "Let's have another." Can I pick one?"

"Slow down, Erasmus," the bookman said. "Try this on for size." He picked up a small, black lacquered box and opened it to take out a pamphlet-sized volume bound in rough green leather that crumbled and left a minty powder on his hands. He dropped it on the platter and sealed the hood. "No fair peeking," he said and impatiently gestured for Jim to put on the mask.

This aroma was deeper, darker, sour …Radiator milk and toilet paper with splinters in it. Rawhide and harsh dye and wildflowers and the ripening loneliness of a sickly child.

OUR BUSINESS IN LIFE

A leaden rosary of blank verse like something burned into stone tablets poured into his head, writ large as the weird designs on the Nazca Plain in Peru, far too vast to read, too great to comprehend. He crawled over them like a bug on a Bible. Sleepy curlicues of art nouveau carnations bloomed and became the perfect pink rose of a woman's lips commanding him to drop his trousers.

IS NOT TO SUCCEED

It took an act of will to rise up, to grow until he could read the words. But even as their meaning flowed into him like cold concrete soup, he felt a sudden sting with each line of verse, a rush of wind and a slap on his ass.

BUT TO CONTINUE

It hurt so bad he could suddenly remember his name.

TO FAIL IN GOOD SPIRITS.

Was the owner's brother spanking him?

He came to jumping out of the chair. His ass stung like he'd been paddled with a squash racquet. He looked around for something to throw at the bookman. "What the fuck was that, man?"

The owner's brother cackled and coughed and wiped tears from his eyes. "Oh my God, that never gets old."

Jim ripped off the mask and came at him. "The book, what's wrong with that book?"

Taking the slim leather booklet out of the hood, he held it up. "A Task" by Robert Louis Stevenson—the kind of little token filled with aphorisms that one would give a young boy passing into manhood, circa 1910. Slipping it into the black box, he held it up to show how the sheen of lacquer had worn off in the center on both sides, and how the corners were crinkled with the sweat of many gripping hands. "Don't know why, but the book became a family heirloom, used by three or four generations to spank their kids. Maybe they thought the wisdom in it would soak in at the other end, if it couldn't get into their heads."

Jim picked up the box for just a moment, smelled the oddly endearing funk of mold and degraded dyes masking the sweat and tears of angry parents and ashamed or unrepentant children. "That was a dirty trick."

"You had enough?"

"I should get back to the counter."

"I'll let you try one more."

Jim's eyes narrowed with suspicion. "Which one?"

"Anything you like … pick something you've never read, though. And something short, without too much wear. You're still a baby."

Jim went back out into the stacks, giddy, excited until the enormity of the store reclaimed him. Which one? His eyes couldn't rove over a single shelf without getting hooked by a title, a byline, a spiky font.

He could ask the guys, but Baird would hand him another moldy slice of Mencken. Cowboy Cal would recommend Lord Dunsany or Zane Grey.

He felt giddy, in possession of a secret, a real one, bright and dangerous in its implications, like a diamond wrecking ball. So much now made sense. The burnout collectors who got the red carpet treatment from the owner, conducted into the back for extended private viewings of extraordinarily rare books, who invariably walked out empty-handed while the boss counted cash. The spacey, uneducated weirdos who wandered the store discussing metaphysics and philosophy like refugees from the School of Athens. The blind guy who bumbled in every so often and bought art books, though they had nothing in Braille. People tripping on knowledge they never could have acquired the hard way.

He was tempted to try smoking a box set—either the 1949 *Encyclopedia Britannica* in the free box on the front steps, or the complete series of *Man, Myth & Magic*—but nixed it. Practical knowledge absorbed like a dream would be incredibly vivid, but difficult to process and recall in waking life. Bits of trivia and bowel-squashing slabs of sensation would resurface like flashbacks, but never on demand.

Maybe something a little more focused, like Bunker Spreckels' surfing manual, or Neil Armstrong's memoirs or *The Techniques of Supermaxillary Surgery*. Maybe all three at once …

The more he looked, the more questions he had. Would he have to live through everything, every trauma, every triumph, every death, in a book? And what about the author? This looked like the perfect opportunity to finally get all the way through *Infinite Jest*, but he didn't want to become suicidally morose. Could he understand *Finnegan's Wake* or *Ulysses* without his liver spontaneously failing? It didn't seem worth the risk.

Nor did he want to risk opening himself up to crazy ideas that could become his own. No *Secret Teachings of All Ages*, no Cayce, Fort or L. Ron, no *Sword of Song* or *White Stains*.

He went to his hold shelf and studied the books he'd picked to buy with his next paycheck. He was currently saving up for a Borges omnibus, a coffee table book about Dali's 1939 World's Fair exhibit, four trashy noir novels and a dog-eared copy of *Cards As Weapons*. The latter was seriously tempting, but the odd brown stains throughout promised to show him things he wouldn't want to live through.

Baird was on the phone with the OCD customer who had to have a new and unique edition of the *Rubaiyat of Omar Khayyam* every month. He assured the caller that his collection so far was "obsolete trash," because the new Atwater translation rendered all previous interpretations "laughable at best." He didn't notice Newcomb grabbing the Indian love poetry book out of the safe.

Jim slipped back through the store to the back room. The owner's brother was slouched in an egg chair in the corner, wearing a heavier mask like a deep-sea diver's helmet. The pumps shook and made unsettling sounds like plumbing in a condemned house. Jim went over to the vaporizer dome. It was too fogged up to see what was inside, the inner surface dappled with condensation.

He turned and tripped over a hose. The owner's brother helped him up. The hood made a vacuum-pop when he took it off. "Dude, that one was sick …" His eyes were glassy, his face blotchy and badly embalmed. "You ready for another one? Lemme see."

Jim held out the book, his neck twisted around to peek under the dome. The owner's brother popped the seals and swapped out the books like a veteran club DJ.

Jim fingered the little mask he'd used before, but his eyes strayed to the helmet. "Go ahead, but if you puke in it, I wouldn't wanna be you."

Jim settled into the egg chair and let the owner's brother drop the helmet on his head. His ears popped when the seals clamped down on his shoulders. The tubes behind his ears gurgled and burped the stench of black licorice. The faint, cloying musk of night-blooming jasmine leaked in, but it was soon overwhelmed by a deeper, darker odor, utterly unlike perfume and flowers.

Jim stood up, but he was already disintegrating.

The cloudy glass window in front of his face was so fogged over he could barely see the spear of burgundy sunlight piercing the gloomy room when the owner's brother opened the back door. "I'll be right back, man. I gotta see a dude about some Bibles ..."

Right away, it went wrong.

He skated for a sweet moment on a ribbon of quaintly fake exotica penned by a guilty British officer who took part in the Amritsar massacre. Printed on paper made from the fiber of opium poppies and inscribed with hypnotic meters that made its corny verses into a campy Song of Solomon, it was a pure pleasure to inhale, but it was the residue of the previous book left over from the mad bookman's session. If not for the lingering waft of love poetry from the book he thought he'd chosen, the book he'd mistakenly inhaled would have struck him dead.

He couldn't see the glass in front of his eyes, but he knew right away which book it was. The endless black Moebius strip, the ghastly chain of naked crime scene carnage, the taste of bile and mucilage and the barrel of a gun.

Like the strata of an archaeological dig, the layers of madness and obsessive misery crumbled and filled him and buried him alive. He was freebasing the blues. It shook him and sickened him like a pint of formaldehyde on an empty stomach. The smell that filled his nose was the stink of his brain burning up in his head, the stinging cordite afterburn of a failed suicide.

How could he miss, when he had the fucking barrel in his goddamned useless mouth ...?

And who wouldn't want to eat a gun, when someone had stolen his book, the one true story he had inside him that he had drained out of himself like slow bloodletting, written longhand in an old journal but so carefully composed, that when his father saw it he would know that his son was an artist in his own right, his horrid has-been literary lion father who cheated on his wife just to have something real to write about ...

He should've known better than to trust him, but he could barely hold it together against the fear that his father would simply *hate* it. When it happened, when the book came out, when the carton of hardcovers still redolent of benzene and treachery arrived on their porch, he thought it was a joke. He looked twice at it to see if his name wasn't tucked under his father's byline. He could barely conceive of his father submitting the manuscript to a publisher, let alone signing a deal for him behind his back. But his name was nowhere in the front matter except in the routinely oblique dedication, the same he'd used in his last three books—*with love and respect to all my sons ... real and imagined.*

And before he could breathe, he was eating the gun and before he could smell his own skull on fire, he was in an observation cell in the ICU at Cedar Sinai, and then a private sanitarium near Lake Arrowhead, where he kept the doctors hopeful for months while he revised his handwritten manuscript. The nurses let him cut up their crime magazines and he diligently revised every word of his masterpiece, made it uniquely his own.

Jim Newcomb vomited into the helmet. On his knees he crawled up to the vaporizer dome, clawing vainly at the helmet seals and screaming for someone to help him.

Blind and drowning in bile, he stumbled into a door and pulled on it and he could barely hear the sound of the vaporizer toppling off the dome and trailing after him over the whine of the fan in his ears.

—

Nobody else in the store was having a good time, either. The owner's brother pounded on the back door, having locked himself out in the back parking lot with a lit joint and a crate of Enochian magic grimoires packed in cat litter.

Cowboy Cal was down the street at the 7-11, engaged in a passionate shouting match with the Somali family working the counter over the proper way to reheat coffee.

Baird was getting robbed.

Baird's voice was a quavering shout. "How do you expect me to help you, if I don't even know your taste?"

"Just gimme the *good* ones, goddamit! The rare, expensive shit, the old shit!"

Baird reached into the safe with a pained grimace creasing his face. "Here's our signed Shakespeare ... But if you take it, you might as well kill me ..."

The thief put down the gun to look over the Reader's Digest Shakespeare Condensed Edition with fake gems embedded in the cover. "It's all old and beat up!"

"What condition do you expect a five hundred year old Book Club edition to be in?"

Jim Newcomb came around the corner screaming for help. In the customized helmet with the tinted, bulging eyepieces and the respirator hose trailing back down the aisle, he looked like a gawky, wasted Space Age Ganesh.

The robber wore a ski mask and a dingy blue tracksuit. He crouched behind the counter in front of the safe, pawing through the counterfeit rarities within as Jim staggered down the aisle, trying to catch a breath that wasn't full of insanity and second-hand death.

A weird, wavering cloud like heat haze on a hot desert blacktop rolled up behind him, full of faces and facts and myths and lies and bountiful breasts and dinosaurs and world wars and Hummel figurines …

And all the ephemera, the divers hands that had left their own marks—a lifetime of stories in every chocolate fingerprint, hair, booger and spot of blood squeezed from the mummy of a flea crushed in the pages, every dog-eared receipt and scribbled marginal Post-It note—*Next time the shark eats somebody, bring me a vodka gimlet?*

He breathed in and his head was a house with 128,000 doors. All at once, they opened.

⁂

Lord Fontanel jolted awake in his seat and saw a deep-sea diver freaking out like a saucer person huffing paint thinner. He looked around for a moment, then lurched over to the wall behind his chair and pulled the fire alarm.

The thief screamed and dived over the counter as he squeezed off a wild shot into the ceiling. The trapdoor in the ceiling dropped open to shower him in petrified rose petals and rubber snakes. Screaming and sneezing, he ran out the front door with the autographed *Reader's Digest Shakespeare*. Lord Fontanel cursed the depraved spirit of the age and went back to sleep.

⁂

The fire engines only took six minutes to arrive. It was a slow night for fires. Baird met them on the steps and explained the emergency. "The store's full of aerosolized teleological poison. You'd better put on your rhetorical gas masks ..."

Baird had been locked out of the store without his keys. He didn't carry a cell phone, and there wasn't a working pay phone for ten blocks in any direction. The firemen broke the glass front door and forced their way in. Baird went into the back door to stop the firemen from chopping anything down.

He found the peculiar helmet in the rare book gallery. The fan was still whirring, but he saw no other sign of Jim Newcomb. He noticed then that everything in the store was covered with a thin patina of creamy, pinkish-gray dust. Baird gagged, covered his mouth and nose and went looking for the firemen.

He found them in the cookbooks. One of them held up a book of chili recipes. "Hey, what's the big idea?"

Baird picked up a book, then another, then went to check the rare book gallery.

"And yet God has not said a word," he said under his breath.

Every page of every book in the store was blank.

MISERICORDIA

The last sounds Laurel Evangeline Wiggins heard were the dog barking, the neighbor kids flying an RC plane in the field out back, like a big, angry hornet, and her mother sobbing.

Eight year-old Laurel had infections in both ears and it hurt so bad she couldn't even cry. Mom had calmly told her to ride it out like the others, but this time, when her ears finally popped like on the airplane to visit Grandma Jean in Florida, all she could hear was a seashell roar or a cold, steely whine, and sometimes a blessed, blank nothingness.

If she had not lost her hearing, Laurel was often asked, would she have stuck with the violin just because nobody believed she could? And would she have become something of a prodigy, a gimmicky teenage sensation, the Deaf First-Chair Soloist? Now touring the world at sixteen, rehearsing in a drafty palazzo in Venice, in *Italy* ...

No, as she limbered her fingers and took up the bow again, she probably would still be in Lawrence, Kansas with some steakhead local boy gunning to nail her down with his name and babies, and nowhere to go but down.

But then she'd be able to *hear* music again ...

While interviewing her on her breakthrough appearance on NPR's *From the Top*, Christopher O'Riley said that she played with an uncanny purity, as if hearing was distraction, as if deafness was her armor, and all her critics adopted and regurgitated it. The laziest ones compared her to Beethoven.

Pity party, she scolded herself, bowing to the empty attic, *and I invited all my friends.*

Milosz, her sparring partner, had left his cello in its open case like a fat vampire, and retired to a couch in the attic practice studio to romance someone on his phone. They had worked on her cues for three hours and reviewed YouTube videos of the conductor and laughed at his ridiculously pompous but critical facial expressions; but in the end, Milosz had been used up rehearsing the tune the Europeans never tired of requesting as a corny encore, "The Devil Went Down to Georgia."

Italy had been almost terrifying in its open adoration, which she had unwittingly fanned when she'd told a reporter her two favorite composers to play were Verdi and Morricone.

The cheap oscillating fan on the windowsill sucked in hot, stifling air redolent of low tide and diesel fuel, but it kept the interior stench of mildew and mold at bay, the dust of renovation from the lower levels.

Bianca, the tour manager, had picked the palazzo to wow her, as well as stash her out of sight while she abandoned Laurel for some private tryst, judging by her black velvet-trimmed cocktail dress and spicy, challenging perfume. Laurel had to work not to get annoyed at such treatment, but the space itself was something special.

The floor was a crimson slab of travertine marble that carried every vibration like a tuning fork, so she could keep up with Milosz's tapping feet even when her jawbone transceiver couldn't pick up the bass.

The builder of the Palazzo della Misericordia was a particularly crafty and crass 17th-century merchant who made it a reliquary for his younger wife, an arranged match who was kept under lock and key and even wore a gruesome chastity belt (on display in the gallery downstairs) when her husband was away on business. She spent her captivity in this very room, where she practiced and became quite a master of the early violin on a collection that included Stradivari and Guarneri pieces. The walls and high barrel-vault ceiling were painted by a desperately down-at-heels Salvatore Rosa or an incredible counterfeiter, feverish sunset scenes swarming with nereids, mermaids and hosts of lusty cherubim, an orgy of suffocating sensuality the horny old patron must have hoped, most pathetically, would turn her on.

They were refurbishing the place, Bianca told her, and the owner was a patron of the local symphony. In lieu of a private tour of the Doge's Palace or the obligatory drink at Harry's Bar, Laurel had asked for somewhere out of the way, somewhere with not so many strange faces swimming up in her view, somewhere she could practice until her mother was asleep back at the luxurious Hotel Daniele, dreaming of all the soap and towels she would steal.

Bianca was supposed to come pick them up at 11. Her purse was somewhere in the room, with her phone in it.

Laurel noodled on her Squier Apostle violin as her mind drifted back to the snatch of a song that occurred to her as they'd enjoyed supper on the terrace. The reeling, vaguely sinister bit of music reminded her of Khachaturian or a Slavonic dance, with its austere yet decadent melody. It stuck in her mind until she hummed it, and it was not until she took up the gold-mounted Nurnberger bow and tucked the violin under her jaw and tried to pick out the damnably catchy thing that she realized she hadn't thought up the weird melody at all.

She'd *heard* it.

Somehow, that crooked little tune had bypassed her dead ears and entered her brain through the small hairs on the nape of her neck, or the membranes of her sinuses. When she'd mentioned it to Milosz and Bianca, they'd looked at her like she was selling them a bad joke.

She found herself scratching it out now, just goofing off until Milosz rallied, but he snored with his phone on his belly and his stubbly blue chin resting on the loose knot of his maroon silk tie. She was caught up in the deceptively tricky change as the melody circled back on itself faster, ever faster, until it tripped her up and she laid off with a nervous giggle.

As she turned to get up to wake Milosz to take her back to the hotel, she saw her little visitor.

He squatted on the faded brocade arm of the divan only a foot away from her. She was too startled even to leap off the seat. She caught her breath and giggled again, but her throat was dry and flat, a cracked straw. She slid away across the seat, took up her only protection, her violin and bow.

He was a little *Commedia d'ell Arte* harlequin in a soiled purple and gold silk tunic with tiny pom-poms down the front and a little peaked cap, and a cherubic face painted white with rosy cheeks and a big false smile and holes for eyes. A mask—no, a rubber doll's head, bobbing eagerly as if it was speaking to her.

Two warring impulses held her frozen. She had been terrorized more than once since she began to perform in public by other people's ideas of "gifts." Stalkers. Fetish-effigies of roses. Dolls, dogs and kittens and more dolls.

Don't freak out. Someone dressed a monkey as a clown and turned it loose in the apartment. Charming.

She looked around for Bianca, but they were alone. Forcing herself to move slowly so as not to startle it, she rose to wake Milosz. As soon as her stocking feet touched the floor, she felt the lurching tempo of the awful new song her accompanist was tapping out.

His soft leather moccasins drummed a spastic tarantella, his instrument unattended on the disheveled bed. He stumbled towards her, flailing his arms trying to catch something running up and down his chest and arms in a blur. She gasped and coughed now, *here come the clowns …*

They were monkeys, only mischievous, masked monkeys. Another one perched on his shoulder in black and white motley dappled with burgundy. It crouched lower thrusting out its rubber clown face in a whimsical challenge and brandishing a straight razor.

Milosz reached up to grab the tiny clown. A stroke of the blade effortlessly carved off a flap of forehead that folded over his right eye, then plowed the bridge of his nose and dropped into the bowl of his eye-socket, bisecting the left eye so its mysterious workings, proof of God's unmistakable grand design, peeked at her before vanishing in a red rush of oxygen-glutted blood.

The other harlequin clung to his herringbone trousers, merrily strumming the backs of his legs with its blade. Hamstring, Achilles tendon, femoral artery. Blinded and blindfolded by his own face, Milosz pirouetted and swooned, facedown at her feet like a smitten suitor.

Laurel spun on her heel and barked her shin against the divan hard enough to make her vision go to water. A blade-wielding monkey leapt at her just as the lights went out.

She took a step backwards in her stocking feet, shrieking and blindly swinging the violin, flinching when it smashed into something and flew apart, the jolt of mangled notes shooting up her arm. A great stone mass, a plaster bust of some eyeless Greek philosopher, crashed to the floor like a bowling ball at her feet.

Laurel jumped back, overbalanced and tumbled on her butt as something flew past her face, clawing at air, tail switching. Her whole body opened wide and screamed. The effort left her gasping, deafened by the thud of her racing heartbeat, inhaling icicles on elbows and knees crawling in the yellow-green murk from distant streetlamps, like an acid that seemed to slowly corrode, dissolve everything in its glow.

They say the other senses are enhanced to compensate when one goes deaf or blind. "They" are assholes. In her terror, with no idea what was in the room with her or what it wanted or even where the fucking door was, her whole body tried to be an ear, but the overwhelming riot of information left her going in every direction at once, flinching and twitching across the floor seeking anything at her back that wasn't alive.

She banged into something and a body hove out of the dark and fell on her. Shriek, kick out, flailing sideways and the hollow, voluptuous body of Milosz's cello throbbed with outrage as she knocked it out of its coffin.

Milosz—

She called his name. She was swimming in sticky black blood. Springing to her knees in hysterical disgust, she got up and staggered towards—no! away from—the light that fell on the overflowing flowerboxes on the windowsill.

The windows were on her left, so the stairs were on her right, at the far end of the barrel-shaped attic chamber. And there were three floors of empty, dark, mildewed rooms sheathed in plastic and bolstered by scaffolding between her and the street.

Laurel brushed her bangs out of her eyes and smeared blood across her forehead. Out, she had to get out *now.*

She crawled to the doorway, the neck of her shattered violin in her shaking fist like a makeshift club. She still couldn't see anything moving, but she could *smell* them, the acrid stink of urine and musk dominating the room, either from Milosz or something that peed on him.

Abruptly, she felt a wind at the nape of her neck. She spun and looked over her shoulder as she stepped through the doorway.

Even when her eyes adapted to the darkness, she couldn't see any distinct details in the room but the preternatural white of Milosz's shirt collar on the floor, the gloss of reflected light off the hip of his cello. Tiny arms wrapped around it, throttled the strings, shooting discordant vibrations up her feet, a screech she could feel with her whole face, and something lunged at her.

She pulled the door shut but it resisted, stuck on bloody wads of Persian rug. She threw up her hands as she danced backwards, stabbing with the neck of her violin, skittering down the stairs. The scarlet carpet runner tore loose from its tacks. Something ran just above her head over the rotted *trompe l'oeil* cherubs and nymphs on the vaulted ceiling, and then she tripped on something bigger than herself.

Laurel rolled in a tangle of helpless limbs and bloody black velvet to the bottom of the stairs. Reflex kicked her out of the tangle. She shoved the corpse back across the porphyry floor of the landing, shrieking without breath.

Bianca's throat was cut down to the vertebrae, her eyes gouged out, her purse slashed open and thoroughly rifled. They had taken her only minutes ago, probably when Laurel was still playing, blithely unaware of what was going on around her.

Off the attic stairs and she slid on blood-slick stockings into a corridor and hit the shaky railing with her hip, nearly plummeted headfirst down the main stairwell. Rolled off it and pushed, dragging herself by one hand on the splintery scaffolding, ancient paint flaking off under her other hand. She flew down the stairs like a trapped bird.

Molten pain bubbled up between her ribs. She crutched the wall, plaster crumbling like stale bread. She felt for a light switch and looked up, strained at the trickle of dim, iodine light down the stairwell, waiting for any shadow or motion to send her flying over the railing.

She went down to the second landing and the first, the ground floor in an almost robotic burst of motion, until she got off the stairs. A light was on by the door by which she'd come in. A water taxi had dropped them off, and Bianca had promised to return by 11, and she was dead upstairs and Laurel's blouse was plastered to her sides with the tour manager's blood, and nobody else knew where she was …

Laurel sagged backwards on her feet and she was fainting, the blood draining out of her head so fast it might be sluicing over her feet. She had fainted once from pain as a small girl and a couple times from heat stroke—only last week, in Rome, she'd wilted like a southern belle in a corset and hoop skirts in the sweltering heat.

She slapped her face and the sting in her left hand hurt worse than her cheek. Deep, yawning slash in the heel of her hand and a shallower one across her knuckles, from when it leapt at her face. She hadn't even felt it, but now her hands screamed with unbearable pain.

Bianca always walked a half step ahead of her, opened every door, took every hot cup of coffee for her, making the courtesy fluid and invisible, but always the intent was to protect Laurel's moneymaking hands.

No one was here, she was alone and it didn't matter if she understood what was happening. Whether she believed or refused it, they were going to kill her like they killed the others, but if she didn't get out now, she was going to seize up and drop dead, right here.

A broken, mewing cry came out of a crack in her, but she stuffed it shut. You're brave, all the nice reporters say so, because you get up in front of people and do the only thing you're good at, because you can play music you read on paper but never actually hear, and somehow, just not collapsing into a puddle of nerves because you can't enjoy what you make any more than a spider can enjoy the beauty of its web.

Once, she'd told a reporter that she'd rather be deaf than blind, because then she'd always be afraid, but now she was deaf and all but blind in a strange place, and she was more than a little stupid, as well, she might as well admit it. But she would be brave, like the little deaf prodigy that everybody said she was ...

OK ...

She was bleeding. She couldn't bear the thought of searching this place for a phone, let alone a first aid kit. She sat down against the wall and rolled off a stocking, but they were filthy and caked with clotting blood. Hardly the stuff for a tourniquet. She took the scrunchie out of her hair. It was sturdy elastic; it had to be, to hold Laurel's unruly curls at bay. She wrapped it around her wrist, doubling and doubling it until it staunched the bleeding. Instead of swelling up and turning blue, her hand simply tingled and seemed to go right to sleep. She couldn't keep it like this for long, it would start to die and gangrene could set in, and she wasn't into becoming the world's first deaf, one-armed violinist. She had to go ...

Her head whipped around constantly, searching every shadow for the things that killed Bianca and Milosz ...

This house—*palazzo*, remember, this place was nothing like any normal human house—was on a corner, an intersection of two canals, the romantically morose Rio Della Misericordia and the picturesque Rio Ghetto, on the island of Cannareggio. She had come in by a water taxi and then eaten a picnic supper on the little grassy terrace on the corner overlooking the wider canal and the narrow, gloomy gutter that flowed into it. There had to be a street door, a footbridge ...

Fumbling through one room after another, she finally identified the light switches, but they were shut off, or the fuses blown. She found nothing like a phone, but after casing four moldy rooms jammed with furniture older than America, she found an atrium and, at last, a door that seemed to lead out.

It was big as a barn door, with cumbersome locks requiring keys the size of small handguns. She fumbled up and down the door looking for the latch, jerked on it, twisting, squeezing with her right hand, but then she smelled that bitter, musky stench folding over her like an invisible cloud.

Panicked hands slapped and tugged on the bolts until the pain made her cry out, but she was locked in. Turning, arm up for the next attack, she ran into the next room, a dead end little bigger than a closet. When she turned around, she felt it grab a fistful of her hair and yank her backwards. Her knees gave out and she found herself hanging by her hair from a rusty coat hook.

Her eyes watered. Feeling almost relieved enough to laugh, she recovered her balance and untangled the knot of hair around the hook, but a good hank of her curls had been ripped out of her scalp. The pain cleared her head again. If she kept hurting herself like this all night, she just might stay awake.

She doubled back through a kitchen like a medieval torture chamber, and then found the back door. It was low and wide, but had only two simple bolts and a key in the lock that nearly unhinged her before she figured out how many twists it took to make it spring open.

She threw the door wide and stepped out into open air. Her foot splashed ankle-deep in tepid water, slid on slimy stone and waved her arms to catch the doorway, so she wouldn't fall head-first into the canal.

No walkway, no footbridge. Green-black water lapped the steps at her feet. There was no walkway on her side, not even a catwalk. The door opened on the narrow Rio del Ghetto, where a few damp scraps of laundry dangled from lines between the buildings.

A lacquered post projected out from the lintel just above her head, and a little fiberglass boat with a two-stroke outboard motor was tied with a nylon rope to a corroded ring set into the post.

Across the wider canal on her left, maybe thirty feet away, there were cracked cement steps and a deserted promenade lined with moored boats and a gelati shop, a shoemaker, and a boutique that sold wooden toys and music boxes, but all were shut up behind rusty rolldown doors and accordion bars. All the bustling noise and color from which she'd needed a retreat had vanished, leaving only acid-etched white and rose stonework and opaque, oily shadows.

Her backyard in Kansas wasn't particularly big, not even a quarter-acre, but there was one patch of ground in the middle where you could stand and look around and if you kept your back to the house, you could pretend there were no people, anywhere. The stand of willows blotted out the Toops' house next door, and the big sycamore hid the telephone pole and the wires that connected them to everything else. She had her tea parties there, she played explorer there, and she read books there after she lost her hearing and kids stopped coming over to play, but if you were in trouble and you hollered, someone would hear and come running, like when Mr. Toop had come over the fence calling 911 when Laurel fell out of the big sycamore.

This place was as unlike her home as anything she could imagine. Not a natural thing in sight, but no sign of life whatsoever. She screamed for help with her hand on her throat so she knew the sound was coming out, but no lights switched on, no one stirred behind those serried rows of shuttered windows with their rounded arches, the dead eyes of sleepers killed by a sweet dream.

She looked over her shoulder. They were still in there, somewhere. She wouldn't hear them coming if they wore bells round their necks, and she probably wouldn't see them until it was too late, anyway.

She could go try the front door again, but the idea alone made her hand throb and her heart hammer faster. There was no way out but the boat.

Steadying herself against the doorway, she knelt down on her right foot and stuck her left out to step in the shallow puddle of bilge in the floor of the boat. It was the same kind of little two-man skipper she and her dad had gone fishing in when she was little, but she still clung to the doorway with her good hand, lowering herself onto the bench as if it was red-hot.

A shadow fell across her face. She looked up.

It hung from the post over the doorway by its grasping feet and a tail as long as itself. Doll mask askew so white needle teeth and pink tongue glinted under the painted rubber head. Mouth wide in a silent screech, it reached down and grabbed a handful of her hair.

She reared back, raised an angry arm to strike the thing. It was not much bigger than a goddamn cat. The snarl of hair went taut as the boat shifted out from under her.

For just a second, she hung by her hair over the black water of the canal. The tiny harlequin couldn't possibly hold her weight. It didn't try.

The gleaming silver razor flashed out and hacked off the hair close to the root. Laurel tumbled over the side of the rowboat and landed butt-first in the cold black canal.

The water slapped her face and forced its filth into her nose and mouth. Eyes crushed shut, she clawed and kicked. One knee banged the hull of the boat. She turned over, rolling in her own backwash until she thought to follow the surging bubbles all around her.

Her head broke the surface. She flinched, arm coming up to guard her face, but it was gone. The doorway loomed, a gaping darkness. No way was she going back there, but the expanse of the canal now looked a lot wider than thirty feet.

Just around the corner from the kitchen door, she saw another staircase with a cold fluorescent light shining out of a narrow walkway between the palazzo and another crumbling ruin with blank rows of arched windows. She floundered away from the door and the boat and dog-paddled across the canal.

Crawling out onto the steps, she shivered with the chill. Her leggings clung to her legs, and her blouse had swollen to an ungainly drape with the water. She wrung it out, shaking, biting her lip at the pain in her hand.

Her throat was hoarse. She'd been screaming her head off the whole time, from when she first saw it to when she fell in the water, and no one had come. She cried out now, hand to her throat. Not a single light came on.

Maybe everyone was dead in their beds, throats cut by little visitors. It was easy to believe in her current state, and she almost found herself taking comfort in it. For behind every window, she knew, there was someone so deep in sleep or watching American football on satellite that they had no interest in the trifling problems of an American girl being hunted by manlike animals through the open sewers and walkways of their precious city.

Don't think like that, Laurel told herself. *Don't be like that. Don't use your fear to make hate; don't turn what's been thrown at you as a reason to give up.* That's what Mother would do, and she wasn't like Mother. She wasn't like anyone she knew. She would fight for her life, because she deserved to live.

The walkway turned into a footbridge that crossed the canal and went past an ostentatious portico with stained marble statuary around it that could only be the front door to the palazzo. She edged past it with her sodden back against the bricks of the opposite wall, as if it might swing open and they might come leaping out to cut her—

Shaking off her lethargy, she ran down the narrow passage, passing other doors and blind alleys until finally, she came out into a little plaza. The shops were closed up, every chair and display withdrawn like snails and anemones on a colorful reef when the predators swim past. No public phones, no lighted doorways. She passed a kiosk shaggy with posted bills and flyers, tear-away phone numbers for tours, all in Italian …

She screamed for help. The plaza couldn't even muster a proper echo. Venice was a necropolis; in place of the houses, shops and churches by day, now were only crypts, tombs and mausoleums.

She heard the music.

It was coming from three hundred years ago, but it was somewhere nearby. She *heard* it. The skirling, reeling melody looped through the air like cigarette rings, and she followed it down an avenue that tapered until it almost brushed her shoulders, through a pocket park and a deserted farmer's market until finally, she went over a bridge to an oddly shaped plaza with an ancient cistern like a capped fountain in the center next to a pile of rental kayaks.

The austere Romanesque dome of a miniature basilica terminated the plaza, funereal white marble blocks infested with saprophytic shrubs, towering bronze doors between Ionic columns like the entrance to a giant's tomb. A bas-relief circle and triangle on the pediment enclosed a staring eye like on the dollar bill. FONDAMENTA DE LA MADDALENA, proclaimed the guano-streaked legend beside the portico.

The only other way out of the plaza was a charming arch of a footbridge over a fetid gutter of a canal. At the peak of the bridge, she found the music's source.

As on so many other such European landmarks, the railing on the dead-end bridge was encrusted with locks of every description, from cheapo combination jobs to big bullet-proof keylocks, from garish pink heart-shaped locks manufactured for just such a gesture to rusted ingots of indescribable age, tokens of lovers long since gone to dust. She wished she had a lock to add to the others, but she would not name a man when she pledged the token, she would pledge her love to herself and music, and to never coming back to Italy again—

A man—a dwarf or a hunchback, she guessed, as she came closer—slouched against the cluttered railing, his face hidden by the brim of a battered black homburg hat, his body shapeless under a bulky, moth-eaten wool overcoat. One gloved hand turned the crank on a black lacquered box strapped to his chest, and the other steadied it on its single, wobbly leg. The music came out of vents like gills in the walls of the box, where the crank pumped air into a series of pipes to produce the simple but maddeningly seductive song.

Laurel had never seen an organ grinder before, except in a few very old cartoons, and she'd certainly never heard one. She should've guessed it was some kind of recording by the way it looped endlessly like a music box, but she hadn't heard music, or anything else, in almost five years. It was utterly bewitching, and all the more magical for all that she'd been through, since the first time she'd heard it. She almost hugged herself for joy at the sound.

At the *sound!*

She came within ten feet of the organ grinder—was that what you called the instrument, or the player?—pleading for help in her limited Italian.

Out came the lead cup. When she cried, the cup only banged against the box.

She patted herself down and pulled out her travel wallet on its lanyard around her neck. She would toss him a dollar, even a ten, and she would find out the name of the song, and directions to the Carabinieri or the Ospedale.

She didn't know much about organ grinders at all; not how they were outlawed in most of the world as a nuisance until they were long forgotten, and then unthinkable in an age when lawyers pounced on every illegal download and coffee shop singer-songwriter for playing their music. But just as she pulled out a soggy five-Euro note from her pocket and folded it, approaching to stuff it in, she remembered something about the organ grinders in the cartoons.

They always had monkeys.

The organ grinder's gloved hand reached out on an arm nearly as long as she was tall, caught her hand and crushed it around the wet money.

Planting her feet, she gagged on her pitiful scream. She could barely feel it coming out of her, she had so little breath left.

It was barely three feet tall, but she stubbed her toe and helplessly skidded over the paving stones trying to escape its iron grip. He reared up to his full height of over four feet and dragged her closer.

His head tilted back so the dingy streetlight fell on a long, bone-white proboscis and eyeholes painted to look like spectacles. It was a plague doctor mask like you could but at any souvenir stand around the city. It hid his whole face, but not his neck or his steeply sloping shoulders, which bristled with a filthy silver pelt.

She tried to wrench free and run, but she felt something land on her shoulder, yank hair and slash at her scalp.

She saw the mask slip away, saw a mouth big enough to bite off her hand. Canine teeth longer than her ring finger.

It dragged her closer.

She stopped resisting, flew at the organ grinder and brought her knee up into its barrel chest, smashed into his shiny black box.

She felt its roar down her arm, felt the spit-flecked hurricane in her face. The monkey leapt off her shoulder as the enraged organ grinder whipped her off her feet by her arm, popping her arm out of its rotator cuff.

She floated almost over its head, and she thought she could float away on the stifling night air.

She jackknifed in midair as it yanked her down by her tether and slammed her into the bridge railing.

⸙

She woke up in the middle of a Stravinsky overture.

Thunder rumbled in sync with the sickening sensation of being dragged down an endless flight of stairs. She lay on jagged stones and rusty metal that conducted the thunder and shrieking like violins in a woodchipper, howls like someone ran the brass section over with a steamroller. And crushing it all, the hammering of a hundred tympani in a mad anvil chorus in her head.

She struggled. Wet, brine-crusted canvas shrouded her, pressed against her face. Sea-spray stung her arms. She was hanging over the gunwale of a little boat speeding over black water. The surging, bucking motor drowned all other sound, the stink of gasoline and musky reek of her captors. Her leggings stuffed full of rocks.

Hands like pitchforks, knotted with muscle, hoisted her over the rail until she hung by her waist. A wave slammed into her head, soaking the canvas so it clung to her face. She sputtered and gagged, sucked in half a breath of air before it happened again.

Hands behind her back, pinned by a bigger hand grinding the bones of her wrists together, levering her over the edge by her dislocated shoulder.

She screamed and the heavy hands went away and she rolled back into the boat, tossing her head until the canvas fell away from her face and she saw two white-headed monkeys clawing at the organ grinder. Swatting at them, the powerful thing reared up near the bow of the racing boat, nearly capsizing it. Its hat blew off as they sliced away its plague-doctor mask.

Laurel saw its face.

She fainted.

⁓

That *face—*

When she woke up, it was waiting for her.

Eyes like tiny orange beads tucked under a shaggy shelf of brow. Brighter than blood, its narrow nasal ridge was a brilliant scarlet stripe down its massive, flat face, cutting between corrugated ridges of luminous electric blue on his cheeks. Silver-gray fur formed a tuft atop his tapered skull and a yellow-stained goatee framed his crimson lips. His enormous jaws opened wide, baring vicious yellow canines and incisors like chisels, spraying spittle in her face.

Only then did she see the crosshatched cuts on its snout and brow, the dull beads of dried blood dappling its muzzle and matted fur. *Did I do that?* she wondered, and knew she didn't.

Her head hurt, she was terrified and cold, but giving a name to it made it real, something she could deal with.

Mandrill. She'd never seen one in a zoo or circus, but they stole pies in Richard Scarry's big picture books, and she'd seen nasty pictures of the brilliant displays their rumps put on in mating season. Even in the kid books, the creatures scared the shit out of her.

A mandrill was not an ape, but the biggest of the monkeys, and this one was a giant among its kind. Even crouching on all fours in the overcoat, it came up to her waist, if it would let her stand, which it would not.

She was chained to the trailer hitch of a big van inside a big, dark

220

building that smelled of rot and charcoal and piss. A warehouse with a few rat-gnawed packing crates, bulging with damp, piled up where no one would ever come to claim them. A few bars of milky morning light leaked in through high, narrow windows between crooked sheet-metal walls.

The mandrill snarled in her face again and loped away to the other side of a dying fire. He unslung a satchel from his shoulder under the overcoat and pawed through its contents. Gold watches, jewelry, wallets, cash rolls and passports. Its other hand rested on the organ box beside its hip.

Three monkeys in harlequin costumes perched on crates around the fire, gnawing on rotten fruit, rancid french fries and scraps of fetid fish.

She'd certainly not watched a whole lot of her mother's detective mystery shows, but you didn't have to be the *Murder She Wrote* lady to figure out what happened.

Someone put her in the boat and stuffed her clothes full of rocks. She slowly began pulling them out, piling them behind herself. Paving stones and hunks of broken concrete from the plaza. Someone was going to murder her, and she hadn't seen anyone holding the mandrill's leash. There was no one else in the little boat.

A *monkey* had taken steps to murder her and dump her body. She shivered like a cold hand stroked her diaphragm, freezing her bowels. But something stopped him.

There was no one else on that boat, but the monkeys …

Capuchin monkeys, she thought, all credit due to nature shows on PBS. They ate busily, mouths working and seeming to screech and chatter at each other, but they all took furtive sidewise glances at her as they feuded.

She didn't see any signs that anyone human was in charge, here. But someone must've taught them to steal. Animals could learn just about anything, if you were patient enough. She wondered how many lessons the mandrill needed, to do what it tried to do. She wondered why the three little monkeys saved her. She wondered if she wouldn't be better off at the bottom of the Grand Canal.

The mandrill fingered a bunch of gold chains, staring at her. Waiting for her to go to sleep, or for Master to come home. Maybe it could plan a murder, but she doubted it could spend its loot anywhere outside of a vending machine.

The bars of gray light swept across the floor like searchlights as the day waxed and waned. The capuchin monkeys ran in and out of the van, but the mandrill sat on its lurid, callused ass, fingering gold and occasionally baring its fangs.

Given its druthers, it would come over and bite her face off. There had to be a reason.

She cleared her throat and tried to ask him not to hurt her in Italian, then tried Amerslan, International Sign and the little bit of Italian sign language she'd picked up for a reception in Milan where she'd addressed a school for the deaf. *No-me-hurt*, she signed. *I-you-help*.

If she could just get out of her chains, out of the warehouse, she could get away, find someone. There was still a world, there were still people in it, and any one of them would save her …

After a long while, when she had not seen the monkeys and the mandrill had not moved for an hour, she realized it was asleep sitting up, and they were alone.

Rising on her knees with a broken brick ready in one hand, she gathered up the chain in the other to muffle the slightest sound. The mandrill twitched, snarled, bared his fangs at a nightmare.

She couldn't get away and the lock was sturdier than any lover's token padlock. The cuff on one hand and one ankle were heavy old-school shackles. Three guesses whose they were, she thought.

She felt weak and sleepy, but if she let go, she would slide into shock. Her vision was kind of blurry. If you had a concussion, you weren't supposed to go to sleep. Her hand was still numb, though the scrunchie tourniquet was long gone.

She couldn't get away, but she could get inside the van. If she could move. When the time came, her limbs wouldn't obey her simplest commands.

The part she didn't like about being famous was when people who didn't know you said things about you. They always said she was brave. Some critics said she was like a robot, a sideshow act and bad for music, because she couldn't hear the performance, because she only heard her own music in her head. How could such a defective player relate to Beethoven? But they all agreed first that she was very *brave*, so they wouldn't look like assholes.

Music had always been her comfort and her compass, a way of ordering her mind, her life and the world, when everything else was a dirty, maddening tangle. She had always wanted to be a great musician, for as long as she could remember. Mother always told her so.

When she was sick, when the fever got so bad that her auditory nerves died in her head, she wasn't brave. She had gone so far past asking God to take her life, past thinking God must not care and maybe might not exist at all, to a place where none of it mattered. The Fever would burn it all in the end, even God, if there was one. When she woke up to find herself alive in the quiet place and Mother talking to the doctors and then to reporters about their decision not to vaccinate Laurel, she went on and on about how brave her daughter was, and Laurel's first conscious thought upon recovery was that Mother didn't know her at all.

Laurel wasn't brave, then or now. She was pretty sure she'd peed her pants, but anyone else would've done the same. But anyone else would get up and do something, she goaded herself.

Her arm tucked under her head was asleep. At the slightest motion, the needles in it turned to teeth. She choked down a hot green scream behind her tingling fingers.

Rolling onto her hip, with her eyes on the mandrill, she put her hand on the rusty bumper of the van and reached for the loading door. It hung just slightly ajar so the monkeys could get in and out, but she didn't see them. They were probably inside. She thought of what they did to Milosz and Bianca. Her stomach revolted until she closed her eyes and willed it away. There's no one else, she told herself.

Hand on the door. She wouldn't know if the rusty thing made a sound until the mandrill woke and came down on her. She held her breath and made herself look at him as she took hold of the door, nudging it wider with her shoulder.

He growled, flinched and brushed away a fly.

Swallow. Breathe. *Push*—

She levered herself up into the van an ounce at a time, feeling every incremental shift of the derelict chassis on its blown-out shocks.

Inside smelled—surprise surprise—like a monkeyhouse. Blocking her nose, she still tasted it on her tongue, coating her throat and burning her eyes. The dark and the musk and piss and dander clung to her and bound up all her senses, so she had only her fingers.

She felt bars.

She crouched there with her hands slowly creeping over cages and cases of musical gear and tools and hardware, racks of silk and burlap and wool costumes, so she thought she knew the space pretty well by the time her eyes adjusted to the light filtering through the filthy windshield.

The three monkeys sat on top of a row of small cages in the corner, motionless, holding their razors. Watching her. She froze, tried to freeze her mind.

Why didn't you kill me? You killed those others ... The monkeys were trained thieves. Murder wasn't what they were supposed to do; they had gotten along quite well doing what they did, but something went wrong last night.

Me.

She thought of the song she'd heard, yes, she'd *heard* it, somehow, that insidious tune that seemed to bypass her ears to tantalize her naked nerves.

The walls of the van were scabby with posters. The oldest ones were for jazz and prog rock concerts in Italy, Portugal and Spain. There were boxes of LP's for said jazz combos and rock bands. The newer posters, still nearly as old as Laurel, were for something called Professor Ugo's Camera Musichanica, which was apparently a gigantic automated one-man band operated by a mandrill in a clown costume and conducted by a deranged-looking man in an antique tuxedo with a crude prosthetic right hand, holding an old-fashioned listening horn to his ear. Little cameos identified the three scampering monkey harlequins as Otto, Lotto and Blotto.

A rack of mothball-stinking costumes hung from hooks on one wall, and an abbreviated workbench against the other was buried in gears, pipes, chimes and cannibalized bits of musical instruments, and the guts of various antique music boxes. A cheap old viola with crude amp pickups rested on a pile of junk, the horsehair bow beside it fitted with a socket that probably attached to a prosthesis. With no hand, an old man tried to keep making music. With no ears, he tried to make music he could still hear. He should have been famous, she thought, and touring Italy. What happened to him?

The smell coming from the big cage in the far corner was worse than monkeys. She had to force herself to get closer. It was in the dark behind the passenger seat and had a cheesecloth sheet over it. She lifted it up but only wafted a gust of toxic dust into her face without seeing anything. Closing her eyes, clamping her mouth shut, she pulled the cloth off the cage.

She felt moth wings brush her face and then a blast of fetor that made her dry-heave onto the floor between her knees. Through watering eyes, she saw a lovingly hand-lettered legend in Gothic script clipped to the cage. IVO, it said.

It had to be the name of the mandrill outside, but the thing inside the cage could only be Professor Ugo.

It was like a shrine, albeit a deeply conflicted one. A skull and a jointed rubber and steel prosthetic arm and a painfully arranged tableau of bones rested on the rags of a rotted black tuxedo like the relics of Saint Mark in the cathedral yesterday, but every one of them was chipped, cracked, broken in half. To get the marrow, she thought. They loved him enough to enshrine his body in a cage, after they ate him.

She wondered whose idea that was.

She looked at Otto, Lotto and Blotto. *See no evil, hear no evil, speak—*

The back doors flew open. Laurel turned. Ivo yanked her chain, dragged her out of the van by ankle and wrist. Her hands grabbed at the junk on the workbench, at something that caught her eye just before she lost her grip on Ivo's cage and flew out into his waiting arms.

The floor came rushing up and she threw out both arms to save her head. Both elbows hit the bumper, the funnybone jolt made her cry out and drop what she was holding.

He dragged her away from the van to the extent of the chain. Laurel rolled into a ball and cowered before him, weeping, waiting for him to crush her, but instead, he took up the organ box and began to turn the crank.

She could hear only her pulse thundering in her head, and then she could hear the song. Rolling and reeling on its circuitous, looping track, the tune infused her limbs with a languorous numbness, a sense that all was going to be okay, that she could roll over and cover herself in dirt like a warm, soft eiderdown and sink into deep sleep and remember none of this when she woke up.

She only sank deeper as Ivo turned the crank faster. The somnolent, inscrutable melody took on a sinister urgency, an inevitability like galloping towards a cliff.

They fell on her, the tiny hands, the shiny razors. Her hair was flayed away and fell from her head like leaves. Her hands were slashed and stabbed wherever they tried to block the attacks. Through her fingers, her whiplashing eyes took in the maddened, automaton-expressions of the monkeys, the mechanical attacks that only seemed to grow more urgent, more thirsty for blood, when she cried out their names.

And then it all stopped.

The music fell off into the old, familiar total silence. The blood-flecked harlequins froze, then shook and screeched, but cowered at Ivo's mute roaring.

The monstrous organ grinder turned the crank, shook the organ box, but something had gone wrong inside it. Ivo and Laurel came to the same conclusion simultaneously.

When she'd kicked it, the mechanism inside had come off its tracks or thrown a gear, and now the music, the last vestige of control, was gone.

The mandrill shook the box and howled, raised it over his head as if to bring it down on Laurel's skull. The monkeys stopped attacking her, but remained frozen in the violent silence.

She had no other way to make herself heard, no other instrument.

So she whistled.

The first notes were quavering, spit-flecked, tuneless. But she licked her lips and blew again, truer, cleaner, feeling the notes coming out through her lips and resonating through her jaw and down in her chest. She whistled the melody as slowly as her racing heart and hysterical mind would allow. She closed her eyes and made herself keep it up when Ivo hit her with the box.

The heavy lacquered wood crashed down on her shoulder, her head, her ribs, but she kept it up.

Something crawled across her. She tucked her chin down into her chest to protect her throat, but the tiny feet raced up the length of her and sprang off her, into Ivo's face.

The mandrill retreated, swinging the ruin of the organ box, sending a torrent of gears and pipes scattering across the warehouse. The monkey clung to his face until he reached for it, then leapt away, and another ran up his back, chopping at his matted pelt with a razor, sending Ivo in a twisting, tail-chasing rampage.

She kept whistling, though she could barely make the sound, barely find the breath. One of them crept up beside her and pushed it into her hand, then. What she'd had in her hand when he dragged her out of the van. She'd only had a moment to notice it, but it had all come racing home in her head.

Why they came for her and took Milosz and Bianca, but protected her from their fearsome master.

They came when she played the song. Seduced away from their rounds among the open windows and unwary tourists of miasmal Venice, they had come for her because she summoned them, when she played their song.

All the crazy things in the back of your mind that you think an audience will do to you, if you fail them. Laugh at you? Pelt you with shit and garbage? Rip your clothes off? Kill you and eat you and make a banner of shame out of your skin? All those buried nightmares had come true at once, but at least she didn't have to listen. She closed her eyes, she tucked the cheap gypsy violin under her chin and began to play.

At first, she scratched out the melody as she had before, finding her way on the woefully untuned instrument, but as soon as she had taken its measure, she put the melody through cycles of variations, tightening it from its playful menace to something colder and sharper, turning the drunken slurs into spiky pizzicato spurs, wintery flourishes that spurred it ever faster. As good as she was before an orchestra, the critics were right. She couldn't hear anyone else, and that held her back. Now she opened her eyes and no one was conducting her. The music poured out of her and played the little monsters like her own fingers.

She felt Ivo's pounding gallop approach her. Blood flew from a hundred tiny cuts. He raised a paw to grab Laurel by the throat. Lotto ran up under the overcoat and cut something inside the mandrill's armpit. The massive arm swung from its socket, throwing him off balance. Ivo roared. His other paw caught Lotto by the neck and crushed her skull like an egg.

Licking the mess off his paw, he turned on Laurel, cradling his useless arm like a dead baby, bared yellow fangs and charged.

She lay on her injured side, knees huddled up to her chest, playing their song as fast and as hard as the strings would allow.

Otto clung to the mandrill's shoulder, swung around his face and shoved his straight razor into the gaping maw. Ivo bit down on it, taking off the arm at the elbow and swallowing the razor.

Ivo skidded to a stop against Laurel and then sprang sideways to land on his back, thrashing and vomiting bright blood in crimson Catherine wheels, all over Laurel and the walls and the floor and the fire.

She lay in the dirt and cried and when she tried to get up, she couldn't.

She woke to them poking her. She crawled backwards. The light from outside was yellow and fading to orange. Outside, people could be passing by in cars and on foot, and she would never know.

Otto had a little hook wired to his charred stump, and a ring of keys in the other. She held up the lock but Otto only shook the key and pointed his hook.

At the violin.

Shaky, wheezing around broken ribs, she reached out for it and picked it up. Just out of reach, he shook the keys again and pointed at the bow.

"Let me go!" she screamed. She tried signing it every way she knew how, but the problem wasn't communication. He knew what she wanted.

Something crawled up on her shoulder. A prehensile tail tickled the crook of her spine. Blotto, the third monkey, still wore his rubber doll mask. He showed her the razor.

Shivering, she tried to play their song.

At the first wrong note, Blotto chopped off half her right ear. She jerked and screamed, grabbed for him, but he was gone.

A slash opened down her shoulder blade. Her hand recoiled from upon finding the naked grin of bone. She was fading into shock, and he would keep cutting and biting her until she played, and they didn't want to hear the organ grinder's tune ever again, now they were the masters.

She made herself put away the pain and the terror, and started to play the opening Verdi piece for tonight's concert.

Her audience ate it up. When they were happy, they fed her as she played, and when she couldn't stop crying, they let her play something sad.

When the sun finally faltered and faded and purple shadows seeped out of the corners of the warehouse, the monkeys scampered up into the rafters and out into the night. Laurel howled her throat raw and passed in and out of delirium. The cuts on her body had stopped screaming and now merely moaned with a sickly weight she knew was infection. She made herself crawl to the extent of her chain because settling down would mean falling asleep and probably never waking.

Surely, someone would have come to the palazzo looking for her and found the bodies, surely the police were looking for her, surely her mother—

Even if they were hunting high and low, they would never find her in time. In the far corner of the warehouse, where the stench of damp and fish was worst, she noticed wires hanging out of a hole in the wall near the floor. She thought of a TV movie she'd seen once with her parents, where a girl was kidnaped and stuffed into a car's trunk. She pulled the wire out of the taillight and used it to make the lights flash S-O-S until someone called 911 and the police saved her.

Whatever the cables were, the damage looked fresh, and the cables themselves stirred something in her. A twinge of familiarity.

She was jerked off her feet by the taut chain, and had to drag agonizingly on it to acquire enough give to reach to the cable.

It looked like a bigger, older version of the voltage cables in the big old Tannoy amplifiers in many concert halls. It had been disconnected from a hardwired power outlet, and ran into the back of a big amplifier box set into the chilly exterior wall, so the speaker projected out over the canal.

It had to be some kind of alarm, but it was too big for a fire bell. Then it occurred to her, something Milosz told her just before they sat down to rehearse tonight, about the horns that blared a low, mournful drone at high tide. They must have disconnected it to silence the horn. They must have hated the sound. It might drive them berserk if she could reconnect it, but to what purpose? They would take their rage out on her, and she wouldn't even know for certain if she could make the horn go off, or if anyone would notice.

She fumbled with the amplifier, prying at the rusty panel on the back until she managed to get it off. The components weren't so different from a concert hall system, except for the lack of input jacks, but a plastic component with variable pitch controls on it was clearly the tone generator module, with a thick soldered cord running to the back of the speaker cone. She ripped the end out of the tone generator, stripped away the rubber sheath with her teeth and wound the silver and copper wire cores around the pickups on her violin.

It looked crude but functional, but the brutally severed power cable, with its snarl of exposed copper wires, left her petrified. In the end, she told herself, she was wearing rubber-soled shoes, and that meant she was insulated … right? It was scant comfort, but she had seen her father connect batteries a hundred times. In the end, she told herself, if she was electrocuted, she might die before she felt it, and surely a lot faster than the monkeys would let her.

She bit her lip and picked up the cable, pulled the severed plug out of the outlet and braided the copper together, then gingerly snugged the corroded prongs into the oversized outlet, eyes squeezed shut, waiting to explode.

The plug spat sparks that sent her jumping backwards, but it didn't strike her dead. The low throb of the hot channel tingled her hand when she touched the back of the amp.

Now, she looked long and hard at the wired violin. She had to force herself to reach for it and take up the bow, holding it by the awkward socket screwed onto it for the use of the unfortunate Professor Ugo. The strings crackled under her fingers, the feedback loud enough she felt it in the bones of her ears, even if she couldn't hear it.

Whatever she did, they would come back for her. They had killed their masters, human and animal, and they wouldn't risk her escaping them. She was all the music they had left. She might be able to control them if she played their tune, but she doubted it would protect her, anyway.

So she played the last song she'd rehearsed. "The Devil Went Down To Georgia."

The wounds in her hands sang grand opera, split open and blood streamed down her arms, but she leaned into the dizzyingly complicated redneck aria that the Europeans always requested.

She could not know if the amp was relaying her performance out over the water, or if the monkeys had shredded the speaker and she was just entertaining herself, she would never know …

Before she got to the Devil's solo, they came.

One of them pounced on her back and immediately sliced her shoulders and neck. She hunched over and threw herself back into the wall. The monkey ran down her arm, slashing at the neck of the violin.

The other monkey ran up the back of the amplifier and took hold of the power cable with its hook, then chopped through the cable with its razor.

The flash blinded her. The concussion flung her away from the amp, but the purple image of the one-armed harlequin attacking the cable floated in the darkness with her as she rolled over and over, flailing at the other blood-mad monkey. She was a mask of blood when she caught it and trapped it under her weight and throttled it in her hands, and she was still strangling the lifeless little doll when the Venezia carabinieri came blundering into the warehouse, drawn by her song and then by the guttural growling screams she didn't realize she was making.

They bundled her up and put her on a gurney, but someone thought to give her the violin. The strings were severed and smeared with her blood, but she clung to it, humming the hypnotic song and wondering in the last little sane corner of her mind, what would happen when she played it for Mother.

OF A THOUSAND CUTS

Only in the final, volatile moments of the ludus, when vows made by will are broken by flesh, does the Samurai forget himself and mar his hitherto flawless performance by trying to die.

Dragging his left leg, javelin jutting from butchered knee, hastily resected bowel waving like a gory pennant, yet the Samurai circles his remaining opponent with calculated poise, herding him downwind of the black, creamy smoke wafting from the pyre of his identical twin.

Frenzy and fatigue vie to take the Roman even before the Samurai can close with him. Plunging his broken *katana* into the smoldering corpse to goad his enemy, the Samurai presents his *wakizashi* like a gift and settles into a waiting pose.

The Roman has abandoned all technique. Draws a whickering, whooping breath into the broken basket of his ribs, roars hollow, blood-flecked hate and charges through charnel smoke, gladius swinging in a blind woodsman's *coup de grace.*

And then the moment that puts the lie to perfection, proclaims it the act not of a masterful athlete, but of a slumming, drunken god, or a troubled automaton. Samurai bows his head, arms out in supplication. Throws up an arm, not in defense, but to tear off his helmet. Impossible, of course …

The Roman's chopping stroke shears an antler from the Samurai's helmet and glances off his leather cuirass. Overextended, he tramples his opponent and lands among his brother's blazing remains. Before any outside his inner cadre have recognized his mistake, the Samurai recovers and hamstrings the Roman. Wakizashi eagerly swims up hyperextended calf muscle, flensing meat catbox bitter with lactic acid from spiral-fractured bones.

The Roman turns, seemingly revived by blood loss. Brings the gladius down on the Samurai's shoulder, splitting the torso down to the solar plexus. What little blood comes out at all is almost black.

The wakizashi quivers, sheathed to the hilt in the Roman's kidney.

Samurai's hand touches but can't grasp it. The Roman's spade-shaped sword twisting in the burst balloon of his lung. With his other hand, Samurai draws the javelin from his knee. Nearly faints, but somehow he drives the long spike up through the corded muscles of the Roman's neck, penetrates the ribbed vault of the hard palate and into the cavernous echo chamber of the gladiator's brain.

It takes nearly another minute for the Roman's body to get the message.

It takes the surgical team another seven minutes to separate the bodies and check vital signs to certify the winner. The Roman called Pollux, though stabbed in nine places and burned to the third or fourth degree over ninety percent of his body, almost survives the night.

Shot up with painkillers and adrenochrome, the Samurai lurches out of the arena using the Roman's enormous gladius as a crutch, to the muted cheers of the small, select audience.

⸙

In the time after a battle, is when it gets worst. He can almost remember who he is.

He knows he had a name.

Before this.

His name.

It was … something.

But in the Pageant …

Now … again and forever … he is the Samurai.

Rumors swirl about the champion few choose to fight, relegated to sideshow matches in pariah state secret circuses. All but destroyed in six of fifteen matches in nine years, but undefeated, and none have ever seen his face. Even in the pitch-black demimonde of the Pageant, the Samurai is a cipher, his identity insignificant next to the paradox of his survival. Students of the art point to the many awful injuries sustained; not even the Pageant's surgeons could rebuild such terrible carnage. Indeed, from one match to the next, the Samurai gains or sheds weight and height. Lord Sun makes no promises regarding the identity of the Samurai. Only the masked helmet and the mated swords and the implacable, elegant butchery remain the same.

And yet, the obligatory devil's advocates must insist, compare the perfect discipline, the rigor of technique maintained even unto dismemberment, the reflexive disdain for mere mortal injury, the true absence of fear of death or pain. No matter how many bodies he's gone through, it could only be the same man.

After Lord Sun has viewed his champion and given his orders, the surgeons take Salazar off life support. From behind his mask, he can see the locker room and the masked doctors slick with his blood, drugged with his secrets.

"We've learned so much from him, but all of it useless." Tsukue, the surgeon, changes his gloves while his nurse fills a Styrofoam cooler with ice. "A doctor is wasted on this one. He only needs a seamstress."

He knows he is a freak. No other bodies share his readiness for transplants. He knows they've tried to make a transplant enzyme agent from his blood.

When he can remember, he tries to spare his opponents' limbs so he'll have a ready spare parts bank in the locker room. Two out of three donors are compatible with any body with his blood flowing through its veins, and anything that can be laser-stitched together can be walked out in, and might not be rejected for weeks.

Dr. Balance wears no blood, but Salazar's stink is all over him, oozes out his ears. The hypnotist is as responsible as the surgeons for the miracle of the Samurai. He smiles and dangles a pendant that swings and makes fiery mandalas of the light. Tsukue catches himself staring at it and curses. He takes a phone call and immediately waves to the hypnotist, pointing at Salazar as if he can't see.

Salazar tries to talk around the tubes down his throat. "I can … come back …"

They cannot fix him in time for the next ludus. Even if the bowel could be bypassed, the torso is cracked. *Look down, boy. That blue shirttail … That's your lung, the one that still works.*

"I can't feel it …"

The hypnotist bows. He must prepare Salazar.

"You can replace everything. They know I won't reject it … He just wants to send me … back there …"

Holding up the pendant, he sighs. They have a comprehensive donor. Perfect match, and as he understands, a young Caucasian, and even uncircumcised. Congratulations are in order. Salazar is going home, after a fashion.

Salazar reaches out, twisting the hypnotist's wrist. He could break it and do many terrible things with a greenstick fracture before the hypnotist could even scream.

But Dr. Balance would not scream. He would have only to utter a control word and all the memories Salazar has carefully buried, that should have killed him by now, would rise up to crush him.

"Set me free."

The hypnotist shakes his head. "I have tried to teach you …"

Breathing exercises. Counting sheep. "I can't … Go back, I … Won't …"

"Please." Red hands free, the hypnotist waves away the surgeons and the bodyguard. "Are you an enthusiast of haiku?"

"I hate poetry."

"The haiku is a perfect translation of a dream of a moment. But a moment, as you must know, may contain lifetimes …"

Salazar begs. "Just let me loose … His own people despise him. They won't kick once he's put down. I don't want anything but that. You can have it all …"

"I am sorry not to oblige, but I already have so much more than I want in this life."

"I can't go out and come back, again … all over again. I can't …"

"But you can. You have and you will. This is your seventh body, after all. What a wonder you are! You have cheated death, but who would share your secret?"

"Fuck you … Set me free. Kill me …!"

"Matsuo Basho's haiku lose nearly all their potency in English, but listen carefully." Swinging the pendant in front of Salazar's remaining eye until it defocuses, he recites,

"A cuckoo cries,
And through a thicket of bamboo,
The late moon shines."

Salazar's agitated, bubbling wheeze subsides to a soft, circular rasp.

"Did you hear the cuckoo?"

Salazar nods.

"Did you see the moon shining through the bamboo?"

Choking, he trembles and says, "Yes."

"Then you are free." Pocketing the pendant, he nods to the surgeons, who winch Salazar down and pump a cocktail of drugs similar to that used in California's Death Row into him while a third technician enters with a portable guillotine.

***

The Dark would be nothing to fear, if only it were empty.

His Darkness is an invisible orgy of bodiless abominations. Hardboiled horrors within soft-boiled eggs. Cracked and showing him unbearable visions, the worst of all possible worlds …

His.

Amerasian war-trash, street-raised in Saigon after Papasan went home with Uncle Sam and killed himself without producing a legitimate male heir. Suddenly, the family came looking, and eventually got Salazar immigrated to the United States.

He made them pay, though whether for neglecting him so long or for dragging him into a world he could never understand, even he never knew.

Boxing cultivated his skill for inflicting harm into a genius. He acquired a rep for cracking skulls with his fists. Bad temper got him blackballed, sold downriver. Gray-market cage-fighting. After he killed an opponent in a practice bout, he was jailed and forgotten.

Salazar in Folsom lockdown, a walking death penalty. Gladiator school. Shivved seven times; disciplined for nine jailhouse murders, thirty assaults. Recruited into the Pageant at twenty-two. For nostalgic value, he is christened the Cong.

His signature move: crack the chest and cut out the beating heart. Fuck Vietnam. Fuck America and absentee Papasan.

Call me the Aztec.

Twelve main events … and then a brutal, pyrrhic championship that left him unable to defend his title until a tissue donor could be found to give him new hands. When his cumulative injuries couldn't be repaired for competition, he was retired.

Burning with bitterness, denied a glorious exit, circling a funeral pyre. Out of his search for the ideal death, he found the cult of the samurai. He acquired a sword and a book of Mishima and a promise of inner peace.

It didn't last. Lord Sun's people found him in a Myanmar prison that had exploited his talents to relieve overcrowding. Lord Sun bought Salazar from the prison and took him in as a bodyguard for his family.

Under Lord Sun's wide, shadowy wing, Salazar trained fighters and courted wisdom, but when he expected it least, his anger was abruptly snuffed out.

All his life, he had paid for the damage inflicted by his anger. But it was his first true act of love that condemned him to *ling chi*, the Hell of Slow Slicing.

Just like his father, the new dictator has his guests waited upon by starving, malnourished servants. Jaundiced eyes slather every sumptuously overloaded platter with longing and loathing like an exquisite condiment, complementing the savory spice of terror infused into every dish by the slaves in the kitchen.

Salazar eats with his handlers in a bunker beneath the arena in a subterranean athletic complex that could adequately host the Olympic games, if it were not in an insane dictator's hermit kingdom, and if the Olympic committee was more receptive to bloodsports.

At least twice that Salazar knows of, he has been served human flesh, this time in some weird approximation of beef bourguignon with plum sauce. He recalls a period when gray, freezer-burned pork was a daily staple. Rancid, but he devoured it grimly and doesn't remember why it was so important to have it inside him …

Tsukue worries that Salazar shouldn't try to eat, that intubation is the only sure way to stave off infection of the ridiculously elaborate tapestry of microsutures and meat-glue holding together his new head. But tonight, Lord Sun has made an exception and provided every comfort. Even his owner expects him to get demolished by whatever's ripping the plumbing out of the concrete walls of the adjoining bunker.

Only two days in the Dark this time, they told him. Only two eternities. After the third transplant, he has never come all the way back. The surgeons tirelessly recorded his impressions. He no longer registers colors, except in sporadic, terrifying bursts. Pain is a capricious and fickle liar; sometimes a grievous wound goes unnoticed until he slips in his own blood, but phantom agonies like being burned alive suddenly assail him in his sleep, as if his well-traveled nerves had become some sort of shortwave for picking up the world's pain. His motor skills, however, have become uncannily refined. Dr. Tsukue credits his revolutionary dendrite braiding technique, which might've rendered spinal injuries curable, if anyone in his peer review group thought cripples were worth saving.

Salazar wants to stab someone. Something in a time-release drip makes him drop his fork. His hands slur across the table like drunken crabs. Dr. Balance comes in and the food is taken away. The hypnotist gives him another haiku, repeats it until Salazar can see the moon and his breath as crystals …

While he is distracted, they put the helmet on. An authentic but heavily rebuilt Edo Era helmet of bronze, steel and lacquered wood sheathed in a carbon fiber mesh, with a bronze facemask. Lord Sun's engineers reinforced the dome of the helmet to stop anything short of a sniper's bullet.

Lord Sun has invested more in Salazar than in the rest of his stable combined, but not to bring victory in the Pageant. Lord Sun would give his whole fortune to insure that Salazar will continue to survive and suffer forever.

The technician takes the surgical steel screws out of his breast pocket and closes his eyes to fight down panic. The gong has sounded and it'll be his ears if the Samurai misses his entrance. He fits the first screw on the 1/16" Phillips driver of a two-speed cordless drill and sets it into the recessed guide over the insulated hole in Salazar's left occipital bone.

The senior engineer usually uses an ordinary manual screwdriver to remove and attach the Samurai's helmet. His trainers use a penlight-sized screwdriver.

Though Salazar is heavily sedated, he jerks as if stabbed in the face just as the technician applies the screw.

The spinning steel screw sinks up to the hilt in Salazar's left eye. Already grimacing with phantom pain, his face freezes, set in concrete.

The technician drops the drill. The surgeons fulminate but immediately take X-rays. Lord Sun's staffer orders the orderlies to seize the technician and reluctantly picks up the phone.

Dr. Balance seems amused. Dangling his pendant, he asks the technician if he has ever been hypnotized.

"You can't take it out on me … you can fix him, you fix anything!"

"We *will* fix him," Tsukue says. "He is most important. While you …"

"Please, I didn't mean to … Just fix it, it's just one eye …"

Somewhere overhead, a deranged marching band strikes up nobody's national anthem. Salazar will be the opening event.

"Indeed," says Tsukue. "Only one eye …"

Dimly, he recalls his last North Korean ludus. As an environmental hazard, the match took place amongst twenty blind men with chainsaws. Political prisoners, eyes burned out with lye. The chugging Honda saws drowned out all sound and choked the air with smoke and gasoline vapor.

Balance whispers something to the technician, who relaxes into the chair and lets himself be restrained. Tsukue selects a tool like a notched melon baller. If Salazar's vaunted immune system will cooperate, he observes, this should not delay the ludus at all.

A nerve is just a wire made of conductive organic cells. A conduit for binary electrical signals that aggregate to form the touch of a lover's skin or the impulse to smash an enemy's face.

Just as wires can be spliced together, severed nerves may be introduced to other nerves and new synaptic chains induced. While no mortal surgeon could manually join every nerve in a severed spinal cord, the doctors of the Pageant have found it quite easy to mesh them together with an enzyme derived from nameless Amazonian botanical products and animal donors like Salazar. Gradually over successive transplants, the surgeons have rebuilt Salazar's skull with steel reinforcements and lead shielding, and made it into a module as easily plugged into a new network as any portable hard drive.

Replacing an eye in this improved cranium is as simple, then, as swapping out a burned-out headlight. Before the local anesthetic has entirely worn off, Salazar begins to see through the technician's eye.

At first, white flashes and stabs of neuralgic fire, but a psychoactive cocktail of neurotransmitters and mescaline induces a kaleidoscopic optical storm and then a disturbing razor clarity.

After the initial shock wears off, he insists the eye is working properly and takes up his swords, eager to enter the arena.

Only the hypnotist notices something furtive in his manner. After every transplant, he has warned Lord Sun to expect the Samurai to wither and die. The experience of a brain finding itself in a new body dwarfs even the upheaval caused by a massive stroke. The surgeons themselves predicted years of rehabilitation before he could perform even the most rudimentary physical routines. But always, the Samurai rose from his bed and took up his swords with new hands. Even if the brain could not always feel pain or recall itself, no matter if those strange hands had never hefted a weapon, he made them his own in less time than another man might break in a pair of shoes.

Though he is too stricken to betray any sign of it, the first things Salazar sees with his new eye make him try to claw it out.

He sees ...

Ghosts—the dead serve the living—Lord Sun drinks with the dictator—parades of zombie military slaves, peasant serfs and at his side—

Her.

His hands claw at his face, but with his gauntlets on, he can't get through the mesh screen joining his snarling demon mask with the brim of his helmet. He tosses his head as if the helmet is full of hornets, but after a shaky moment, the Samurai rolls his shoulders, bows his head and strides up the corridor toward the blinding lights and the flatulent blasting of a blind marching band.

Nothing in this life was his, but his body and his hatred.

With her, he lost even those.

An impromptu *ludus* resulting from an awkward ejection of a boorish houseguest. Her face, painted white geisha accessory, carved with tears at first sight of him. Red with blood shed defending her honor. Alone in a sea of howling mouths.

Always, he'd felt as if his nerves extended out of his body. All the world too bright, too loud, in need of a beating. At last he knew where his nerves ended.

Where his true, secret heart had always been.

With his master's wife.

Lord Sun, bastard offspring of a Manchurian "Daughter of Joy" and an anonymous Japanese officer. Master of Hong Kong's black market and a ferocious opponent of Nippon. Builder and destroyer of fortunes, with a stable of gladiators unequalled in the eastern hemisphere and a harem culled from the world's nightclubs and brothels and nunneries with a zookeeper's methodical thoroughness. All but forgotten among the graveyard of discarded human toys and trophies, the Lady Sun.

Assigned to guard her wing of the palace, Salazar did not see her again for the first year of his service. He stood watch outside her garden. He heard her sing. He fell in love with her before they had spoken, before he knew anything about her but that she was also American, and the father of Lord Sun's only true offspring.

Like the birth of a cold, sorrowful star in the void of Salazar's heart, his love for her transmuted his nature. But almost before it was conceived, his new universe began to collapse under its own unstable gravity.

He could not resist her. She seduced him with horrors. Lord Sun was a cannibal who ate his own unborn children. She had become his lawful wife because she bore him two male heirs. When the boys came of age, he would make them fight to the death, and he would have his brain transplanted into the body of the victor.

Even so, Salazar was not without honor. They waited until his indenture to Lord Sun was paid off before he betrayed his master.

***

Lord Sun's wife leaves Hong Kong only twice annually, once to shop in Paris, and once for the family trip to the seashore.

Lord Sun predictably abstains, but insists they get off the continent and buries them in extra security. A surge in threats from various Triad factions with the imminent handover of Hong Kong, so Salazar accompanies her and the boys to Brunei. He bought her a private island in the Maldives, but she won't go. Just once a year, the children will at least see normal people, and play with children whose parents don't aspire to be gods.

A terrorist bomb in the lobby of the Hilton Darussalam kills twenty-two, including the entire family party. None of Indonesia's menagerie of Islamic terror groups step in to take credit for breaking the unprecedented truce, but it fits the profile of past bombings almost perfectly.

Even in the midst of such a devastating tragedy, Lord Sun is not without suspicions. Allowing for the possibility of his having lost his entire family—wife, sons—and several of his most trusted staff in a tragic accident, he cannot help but look to his enemies. Within hours, a team of private operators is dispatched to Indonesia to meet with the Royal Brunei Police Force, insurance investigators and the Sultan's security staff, and repeat the same message: *Deliver them.*

The heat, the humidity, it's like breathing steam. On a rundown former plantation in the jungle above Sipitang, Salazar hides with his bride-to-be. They make plans, they fuck and they fight. Did so many have to die? Stand-ins for each of them accompanied the party into the hotel. The device planted in her luggage. The children and their nanny, the security detail, all expendable. It shocks him that he mourns more for her sons than she does. She rakes his face with her nails, tries to slash him with the neck of a two-thousand dollar bottle of champagne. "He made them," she screams. "He took them out of me and he made them dirty and they … as soon as they were old enough … they tried …"

What she tells him then about her boys makes him sick up the last of his remorse.

Before dawn, a truck driver smuggles them out of Brunei on mountain forest roads for ten thousand dollars. From Tarakan, a fisherman is to take them across the Celebes Sea to Sulawesi, but Salazar plans to hijack him to the Philippines, where they will use new passports to fly to Mexico City and vanish in South America. Even if their scheme unravels and the authorities prematurely discover the truth, Karen tells him, they'll never be caught. She knows of plastic surgeons in Mexico; she has the numbers for holding accounts into which she's siphoned petty household cash for years. Millions. Enough to hide for a long time, or live well for a while.

They're going to get away because they are young and in love, and they are going to grow old together and the story of their romance and heroic escape and flight will become a fairytale, and lovers never die in fairytales.

She says it again and again, and when he goes out to the beach to signal the fisherman, he believes it. If there is any balance, any order, any meaning to the universe, his life has been darkness and blood, a slow whittling away of all that he called himself. He believes now that the dawn must come, for he has earned it.

And he thinks this right up until he goes back into the beachside hut to find not Karen, but only the bloody obsidian knife that was the Aztec's chosen tool, the shard of volcanic glass with which he cut more throats than he cared to count. It drips fresh red on the grass mats, still damp with their sweat.

He takes the knife and runs from the hut, through the village and into the mountainous rain forests of Kalimantan.

Lord Sun discovered the whole architecture of their ruse before they got out of Brunei, and identified his wife's location by the GPS chip implanted in her skull.

Lord Sun's hunger for vengeance is no less than any reasonable man's would be under the circumstances, but he gives Salazar eight hours to go to ground in the trackless highlands before he and his operators come searching. After all he's invested in Salazar, he might as well get one last bit of sport out of him.

The Mongolian storms the arena like a minotaur on ketamine. Trainers remotely spike his adrenaline drip and drive him through the gate with cattle prods, dropping the portcullis behind him. With a seven-foot axe, he splits a peasant retainer to the waist, kicks the underfed kindling off the blade and basks in scorn. The audience of local Party elect shriek like electrified lab rats. In an imperial box fortified by ballistic glass, Lord Sun sits with their host and the other patrons and a group of bored, constipated old men who can only be Chinese dignitaries.

When the Samurai enters, the crowd settles into an unsettling hush, as if refrigerated narcotic gas has filled the vast underground arena. Like something frozen, limbs tightly coiled, he pads into the murkily lit center. Shivering, staggering. Stripped of poetry, of technique, he advances like a praying mantis intent upon mating.

Obscured behind a veil of chainmail, the Mongolian's welcoming grin is almost audible as he beckons. Nearly twice the Samurai's weight and with a good eighteen-inch height advantage, he is a bear to Samurai's skinned rabbit.

A few desultory swings of his axe and jerky feints with a steel net fail to draw any notice from the Samurai. A fusillade of fireworks spray the field. A rocket vomiting green phosphorus sparks cuts between them. The Mongolian must expect the Samurai to be blinded, for he avalanches the smaller man.

This is where the battle typically becomes a dance, where the Samurai's elegant minimalism seeks parity with the Mongolian's bombastic onslaught, and a whole new art form is invented.

Even the Mongolian must realize that something is wrong. What he lacks in tactical skill, he more than compensates with his apparent knowledge of Samurai's eye injury. Circling clockwise and feinting with his axe, he drives to get into Samurai's blind spot.

Instead of his customary dual-wielding *nitoken* technique, the Samurai has forsaken his *daisho*, holds the 74cm katana close to his chest like a precious thing sure to be shattered. Samurai checks the Mongolian several times, then a bloodcurdling scream rips out of him and he flings himself, swinging the katana like a baseball bat, headfirst into the heel of the oncoming axe.

The audience leaps to its collective feet. Shock quickly sours into outrage. This isn't what they came to see.

Samurai reels backwards and falls like a doll to the ground, still holding his sword in the same awkward two-handed grip. Mask split wide open, revealing a one eyed, slack-jawed Asian face. Drooling, tripping his head off on ketamine administered directly into his surviving eye, the technician doesn't even know he's losing a fight. Arms flopping frenziedly, trying to drop the weapon glued to his gauntleted hands when the Mongolian tramples him. Katana snared in steel net and he's slung into the air and slammed into a stone column but still he won't, he can't let go——

Irate Lord Sun calls his trainers, surgeons, hypnotist, security staff.

Message center.

Calls up security camera view of Salazar's bunker on a laptop.

Red.

The hypnotist calls back. He's left the compound for the night, and when he left, everything was as it should have been——

The doors slam open to make way for a headless bodyguard. Screaming like sheep downwind from the slaughterhouse, patrons on their feet amid bodyguards and concubines.

Salazar slides into the box and moves through them like a gardener among windswept trees, artfully pruning limbs with his short sword. Through the boiling crowd, he cuts a path to the front row and a phalanx of Triad soldiers backing Lord Sun into a corner. One of them tries to shoot down the glass. The bullets bounce off the walls until they hit one body or shatter and maim several.

One far more astute bodyguard, using two ceramic-silicon automatics the size of credit cards, pump sixty-eight .12 caliber rounds into Salazar. Half of them glance off his naked steel and bone cranium, trailing drug drip tubes and leaking exotic fluids. His new left eye is so dilated that it looks like a black coin, a mouth overflowing with the Dark.

The host disregards his own prohibition on firearms and draws a massive Glock with a laser sight, shaky with the prospect of firing a shot in anger. He shoots two of his own bodyguards before the survivors sweep him out of the box.

Salazar chops down the last Triad guards and lays bare his nemesis.

Here, some small demonstration of his humanity, of the tenderness that cost him everything, would vouchsafe him the role of hero in this confrontation. And if there were gods who cared not for morality plays but only fed greedily upon empty human trauma, then Salazar's sacrifice would be accepted and miracles would abound.

Lord Sun, a sickly ancient, bald as an egg, blue veins bulging with sluggish blood, clutching his chest with one palpitating claw, takes out his phone with the other. A vile, boneless creature shucked out of its shell of mercenaries and unmasked at last for a coward, squirming behind the last living body left in the box.

Salazar does not act. Less a warrior in repose than a machine with its gears stripped, arm raised above the last one blocking Lord Sun, cowering against starred glass …

It's her …

But how long has it been? How many fights, how many bodies, how many seasons of rehab and torture …

Ash-blonde hair and honey-gold eyes and her face unpainted unwrinkled uncreased by the sorrows that drove her mad …

She sobs and the musical sound of it undoes him.

"Ka … Ka … Ka … ren …" He reaches out to her. "Is … it is … you …?"

She lifts up a hand to take his. No, she holds out something.

She presses a button.

Salazar's heart explodes.

Death is emptiness.

Death is the void.

Death is easy.

Where Salazar goes, the nothingness itself is alive. Emptiness infested with itself.

When you have nothing left, no *you*, no *I*, the Dark gets inside you and you remake yourself out of it until you're at one with Nature's other face. In the Dark, you become everything eating everything else, eating fucking killing dying in the Dark forever and ever.

In here, forever is a breath.

To keep from going mad, you make something. You build a memory palace and fashion the Dark into an infinity of gloomy rooms filled with shadowy impressions. You move from room to room to keep the lustful turgidity of darkness out. You unpack your memories and burn them for warmth, for light.

Until you only have one memory left.

The body on the steel slab quivers. Salazar opens his eyes and weeps with joy at the revelation of having eyes again, before he even realizes he's on fire.

His screams only suck the flames down his throat. Choking, gasping for air—

Drowning, thrashing for the surface but unable to find which way is up, and the cold and the pressure crushing him—

The hypnotist smiles. "What news from beyond the veil?"

Salazar chokes on air, gags out noises that no one else would recognize as words.

"You were in transit for nearly eighteen months. Much has changed while you were away."

His arms are lead with rubber bones. Try to strangle Balance, they roll off his torso to hit the steel like shit in a bedpan. More noises.

"You are in no condition to fight. That part of your life is behind you. As punishment for your actions, Lord Sun has elected to subject you to the most terrible suffering he could imagine."

Salazar's eyes nearly roll out of their petrified sockets when the hypnotist shows him a hand mirror.

His face is sunken, jaundiced, withered, wreathed in yellow-white beard like dead roots from an uprooted onion. It is the most hateful face he has ever seen.

He is Lord Sun.

"The old coward finally took the plunge," Balance says, smiling. "You gave him a reason."

Make him grimace and shake. Make his jaw drop like he is trying to throw up. His hands try to crawl away.

"His son, the one who survived the bomb … His father let the world suppose he was dead, and raised him for this. I never believed he would go through with it, frankly …"

Salazar wonders what he should feel. Nausea, exhaustion, the gravity of despair crushing this ruined, used-up vessel … Still, does it lighten his load to know the boy survived his mother's murder attempt? Perhaps he yet lives. The son's brain could be living in his old suitcase. Meanwhile …

"Where …? Let me …" Stick out his tongue. Swallow it. Choke on it.

"It is impossible. You will have no chance. We have worked for months to resuscitate you after the operation. It was nearly a failure, but no one was surprised you pulled through. Some part of you, at least, clings to life. But now you are alert and in full possession of your faculties, you will finally be executed …"

A spray of spit. Black spots swarming over Dr. Balance's sad smile. Salazar clings, body and mind, to this rotten raft until the Dark subsides.

"Of course, at the moment of expiration, every effort will be made to recover your brain and transplant it again and … well, it is obvious. If he has his way, you will never stop dying."

Bow his head. Try to gouge out his eyes. "Ssssaaaaaw … errrrrrr …."

Balance touches his widow's peak, dabbing at his nose. "That is too bad, my friend. She … is not the one … but the resemblance *is* remarkable, no? That is no doubt why he took an interest."

Make him shed tears. "Sssssshhhhh …"

"She … is her mother's daughter. And the father … it's complicated, but … biologically speaking …"

MAKE HIM BREAK FREE MAKE HIM STRANGLE—

Balance easily pushes him back and cinches the straps around his concave chest. He's not going anywhere.

Lord Sun lives to inflict pain. Why would he throw her away? Especially when he learned she was ripe with a seed he could nurture and nourish to become what he'd always wanted ...

"Put all dreams of vengeance out of your mind. They are worlds away from this one. Now begins as many lifetimes of suffering as your soul can withstand ... but you need not suffer any more than you wish to."

The hypnotist draws close and recites the haiku that he taught Salazar.

Eyes gleam. Pupils dilate. Breathing subsides to a tidal purr. Make his ears *listen*.

"You have learned at great cost that you are not your body. How much less difficult, indeed how liberating, to grasp that you are also not your brain?

"You are a dream your brain has always dreamt, a story it tells itself. But a tale once told does not belong to the teller, but to the reader, the world. Compose your story, and you may not only withstand the pain and the darkness, but you may escape your body altogether ..."

Make him look again at the face in the mirror. Salazar tries to tear it off his skull and eat it.

⁕

The ancient Chinese practice of *ling chi* or "slow slicing"—more popularly known as the Death of a Thousand Cuts—grew in the occidental imagination into a nightmarish ordeal of precision torture which dragged on for days or even weeks. Like the infamous, equally exaggerated "water torture" and similar techniques involving ants or swiftly growing bamboo, it fueled Western paranoia about the inscrutable patience and eerie cruelty of the Oriental mind long after it was banned under British colonial pressure in 1905.

In reality, *ling chi* was reserved only for the worst criminals—traitors, fratricides—and not even the most skilled Chinese executioner could stave off death beyond a few hours.

Dr. Tsukue tells Salazar right away that he's going for a record. Perhaps never in history has such painstaking care been taken to preserve the life of a patient slated to die by torture.

Two pit crews of three technicians will see to his dismantling. Dr. Tsukue conducts the primary excruciation, while his apprentices follow along, debriding and dismantling tissue, cauterizing or clamping critical blood vessels until the maximum amount of agony has been milked from each limb and amputation can proceed; and an antianesthetist with two nurses are charged with keeping Salazar paralyzed with suxamethonium chloride in an intratracheal drip along with epinephrine and acetylcholine to keep him exquisitely alert, yet just below the threshold for shock and cardiac arrest. The pain manager has the most difficult job. Lord Sun abused his body as if certain he would someday get a new one, but in his new incarnation, he is equally adamant that his discarded body survive long enough to satisfy an impossible grievance.

Traditional *ling chi* customarily opens by dramatically mortifying the pectoral muscles and the fronts of the thighs in shallow, gaping wounds that lay bare the ribcage and straps of skeletal muscle. Tsukue is wary of blood loss and premature myocardial trauma. Still, this is an operating *theater*, and just as in the Pageant, all must perform here for a demanding audience. Using a Blumlein ablation knife, he digs into the chilled, rubbery flesh of the chest like a pudding, plowing out jaundiced scoops of skin backed by pale adipose jelly and dropping them in a steel bowl.

Fully alive to all that is inflicted on him yet unable to move beyond the feeblest galvanic twitch, Salazar seems to slip immediately into shock. The pain manager calls for a recess. Observing from his own hermetically sealed recovery ward, Lord Sun demands escalation. Burn his genitalia off with a laser to wake him up, or better yet, peel and invulse them, making a woman of him. But only after coming within a hair's breadth of triggering a heart attack does the pain manager recognize that Salazar is quite awake, yet in a meditative trance.

The next incisions begin at the fingertips and the soles of his feet, long, sweeping slices with a fluted scalpel that turns up the lips of the wounds like furrows of tilled soil. A few nicked capillaries add only stray trickles to the slime of cold sweat beading on Lord Sun's mortified castoff body. Nerves assaulted, jolted to twitching overload, but never severed. Exhausted parchment skin peels away from flaccid fascia, livid and throbbing with terminal arousal.

Goosepimpled flesh shivers in restraints as slices become slashes, as digits in all four extremities are systematically de-gloved and filleted. So adept is Dr. Tsukue with scalpels, lasers and forceps that even when he strips muscle and sinew from the nerve-rich fingertips, exposed nerves linger on, clinging to barren bone, still aquiver with apocalyptic pain.

The medics constantly check Salazar's mental acuity. He remains lucid throughout, gritting his teeth whenever he is queried, but more with the air of a man upset at a distraction, than one in the throes of trauma.

While they flay him, he loses himself in words, recalled to the torments of his body only long enough to stretch out to pick up several larger scraps of his own skin on his outthrust tongue and ball them up in his mouth. Dr. Tsukue notes this gravely, but says nothing to the pain manager. If he is not truly paralyzed, so be it. In the longest recorded *ling chi* executions, the victim would be allowed only his own discarded flesh for sustenance.

But Salazar does not swallow.

After sixteen hours, a recess is called for Tsukue's sake. While he rests and self-administers extensive acupuncture, Salazar is wheeled into his closet-sized cell, suspended supine on a trolley, slathered in ferric acid and industrial Neosporin, to rest.

Before Tsukue's hands have stopped shaking, he returns to the theater. Lord Sun is most unimpressed so far, but even his most aesthetically drastic efforts fail to arouse any perceptible reaction from Salazar.

Waves of pain pass far above his head, but he barely notices them now, like distant traffic through a sealed window.

Salazar is making a new body, a new palace in the Dark, out of words. Literally, he composes himself, weighing words, images, snapshot reminiscences that well up from the seemingly emptied void of his memory. Paring away fat and redundant and flat impressions to vivisect the image, the idea, of himself. Within the rigorous latticework of the haiku, he distills himself into a flow of words and images that set him free and bind him in the surge of red darkness to an anchor. Reciting the words, he holds the walls against the deeper darkness that hungers to reclaim him.

With only three recesses, the ling chi of the gladiator Salazar lasts six days and three hours. Dr. Tsukue has his record, but he hardly seems proud of it, now.

Salazar's brain is pitted with lesions and dull, partially decayed parts, but still emits a stable comatose EEG when reconnected to the monitor and nutrient feeds of his second home, the suitcase.

Only Dr. Balance examines Salazar's cell with any diligence once the last remnants of Lord Sun's corpse are vacuumed away. At first, he mistakes it for a bit of misplaced gore, even as he searches for just such an artifact as it turns out, upon further inspection, to be.

Opening it, he closes his eyes at the first glimpse of its contents.

Salazar has transcended himself. No longer merely a gladiator, now a poet.

The elite box of Hong Kong's Kuan Yin Arena more closely resembles a parliament conference room, with sensibly upholstered chairs arranged within horseshoe tables on a steeply tiered gallery with scarlet porphyry floors and columns.

The reincarnated Lord Sun sulks with his retinue, alone. Less than a year after the operation, he is still a hostile occupier at war with his son's unconquered body. His lipless rictus and incessant stammer freely betray the deranged ancient hiding inside the teenaged body, but the fault lies with all the immunosuppressors and hormones and the many arcane drugs required to maintain even infantile control over the body's basic motor functions. Frustrated with the headset he uses to communicate with the servants waiting outside his inflated plastic hyperbaric bubble, Lord Sun raps angrily on the interior wall, demanding to see the hypnotist. His servants hardly hide their sneering expressions. They think him weak. They see his imminent demise and their greedy enrichment. He's surprised them before.

Dr. Balance finally arrives, looking uncharacteristically excited. "Your new Samurai is prepared for battle. I think today my Lord will enjoy a most interesting match."

At last, Lord Sun recalls some spark of vitality. "The odds. What odds does she command?" A string of drool wiped away by rash-ravaged hands.

"Twelve to one, my Lord."

A young man's lungs vapor lock on old man's laughter. "She will … destroy … them all …"

Dr. Balance locks eyes with Lord Sun, guides him to a relaxed state. By his own insistence, Lord Sun is immune to hypnosis, but Balance's relaxing influence has made him the only one he can trust with the care and feeding of his most prized possession.

"They underestimate you at their peril, my Lord. But not entirely without cause. For far too long, you have pursued your vengeance to the detriment of your business pursuits and your stable. You've become known for vulgar exhibition matches. But your reinvention as a patron shall be as dramatic as your physical reincarnation."

Nodding until he swoons with dizziness, Lord Sun breathlessly agrees. "If he knew … it would destroy him utterly. He should have been revived in time to witness this moment."

Around them, the crowd thickens, patrons and prostitutes take their seats as the lights over the arena brighten. The first event is hardly a title match, but it marks the first appearance of a female gladiator in the history of the Pageant.

"I know you have misgivings, my Lord, but it is best that you not allow yourself to become … compromised again. She is her mother's daughter, full of defiance, but also her father's, and so a formidable contender in the games. Her natural anger channeled in that direction will yield you great benefits, instead of bringing further trouble to your house."

Lord Sun's mouth says something Balance misses because his hand moves to cover it and slap it repeatedly.

Best get this over with. "As luck would have it, I have uncovered a token which was no doubt meant for you. Whether as act of surrender or a last gesture of defiance I leave to you, but I think that once you hold it in your hands, you may find the contentment to leave the issue to the past."

Knowing he treads on rice paper, Balance quickly proffers the tiny pillow book.

He has trimmed its chewed borders and replaced the haphazard binding of hair and detached ligaments and perfected the botched curing which Salazar attempted with his own urine. In spite of some shrinkage, the painstakingly inked words are still clearly legible when he holds it up to the convex belly of Lord Sun's bubble.

赤い風泣くこと

Trembling, Lord Sun reads, unblinking.

私の体は本です

Eyes screwed shut, Balance turns the pages as Lord Sun consumes each inhumanly compressed line.

私の名前は剣です

Eyes riveted upon the unwritten *kereji*—the "cutting word" upon which the last line turns, he says the Samurai's true name aloud, curse turned into prayer.

His eyes go on roving behind closed lids, as if in deep REM sleep. His lips go on reciting the haiku.

"*Akai kaze ga naku …*"

Repeating the mantra until its resonance overlaps with the endless repetition out of the Dark behind every closed eyelid …

"*Watashi no karada wa hondesu …*"

The cutting word picks the neural locks of the door at the back of every brain, the door that drums, drugs and blood alone can open.

"*Ken wa kotobadesu.*"

The crowd rises to its feet at the first sounds of the ludus … not the expected horns or strident martial music, but a piercing black static scream of inhuman desolation that rebounds through the cavernous arena.

Lai's opponent enters the arena to distracted applause, but some of the more astute patrons turn to the back door when they notice that the screaming is getting louder, and it's not coming from down on the dirt floor, but from somewhere much closer. From down in the catacombs where Dr. Balance only minutes ago placed Lai Salazar in a deep trance before showing her the Samurai's pillow book.

Only the hypnotist can recognize the name the newly resuscitated ghost is trying to speak with both Lord Sun and Lai's lips.

Before any can react, the screaming becomes a chorus. Lord Sun claws at the walls of his bubble. His screams tear the microsutures in his scalp, man becoming madman becoming God.

Even Dr. Balance cannot tell, looking into those streaming, alien eyes, whether he is observing his favorite patient in the ecstasy of his hideous miracle—the impossible, the unspeakable, coming true twice-
-or the Darkness, incarnate at last and utterly devastated to find out how incredibly overrated being alive is …

Yes, he thinks as the doors fly open to admit a chill steel wind, *it promises to be a most interesting match.*

NIGREDO

Few cult deprogrammers these days would even try to take someone from Ex Libris. Hardly any even call themselves deprogrammers, anymore. "Exit counselor" is the warmer, fuzzier new title. A human brain must be more than just Descartes' materialist cognitive model, or its feelings wouldn't get so hurt by the truth.

My methods were not popular, but they worked. Most of my business was by referral. My clients had exhausted every other hope. When I could not convince them to accept that perhaps their loved one was better off in their new lifestyle, then I had them sign my waiver and went to work.

Ex Libris was a hard target. They didn't greet at airports or convention centers or lurk outside euthanasia booths. They didn't panhandle or turn tricks. Mostly, they meditated to the Master's audiobooks while toiling in digital sweatshops up and down the coast.

Their leader was a creative writing professor. Dr. Preston Marble used the classics—"guided" meditation, hypnosis, sleep deprivation, protein starvation, mild hallucinogens and traumatic writing assignments. Ex Libris grew out of Marble's intensive writing seminars and his "Awakened Editions" of classic books annotated for neurotics desperately yearning to become psychopaths, harvesting the most hopeless wannabe's, fans and impressionable victims into a militant bibliomancy cult.

Marble's guide to story structure translated more easily into a practical bible than the Bible, complete with interactive commandments. Every devotee had to compose an "antibiography" of everything they were not, and never would be. On average, they ran to five hundred thousand words composed on no sleep and amphetamine-laced oatmeal. When your Editor finally approved your antibiography, you had to burn it and throw the ashes in the ocean or eat it.

If they used Allah, Buddha or Jesus, they'd be on FBI watch-lists, but to the outside world, they're just a fucking book club.

Sometimes, I can dress up as a senior cult official and pull them out with no headaches. This outfit had no such slack to exploit. Four devotees in each one-bedroom unit at all times. A van came every other day to rotate them out. Eight more places like this, just in this part of town.

I cut their DSL line, then knocked on their door. Cable guy uniform. Tool belt. Wig and mustache, cotton plugs in my cheeks, lifts in my shoes. I chloroformed the geek who answered the door, caught him, threw the deadbolt and dragged him into the living room.

No furniture except for four workstations and a couple futons in the corner. Lysol, incense and macrobiotic farts. Two were awake and pecking at their boards. Another lay on a futon with headphones on. The one I wanted.

She wore a biofeedback harness and a Cranio-Electrical Stimulation cap. She listens to his heartbeat and EEG mixed with his endless lectures while she works. The more her brain activity conforms to Marble's template, the more mildly pleasurable zaps she gets from the cap.

And all while copy-editing or revising the mass media equivalent of lead-painted, asbestos infant's teething rings. If you've ever watched a slab of direct-to-video dreck or mind-numbing scripted reality show patter and wondered how sane human beings can create such empty noise, well … sane people don't.

The system also tracks bodily functions and location for the home office. Anyone unplugging their unit or wandering out of range triggers an alarm, and the Editors come running.

I unplugged her and took off her headphones—Marble's sleepy bullroarer voice reading something about an anarchist exploding himself at Greenwich Observatory. She was semi-catatonic, dead on her feet. I didn't even need the chloroform. I stood her up and escorted her to the balcony.

Someone knocked on the front door, then tried the knob.

Out on the balcony overlooking the alley. My assistant Carl waited on the roof of our parked van, ready to catch the product. I bagged her and lowered her over the railing.

Carl caught the bag and gave me a hand down onto the van, then jumped off and caught the product again, dropping her in the back. In and out in less than two minutes.

We took her to Imperial County, to the Olde Desert Inn. It was abandoned long before I set up shop, and no one ever happened by. Two miles off the Interstate, at a dead place that never quite became a town. You can see anyone coming from five minutes away, watch satellites pass overhead at night.

As soon as we got the product strapped down in the honeymoon suite, Carl went home to his family and I got busy. My client had paid a big premium for a rush job. He wanted his wife back. I had to open up the product and find her.

She had the kind of bright, nervous beauty that you feel sparking at you just before you look her way. Smart, fine features; good bones showing too starkly through her pale, jaundiced skin. Avid, hungry eyes.

Real deprogrammers, the old-school guys, kept their techniques under wraps like stage magicians, but it's almost always some variation on the classic aversion therapy interrogation model. I didn't have any tricks or training, and only one dirty little secret.

I didn't break them down the way the burnout FBI agents and MK-ULTRA stooges who started our game did it. I didn't have to. I was more of an assassin. The product died and the person was reborn, saved by the Elixir.

I liked to measure out dosages not just to body size, age and health, but to degree of indoctrination. I usually interviewed the product before, but this one was unresponsive. Semi-catatonic. She'd get up and go where you pushed her, but there was nobody home.

A quick physical turned up scalp scabs from constant electrical shocks and bruises from recent IV abuse. Her pupils were responsive and pulse fine, but someone had already worked her.

I wanted to wait, but I gave her the shot. Her pulse spiked, then flattened out. I checked her restraints. If she didn't come around in an hour, I'd give her the second dose.

It wasn't therapy. I studied psychology, but I'm no doctor. Nobody can teach you how to raise the dead. To join any cult, from the Masons to Aum Shinrikyo, you have to die. The old You dies and is buried inside you to fertilize the budding of the new You. To resurrect them, I just had to go digging. The Elixir was my shovel. It's just easy enough, the results miraculous enough, that I'd kid myself I knew what I was doing.

Under the Elixir, you are outwardly conscious. You speak when spoken to. You obey. You don't ask questions. You know nothing but what you are told. You are utterly suggestible. I could make you blow me, hijack a bus and drive it into a nuclear power plant. It's not like hypnosis, where the idiot on stage *wants* to act like a chicken. What the product wanted, who they were, what they would or wouldn't do … all of it erased. In its place … whatever I put into them.

But she was doing it wrong.

She took me so completely by surprise that I almost didn't see that I'd found what I'd always been looking for. Someone who could show me what it was like to be nothing.

She babbled in French, faster than I could understand. Then, "*See the stars beneath the sea* … Do you remember before you were born? You remember what it was like …? I'd give anything if you could send me back …"

Usually, the product has to be coaxed out of the clouds. Sometimes it helps to guide them out with imagery; childhood snapshots as stepping-stones, recreating history with a big red editorial pen.

She didn't need me to set the scene. I couldn't stop it. The walls of the motel room turned to stained canvas flats in the wings of a musty black cathedral.

The ceiling vanished in a jumble of scenery dangling from cables. Some I recognized—the apartment, the Ex Libris Chapterhouse, the beach at night, a Hillcrest townhouse—but there were hundreds of others, an armory of scenes. Flakes of corroded varnish fluttered down to settle on her hair like golden snow.

"Before your script was written? Before the Plot had sharpened and bent and broken you to its ends." She winced, trying to smile. "If you're here, you must be an actor …"

"Then you're an actress?"

Her laughter shivered flurries of paint flakes from above. "If you're alive, you must act. Are you so sure you're alive?" She tossed her head and fussed with the ash-roses embroidered in the sleeves of her gray gown. The fabric was dull yet subtly iridescent, like a shed snakeskin. "I like this one ever so much more than the last play …"

"What play was that? What was your role?"

"I was a mirror for a man to admire his own mask. So few real roles for women, now as ever … I loved my Lord the King more than my husband. I had forsaken all others to become a thought in my Lord's mind. But then he revealed to me my particular purpose …"

"And what purpose is that?"

She knelt before the pool that had been only a square chalk outline on the floor of the stage. "To murder him," she said. The buckled, warped boards were now pitted umber flagstones, the corsages of stained paper extravagantly sexual lilies on still, emerald water.

"Do you want to be free of him? Of … all this?"

"Oh, he's no burden. His sinister hand stopped my dagger as if it were a feather. By his fear and by his blood, I knew he was but a pretender. No, the one I want to be free of, no one can escape."

"Who's that?"

She leaned in close and whispered, "The Plot."

Looking up into the gallery, she hunched closer to me. I could feel my warmth leeching away into her. "I like this one ever so much better. So many places to hide … Do you not know the French Play?"

I shuddered and told her no.

"No matter, the lines read *you*, as it were. But we must enter! The call! Here, you must don your mask!"

The theater throbbed with the tolling of a vast, leaden bell. She shoved the cold, dry thing into my hands. Before I could look at it, I had pressed it to my face. Shadowy hands came out of the dark to guide us up twisting stairs and through a velvet miasma of rotting curtains into a cold white light …

We lay side by side upon the bed. Her pulse was steady. Her eyes were empty.

I thought better of giving her the second shot, decided instead on a serious sedative. But when I turned around, the syringe was gone.

It was in her hand. Then it was in my neck.

Before 9/11, the airport was much more than a place to wait in line and get searched. It was also really easy to steal people's luggage.

I did it to pick up quick cash after I dropped out of college. It beat waiting to be expelled once my misuse of the clinical psychology department's resources was uncovered, or the new law requiring piss tests for financial aid went into effect.

At LAX, the passengers would crowd up to the belt even if their luggage was nowhere in sight, so if something went round the loop more than twice, it was probably unclaimed. Missed passenger connection, misrouted baggage, or maybe just a protracted restroom visit. Regardless, within ten seconds of spotting my quarry, I could have it out the turnstile door and into my friend's waiting car.

My friend. Naomi was philosophy on a pre-law track and still doing swimmingly. We had little in common except she enjoyed drugs even more than me, which pretty much guaranteed her at least some sort of regional title. Strikingly homely, smarter than me, and a fry-guide *non pareil.* Any time you wanted to drop acid and go walkabout up the coast, she was down, if she didn't have a term paper due. I told myself she hung out with me because she was writing a paper about me.

So this one time, I cased the claim corrals in the international terminal, which was always sketchy and seldom worth it. Flights from Hong Kong, South America or the Middle East, where customs or immigration might hold them up for me, were also searched the most often. Even back then, they had cameras everywhere, and sometimes someone was watching them. I did a paper on recognition cues that guide our treatment of people we see as young/old, rich/poor, ugly/pretty, hostile/friendly, threatening/helpless, etc. The grabs started as part of those experiments. Everyone is a bigot, but a memorable prop or stereotypical mannerism was a cue that one noticed even above gender or race. I got a C+ and a journeyman's degree in spycraft.

We kept a suitcase full of Iranian currency—Fifteen hundred dollars after exchange—and two pounds of hash. We pursued the experiments elsewhere—shoplifting, dining and dashing, pharmaceutical burglary, etc. Much was learned.

But this last one … it was everything we hoped for and deserved.

I saw this long, odd-shaped, expensive-looking case on a played-out Cathay Pacific from Bangkok and figured it for something fun. Maybe a musical instrument. I wasn't looking for money, though I was broke and hungry. I wanted secrets.

I was dressed in a distressed linen suit, perfect for humid tropical climes, and a Panama hat with a snakeskin band. The dissolute young sex tourist, bringing back only viral contraband incubating where no customs agent dare search, or the callow expatriate, returning to liquidate a deceased parent's estate before returning to kick the gong around with the ladyboys of Patpong.

Already a scrum of vultures from the next flight were converging around the belt, providing plenty of cover from airport security.

I was on the far side of the belt with a clear shot for the doors. Naomi waited at the curb in her ketchup-red Sentra with a bungee-cord holding the trunk shut. I passed "security" when I noticed I'd grabbed the wrong bag. This one was beat up, dull matte-black brushed steel with three key locks on it. It was too late to turn back, so I ran with it.

Three guesses what was inside.

Naomi and I went to a Shakey's Pizza in Culver City. Her dad was a retired cop upstate, but she learned how to pick locks to steal her classmates' Ritalin and weed in middle school. She got it open before our pie arrived and I lost my last ball on the ancient Zardoz pinball machine.

Neither of us knew French, so we couldn't read the greasy, piss-stinking diary. We got disgusted by the pictures of naked or near-naked Thai boys posed in rice paddies, in muddy alleys, in brothels, coatrooms, and riverbanks. Everywhere this guy went, he must have paid boys to drop trou for a photograph, prologue to fuck-knows-what. Maybe he paid them in something other than money, for all of them had the same dreamy, vacant expression, eyes drooping shut or fixedly staring up at the contents of their own skulls. I was never so fucking glad I couldn't read French.

I wanted to go back to LAX and play our other favorite game, Spot the Pervert, but he wouldn't make it easy by going to security. He'd run straightaway he suspected they were onto him, and anyway, I got to the bottom of the suitcase and found the big bottles of weird yellow-gray powder.

Naomi wanted to snort it. I wanted to consult the diary first. Only the thought that it could be cremains, deadly insecticide or uranium dissuaded us from a trial bump.

And the rest, as they say, is history ... When they don't want to talk anymore about how the chance discovery became destiny, or whom they ran over, on the way.

In less than six weeks, I had learned enough French to know what I had, and what kind of monster I took it from. Don't believe that I tried to turn evil to good, to redeem it or myself, by going underground and turning the Elixir to a cult deprogramming tool. I could've become the greatest pornographer in history or a revolutionary therapist, a salesman, anything … But I only wanted to learn what people were made of.

Another experiment.

In the interest of science, Naomi and I tried an intramuscular injection of fifty micrograms in solution of the Elixir. That was his name for it.

I don't remember anything after that. Naomi was gone when I came down. I never saw her again. I freaked out and took off and I hid out here and there and everywhere, shedding myself on the road until I was only the Deprogrammer. I believed that the euphoric migraines that overtook me like menstrual clockwork every few months were flashbacks, withdrawal symptoms, but I never tried it again.

Using the powdered Elixir, I delivered fifty-two prisoners of cults and successfully converted all but two of them into reasonable facsimiles of their old selves, minus a traumatic scar or an empty hole · that made joining a cult seem like a good idea. I fixed them.

After four years, my supply of the Elixir was nearly used up. I had a sample tested once and learned it was a fungal derivative, but I'd never get spores to grow from it. Nowhere near close to having learned anything real, I was looking at retirement.

Carl came within seconds of my paging him. This was because he and his family lived in the motel … and also because his "family" didn't really exist, except as an elaborate skein of posthypnotic suggestions. Carl was my first product. Mistakes were made …

Nothing like this, though.

Carl let me get it out of my system. Just apologized and said he didn't see her leave.

Nobody ever escaped from the motel before. An unrehabilitated product would go running back to the cult, which might go to the police or come after me. I would have to call the client to let him know his wife was missing with a head full of nameless psychogenic drugs.

Richard Resley, PhD, was a professor of nothing so mundane as one discipline, a postmodern *enfant terrible* who could never be contained on one campus, let alone one bed. The first article pulled up by a

Google search called him the Deacon of Deconstruction. I had to get into the double digits to find things I wished I'd known before I agreed to abduct his wife.

I deployed Carl to look for the product and drove into the city to meet Resley.

He was being interviewed at the local public radio affiliate, but agreed to give me a few minutes between demolishing patriarchal dialectics and delineating game-changing paradigms for a chubby ash-blond postgrad who looked ready to jump his boring bones.

He took it well.

"So, she is no longer your responsibility then." He nodded to me, turned to go. "She is very headstrong. I trust you did your best."

I took his arm, sure he wouldn't want his pet coed to hear what I had to say. "I won't try to complicate the situation any further, if you'll just tell me why you'd pay good money to have your wife deprogrammed from a cult that *you* still belong to."

His face tightened. "I suppose there's no point equivocating. My interests and Preston's are still deeply entangled, though I was never as devoted to his philosophy as my wife." Air-quoted *philosophy*, the prick.

Resley coauthored three major studies of "psychocultural engineering" with Marble two decades ago, just before the guru left UCSD and started his sewing circle. Never publicly connected to the cult, but the pattern was there, if you were paranoid enough to see it. "So, you get all the benefits and none of the starvation …"

"My antibiography wasn't all that long. Preston is doing some extraordinary things with expanding human potential, and I've been privileged to witness some of it. Listen, this is beginning to sound like some sort of blackmail attempt …"

"It's not. Your wife disappeared in the middle of a session. She's extremely suggestible …"

"I could've told you that," he said. "Listen, if you're so concerned, why not go to the police? I'm sure they'd be very thorough in locating her, once they sorted *you* out." Impatiently, he sped up and crossed the street just ahead of a truck loaded with liquid CO_2.

I gave up chasing after him. Just stopped and shouted in the street, "Was it you or Marble who turned her onto the French Play?"

"Jesus fucking *Christ*!" Resley whirled and came back to me where I waited on the curb.

I couldn't resist. "She dreams she's acting in it. Says she was in another play, too, where somebody tried to get her to kill somebody else—"

He hit pretty hard for a middle-aged college professor. The punch folded me into his shoulder, which shoved me back onto the curb.

His face was frozen milk. I smelled urine, and it wasn't mine. "Stay the hell away from me or I'll call *my* police. Would you like that?"

I watched him walk away. The postgrad skipped after him, looking sideways at me as she followed him to his office.

I could've left it alone. Nobody was paying me to press further. I didn't like being used, but if Ex Libris wanted to play games, they would have been subtler about it. The easiest explanation, that Mrs. Resley had been a plant to spy on my methods, would explain it all, if anyone had ever gotten up and walked away in the middle of an Elixir session.

But one person had, and I never saw her again.

No one under the Elixir had ever successfully dragged me into their head. And I had heard only once before of the French Play, in the journal I found with the Elixir.

"And the games! Such delightful entertainments our pretty toys gave us … Never has the French Play been performed with such abandon, as my little troupe put on for the Khmer Jaune Festival. Every performance consumed a raft of Cassildas, a platoon of Thales, and taxed my art to its core. Such ecstasies, such wondrous pitiful pain! My dolls laid so bare the veiled face of power and desire that the Pallid Mask wept tears of priceless ichor and the Hidden City beckoned beyond the rotten red moons … We all saw it, and beheld the colorless, cold corona of the Crown of No Nation … "

The King in Yellow was only one more bullet point in an inventory of depravity that yawned at mere pedophilia and cannibalism. I tracked down and attempted to read it back when I was still trying to find out what I had, but I couldn't tell you what the big deal was. My memory of it was like a hole in a pocket. I ran down a copy at a Xian Science Reading Room where the curator owed me a big favor.

I put out an underground APB on my car with some contacts in the repo and private security industries. I prowled the Ex Libris chapterhouses in Ocean Beach and Encinitas. I got nothing and nowhere, and hoped for better news from Carl when we met at a taco shop on PCH. He had ignored my calls all day, so I assumed he was either busy or had lost it. He was always losing things when I forgot to remind him.

He looked like he'd lost a lot more than his phone. He sat down next to me on a picnic bench out front. The surfers and landscaping grunts had all gone and the shop was deserted. On the wall, they had that mural in every taco shop, of the dead Indian prince on the woman's lap, an Aztec Pieta …

"I found her," he said.

I lit up. I asked her where, how, why didn't he tell me on the phone …?

He rubbed his eye, looked absently at the smear of blood on his fingertip. He took out a picture. It was creased and faded. He stared at it, cupped in his big, shaky hands. "Why didn't you tell me …?"

Where was she? I asked him.

"She's everywhere," he said, and dropped the picture on the scarred wood table. It wasn't Regina Resley. It was a picture of an emaciated, bald effigy that it took me several seconds to recognize.

Naomi—

It was hard to make out just what he was saying. Words didn't come easy, but he wanted to know what I did to him, to his daughter. Why did he have false memories of another family in the desert, and what was his real fucking name, please?

Before I could think of an answer, he let out a desolate sob and lunged at me, hands around my throat.

⁙

Did I leave that part out?

Carl. I didn't let myself think too much about who he was or where he came from. It was so upsetting, I resented him if I even thought about it, because it never bothered him, and if I could fix myself so I didn't remember Naomi either, then I would have. I was jealous of Carl, because he had someone to fix him.

Carl came looking for his daughter about a month after the Incident. I had split town and was hiding, but he was a retired cop and a widower with nothing else to do. He wanted to know where his daughter was, and since nobody else knew and I was her good friend and had fled right when she went missing, I had a lot of explaining to do.

Instead, I stabbed him in the neck with a syringe of Elixir. I was still haphazardly translating the journal with a big Larousse French dictionary, and I was seriously considering throwing all of it in the ocean and starting over.

But then I had an ideal subject. It was easy to erase memories, but putting something in its place ... that took nuance. Starting with Carl, I had gone from something resembling a sleepwalker to someone who believed quite firmly in the fantasy I had given him, who enjoyed the love of a family in his head every night while he lay alone in a motel room. He was happier with my lies than with his real wife and daughter.

But try to tell a man that when he's strangling you.

None of my safe words worked. Not even the nuclear one, the name of his daughter. Breathless, I gasped them in his ear, but he was a me-killing machine. More in sorrow than in panic, I took out the injector pen I'd mixed for Mrs. Resley and stuck it in his left armpit.

He went limp, crushing me on the table. I rolled out from under him and sat down, composing my thoughts. The taco shop workers watched me through the window. Cars passed on the street.

All my work ruined. Her name should have shut him down, but he had found it, and come back for me. I couldn't accept that my programming had simply come undone.

To rebuild Carl would be impossible ... his identity was a patchwork stitched together over the last four years. I could leave him blank, but someone would come looking. A man with no memory is interesting, while a man with sad memories can't be buried fast enough. Far easier to restore him to where he was when I found him, with a few hasty updates to account for the missing time.

You've been drinking and drifting ever since you found out your daughter Naomi died of a drug overdose. But now, it's time to go home, to pick up the pieces and live your life.

I gave him a little more off the top of my head, then put some cash in his wallet. I asked him who did this to him. Who gave him this picture of Naomi, digitally dated four years ago.

Even under the Elixir, he could not, or would not say. The words he seemed to mouth but could not speak aloud, I could only guess that they were: *Your Master.*

I spent the next several hours hiding out from the Plot, trying to figure out what to do next. Waiting to see who'd try to fuck me up next.

Reading the French Play.

Like naked celebrity photos or instructions for making a nuclear weapon, you can find no end of fakes and fragments of the French Play on the Internet. But all the versions out there are counterfeits, malware or worse. Even the most scandalous English translations omitted much, and if an editor only suffered a stroke or a nervous breakdown in the process, he was lucky.

I felt something for Regina Resley that I had not for any of my other products. She was beautiful and smarter than me and she stood at the heart of everything I had thrown away my life to discover. How could I not fall for her?

That's what I told myself, but I loved her as I loved mystery, and because chasing after her lost me in a story less pathetic than my own.

There's just the stories, and people who weave them to trap a bit of reality and tame it, and people get trapped in them and think they're taming the world and playing it like a game to get what they want, like shaking a gourd and doing a dance to make it rain. Sympathetic magic. Spill blood so it'll rain blood.

Stories do all that for us, and what do they ask in return?

I didn't own a copy. But I figured I for sure knew who did. The condo in Hillcrest had three pet grad students in it. None of them were wired Ex Libris drones, just the new crop of coeds from which Resley had once picked Regina.

I didn't have to search Resley's office. It was on the desk in plain sight, nicely annotated with Post-it tongues sticking out of the crumbling, acid-etched pages. He was nowhere to be found, so I sat behind his desk, donned a pair of rubber gloves and started to read. I don't think I got through the dramatis personae before I blacked out again.

I sat upon a threadbare throne hidden behind a moth-eaten screen as the curtain fell. A river of parchment skin and brittle bones rattled applause out of the void beyond the footlights.

"You were marvelous," she said. She took the gold-trimmed tails of my cloak and slit them with a straight razor.

My hands went to my face and touched the mask. It wouldn't come off. Her hand on mine was colder than the razor. "It's a short intermission. Do you want them to see your naked face?"

I had to search for my own voice. The Lines hung in the air like the promise of plague. "In the ... in the last play ... your husband hired me to turn you against your master ..."

Her hands went to her face. The razor sheared away a wing of her bangs. "Oh, look what you've made me do ... You're gnawing at my motivation again."

"I'm sorry, Regina. I only wanted to know ..."

Her eyes went blank and blind. "We're here now, and that's all that matters. We don't ever have to leave ... *so long as we play.*"

She returned to tattering my wardrobe, hysteria whickering in her throat so I didn't dare press. "All of this to be gotten through ... all these scenes ... As if any of it matters ... But our reward ..."

"What do we get? What comes at the end?"

She looked up from her work and kissed my frigid mask. "Why ... *you* do!"

"In the next act ... I can't recall the lines ... but you ... you're going to murder someone ...?"

"Imagine that! I couldn't murder my own shadow ... Even when She almost ... but no ... No, you won't ..."

Agitated, she cast about with the razor. "He's not going to find me here. You won't tell, will you? If he doesn't, if we get to the end, then we can go and live where everything has already happened, but we'll remember, won't we? The black starshine won't erase us ... The sun beneath the sea won't forget us, because we'll stop it, we'll never have to be born again and we'll stop them, the stopping stoppers ... stop ..."

The words seemed to come apart in her mind. She looked at me in alarm, the razor clenched in a white, birdlike fist, her soft white wrists cobwebbed with hesitation scars. "Oh my Lord, I'm undone … I have forgotten my lines! He's coming to correct us …"

The screen around us was hoisted into the gallery. The throne withdrew on whimpering casters with me on it, leaving her trembling alone on the boards when the curtain lifted. She threw up her hands and told me to run just before she dissolved in the pale yellow light.

I looked up from the book, my thumb jammed into the last act. He must've come while I was … reading? Sleeping? He sat on the leather couch under the picture window overlooking the ocean. He was wearing the same plum worsted wool suit he had on at school, which was fortunate. It hid the stains.

Resley had no face. Everything from ear to ear, from hairline to chin, was stripped away in a frenzy of slashing, flaying strokes that left only ribbons of gristle dangling from his naked skull. The worst of the mess lay strewn across transcripts of phone conversations with me piled in his lap.

Two grad students were waiting in the hall. "We've called the police. You really should wait here." They didn't stop me leaving. They shot me with their phones as I fled the scene covering my face with the French Play.

Marble was slated to speak to a few thousand at the Extensions Festival, a massive New Age, human-potential snake oil block party on the Prado. I left my car in the zoo lot and cut through eucalyptus groves and twisting canyons to the backside of Balboa Park.

Yellow-gray clouds draped over the park, clammy fever sheets gravid with rain that couldn't fall. Shadows seeped up out of the decaying Spanish colonnades, alcoves choked with morbid satyrs and defaced saints, faces gouged off and bearded in graffiti and guano. Hotter in the shady arcades than under the stricken sun.

I heard the watery echoes of Marble's voice lapping at the walls everywhere in the park, but it took me a long time to locate him. A cohort of grad students surrounded the Spreckels Organ Pavilion and Ex Libris had bussed their dupes in, so the crowd overflowed the pavilion and swamped the Prado and forked around the goldfish pond to back up against the botanical gardens. Everywhere among them, you could see the earbuds and skullcaps of the ones already listening to his voice, his brainwaves, telling them how to be not just the heroes, but the authors of the story of their lives.

They followed me into the Model Railroad Museum. One of them shot me in the hand. The projectile was the size of a pub dart. My hand went rubbery and spasmed out from under me as I climbed onto the tabletop model. I tripped over Cajon Pass, kicked a hole in Mt. Palomar and wrecked the Santa Fe Super Chief. Ancient volunteer engineers in blue caps tried to pull me down, but I staggered towards the HO-scale downtown, intent on stomping Balboa Park, crushing the shoebox-sized replica of the Organ Pavilion and its tiny plastic Preston Marble before Regina could find him. I only made it as far as Fashion Valley. I collapsed on my face and had to be dragged out, numbly clutching many broken boxcars.

Tranquilizer darts. Seriously. It's heartbreaking to devote your life to abducting people efficiently and safely, and then to be taken by sadistic amateurs.

"D'you know how you can tell you're trapped in an inferior writer's universe?" someone said. "Nobody can speak more than three sentences without sounding exactly like the narrator."

I woke up in a tiny, dusty tea room. The only window was covered up by a faded French, maybe Belgian, flag. I was a prisoner in one of the Houses of Hospitality.

Two big men with thick glasses blocked the door. A stocky man with doleful eyes and no hair of any kind on his head except for a full white handlebar mustache that hid his mouth, so his deep, overly familiar voice could have been coming from anywhere. His left hand rested on his lap like a dead pet, bandaged and splinted as it would be for a deep wound. Say stopping a knife—

"Do you know why cultures die, Mr. ———?" He took a cup of tea from a bodyguard with his right hand. Nobody offered me one. "The Native Americans saw their narrative arc demolished by the more dynamic European colonial dialectic. Their myth, their story-way, was gone, and they soon followed it. They were dead inside, long before we put them on reservations.

"Same with modern America. All our myths gone to rust and reality TV. Fantasies of quick fame and fortune, of swift and brutal retribution on the lazy, the stupid, the poor. There's no mythic resonance to daily life. That's why everyone dreams of writing a book or a screenplay.

Everyone feels one in them, that never gets out. That story they can't tell is *themselves!*"

A bodyguard handed him a napkin to blot the spilled tea. "More powerful than drugs, than God or death or fear itself, are *stories*. With less instinct than any flatworm, we look for them to tell us what to do, how to behave, how we're going to end up. There're plenty of atheists in foxholes, but none without a personal mythology that gives them meaning. When life seems long and meaningless, stories make it short and exciting, make every accident into a test, into enemy action, into a *Plot.*"

My head throbbed from the tranquilizer. I still couldn't feel my hand. Trying not to stare too fixedly at the teacup, I said, "I'm falling asleep again, you dick. Bullet points, please."

"Exposition is death," he admitted. He tossed his empty teacup into the cold fireplace.

"Would it kill you to give me something to drink?"

The bodyguards looked at each other. One went to a tea service in the corner and graced me with lukewarm bottled water that wasn't French. It tasted like a kiss from someone with worse breath than mine.

"People call what I do a cult, and that hurts. I help people tell their stories. I teach them to see the mythic resonance in their daily lives. I tell them the world is full of shit, and I'm right. The disciple pays for wisdom with submission. But this isn't a cult. Nobody here worships me. I don't tell anyone what's going to happen to them when they die.

"Everyone who comes to me, I help them articulate their One Story, their narrative arc, and I don't just help them create a marketable masterpiece. I help them tell their story compellingly, because *that* is where they will go when they die."

My sleepy hand wouldn't cooperate with the clapping. "You should say that up front, more people would join up. What's this got to do with the Resleys? You know he hired me to deprogram Regina so he could try to get her to kill you."

He looked delighted. "Of course. He was only following my outline. Do you know the difference between a fringe cult and a legitimate religion?" He anticipated my obligatory smartass answer. "One dead messiah."

"It's hard to believe you're having a hard time getting someone to kill you."

"With respect, you're not a storyteller. Regina was addicted to escapism and had no real story of her own to tell, so she naturally insinuated herself into mine. Easier to be the villain in your own story, than trying to be something you can't imagine. At least you know where the end is."

Pointing at his mangled hand with mine, I asked, "Why didn't you let her finish you off when you had the chance?"

"Timing is everything. Our lives are like coal. Shaped for eons in darkness to be used up in an instant. Stories are the heat, the light, they emit as they burn."

"If we're lucky. So … your … *arc* comes to a dramatic end, cut down by a traitorous disciple … I think I've seen it before."

"Then you know how it ends. Preston Marble the Man dies, but Marble's Word lives on in *every* man. She'll play her part."

"She's playing it now. She killed her husband, less than an hour's walk from here."

"Nobody seems to have seen her there." He held up his phone to tab through a slew of amateur paparazzi snaps of yours truly fleeing the condo with a gray blur like a struggling dove trapped in my hand. "Just you."

"You don't know where she is."

"We thought you had her, but wherever her body's gone to ground, we're confident she'll rise to the occasion when the curtain goes up."

"Why *The King*—"

Shaking his head vehemently, "Don't." He gathered his thoughts, fetishism warring with fear. He told his bodyguards to wait outside.

"Few can bear to read it at all, and most give up or are thwarted, and everyone who claims to have read it has described a different ending, with variations large and small, but no two alike … because no reader or actor has ever *truly* finished it …"

"But that's not possible. It's just a play, for fuck's sake. How hard can it be to get to the end of a goddamn book …?"

"Every reader must enter the text alone. None emerge unchanged. Some never return at all. Regina is that most *rara avis*: a *pure* reader. Only the most extreme spheres of abstraction satisfied her, but once dug in, she was impossible to shake out again.

"To reach her … to break her out of her fugue and quicken her to her purpose, we needed some radical outside element to catalyze the last act. You'll continue to serve our plot until your arc is complete."

"And your arc will end with her killing you … to try to make Ex Libris a mainstream religion …?" He shrugged, all false modesty. A bodyguard watched us through the porthole window in the cottage door. I tossed my water at him.

The door flew open and they were on me before it hit him. My head hit the wall, but I saw how he caught it with his bandaged left hand. It seemed to hurt him a lot less than if someone had just stabbed him there.

"You're not Marble," I said, feeling brilliant.

"Well, of course not … But I've played him for many years, and I've only ever quoted the Master. Professor Marble retired from public life three years ago, and communicates only through bibliomancy and doubles."

Quotations selected at random from his own books on writing. "You're willingly going to die just so he can attend his own funeral?"

It was pure hell finding something that didn't make him smile. "He will be alive and yet mythologically dead. He will be, in point of phenomenological fact, a living god."

"And did *you* have any say in how this would … will … happen?"

"*The Secret Agent*, by Joseph Conrad. It's one of my favorites. Have you ever …?"

I shook my head. I lie a lot. "You're so tight with the, ah, Master … What's he really like?"

"Could you ever hope to attain mastery so complete that when you close your eyes, your disciple opens them, not merely believing in, but *being*, you? That's what he's like. I pray to him: TEACH ME TO BE YOU. And silently, wisely, he has."

Outside, the pipe organ was crushing the exultant final movement of Saint-Saëns' 3rd Symphony. A timid knock at the low, rounded door lifted Marble's double out of his chair. He shuffled through ankle-deep dust, looking over his shoulder at me from the open doorway. "I imagine you're about to be overwhelmed with remorse when you find out what your last patient has done. You're going to become very emotional over the undoing of your perverse amateur brainwashing operation, and with the police at your door and so many ruined lives in your wake, you'll be doing the world a favor. A real one, not like the sick games you played with helpless, vulnerable people's minds."

I couldn't help but nod along. "That does sound like me. Did you write it all out?"

Slapping his forehead, he produced his trademark overstuffed spiral-bound journal and shook out a slip of paper from my motel. Someone had surely meditated very deeply upon my choppy block capital handwriting. "How much do I owe you for this?"

Chuckling, he nodded and walked out into a monsoon of applause as the organ symphony reached its crescendo. Three bodyguards came into the cottage once he was clear and escorted me to a limousine. The bitter tang of mildewed paper and incense. I got in without making a scene.

The book was gone, but I didn't need it. A bodyguard got in with me as the limo pulled away from the curb. He crushed me against the passenger seat. I hit and kicked to no effect. Try as I might, I couldn't even bruise myself against him. I wasn't there at all by the time he hooded me in a two-ply plastic yard waste bag and wrapped his arm around my neck in a truly professional sleeper hold.

⁂

I was back in the gallery. I wore a soldier's uniform. Regina wore a tattered ochre cloak made from an asbestos fire curtain.

She pulled back a drape hiding an alcove and a tarnished brazen bell cover. She lifted the cover and showered us in verdigris-hued light that seemed to rot all that it illuminated.

Underneath it, her husband's severed, faceless head. Upon his brow, cruelly piercing it, the source of the dismal glow—a plain golden circlet transfixed with barbarous, spiky coronal flares.

"A cabal of Spanish conquistadors who sought the seven cities of gold from California to Patagonia made it with all the gold they found. In their bitter madness, they dedicated the crown to Cibola, a kingdom that never was.

"A crown must be ritually consecrated by blood and soil to bind the land and the people to the ruler's bloodline. It was drowned in blood, but never has it touched earth. Outside, it's only a curiosity, but because it's here, the play has outrun the Plot. Whoever claims it becomes King of Hastur. They shall don it and declare a state of war and lay siege to Carcosa … And bring the curtain down upon us all. If he is not stopped … Take it."

I knew it would burn and mutilate my hand. It hurt to touch it, until I realized *I* was hurting me. My fear of it turned to raw, phantom agony, an almost magnetic repulsion.

"Now, I must play my role." The slip of paper clutched in her hand bore a strangely unfinished, yet overripe symbol, a kind of three-headed question mark rendered in saffron ink upon ivory foolscap.

I took her hand. I had no idea of how it ended, but I would do anything to stop it.

I pulled her close and kissed her. Her lips trembled and she clung to me until her passion dissolved into hysterical laughter. "He's coming! If you don't let me go and perform the scene, then we'll all go into the void …"

"No, let's go." And we ran.

Somewhere, a pipe organ swung deliriously into Saint-Saëns' *Danse Macabre*, with the slap of whips on flesh for percussion.

I leapt into the nearest canvas flat, but instead of ripping through painted fabric, I pancaked against immovable stone.

The chamber at our backs was crowded with broken statuary, headless kings and limbless nymphs, clothed in drifts of crematory dust. The flagstones were gray-veined yellow marble, pitted with tiny marine fossils and worn down with centuries of pacing. Fumbling along the wall in the dark, I clung to her arm. I nearly lost her when a long butcher knife slashed through the *trompe l'oeil* scenery on brittle canvas.

Cassilda cried out and ripped her hand free, so I followed her.

We raced down a flight of stairs and through a courtyard of leafless trees; a cavernous library of books that disintegrated in a whirlwind of debris at our passage; a feasting hall with a bowed table buried to the rafters with uneaten, rotten meals; and a ballroom where the blindfolded organist attacked the climax of the delirious, reeling tune in a spastic frenzy. And behind us, just as we escaped each monumental, empty chamber, the butcher knife pierced the canvas and shredded it and our hooded pursuer staggered into fleeting, panicky view.

Breathless, at last we broke through the tall glass doors of the ballroom to end up on a wide balcony overlooking a lake still as stone under two moons. Almost annihilated by the discordant shower of moonlight, on the far shore of the lake and yet somehow further away than the moons, I could see the spires of a city.

Cassilda threw off her robes and cast the Yellow Sign onto the water with a shiver of bravado. "Can you swim, my darling?"

I looked down, shaking my head. "It's not even water …"

She looked at my hand. Only then noticing the crown cutting into my fingers, I threw it after the Yellow Sign.

The ripples from our offerings passed like the quivers of sleeping meat. Deep within it, I could see sepulchral gray lights of unborn ghosts.

The now-familiar purr and crack of steel ripping through canvas and petrified wooden struts echoed through the ballroom. We had been lost, but now were found.

She climbed onto the railing, fingers dug into the eyeless mask of a caryatid. "Come, darling, if we are true, then we shall prevail and gain the far shore …"

She kissed me and took my hand. "Quickly, before the sun rises beneath …" I climbed up onto the rail alongside her, looking down into the depths of Hali and seeing those imprisoned souls whose dull glow bored up through the queasy sheen of doubled moonlight on the skin of the water like the moans of the damned from an orchestra pit.

I kissed her one last time, and pushed her.

She did not grab me, but fell gracefully into the water, like a knife.

I watched her dissolve in the darksome gray deeps and heard the chemical scream of her undone body and defiant soul, a pure peal of doomed beauty like an echo of the emptiness of Heaven. She would have to do it all over again, when next the curtain rose.

⁂

I jolted awake to find the trash bag slashed open around my neck, sodden with vomit. The man who'd been killing me only a minute ago now sat with his hands in his lap, looking out the window, pointedly oblivious to our other passengers.

A shrunken, careworn version of the man who'd dictated my suicide note sat across from me. He wore burgundy pajamas and a baggy cardigan with leather elbow patches, bulging oddly, like he had a bulletproof vest underneath. Resley's copy of *The King in Yellow* lay on his trembling knees, open to the beginning of the last act. His bandaged left hand upon it looked like a chicken's claw. His eyes were closed, his head bobbing in time with the whispers of the man who sat next to him, who had no face at all.

It wasn't that I can't recall it now, so much as that I simply could not perceive it, except as a colorless glass mask. He enveloped Marble, whispering in his ear. Sheepishly, Marble nodded. The bodyguard on his other side looked right through me when I mouthed his name.

The limousine stopped and Carl got out to open the door. Marble shuffled out in corduroy slippers, out of the crosswalk and up the ramp to the Prado.

"It was you," was all I could say, "in the … in the play …"

"We've never really been apart," said the faceless man, "from the day you took what was mine."

I stared at him, really *tried* to see him. He smiled. I looked away. For just a moment, he had a face, but it was mine.

"If you knew where I was and what I was doing," I said, "then you could have stopped me … Why didn't you?"

"I could ask you the same question." He turned and rapped on the partition, whispered briefly to Carl. "You could have brought me to the attention of the authorities. We kept each other's secrets admirably. But now …"

I was unable to speak. Was there ever a time when I had not been a puppet of the Plot?

He pointed at Carl. The bodyguard slid across the suede acreage of seat to mix a drink.

"When you stole what was mine, I was beside myself, but then it occurred to me that I might learn more from making a gift of it. And how much you have taught me …"

"I never used it the way you did."

"I know! You attempted to redeem my Elixir! A dismal failure as an alchemist, but what a failure! The raw material, you refined away all the wrong properties. In my own experiments, I called them my angels, because they lacked free will, and were innocent of desire. Your first instinct was to use it to discover, to learn, to interrogate your angels, but you deluded yourself you set them free.

"Your choice of career was, of course, my suggestion. But you deserve credit for the basic decency that gave me the idea to let you … help people with it."

Help people. Learn things. Lies within lies. He didn't even have to erase my true motivation, I did it myself. I wanted what we all want, love and revenge. A cult orphan, nobody's child in a generic post-acid hippie personality cult where children were assigned to adults as punishments. With a different broken, grudging parent every few months, you get to learn ulterior motives like the Eskimos know snow.

"Well, you're too late," I said. "It's all gone. I couldn't figure out how to make more."

Now, I could see his smile, but without eyes, it wasn't much comfort. "The Elixir's potency comes from the ease with which it penetrates the brain, and that is the secret of its rarity. It only propagates in human cerebrospinal fluid and brain matter, and its progress is exquisitely slow. In my home country, we would keep 'cows,' angels too used up to give pleasure, and milk them, but only a few milligrams can be had every year, unless it is allowed to ripen. This takes—"

About four years, I thought, touching my forehead. The headaches weren't withdrawal. The drug I had come to crave was already in my brain.

"It's not working inside your head, of course; there's a lengthy process to activate it, but you've given me a sizable start on a plantation in this country."

Fifty-two clients. Maybe the last few were just starting to have the headaches. Nobody had come to my door to complain yet—

"You know," he said, finishing the drink, "the most remarkable thing about the process … is that, as the fungi gradually digests it, the cow experiences some diminished function, to be sure, but remains a dutiful farm animal long after the brain is little more than a stem.

"The Elixir is far more potent, however, from a patient who enjoys at least the illusion of free will. Your associate Carl has no forelobe to speak of at all, and yet …" He took his drink from Carl, who'd been waiting to deliver it. "How is the family, Carl?"

"Doing real good, thank you, sir!" Carl, smiling.

"So you see, the Elixir makes its own use of the brain, and yet the mind goes on, like a ghost in a haunted house. So long after you have grown weary of your own purpose in life, you may still serve."

He held up a grotesquely long syringe. Carl took hold of my head and pressed it firmly against the opaque black window. "Hold still," he said. I was unable to move it at all even as the needle slid into the soft tissue beside my tear duct, up behind my eyeball and into my skull.

It hurt like being sucked down a black hole, crushed and stretched into a monofilial string. I felt myself surging into the needle's fat reservoir, leaving behind the hapless amateur brainwasher I'd been. I could see the straw-colored fluid dribbling into the syringe. I was being drained out of myself.

When he let me go, I sagged onto a bus stop bench on Park Avenue, across from the zoo. People were running past me and police cars and fire engines surrounded the park. I lay there for a while until a bus came, and I got on and tried to get on with my life.

I spent two weeks in a motel, hiding out and listening. The news made much of Preston Marble's death at the hands of his fanatical understudy. We all saw the video of the disheveled maniac emerging from the crowd to embrace the terrified, charismatic spiritual leader. The black rubber bulb in one hand looks enough like a grenade that two bodyguards move to pry them apart, but somehow, their actions are confused until both men are engulfed in a blanket of white fire.

The vest stuffed with thermite cremated both men on their feet and badly burned thirteen bystanders. The resulting mess was spun to hide Marble's conspiracy, but the narcissistic murder-suicide turned him into another punchline, another hammily-plotted fable that only proved some people will believe anything.

I never saw Regina again, not even in my dreams of the French Play. I hope she reached the city on the far side of the lake. Nobody who's been through what she endured should have to come back.

The alchemist was merciful. He told me that he would come to harvest from me only when he had to. So long as I cooperate, I can go about my business for as long as my brain function holds out. He would leave no memory of his visits, just as he would protect my old patients. He gave me a single dose of the Elixir and told me that if I regretted the way things turned out, I could fix it.

I have recorded a new cover story, a new antibiography, and secured the necessary fake IDs to make it stick.

When I wake up, I will tell myself who I am. But I could not resist giving myself an escape hatch. Next to the tape recorder, Resley's annotated copy of *Le Roi En Jaune.*

Whatever the newborn tenant of this motel room chooses, he will deny you the neat, poignant denouement you seek. He will burn this manuscript and go into the world and write his own ending.

THE MAN WHO ESCAPED
THIS STORY

So, what are we to discuss today, Mister … What is your name today? That would be a good place to start.

No more names, please … Names are lies, except for the one you earn … It's different, anyway every time I try to remember it … and if I gave you one, I wouldn't be the same person I was talking about …

Well then, shall we begin with what you are, right here and now?

That changes too, I'm afraid, and never for the better … Just call me the Protagonist, heh … Have you always wanted to be a psychiatrist?

As long as I can remember, yes. It's my calling, I guess you could—

Calling, sure. But have you ever thought of being anything else?

Everyone fantasizes about a different life, but I'm always a fantasizing psychiatrist. But enough about me … What of the *essential* 'you?' What are you, that never changes? How does it feel to be you?

I'm a whipping-boy. I'm the pain-puppet of an angry, third-rate god … I … I …

Well, now we're getting somewhere. That's a common enough delusion—

That's just the sort of thing one of his characters would say—

So you're convinced that you're just a—

We all are. Let me tell you a story …

What did a guy have to do to summon the Devil?

Mr. Furst was used to getting results, and he'd been trying for a solid month; tried everything he'd seen in movies or read in tabloids and paperback grimoires, even a few new things he'd come up with on his own. But the road to true Biblical evil had been far harder than Sunday school would have you believe.

Even for so naturally immoral a person as he, the descent into mindful malevolence had been harder and more painful than a benevolent soul might find the ascent to sainthood. It was a lonely lookout, he thought as he lit another menthol off the guttering butt of the last, so wrung out he forgot to pick up matches on the way home.

Because of the sacrifice.

He picked up a stray cat that rubbed itself against his trouser leg in the park at midnight. Taking it for a sign, he'd bundled the vermin up in his coat and run to an intersection, where he'd cut its head off with a pocketknife and used the carcass as a brush to paint the sigil of the Ascending Dragon just like in the Pocket Books *Necronomicon*. Then he'd waited, reciting some Babylonian nonsense and some backward Iron Maiden lyrics, but nothing came of it.

He sneezed out the cherry on his cigarette. The cat hair on his coat had triggered an allergic meltdown. Now his cigarette was out, and not even two sticks to rub together for a flame. Same old shit, again and again ...

"I know you're down there watching," he roared at his apartment. "I hear ya laughing at me so much, it sounds like my own goddamn laugh! Church makes out like you turn up whenever a guy spits on a Sunday, but I done the works for you, and I got stood up! Whattaya, scared to do business with a real player? One salesman to another? Think yer better'n me? Please, *fertheluvvaGod ...* "

As his first sacrificial tear hit the naked concrete floor, his front door opened, without any of his locks unlocking, without tripping any of his traps. Just opened. And in walked a blasé, coolcat sonofabitch in a Botany 500 sharkskin suit and scuffed black oxfords. No horns, no red warty skin or forked tail ... not even a sinister beard.

Where a lesser man might've fainted with repentance or relief, Mr. Furst was beside himself at the lack of ceremony; ignore a guy's heartfelt pleas and backbreaking toil in the service of blasphemy for a whole month, only to breeze in the front door dressed like a used-car salesman, without so much as stinking up the joint with brimstone? It rankled, but Mr. Furst wasn't the sort to jump down a guy's throat about details. Cut it and drink from it, maybe, but never jump down it.

The coolcat sonofabitch took a fierce hit off his cigarette like he was sucking poison out of a snakebite and said, "Imagine if you will—"

"Shut up. You gimme a cig first, then we'll talk turkey, and I'm gettin' extra gravy on mine, on account of how long you kept me waiting." He tapped his imitation Rolex to drive home the point. Mr. Furst was never one to let a mark get the first—or the last—word in. He didn't get to be Senior Appliance Salesman at *The Good Guys* by letting goons off the street dictate terms to him, and damned if he'd do business any different with the Prince of Darkness.

"Ah yes," the Devil smiled like a guy looking into a TV camera that only he could see. "Mr. Emil Furst. Takes his business brief, his drinks out of the bottle and his meals from the lunchboxes of slain virgins."

"So you *were* watchin'. I was wondering what it took to make you come around."

"What it takes, Mr. Furst, is a far rarer culinary offering, one not properly served since Hector—"

"Soul, yeah, you want my soul. Quit talkin' in circles."

"I do apologize."

"And I wanna smoke."

"Again, I beg your pardon, but I have only this one. But it never burns down." He puffed hard to prove it. "It was a gift from the R&D people at Phillip Morris. Unmarketable, of course ..."

Mr. Furst made a lobster-claw of his fingers and shoved it under the Devil's nose. "Give it here."

The Devil bethought himself a moment, then handed it over. "Yours, as a token of my esteem. As I was saying—"

"You mean this'll never go out?"

"Eternal. It's a long way between convenience stores, along some routes in my domain."

"Can't crush it out?"

"Impossible."

"Dunk it in water?"

"It would not only be futile—"

"Great." He hit the cigarette. Smooth and satisfying. "Get on with it."

The Devil smiled obligingly. "Of course. Now, in all fairness, you must admit that what you bring to the table is somewhat tarnished to begin with, so—"

"Whattaya mean, 'tarnished'? My soul's as pure as the next guy's."

"On the contrary. Even before your campaign of terror to get my attention, your soul was never a Golden Fleece, so to speak. It's a fair bet you'd have been mine anyway, barring some miraculous deathbed repentance."

"A deathbed *what?*"

"Precisely. Had you given it any thought, you might've realized that all you had to do was perform a few outstanding *good* works, and I'd have been at your side with all the theatrics you crave in an instant. Still, I don't get much chance to do this kind of trading anymore—"

"You know, you're not the only one out there buying up souls."

"Oh, I'm well aware of that. The old milieu guaranteed us such a vast market share that we became careless about image, and it's no surprise, in hindsight, that so many clients have taken their business elsewhere. There's more than a few out there collecting, and their offers are tempting, but whom can you trust? They're not bound by the same regulations as I—"

"So what? I'm supposed to cry for you?"

"Remember who called whom, Mr. Furst." Tapping his own fake Rolex.

"Okay, brass tacks. I was gonna ask for money and broads and shit, but then it hits me. I won't 'preciate any of that 'cause I didn't earn it. Then I get depressed, I get crazy, I get dead, and I go to Hell and get the shaft forever and a day, am I right?"

"You've seen right through us, Mr. Furst."

"So I didn't know what to ask for. At least not until you give me this cig, then I get an angle. I wanna live forever. No funny business, no fine print. I LIVE FOREVER. That way, I'll have all the time in the world to earn the good life, so's I can 'preciate it with a clean conscience. Dig?"

"Like a sexton's shovel in 14th century Venice, Mr. Furst. You're the kind of man who lives for the afterglow of towering achievements, and the thrill of still-greater prospects ahead."

"That's me all over."

"I'm just afraid that's an awfully tall order for a soul so shabby, that we'll never even collect on …"

"I'll throw you so many referrals along the way, you'll never want to see me come back—"

"I'm sure if you look at it from my perspective, we can come to a more reasonable settlement—"

"No deal! I live forever, or I walk! Or maybe I go into the soul-collecting business myself …"

"No need for threats. Alright, I think we can afford to take one on the chin, if it'll spark up some life in the market. You'll be sure to tell all your friends, if you ever chance to make any?" The Devil looked almost obsequious as he fished a red leatherette ledger out of his breast pocket.

"I got a secretary back at the store, gave it up to me for a baggie of marching powder, she'd probably sell her soul to you for a makeover. You gonna write up the deal now?" He edged up alongside the Devil; this was when you had to look out. This was when a real salesman screwed the customer, yes indeed. Extended service warranty, delivery charges, and so on. They never read the fine print, and he dragged them to Hell every time.

"Make that 'forever an a day,' just like I said before. And that 'achievements and prospects' bit too, I don' want no boring eternity." The Devil obligingly spelled it out and signed on his dotted line, then passed the pen and ledger to Mr. Furst.

"Not so fast, let a guy read." His lips moving with painstaking care, he perused the contract. It was neither as complicated nor as elaborate as he'd expected—hell, it was simpler and homelier than the form he had to fill out to get copies made at work. "*I, Emil Furst, accept the agreed upon terms entitling me to eternal life on earth in present corporeal state, to enjoy satisfaction of great achievements and grand prospects, in return for my immortal soul, for a term of not less than forever and a day. I understand that all force majeure clauses are herewith suspended, and that this contract can only be terminated by mutual agreement of both parties.*" He grumbled over some of the larger words for a while, then signed it.

"Best deal anyone's ever gotten out of Hell, Mr. Furst. When you spread the word, don't let's be too honest about our terms, please?" The Devil looked around for the first time as Furst studied his carbon receipt for the fiftieth. "Lovely place you've got here. One could spend eternity here, and never want for comfort."

"It's a dump, but I like my privacy. I got it for a song, and I'm tapped into municipal power and water and the neighbor's cable, so no bills. See, Devil? Nobody screws Emil Furst."

"Indeed. Well, our business, then, is at an end ..."

"And I get to keep the cigarette?"

"You and that cigarette were made for each other, Mr. Furst. Don't worry about a thing. An eternity of pleasure and anticipation awaits,

Mr. Furst. A latter-day Sisyphus, you are. All the world at your feet in no time, I have no doubt."

The Devil's logorrhea rolled over Furst like a hot, balmy wind, but he was sharp enough to catch the false note. "D'you call me a sissy?"

"You know, the best kind of deal is when both parties walk away believing they've gotten the best of the other."

"Yeah, pleasure doing business with you, too. Get the hell out."

"Be seeing you," the Devil murmured, and left. The locks relocked, the traps reset, and Furst was alone. He stood there and thawed for a moment, the realization sinking in like the nicotine stain and carbon ink on his fingers.

He couldn't die! The things he'd do, the places he'd wreck, the people he'd settle up with … More, he'd beaten the Devil at his own game. He'd screwed the tits off the patron saint of salesmen, and he'd only go up from there. That crack he'd made about going into the soul business himself had seemed to rattle His Satanic Majesty an awful lot. Maybe he could drive the Devil out of the Devil business. But first, he'd go out to have a drink, celebrate …

Before the door, he fumbled out his keyring. So many keys on it, five for the front door alone, two for the car, three for the store, one for the bank night deposit, and his pocketknife and a bottle opener and a mini-flashlight, besides. It was hard to juggle with the lit cigarette, and, as he often did, he dropped them onto the poured concrete floor.

Leaning over, cursing his keys and their mothers and his own as well, he picked them up. He took a deep, satisfying hit off the eternal cigarette. *Emil Furst, the man who beat the Devil today and who'll do it again tomorrow, can't even hold onto his keys.* He laughed.

And the man who beat the Devil dropped his keys.

And he picked them up.

And took a hit off the cigarette.

And laughed.

And dropped his keys …

⁖

And how long have you been suffering from these … stories, Emil?

Don't call me that! What'd I tell you?

I'm very sorry. But you said—

What's a character's name, before someone invents him? Where did he live? Where does he go when it ends?

Why ... here? Is that what you're saying?

Exactly. As for the stories ... For as long as I can remember. Sometimes, they're all I can remember.

Please elaborate.

I have no childhood, no memories at all except these contrived, cruel situations. I wake up sad because suddenly, I had a child who died of a mysterious disease or a sudden car wreck. I wake up evil because I'm ugly and bad and have a mean name. The only time things seem focused or tangible is when they happen. The rest of the time ... I'm talking to you.

But why do you harbor such disgust for them, if you believe they're real life, and *this* experience only a dream?

As shabby as they are—and the prose that describes them ... God, how I wish I at least had my own words for them—they're so much more real *than anything here. I can't see your face, for instance. Or the plaques on your office wall; they're just gray shades, props with no words on them. Everything is like that to me, Doctor—people, things, my own body. We're not made of atoms, Doctor—we're made of words! There's no pleasure or pain, no hot or cold ... All I can feel is a vague sense of weight and a feeling of repulsion, of animosity.*

You feel that inanimate objects wish to do you harm?

No. Just that this world wants to push me out. It ignores me, it breaks down, it gets lost, gets sick and dies, stands me up, goes crazy, bores me, hurts me, catches fire, gets scratched up by the cat or melts in the sun, and it won't return my calls. Things ... people ... They repel me, they push me out ... into the stories.

At least in the stories, there's some sort of ... meaning. I have a family or a wife or a position of power, though it always turns to shit in some cheaply ironic fashion. Or he makes me a real shitheel who deserves whatever happens to him.

But good or bad, I almost always die. But like ... you know how, in horror movies, people's heads and limbs just come off like they have no skeletons, no connective tissue. That's the real horror, when you're cut open and you realize you were never really alive ...

And you believe that God is to blame for this, that you're some kind of pawn for His amusement.

No, not at all. God wouldn't make worlds like these: flawed, unfinished, breaking down and not there at all when I'm not looking. No, most of the time, I think I'm in the hands of a Demiurge. Do you know Gnosticism, Doctor?

Not as well as *you* seem to …

Heh … God doesn't have anything to do with the Material world. For him, it'd be like playing in his own shit. A Demiurge created this world, and its flaws are a reflection of his tortured, self-hating soul. Everything in it is poorly conceived, and wants to fall apart. We're all puppets made of shit, living out lies. This world is the closet I lie in until he takes me out to make me play his sadistic games.

It gratifies you, however, to be the special object of these episodes. You feel important, as the focal point of his … excuse me, His … attentions.

It sickens me. He traps me in these awful plotlines. No matter what I try to do, I'm sticking my head into the noose, even as I'm crying out for it to stop. The hardest part is, I always have to act surprised when it happens.

Why do you think He does it to you?

Why do little kids draw on the walls, burn ants or pull wings off flies? To prove that they're God, too …

Haven't you invested quite a lot of energy in making these escapes of yours seem real? And doesn't their punitive violence reflect your own feelings of inadequacy, that you can't grant yourself even the boon of a rewarding fantasy life?

No! Nobody hates themselves this much! You don't know what it's like … Oh God, it's like—

⁘

Jarvis Glaublich felt empty inside, a hollow shell against which events flailed and battered, like machines on a disassembly line. The faith of his parents offered no revelations to fill him with light, only deeper shadows that covered the secret workings of life in malicious mystery. Hadn't they themselves been deprived of all but the knowledge that they were flawed and dirty vessels, speaking of nothing with passion and enjoying sexual congress only through a hole in a sheet?

He walked the earth in the trappings of a beast of burden, but without the serenity of a beast's serene understanding of its true role. If there was a truth which could fill him, he would gladly pledge his soul, kill or die for it, and rest in peace. But his was not a seeker's nature, and though his hunger for faith gnawed him inside, he settled for it, because it was not emptiness.

One thing which Jarvis's inherited faith did instill was an assiduous work ethic, which propelled him to a position of median responsibility at his job without any real effort. So it was that, laid over in a strange, fogbound city long after midnight while on a business trip, he was chased down a dim side street by a rampaging psychotic with pendular throat tumors like the wattles of a frilled lizard, who chanted, "*Beatupwhitepeople, taketheystuff,*" in time to the rhythm of his fist pounding the side of his own head. Terrified, Jarvis dragged his suitcase by its leash even after the wheels had all broken off. It skipped behind him like a runaway sled, and swept his feet out from under him when he stopped at a lighted street corner.

A woman stood beneath the lamppost, wearing a long woolen coat and a stocking cap. She held a clipboard in one hand and reached out to Jarvis with the other, her warm smile smothering his primal terror like a security blanket.

"You look like you could use some help," she said. "Would you like to come inside?" When he turned, he found she'd dispelled the maniac. Still, it was out of fear for his safety that he accepted her invitation.

She explained as she led him up the street that she was a member of a nondenominational outreach program dedicated to self-discovery and improvement. They stopped before an office building that, alone among all the buildings on the block, glowed with interior lights and hummed with activity. People moved about behind the windows, animated by a sense of purpose and imbued with a radiant wellbeing that struck Jarvis harder than his suitcase.

"Have you ever felt empty inside, Mr. Glaublich?" she asked.

"What do you want me to do?" he asked.

"Only to take a brief personality test, like a survey. Then, if you're interested in what we have to tell you about yourself, you can learn more." Was it the hunger of his faithlessness, the warm, smiling woman beside him, or the cancerous monster skulking beyond the glow of the lamp that set Jarvis Glaublich upon his path? (Or was it you, ungentle Reader, without whom he might never have existed, at all?)

The survey only took fifteen minutes. Jarvis had taken personality tests in college that lasted for hours and well over a thousand questions, and offered funhouse-mirror reflections of himself. But with twenty questions, the nice lady effortlessly parsed Jarvis Glaublich's Gordian angst. She catalogued him and his mountainous freight of woes in the third person, and he wept to hear this miserable stranger's trouble. How did he live? On what shared article of faith did the cells of his organism agree to slog through his life, and not fly apart to lead successful, solitary lives as dust-eating amoebae? What was it all for, anyway? The questions burned holes in his brain, spilled out of his mouth.

"You can't find the answers to those questions in your fleshly body. The mortal senses cannot comprehend the truths of the universe, any more than a cell of the body can comprehend the larger purpose of the whole."

"I can't accept that. Everyone wants you to take it on faith that there's a meaning, that you'll know, but only after it's too late. How can I know *now*?"

She told him about the subtle energy fields that inhabited matter and gave it form. Consciousness was no more nor less than an energy field that recognized itself. A weird fusion of quantum physics and animism, her pitch swallowed every tenet of modern science that conventional religions choked on; evolution, the Big Bang and extraterrestrial life were not anathema, but scripture. And this was only the skin of the truth, she told him. In this lifetime, they knew all the answers, and knew what even spiritual seekers, when the day was done, had to take on faith. She offered him a book, *Out of the House of Matter*, free of charge, and called him a taxi.

Jarvis began to read the book on the flight home. At first, he was disappointed. Where the lady had hinted at miracles, he found breathing exercises, meditation schemes and a lot of yogic nonsense that proceeded from the baseline state of inner tranquility that he was seeking, rather than offering a way to reach it. Angrily, he stuffed the book into the magazine caddy jammed against his knees and tried to sleep.

As his mind drifted into that fleeting phase of hypnagogic association that the book called the *theta state*, the breathing exercises rose unbidden to his mind, began to set themselves in motion, and Jarvis was cut free for the first time in his life from maintaining its operation, indeed cut free from the body itself. He saw himself cramped in the tourist class seat as he had been trapped inside his body for so long, and realized what he had become.

A being of pure intellect, the ghost free of the machine, but to what purpose? He drifted about the cabin, testing new senses, seeing the stunted, insensate energy fields of other travelers writhing like sodden laundry in damaged, dying washing machines, unaware of their own divinity, unable or unwilling to respond to his reaching out.

And what of the world beyond the airplane? Infinity yawned outside, yielding no answers, no purpose. So the soul was an independent entity from the body; what good eternal, bodiless life in an empty universe, like a lone insomniac in an eternally sleeping city? It was a small, unsatisfying truth in the end, but a large enough revelation to hint at others beyond. Practice the breathing exercises, master the meditational disciplines, and perhaps a greater truth would one day reveal itself, and fill him with what he sought. He remembered to retrieve the book before he deplaned.

In the months that followed, he worked to strengthen his grasp on the elementary principles of astral projection. He learned to bring about the escape at will, and to manipulate his energy field so as to travel, not merely drift. But new lessons brought him only greater confusion, raised only deeper questions. Separation from and objective viewing of his empty body tore away his previous conception of self: he was not the snub-nosed, colorless little man slumbering on the couch, any more than he was the boxy little car that little man drove to work every morning. What was he, then? A lonely, bodiless traveler in a strange, featureless country bereft of inhabitants from whom he might gain some perspective on his own true nature. He considered and rejected again and again the notion of contacting the people from whom he'd received the book. He would not give up his new understanding for a place in an organized religion, which guarded and doled out revelations that should be his alone. He became a seeker at last, but his steps were halting and uncertain, and seemed to lead him only into deeper doubt.

For a while contented himself with exploring his apartment building, his city. This soon proved tiresome, for the few bright souls he could even perceive were like the atheists in Dante's *Inferno*, willful prisoners in mausoleums of flesh and bone, dumbly denying their own torment.

In the flesh, he tried to introduce his breathing exercises to a few neighbors. Small wonder that they stopped their ears to his proselytizing, as his manners and appearance had suffered for all his astral wandering. His job, too, had gone on without him. Returning from a jaunt of some days' length, he found his shelves bare of edible food, his utilities switched off, and his body in an advanced state of abandonment. Bitterly, he saw to its needs and disposed of his automobile to pay his most pressing debts. He thought about selling a kidney, if he'd have to wait around that long.

He had reached the far turn in his quest, that his emptiness had only enlarged itself to encompass an empty world. When he transcended it, he would come upon the inner truth that held the universe together, and would enable him to return to his body and live in the world like those happy pilgrims at the outreach foundation.

As his skill at astral projection grew, he developed new senses and rediscovered the universe unbounded by the time and space traps that snared his material self. He could span any distance as an act of will, compressing time so that a journey anywhere in the world could be made in a single session. Still, his jaunts were empty affairs, for no one appeared to guide or enlighten him. Was he an aberration, alone in the universe in his ability, or were they hiding from him, perhaps until such time as he could comprehend on his own the mystery he hoped to unravel? He understood that though the universe was indeed boundless, the domain of matter had definite and unforgiving boundaries, folded upon itself like a Chinese puzzle box to give only the illusion of infinity. He slipped beyond it one night, and held it in his hand. Beyond it lay a greater emptiness, a space beyond all space which he could not hope to traverse and ever return, and which offered no emissary to lead him to his destination. And that is when he saw the Other.

At first, he took it for a star, though he had traveled beyond stars and, indeed, grasped all the stars and space within himself. A pulsating light of unbearable intensity, it plummeted out of the absolute void and flashed past him, brushing against him with the unmistakable vibrations of consciousness, its edges unblunted by the material ties which had left him so skewed and alone.

At last, intelligent life! He attempted to communicate, but found this faculty had not progressed beyond the infantile in his evolved state.

He struggled to follow the Other, plunging down into the net of matter he'd so painfully escaped, down through spinning galaxies, constellations and suns, all the way down to his world, his land, his city, his apartment, his living room.

He entered his room, but the Other was gone. Despondent, he approached his body, which in his absence had soiled itself.

He could not get in. Something pushed him out where before he had found entry automatic, like succumbing to a vacuum.

Sleepily, his eyes opened. They regarded him with benevolent comprehension, alert perception wedded to placid understanding of the arcane truths he'd found unattainable. Then they looked away. He watched as his body arose from his stained couch, cleaned itself, set his apartment in order, and called on the telephone.

"Yes, I understand. I'd like to open an outreach franchise in my city. Yes … Very good." Jarvis Glaublich's body regarded him again, his careworn face beaming on him with cosmic pity.

"The truth shall set you free," the usurper of Jarvis Glaublich's body told him, and blew him out of the house of matter, to find it.

⁓

Your episodes seem to share common themes …

What is this, self-serve analysis? You want me to spell them out?

You have a morbid fixation on spirituality and the occult, which is a coping mechanism for your uneasy atheism. Your preoccupation with paralysis suggests a metaphorical dialectic to interpret your self-doubt.

Not me, goddammit, haven't you heard a word I've said? It's not me. It's Him. Everything is Him.

I've urged you to get out more. What did you do last night?

I went to the movies.

What did you see?

I don't know … it doesn't matter, does it? I sat in the front row, and I cried, because I knew I was a fictional character, too. Only the stories I live in are cheap little sacks of pus and petty dread for sick freaks who can't wait to be dead, but they're still scared to die. And I couldn't take it anymore. I climbed up onto the apron and tried to break through the screen, to get into their story, any story but this one.

This one? You mean you believe we're in a story right now?

That's all there is here, is stories. This one is shabbier and even less developed than the rest, but it's a story. Or a journal, I don't know … My Demiurge is a hack writer who thinks too much, and loves himself too little. He's you, Doctor.

OK … this has gone far enough—

Don't look at me like that! You're probing me, trying to wring another drop of anxiety out of me for a story. I'm not your whipping boy, anymore. I can escape you, go where you'll never find me again.

You know the best way to exorcise these kinds of delusions, don't you?

Oh, if I only could. Someday, I'd like to write a story about HIM.

Where do you get your ideas?

People often asked O———, as they always did when stuck in a dead-end conversation with a writer. And as any writer trapped by such a profoundly stupid question would, he held forth about how *anything* could inspire a real writer, but he always looked around first to see if his cousin the clinical therapist was in earshot.

Out of the hundreds of books on writing that O——— had read, he found only one piece of advice that ever helped. To write, one must have a "capacity for invention," which enabled one to "articulate inchoate feelings and impressions into plots which enveloped characters imbued by the deft deployment of a few poignant details with the semblance of both vitality and archetypal universality." But if one lacked such a capacity, one had only to "invent the capacity for invention."

Pure genius! O——— left off trying to write mere stories, and committed himself to reimagining O——— the professional writer, who sweated brilliant ideas and transmuted the raw offal of life into golden eggs of art.

When years of self-invention failed to pan out, he cast about in such desperation, that he started listening actively to people around him for ideas.

"Some of the shit they say, man," said his cousin, at a backyard barbecue. "They'd give you enough nightmares for a thousand stories."

Tight, but not yet drunk, so O——— poured him another margarita. "Play some of the tapes," he pushed.

"This one is especially twisted. Poor fucker's got three or more degenerative conditions eating him alive, but he has these nightmares that have him convinced him he's God. He's here because he's punishing himself …"

O——— killed his drink. "I gotta hear that."

Suddenly sober, his cousin remembered his oath. "Wait, man—"

"It's not some celebrity. It's a *nobody*, a sick man. You said so yourself."

"Then what does it matter?"

The patient was only a rasping presence, like the sound of a dying fire, as the session began. "He clams up sometimes, then comes out swinging. Just wait for it."

O——— killed another margarita and read the case notes as the tape played.

Patient 75535 had nightmares, but the nightmares were more real than his waking life. Though they threatened his grip on reality, they seemed to offer the only relief from an existence devoid of any pleasure or rewards. He previously saw himself as a one-dimensional persona floating in an ill-conceived limbo until the next time his sadistic creator hauled him off the shelf, nailed him to another name and place, and dangled him before a crudely crayoned cyclorama of petty dread.

Patient 75535 knew this sounded insane. Naturally, if he was an archetypal victim-character in a writer's mind, he'd be incapable of recognizing it. God is always beyond understanding. *His* god would remain veiled in the inconceivable, free to torture imaginary Sea Monkeys in the dungeon of his mind.

He feared that his whole unbearable life was but another story, and when its telegraphed twist ending had unraveled, he would fall into the infinite void of true limbo and be forgotten. Only natural then, to concoct this fantasy of being God, trapped in His own creation.

But the rest of it—deals with the Devil, astral projection nightmares, and unclassifiable shit like this …

"*I'm a girl in a plain homespun frock, surrounded by larger versions of same. We go to Hometown Buffet in a big group and we clean every tureen and steamer table at the buffet. Stuffed, ecstatic, we pile into our school bus and hasten to church praying at the top of our lungs.*

"*The sermon is brief and interrupted by the first spasms of sickness from the crowd. My grandmother is among the first to rise up and testify to the evils of this world. Her speech is a long, wordless yawn of vomit that sprays over the pews and her fellow parishioners.*

"*The smell is on us all now, and the expulsion begins en masse. Bile flies in fine spray while glutinous clods of half-chewed chicken and fish and tuna casserole coat the floor like hail. Those too sturdy of constitution to join in force fingers down throats to add to the Technicolor chorus, until all of us lie spent and skeletal, swaddled in stretched-out, empty skins.*

"*The deacons crawl through the mess, pawing each morsel and pool of bile and every so often, one of them finds a holy relic. Each discovery is brought to the altar, where a great glass case lined with white velvet holds an almost complete human skeleton. Many "finds" prove to be chicken or pork bones, but one blind old man has expelled the last missing metacarpal of the right hand, while a massive, toadlike woman in the back quite effortlessly heaved up the right half of the pelvis.*

"*The priest is in an ecstasy as the bones are added to the reliquary. But the prophecy has not yet been fulfilled. Only the skull has not been delivered.*

"*I alone have not been sick in church. All eyes fall upon me. All hands interlock to bar the exit. I look down at the bulge of my belly, and I try to stifle my impulse to speak in tongues …*"

It was a goldmine. To be sure, he had never aspired to write horror stories. He liked crime fiction where the hero was the villain, so you didn't have to work out a tricky mystery. But he knew he'd never find better material. O——— took notes, filling both sides of twenty pages of his notebook. His wife had to drag him away from the barbecue. His cousin wouldn't let him borrow the tapes, but he promised to let him review further sessions.

His first efforts were halting, inert lumps of laundry-list prose until he just recycled the patient's exact words. The patient's own palpably mad, hopeless voice was the only way to sell these appalling tales of surreal dread. But even when plagiarized verbatim from the tapes, the completion of each one was less like creative labor than the lancing of some psychic carbuncle, the product devoid of joy beyond relief at its expulsion.

For the stories had their way with O——— before they found their way out, poisoning his capacity to enjoy his success. Indeed, the stories and their anonymous dreamer had reimagined him, so that when success came with much fatuous heraldry at his "discovery" and "arrival", he mounted the public stage with suitable detachment and the haunted decorum born of second-hand despair.

Though he never had cause to suspect that 75535 was aware of his nightmares' spectacular popularity, O——— sometimes wondered if the nameless patient was toying with him.

One recurring nightmare involved a writer who keeps penning masterpieces, only to discover that they've all been done before by an ingenious but obscure writer whose final story before he disappeared was about a writer who learns to see into the future, and uses his gift to steal our hero's ideas.

Horror stories about writers were all the rage at the time, and O——— —'s novel about it was his first to crack the bestseller lists, but he was sued by some ancient nobody who'd written a story with the same premise, that O——— might've read in a textbook in grade school. In 75535's dream, the hapless protagonist had written the final scene, powerless to stop his typing hands describing the hideous apparition of the time-ravaged plagiarist even as it crept up and slipped its fleshless talons around his throat. In real life, O——— quietly settled out of court.

Another recurring nightmare was about a man who witnesses something in the middle of a riot. He tries to tell a girlfriend, but she almost immediately commits suicide. The protagonist keeps the horrible secret to himself, but its sheer toxicity leaks out his eyes and causes anyone he makes eye contact with to snuff it in the most spectacular fashion possible. He learns to spot potential victims by a cloud behind their eyes of sadness and buried pain and an unacknowledged hunger for self-destruction. Finally, he gouges out his eyes to bury the secret, but the toxic cloud pours out of his eye sockets and poisons the world.

With some work, O—— was able to turn the bleak vision into *Victim Eyes*, a rousing 600-page doorstop of paranormal suspense.

In his dream, 75535 had seen a horde of towering puppeteers looming over the crowd, working their passions, stoking their bestial rage by slim quicksilver cords that plugged into their brains. The phantasmal puppeteers were themselves but the tiniest digital extremities of a forest of intangible limbs which converged on a headless, hundred-handed leviathan hovering over the city like a bloated spider preparing every mind to be drained of its essence, leaving a legion of impotent, hungry husks.

75535 hadn't given him much to work with at all. Bleak stuff, true, but at least it offered something concrete for the hero and his ragtag surrogate nuclear family to defeat, if only 75535 would tell him what the hell they were.

Just when O—— needed him most, 75535 refused to confess any more material. After much coaxing from his therapist, he finally exploded, "What kind of hideous new metaphor do I need to conjure up for you and your friend, to rationalize the sickness I feel? It wasn't a vision of Hell or the outer spheres that cracked me. In my worst nightmares, I'm still here! It was *this* place, this species, these sick, sad, hollow cells of a broken, self-murdering monstrosity that each believe they're seven billion demigods. *We* are what's wrong with the universe. If only there *was* a god or a monster out there to crush us before we remade the whole world in excrement, then maybe there'd be something left for the monsters who'll come after us. That's what I'm most afraid of. This world is the horror story too terrible to tell, and any attempt to modify it for public consumption would make it into a joke or pornography. Or worse … scripture."

The public devoured *Victim Eyes* and its author with blind, idiotic gusto. He soon found success a hundred times the burden that obscurity had ever been, and yet he doggedly persisted in harvesting 75535's nightmares. For though he had become a "dark prince of paranormal suspense" for an adoring, outraged public, he still could not invent an interesting cocktail party anecdote without recourse to the tapes.

As movies and TV elevated him to an iconic status that extended to those incapable of reading, he insulated himself from the world, and so it was not entirely unbelievable that he did not hear the stories in the news, or the suspicious coincidences that began to surround his work.

His agent and manager weren't going to be the first to bring it up. It wasn't until his cousin finally tried to cut him off that he was forced to confront the awful truth.

The story was about a church in a small Southern town where a girl had perished as a result of massive internal bleeding in the midst of a fervent church service. The article was maddeningly short on details, but police were investigating the source of a "foreign object" which hospital officials said an X-ray disclosed. The church was under investigation, but had retained a lawyer to recover the "object" pending an autopsy, which they claimed had "powerful religious significance."

O——— had a good idea what the object was. "How did this happen?"

"It didn't happen until you wrote it."

O——— got a beer from his cousin's fridge. Most of it spurted out as foam when he cracked it. "Goddamit, it was just a story ..."

"It was *his* story."

"So what? It came true? Life imitating art is the oldest cliché in the book. You tell me how I could put a human skull in that girl's belly."

"It wasn't the only one, man."

He showed O——— a pile of clippings. Strings of random public suicides were the most recurring theme. "D'you have anything stronger than beer?"

"You didn't know? How could you not know?"

"I don't look at anything unless my assistant vets it first. I can't go out there. You don't know what my fans are like ..." He swilled his drink without tasting it or caring what it was, leaning into his helpless rage. "I mean, what kind of people need this crazy bullshit just to give meaning to their lives? How empty do you have to be ...?"

O——— noticed how his cousin was staring at him and asked, "How long have I been in therapy, here?"

His cousin didn't laugh. "Nobody's blaming you for any of this. If anything, it's only added to your mystique. But I can't do it anymore."

For a moment, O——— felt sickening relief. "You can't just cut me off—"

"I didn't. He did. He's stopped coming in. Cancelled all his appointments."

"Do you think he knows?"

"He doesn't watch TV or read the paper either, but I've always suspected that he was playing with us …"

"Where does he live? I've got to meet him."

"You've got to stop writing these books! Somehow, you're both making this happen—"

"Or we're revealing it before it happens." O——— killed his drink. "No, *I* don't even believe that."

"I can't tell you where he lives. It would—"

"It would out us both, I get that. But he always goes to the movies."

The stores were all closed on Christmas day, but the movies stayed open. Without the cinema, with its multiplexed portals to more meaningful, heartwarming universes than ours, the suicide rate on Christmas Day would go through the roof.

O——— waited in his car across the street from the rundown multiplex for ninety minutes. When the old man got off the bus and shuffled to the box office, O——— instantly knew it was 75535.

The patient bought a ticket for a holiday family film. Dysfunctional as they had to be these days, the family looked nice in the poster, safe surrogate company for those with no families at all. Not like the morbid orgies of negativity that he'd vomited into the communal consciousness …

O——— took a seat two rows behind 75535 and watched him as the lights went dim. Three other people wandered into the theater. Two were employees who immediately lit up a joint and started making out. The third fell asleep during the trailers. His snore was like a bandsaw cutting blubber.

75535 covered his face in his hands through the credits and the first scene. They were having a lively holiday dinner, lavishly catered fare sizzling under sparks of jolly sarcasm. O——— had almost forgotten why he'd come when, with a pitiful wail, 75535 hurtled out of his seat and rushed the screen, bounced off the silverized nylon and fell to his knees before it, pleading and praying.

O——— got up and intercepted the man before he could get up and try it again. "Not as easy to get out of here as in Roman times, eh, old timer?"

"Don't touch me! I won't have it ..." The old man shook him off and crawled to a seat in the front row. "Why do you, why do you do it?"

"I care. I wanted to give the world something ..."

"You're a thief, and worse. You all are ..." The movie was reflected on his cloudy, sightless eyes. His cousin never told him 75535 was blind.

Nobody told them to shut up. O——— tried to get 75535 to sit down. "I thought we should talk ..."

"It's too late. You know, God was invented to help you accept the evil and ugly things in the world. But what of all the awful things that God *didn't* put into the world? All the things too terrible to contemplate, that crowd His mind? You didn't make them grateful for what they have. You only made *reality* seem boring ..."

O——— had rehearsed praising and charming this man, intimidating him and having him silenced. But now, in this smoky dream den, he had lost the meaning of words, let alone the power to persuade.

The screen went black, and then it got *darker*. Pinpoints of violet light swarmed and smoldered as his eyes struggled and failed to process what he saw on the screen, which had become a window into a festering void, crawling with arcane shapes of deeper darkness like septic constellations ... restless, colossal, empty *words*. And behind *them*—

"You have no idea what it's like ... to be constantly recreated by your creation ... Every living thing creates and destroys. Until you are moved by disgust to drown, burn and crush your own creations to save yourself from becoming like them, you have nothing in common with God."

"You're no more a god than I am—"

The old man laughed, a sickly seizure of a sound that somehow made him taller and sucked the heat out of the theater. "I've walked among you for as long as I could stand it. You're all just praying to yourselves, anyway."

"You have to tell me—"

"You want answers, why don't you ask that asshole?" And the blind man pointed at the cosmic logorrhea behind the screen, pointed directly at you.

O——— reached out to hug the old man, to throttle him with questions. "Why do you hate us so?"

"Because *you created me*!" Shoving O——— back into his seat, 75535 turned and hobbled into the screen. For just a moment after he passed through, O——— saw His true face.

So much evil to undo …

He had so much to repent of.

He started with his eyes.

⚜

Stop it! For the love of God, let me out!

Settle down, please, these restraints are for your own protection. You have to go all the way through it to find yourself.

But don't you see? Don't you understand, even now? We're both *him … He's using you to tear me apart … He's doing it now! I'll hold my breath. I'll just hold my breath and … NO …*

Wake up! You can't … You've got to wake up. Mr. Furst? Mr. Glaublich? Mr. O———? Come back … you have to finish …

Please … You, out there …? *God, please don't stop reading … Please don't turn the pa—*

ABOUT THE AUTHOR

CODY GOODFELLOW has written five novels, and he co-wrote three more with *New York Times* bestselling author John Skipp. His first two collections, *Silent Weapons for Quiet Wars* and *All-Monster Action*, each received the Wonderland Book Award. He wrote, co-produced and scored the short Lovecraftian hygiene film *Stay At Home Dad*, which can be viewed on YouTube. He is also a director of the H.P. Lovecraft Film Festival–San Pedro, and co-founder of Perilous Press, an occasional micropublisher of modern cosmic horror.

ACKNOWLEDGEMENTS

PURITY BALL appeared in *Flesh Like Smoke*, April Moon Books, 2015.

LIFE COACH appeared in *Psychos: Serial Killers, Depraved Madmen, and the Criminally Insane*, Black Dog & Leventhal, 2012.

HOWL OF THE SHEEP appeared in *Werewolves and Shapeshifters: Encounters with the Beasts Within*, Black Dog & Leventhal, 2010.

BLIND ITEM appeared in *Undead & Unbound: Unexpected Tales from Beyond the Grave*, Chaosium, 2015.

NATASHA HATES A VACUUM appeared in *Demons: Encounters with the Devil and His Minions, Fallen Angels, and the Possessed*, Black Dog & Leventhal, 2011.

THE TELLTALE PARTY is original to this collection.

AND THE ANGELS SING appeared in *Horror for the Holidays*, Miskatonic River Press, 2013.

WE WILL REBUILD appeared in *Zombies: Encounters with the Hungry Dead*, Black Dog & Leventhal, 2009.

BLOOM WHERE YOU'RE PLANTED appeared in Allen K's *Inhuman #5*, 2011.

THE FREE SCHOOL appeared as a chapbook from Dim Shores Press, 2016.

DUST MADE OF WORDS appeared in *A Darke Phantastique: Encounters with the Uncanny and Other Magical Things*, Cycatrix Press, 2014.

MISERICORDIA is original to this collection.

Of a Thousand Cuts appeared in *The Children of Old Leech*, Word Horde, 2014.

Nigredo appeared in *In the Court of the Yellow King*, Celaeno Press, 2015.

The Man Who Escaped This Story appeared in *The Grimscribe's Puppets*, Miskatonic River Press, 2013.

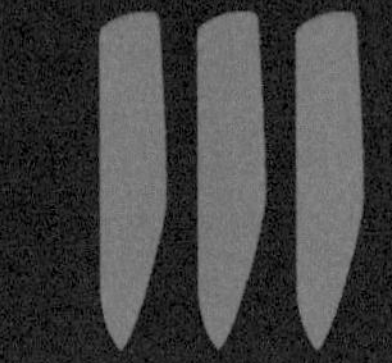

DARK CARNIVAL
BY JOANNA PARYPINSKI

CALCUTTA HORROR
GRAPHIC NOVEL

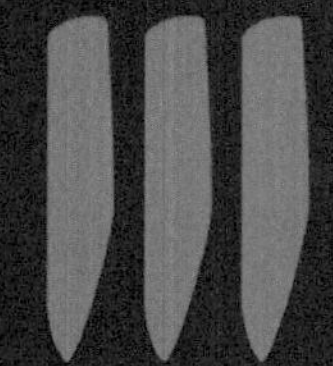

NARAKA
BY ALESSANDRO MANZETTI

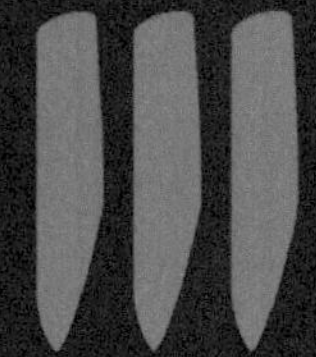

LATEST RELEASE

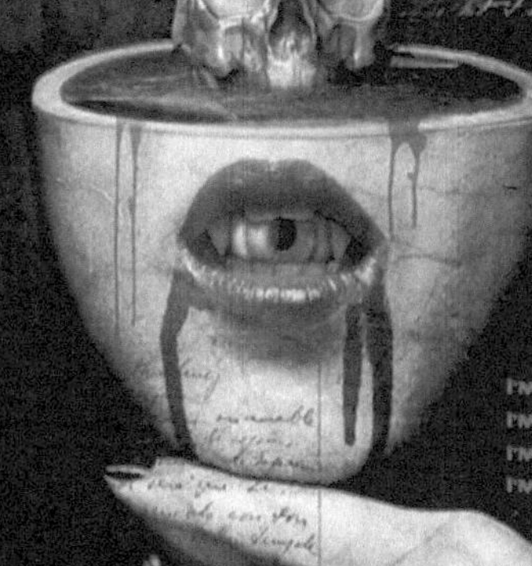

DARK MARY
BY PAOLO DI ORAZIO

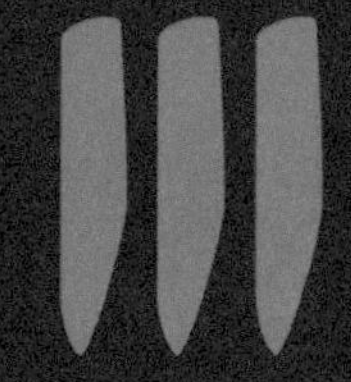

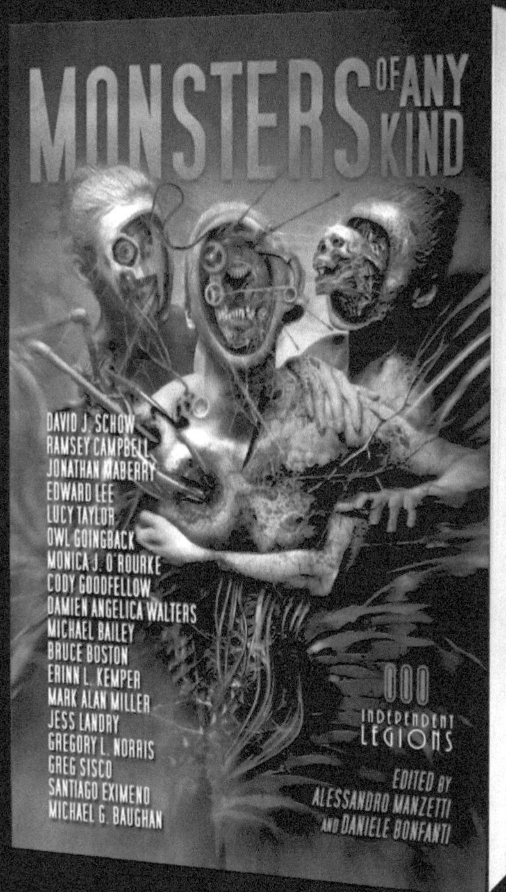

MONSTERS OF ANY KIND
EDITED BY A. MANZETTI & D. BONFANTI

AVAILABLE BOOKS

Our publications are available at Amazon and major online booksellers. Visit our Website: **www.independentlegions.com**

B̲OTH P̲APERBACK & D̲IGITAL P̲UBLICATIONS

DARK CARNIVAL
by Joanna Parypinski

HORROR CALCUTTA (GRAPHIC NOVEL)
by Alessandro Manzetti & Stefano Cardoselli

COYOTE RAGE
by Owl Goingback

FEARFUL SYMMETRIES
by Thomas F. Monteleone

DARK MARY
by Paolo Di Orazio

TRIBAL SCREAMS
by Owl Goingback

MONSTERS OF ANY KIND
Edited by Alessandro Manzetti & Daniele Bonfanti

KNOWING WHEN TO DIE
by Mort Castle

ARTIFACTS
by Bruce Boston
NARAKA THE ULTIMATE HUMAN BREEDING
by Alessandro Manzetti

A WINTER SLEEP
by Greg F. Gifune

SPREE AND OTHER STORIES
by Lucy Taylor

THE BEAUTY OF DEATH 2 – DEATH BY WATER
edited by Alessandro Manzetti & Jodi Renee Lester

THE LIVING AND THE DEAD
by Greg F. Gifune

THE CARP-FACED BOY AND OTHER TALES
by Thersa Matsuura

THE WISH MECHANICS
by Daniel Braum

CHILDREN OF NO ONE
by Nicole Cushing

THE ONE THAT COMES BEFORE
by Livia Llewellyn

ALL AMERICAN HORROR OF THE 21ST CENTURY: THE FIRST DECADE
Edited by Mort Castle

BENEATH THE NIGHT
by Greg Gifune

SELECTED STORIES
by Nate Southard

DIGITAL PUBLICATIONS

TALKING IN THE DARK
by Dennis Etchison

THE BEAUTY OF DEATH VOL. 1
Edited by Alessandro Manzetti

THE HORROR SHOW
by Poppy Z. Brite

DOCTOR BRITE
by Poppy Z. Brite

USED STORIES
by Poppy Z. Brite

THE CRYSTAL EMPIRE
by Poppy Z. Brite

SELECTED STORIES
by Poppy Z. Brite

THE USHERS
by Edward Lee

SELECTED STORIES
by Edward Lee

INDEPENDENT LEGIONS PUBLISHING
Via Virgilio, 10 – TRIESTE (ITALY)
+39 040 9776602

WWW.INDEPENDENTLEGIONS.COM
WWW.FACEBOOK.COM/INDEPENDENTLEGIONS
INDEPENDENT.LEGIONS@AOL.COM